To Suzanne Lee

Enjoy

Stephen Finlay Archer

6-29-2016

W9-BYH-319

TESTIMONIALS

Searchers: The Irish Clans is a rollicking ride through Irish history in 1915, which set the stage for the 1916 Easter Rising. Parallel adventure stories in America and Ireland unfold through endearing characters based on actual historic individuals and related fictional Clansmen and women. As we follow them in this action-filled and at times swashbuckling journey, we cannot help but wonder when and how the twain shall meet. The tease works well, and I look forward to experiencing all that is served up in Books 2, 3 and 4.

—Sally Kaplan, writer of fiction and non-fiction, and Documentary Film producer at Backcountry Pictures

Searchers: The Irish Clans weaves an intricate and gripping tale of parallel families destined to fulfill an ancient Clans Pact. This is the first novel for this talented engineer-turned-wordsmith, one that is skillfully wrought, well-researched, and authentic in voice and spirit. The romantic adventure tale dishes up authentic Irish history, weaving in ancient clan lore and historic events into a saga of epic proportion, with upcoming books lining up for release.

—Monika Rose, Director, Manzanita Writers Press

Stephen Archer's, *Searchers: The Irish Clans,* the first of a four-part series centering on the drama of the Irish Rebellion, is the best kind of historical novel, a tale told in the heart-stopping tradition of *War and Peace, Gone With the Wind, and Wolf Hall.* Come breathe the very air of Ireland as its gallant citizens struggle for autonomy against hostile Brits who've held them in virtual slavery for hundreds of years. The stakes are high, the chances slim, but brave men and women will take up the cause. Many will be martyred, but Archer weaves an unforgettable tale of courage and inspiration that sweeps up the reader in a stirring drama that will long be remembered.

—Antoinette May. author of The Determined Heart, The Sacred Well, Pilate's Wife, and Haunted Houses of California

Searchers: The Irish Clans
Book One of Four Novels

Copyright © 2016 by Stephen Finlay Archer
All rights reserved.
Printed in the United States of America

ISBN: 978-0-9908019-3-1
Library of Congress Control Number: 2016902266

Publisher: Manzanita Writers Press
PO Box 632, San Andreas, CA 95249
www.manzapress.com

Cover design and Interior Layout: Connie Strawbridge
Cover photos credits:
Front cover: The Sinking of the Lusitania painting, courtesy of the Everett Collection
Back cover: The Cumdach of the Cathach, in the National Museum of Ireland, Dublin
Inside back cover: Author photo by Kathy Archer
Rising front cover: The GPO in Flames painting, courtesy of Norman Teeling, artist
One of a commemorative set of paintings for the Easter Rising centenary
Revolution front cover: The Temple Bar, Dublin, Ireland, photograph by author
Revelation front cover: St Columba's monastery on Iona, photograph by author

This is a work of fiction. Any resemblance of my fictional characters to real persons, living or dead, is purely coincidental. The depiction of historical persons in these novels is not coincidental, and to the best of my knowledge, is accurate to events and their character in life. Some historical aspects may be augmented or adjusted for dramatic purposes.

Searchers

The Irish Clans

Book One of Four Novels

Stephen Finlay Archer

Manzanita Writers Press
San Andreas, California

AUTHOR'S NOTE

As Mr. Frank Delaney, in his marvelous book *Ireland: A Novel* so eloquently writes, Ireland's early history was not written down, but taught verbally by *Seanchai*, migrant storytellers who carried the messages of the ages to the citizens far and wide. In Medieval times when most of Europe was plunged into literary darkness by the barbarian hordes, Ireland uniquely maintained a network of ecclesiastical monasteries of very high academic knowledge for their time to which Europeans flocked for learning.

When the English chose to invade and conquer Ireland in the 1500s and the early1600s, they did so in the name of their new religion. They were very successful in rooting out and destroying most of the precious and tangible relics of the Irish civilization, including castles and Catholic churches. During this process, there were some valiant efforts to document the past, for example the Annals of the Four Masters, which were created in what had recently been the O'Donnells territory of Donegal. Then England imposed such punitive laws on the native citizens that they lost their lands, their lives, and their civilization for centuries. But the Irish men and women did not lose their innate will to overcome this oppressive domination and to restore their own self-governed civilization. Note asterisks for further history, located in the back of the book.

It is after all of this mayhem that modern scholars, much more learned than I, have attempted to stitch together the important threads of Irish history in the total scope of human existence, before and after the advent of Christianity in Ireland ushered in by St. Patrick. Yet much of it before 1600 is speculation in the mist of time, which for an author is grist for the mill, as they say.

And so it is that I, a would-be historian of Irish ancestry, have examined some of the few remaining treasures that escaped the purge in an attempt to weave a plausible tale of secular and religious Clan intrigue that spans the period of civilization on the blessed Isle, which was once known as Scotia, but is now our beloved Ireland.

Searchers – The Irish Clans Book 1 begins the tale in the context of 1915 Ireland, when the funeral of O'Donovan Rossa afforded a golden opportunity to fan the flames of revolution.

DEDICATION

There is a woman wise and free,
Who is the only love for me,
She is my muse, my soaring wing,
My Kathy Ann, my everything.

ACKNOWLEDGEMENTS

It may seem odd that I would start so far back with Major Bull, that wonderful high school English teacher, who somehow taught us budding scientific mathematicians, back at the birth of the Space Age, that there is more to life than slide rules and protractors—so much more. Tennyson and Brontë, Joyce and Thurber, to name a few. Oh, how my heartstrings vibrated that senior year before I was launched into my hi-tech, button-down aerospace college and career life.

Why do people always seem to compare task complexity to rocket science? True, it is an exacting and complex trade requiring strict design, production, and mission execution. But I can tell you now, from experience, that it doesn't hold a candle to the art of authorship, the precision of language, the complexity of character development, and the mission of creativity.

Thus, at the end of an aerospace career that was full of memories of successful teams who brought complex earth sciences, communications, and planetary probe space systems into fruition, it was fitting that I should tackle a more daunting challenge, namely a second career as an historical fiction author. Jeanne Robertson refers to her husband by name in her comedy sketches as being left-brained. Hilarious. I can relate. It was drummed into me over the years. Double digit accuracy trajectories.

So, dear reader, you can see that I have many, patient right-brained thinkers and trainers to thank. There are my mentors at The Long Ridge Writers Group who guided me through short story and novel correspondence courses—in particular Lynne Smith, who soldiered on to become my editor beyond the courses until it became too much to bear. Thank you. And more recently here in the Mother Lode hills of California, Sarah Luck Pearson, through her Creative Non-Fiction Workshop series, tried to help us novice writers develop a character's creative arc among other writing skills. Thank you for showing and not telling us.

Further, I wish to thank the very skilled members of the Manzanita Writers Press in Angels Camp, directed by Editor Monika Rose, without

Acknowledgements

whose enthusiastic and creative guidance this book would never have been completed. Her entire team, including Connie Strawbridge, Suzanne Murphy, Joy Roberts, Jennifer Hoffman, and on this project, Sally Kaplan, have been instrumental in my right-brain development, such as it is, and in the editing and production of this novel. Thank you, ladies.

I also wish to thank my readers, Kathy Archer, Amber Herron, Victoria Bors, Bob Kolakowski, Michael and Virginia Finlay, and Bob Blink for their inputs and moral support.

Mr. Eamonn Casey, renowned Irish historian, has been kind enough to provide some historical perspective of this tumultuous time, and Mr. Tom Cleary, owner of The Temple Bar in Dublin, has been supportive of a tale that integrally involves his establishment.

Most importantly, my wife Kathy Ann has been my guiding light, always understanding and supportive of a guy who chose the rigors of writing over retirement relaxation. To her I owe everything, for so many reasons.

Finally, the front cover art showing the travesty of the sinking of the *Lusitania* by U-20 in May 1915 has been graciously provided by the Everett Collection, NY, NY., and the photograph of the *Cumdach of the Cathach* on the back cover, taken by the author, one of the precious remaining relics of the glorious Celtic civilization, is currently housed and on display in the National Museum of Ireland in Dublin.

Contents

Contents

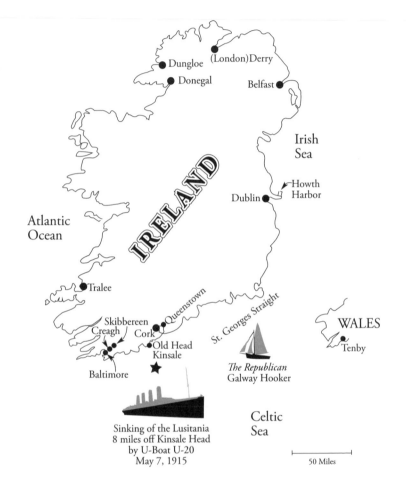

Dungloe

(London)Derry

Donegal

Belfast

Irish
Sea

Howth
Harbor

Dublin

Atlantic
Ocean

IRELAND

Tralee

Skibbereen
Creagh

Queenstown

Cork

Old Head
Kinsale

Baltimore

St. Georges Straight

WALES

Tenby

The Republican
Galway Hooker

Sinking of the Lusitania
8 miles off Kinsale Head
by U-Boat U-20
May 7, 1915

Celtic
Sea

50 Miles

PROLOGUE

October 4, 1600 AD
Donegal Town, Ireland

*F*rom the battlements of the castle keep, Red Hugh O'Donnell saw one of his southern countrymen emerge from the distant woods heading for the town. The two leaders had arranged this unusual and critical meeting and conveyed its purpose through secret correspondence. Red was not convinced that this type of planning was necessary yet. True, the English enemy had recently managed to attack and destroy portions of Derry, his northern stronghold town, continuing their vile kill and burn tactics. This fact troubled him greatly. With this thrust the heretics were attempting to split the two remaining northern Clan armies. But this wasn't what angered him most. His own miserable cousin, Niall O'Donnell, was siding with the enemy and guiding them in their ruthless attack.

Red, the charismatic, flaming-haired chieftain, just twenty-seven years old, had already broken out of the enemy's jail and liberated his people in several successful battles. All of these skirmishes were fought in the name of his God, with clemency for his vanquished foes and compassion and comfort for his army and allies. Ten centuries before his birth, Saint Columba, born to lead the O'Domhnaill Clan, his clan, had prophesied that Red unite his people and lead them to freedom at last. By the will and grace of God, his goal remained—he still intended to do just that.

"Sentry," he yelled when he spied horsemen peering out from behind the shops down in the town square. "Summon the guard. Open the gate."

Before the sentry could act, Red had bounded down from the keep and was heading for the gate, sword in hand. "Sound the alarm," he cried. As the gate cracked open, he squeezed through and made a dash for the square. From his position he could see that the visiting Clan chieftain was just about to reach Diamond Square where the horsemen were hiding, swords drawn.

The alarm wailed and the horseman, startled, turned towards the sound. At that moment he recognized his cousin in the stirrups. "Traitor!" Red cried.

How did they know about this meeting? From what he could see of the enemy, the two warriors were outnumbered five to one. He gauged correctly that it would be too late by the time his guards arrived. His visitor would be cut down before he had a chance to defend himself.

He knew that by killing his ally, Florence MacCarthaigh Reagh, within sight of the castle, this tip-of-the-spear enemy column hoped to demoralize the clansman's people. *I've got to draw them into the open before Florence arrives at their ambush site.* So, instead of attacking the enemy, Red raced down towards the center of the square where he would be in plain sight of the advancing visitor.

Florence heard the wailing from the castle and knew that they must be under attack. He spurred his horse on, never thinking that danger loomed in the village square. Suddenly, from out of a side street a hundred yards ahead, he saw a lone countryman running out into the square waving his sword frantically. He was yelling something that Florence couldn't understand over the piercing noise.

Then, from the opposite side street, a band of enemy soldiers ten strong rode out to attack his countryman. He knew the bastards well by their shiny armor and colorful breeches. They were more of the same murderous devils that were laying barren his own territories. He yelled at his horse as spurs dug in. The steed propelled him forward.

Florence saw his countryman engage with the heretics, his sword slashing like a whirlwind and finding its mark. Two of the enemy had been knocked off their mounts, yet they were still fighting on foot. They had encircled the lone defender and two, still on horseback, had turned and were heading out to engage with him now. He recognized the countryman to be none other than the Chieftain he had come to meet. *Red!* He attempted to cut a swath through the throng. In the process he was knocked off his horse, and he arose amidst the circle of terror, right next to his ally.

"Glad you could join me," Red roared, as he slashed at another heretic to keep him back. "How do you like my welcoming committee?"

"You really set out quite a banquet," the MacCarthaigh said, noticing the red-stained cobblestone square around them.

"Bloody right." Instinctively they fought together back to back.

"Burn in hell, cousin," Niall shouted from the background. "I will take my rightful place as head of our Clan."

"Cowardly fool," Red spat back. "This is our enemy. They will overrun you and all of our people."

Although the two companions had killed two of the enemy and wounded three others, Red knew that they could not hold them off forever. *Where are my guards? Two more minutes, and it will be over.* Some of his blood from an arm wound was already running into the cobbles. "Our God in heaven, deliver us from our wicked enemies," Red cried out in desperation.

Suddenly, from all sides on the square, villagers poured out of dwellings wielding pitchforks, axes and, in some cases, sticks and brooms. It had taken them a few minutes to react, but now they were here *en masse* to save their leader. Red likened it to red ants swarming to the defense of their ant hill, totally engulfing and annihilating the invading insects in a matter of seconds.

Outside the fray, he could see his treacherous cousin cut and run like the coward he was. Red and his ally pushed outward, and the villagers attacked inward.

It was over in less than five minutes, leaving nine enemy soldiers dead and mutilated beyond recognition, their horses either maimed, dead, or bolted.

The villagers cheered, raising their hero and his ally up on broad shoulders, singing songs of heavenly praise as they carried them out of the village and into the safety of the castle.

Alone together at last in the great hall, the two leaders conversed, warmed by two flagons of ale between them. In the center of the side wall a hardwood fire roared in the massive stone fireplace, its stone corbels rising up to the beamed ceiling framed double stone shields. Florence could see the crosses on them and remembered the O'Domhnaill legend. The great St. Columba, one of their own back in the sixth century, had admonished their chieftain to always go forth into battle with the red cross of Constantine on their shields to ensure victory.

That reminded him. "Do you still use the Cathach of St. Columba in battle Red?"

"Aye, since brother Columba left for Hy, more than ten centuries now. We swear by it. I'm having it brought over by McGroarty."

"Good."

"Why are you here, Florence?"

"The situation is grave in the south, Red," Florence explained, unbuckling his scabbard and laying his sword on the ancient oak table. He rolled out a crude sketched map of his south-west territory from under his tunic. "See here," he pointed. "We are being overrun again. The heretics, driven by their heartless foreign queen, are committed to the destruction of the sacred way of life of our people."

"I experienced that first-hand, right enough," Red wiped his mouth after drinking. "But what is to be done?"

"Oh, the true believers will continue our fight with guerrilla tactics, which may slow down the onslaught. But in the end, I believe that our lands, our worldly possessions, our loved ones, and our religion, will certainly be stripped from us by the savage horde." Florence gripped his cup firmly with one hand but didn't partake. "How ironic that the enemy considers our noble race to be vermin to be exterminated. Our glorious civilization was the center of learning for the known world five centuries ago."

Unsheathing his dagger from his thigh, Florence stabbed and then carved a hunk of the overripe cheese on the table plate, flicking it up into his mouth and chomping down hard on the rind.

"But what is to be done, and why are you the one to tell me?" Red drummed his fingers on the table. He wasn't used to having to ask twice.

Florence lifted the cup and drank, some of the ale spilling onto his shirt. He set the vessel down on the oak table and let go, waiting for the other inevitable question.

"Why didn't you fight with our ally the FitzMaurices in the southwest when we called upon you to do so?" Red demanded, slamming his goblet on the table, sending the scabbard flying onto the wood floor. "Thousands of defenseless men, women and children have been cut down, their heads chopped, and their bodies thrown into the sea for the fishes."

Florence MacCarthaigh gripped the edge of the table with both hands. Staring into his host's black eyes, he smiled and, with measured pitch in his voice, he answered, "We have each been protecting our own territories for centuries. Your family was the same. Under dire threat of annihilation we hunkered down to protect our own. Some have chosen to support the enemy, like your cousin. But we have not."

"Our only hope is to band together, forgiving old animosities,"

Red argued, his eyes blazing. "In God's name, with the help of our Spanish ally, we can free our country of these tyrants forever."

Florence waited, then said, "I will commit to following you in this battle and will strive to bring our foreign ally to our shores. But only if you will listen to a proposition I have for you." He raised his glass to toast, then held it there, expectant, words still forming.

"I am listening, comrade," Red's eyes deepened, shadows forming.

"You are a man of God, with visions of glory," Florence, not wavering, began. "I know that you believe in Divine destiny. I am a devout man of the land, rooted in the harsh reality of our situation. I, too, believe in Divine destiny for our people and I, too, revere the Gaelic history of our nation." The cup lowered but did not rest. "The difference between us is that I believe that this destiny is not going to come to fruition in our lifetimes, nor in those of our immediate offspring, but at some time in the future when conditions are right." He set his cup down hard, some of the ale sloshing onto the table.

"If you are right, and I hope to God you are not, then what's to become of our people in the meantime?" Red drained his flagon, then set it down, pushing it away from him.

"I am not saying that we should give up. Far from it," his companion urged. "But I say we need to plan far ahead. If the worst happens despite our Herculean efforts, then I say we need to hide the treasures of our forefathers for some future generation to find and use to liberate our people when it is their destiny."

Red stared hard at his ally.

"I have chosen your family, and not the others, not only because of your noble and benevolent deeds, but also because of your linkage back to the Saints of our great nation." Florence sat back in his chair, his arms folded against his chest, and waited.

"I greatly value your support in our ongoing campaign," Red opened his clenched hands, revealing strong fingers, calloused and hardened from battle. "And I see merit in your foresighted contingency plan." The warrior leaned into the edge of the table. "How would you suggest that we do what you ask?"

"By cross linking the clues we will plant, this will cement the bond between our families, south and north, for generations to come," Florence explained, "with the firstborn son of each family protecting the trail of clues."

"A blood pact between us, is it?" Red exclaimed. "But how would our future generations know to decipher and share their secrets?" His muscular arms shone in the light as they rested on the oak table, veins pulsing in anticipation.

"When the time is right," Florence responded gravely, "our Lord God will lead them by Divine intervention."

Believing in the supreme deity, Red nodded his head in agreement. It made sense that north and south should be connected in this way. After all, this is what he had been striving to accomplish for the last decade. And besides, he had other buried secrets beyond the wealth of his own family. If the worst happened, then the path would have to be protected by the righteous ones beyond his bloodline.

Taking his knife from its sheath at his side, Red cut a narrow furrow across his palm, then offered the knife to his ally as the blood gushed.

Moments later, their pact, in principle, was sealed by the mingling of their blood wounds in a stout hand clasp.

Alone, the warriors spent three days organizing the details of their pact, neither telling the other where they would hide their family monetary treasures. Florence had brought his measurements. They used acronyms. Both agreed to have the matched interlinked clues prepared. In the end, they alone wrote and signed the pact that now bound them as brothers, for eternity if necessary; two copies on single sheet parchment, signed, folded twice and sealed with both their ring stamps. Then each chose a special location to hide their copy of this all-important document.

At a farewell banquet held in his honor, Florence, the MacCarthaigh Reagh, proclaimed to all assembled, "I commit to joining you in an all-out fight to liberate our country from the heretic enemy. We form an alliance north and south for the future, come what may. Let the Grace of God go with us all and may the wrath of His justice be in our swords and in those who will follow after us."

A clamor rose in the hall, and the throng hailed the new coalition, clapping each other on their backs, boots stamping in approval, cups smashing together.

Behind the floor-to-ceiling tapestry of the Last Supper, the Judas cousin Niall had slipped in, disguised, with the other guests. Upon hearing the Southern leader's commitment, he hatched a plot to betray his own bloodline, his hatred and passion mirroring the enthusiasm of the crowd, but his anger, turned inwards, simmered, muted and cunning.

Chapter One
Running the Gauntlet

May 7, 1915
The Atlantic Ocean
South of the Irish Coast

*C*laire awoke on the last day of their sea voyage to an echo of the stern warning they had all been given the night before by Captain Turner—a chilling reality of the Great War. They were, after all, on the "Greyhound of the Seas," the most luxurious ocean liner ever built—the *Lusitania*. It had set speed records, for heaven's sake, and could easily outrun any of the Kaiser's U-Boat submarines. *Couldn't it?*

Unlike the sumptuous accommodations of the first class passengers, Claire and Doris, budding nurses from New York City, shared a stifling closet-sized 'stateroom' down on F deck just above the boilers. The windowless, sickly green cubicle, with its now-familiar banging of scalding pipes and the incessant drumbeat of the mighty Parsons engines reverberating through the steamy flooring, was barely tolerable, and then, only for sleeping. The heat and smell of coal along with the humidity of the engine room bubbled up through the rivets in the planking.

But Claire didn't mind one little bit. She was free at last and in love with her liberator, Byron. Such a fine figure of a man. Who would have thought just four months ago, when she was still captive in the terrible Providence Orphanage, that she could be on her way to England today as part of a team to demonstrate advanced battlefield triage methods? *How life can turn on a dime, as they say.*

"Get up, Dor," Claire prodded at the lump under the blanket. We've got work to do and Ireland to see as we steam past today."

Although they had only known each other two months at Beth Israel Hospital in New York before this adventure started, they had become the best of friends.

"Aren't you worried about the Germans?" Doris said, peeking out from under the covers.

"Not when you compare it to where we're going, in field hospitals near the allied trenches."

Doris propped her beefy frame up on the bed and started hunting for her undergarments.

"Better dress for a swim," Claire kidded, pulling on her woolen leggings and jumper over her shapely five-foot-seven figure.

"Don't you joke about that," Doris frowned.

"I just meant that we should be prepared, like the Captain said last night at the life boat drill," Claire offered to reassure her nervous friend. "He said it was only a precaution." But Claire sensed that they were, in fact, entering the Great War battlefield already.

"How come you're so brave?"

"Had a tough upbringing, I guess."

"You don't look the worse for wear except for that scar on your chin. Where'd you get it?"

Claire's shoulder-length jet black hair in ringlets framed her sensuous face with smoky green eyes and high cheekbones. She carefully wound it into a bun as they prepared for a day in the nursery.

"From a ring-fingered punch I got one time. I told you about that, surely." In fact, she had been keeping her past secret from all but Byron.

Doris jumped out of bed onto the postage-stamp-sized floor. "Yeow. That's hot on the tootsies. No. You never said."

"What would you say if I told you I was abducted from Brooklyn when I was thirteen and made a slave, imprisoned in a rat-infested orphanage and worked near to death in a textile mill in Rhode Island until three months ago?"

No, girl, you'd be skin and bones and you're gorgeous."

"How about I tell you that I can't find my Ma and brother since I've been back. They've vanished. Or what if I said that our own Byron saved me when he came to the Mill his forefathers used to own because he saw me tending to an injured lad?"

"Is that where you got your nursing skills, Claire?"

"Somebody had to try and save them, all the injured and maimed ones. And what if I were to tell you that Bryon's life was threatened at gunpoint last week at his home in New York City, likely because of his heroic act?" *There. It's out in the open now, for what that's worth.* Claire felt better for the telling.

"No wonder you're on this assignment and that you don't seem worried about U-Boats. Anyway, you've got Byron to save you, don't you now. I've seen how you look at each other. Did you . . . you know . . . ? she pumped her right index finger in and out of her left circled thumb and middle finger, giggling."

"Heavens no, Dor," Claire cringed and looked away to finalize the line of her jumper. Then she said, "But there was one terrible time at the orphanage . . . a preparation for prostitution later on . . ."

"Oh my God, Claire." Doris threw her arms around Claire's back and held on tight. "You poor girl."

"But now there's Byron, our handsome orderly." Claire said, spinning around and urging Doris to finish dressing.

"Does he know that you love him?"

Claire shook her head vigorously. "No, and don't you tell him."

"Then *you'd* better tell him and soon, you knucklehead."

"We'll see, Dor. I don't want him to feel sorry for me. I want him to tell me first, if he does truly want me."

"*Knuckle—head,*" Doris chanted over and over, grabbing her friend in a headlock and wash-boarding her arched eyebrows with the back of her hand.

"Cut that out. Let's go to breakfast. I'm famished," Claire scolded.

As they headed out of their tiny third-class cabin, Claire was satisfied that for the time being at least, Doris's frown had disappeared.

"The risks are highest now," Captain Will Turner sternly cautioned his bridge officers as the *Lusitania* cruised into the war zone in a Europe that was fully engulfed in the Great War. Although he had no explicit U-Boat warnings from Vice Admiral Coke in Queenstown, Will had seen the German notice in the New York papers before they got underway. The hair on the back of his neck bristled.

He was not new to this business. He loved being an irascible captain, aloof from the prissy passengers and crew. He'd never understood why they all flocked to cruise on his ships. *What was the attraction?* Gnarly and wizened from his many years at sea, Will looked and acted the part of a crusty sailor.

Why the Admiralty had decided to divert his cruiser escort, leaving him defenseless at this critical stage of the voyage, was beyond him. Likely enemy action nearby. Nineteen hundred and sixty-two souls were entrusted to his care.

On this May morning, he bellowed at his men from the bridge, "Double the watch and close all bulkheads! And swing the life-boats out on their davits, just in case!"

He wished they had not finally emerged from a foggy morning into radiant sunshine. They were south of the Irish coast en route to Liverpool, and except for their speed, the ship was a sitting duck. Bowler Bill, so nicknamed for the hat he always wore on the bridge, decided to veer northeast toward Queenstown to be safe.

"Port thirty degrees. Full speed ahead!" he ordered. "Do not zigzag. It will only slow us down."

At one-forty-five in the nursery on a lower deck of the *Lusitania*, Claire still assumed they were safe enough. Claire, Doris and their fellow nursemaids were busy preparing the twenty-nine infants in their charge in case the unthinkable happened.

She watched Byron calmly and confidently secure the babies into wicker baskets. The children made her think of Moses being swaddled and protected as a newborn babe on the banks of the Nile. Byron was a ruggedly handsome man, standing over six feet tall, with gray eyes and an earnest and honest face that mirrored his caring character. Claire had decided to find a way to confess her love to him. She could still feel the tingling where Doris's knuckles had massaged her scalp. But when Claire went to speak to him, all that came out was "Byron, why don't the high-falutin' first-class passengers look after their own babies at a time like this?"

"They're too busy hobnobbing at their high-falutin' lunch, I suppose," he shot back. "Of course some of these babies are genuinely sick."

Without warning, the liner surged to starboard.

"Look out, Byron!" Claire cried, diving to catch one of the baskets as it slid off the table.

Byron watched as Claire deftly caught the infant before the basket hit the floor. It amazed him that she had managed to keep her beauty and svelte hourglass figure in spite of the depravation and beatings she had endured at the orphanage. Her bubbly smile that could light up his heart was hidden now in this hour of uncertainty.

This was no time to revel in her beauty.

"Nice catch, my Irish rose," he said, trying to be chipper.

When he saw worry lines etched in her face, he knew he needed to bolster her resolve. "I'm sure our Captain knows what he is doing. You have been amazingly brave and resourceful, Claire. Summon that courage now, dear one. These children are counting on us, just like the ones you cared for at the Mill and orphanage."

"You're right. We need to be strong now, don't we, dear one." Claire played with those words on her tongue, the term of endearment he had used for her, which had stopped short of the three loving words she longed to hear.

Kapitanleutnant Walther Schwieger was satisfied. He'd had a very successful mission. U-20 had sunk several ships in the Irish Sea.

"We are low on fuel and armament," he reminded his second-in-command, First Wachoffizier Weisbach, "so we're heading home to Kiel."

His men were sweaty and tired, and despite his strict on-board discipline, they were getting testy.

He was running at maximum speed on the surface, charging the batteries. From his perch on the conning tower, he spotted multiple funnel stacks on the horizon. At first he thought it was several ships. When he finally recognized the unique outline of this four-funnel ocean liner, he remembered his orders to seek out and sink her. She was reportedly carrying American munitions for the war effort.

"She is heading northeast away from us, making about eighteen knots," the helmsman, Unteroffizier Fritz Gruber announced through the IMC.

That was double U-20's maximum available submerged speed.

"Dive, dive to eleven meters. Raise periscope!" The Kapitan ordered. "Herr Weisbach, load forward tubes one and two with our last torpedoes in case we get lucky."

Schwieger waited, his pulse quickening, as his silent killer slipped beneath the Irish Sea. And then he stalked his prey.

Through his periscope a few minutes later, he saw the liner abruptly change course to starboard. The ship was now heading on a bearing that would bring it squarely into the path of U-20.

"How fortunate!" Schwieger said to his crew. "We will intercept."

"Herr Kapitan," Obersteurmann Charles Voegele spoke up. "We cannot fire at an unarmed passenger liner with women and children aboard without signaling them first."

Schwieger knew that international marine law did require this courtesy to allow for the women and children to take to their boats, but he would have to surface again to hail them. He had done that yesterday before he sank both the *SS Candidate* and the *SS Centurion*. But, with the *Lusitania's* speed, there was no time. And a submarine on the surface was vulnerable to a ramming attack by its intended target. A flicker of compassion passed over his face. He hesitated, thinking of the carnage he might inflict; then reminded himself that this ship likely carried munitions destined to kill many of his own countrymen. The German High Command had warned Britain's allies that these waters were considered a war zone. Such warnings were posted in newspapers all over the globe. This vessel was fair game.

"Do you question my orders, Herr Voegele?" Schwieger growled.

The quartermaster cringed, but he held his ground. "Yes sir, mein Kapitan. I refuse to fire on an unarmed vessel without signaling them first!"

The liner was closing fast. There was no time to argue.

"*Nein!* Place this man in the brig and load those torpedoes!" Schwieger bellowed. Then, without batting an eyelash, at seven hundred meters closing distance, he shouted, "Fire!"

Weisbach pushed the button and launched a single gyroscopic torpedo.

A lookout high up in the bow of the liner saw the torpedo coming, closing at thirty meters per second.

"Bridge! Bridge!" He screamed up to the bridge through his megaphone. "Torpedo off the starboard bow!"

The wind and the throbbing of the mighty turbines running at fever pitch drowned out his shouts. Only a few nearby passengers, out for a stroll on deck heard his warning. They shrieked with panic and began to run.

The torpedo hit amidships, just behind the bridge at a depth of three meters. It pierced the hull and exploded inward, shredding bulk-heads, staterooms and human flesh. Clouds of debris, steel plating, and water shot upward, knocking starboard Lifeboat 5 off its davits. It sounded like a million-ton hammer hitting the boilers. But Claire and Byron, protected two decks below in the nursery, had no idea.

"Good God, Byron!" Claire cried, rushing to his side. "What was that?"

"I'm not sure," he replied, pulling Claire close to him with an arm around her shoulders. Looking frantically around the small nursery he heard tearing metal ahead and below him and shouts in the outside companionway. "A damned torpedo hit."

A second even more terrifying explosion erupted from the bowels of the ship. Claire shuddered against him, and the babies began to wail. The vibration of the engines died, and Byron could feel the huge liner immediately start to heel over to starboard and tilt forward. Losing their balance, Claire crushed into him as they fell. When Byron pulled her to her feet, he saw the disarray of baskets on the floor. Byron guessed that the ship was mortally wounded.

"Claire, you remember what we talked about. You and the other nurses must get topside." Byron turned her toward him and gripped her arms. "Take two babies each and go now. Board the lifeboats and whatever you do, do not come back here. Dr. Gilroy is up there somewhere in first class. Mr. Frohman, Alfred Vanderbilt, and I will get some of the other men to carry the rest of the babies to safety."

"Oh, Byron!" Claire clung to him, "I love you so. Don't you know that?"

"The words I've longed to hear." Byron closed his eyes and drew her closer, savoring her warmth and softness, but only for a moment.

Then he held her at arm's length and smiled into her green eyes. Inwardly, he was terrified, but he forced himself to stay calm and decisive or they hadn't a prayer of surviving.

"My dearest Claire. I love you more than anything in this world. You are my beacon of hope. You must go now, darling. I need you to be brave and strong and lead the way for the other nurses."

He pressed a soft kiss to her forehead, and felt her stop clinging.

"All right, my love. Hurry to me as soon as you can." Claire drew away and turned briskly to her fellow nurses. "Quickly, ladies. Take two baskets each. We must get our charges up on deck. Byron's orders."

Claire grasped two ten-pound baskets of infants and led the way out of the nursery. At the doorway she paused, looking down at the helpless babies' faces in her charge and thinking about the sons and daughters that she and Byron would have after this was all over. Looking back she gave Byron a brave smile before moving out. Then it was over to the first set of stairs leading to the next deck.

A moment later all the lights in the ship went dark.

Chapter Two
The Unthinkable

"Damage control!" Captain Will bellowed into the ship's intercom from his perch on the stricken bridge. He hoped to hell someone could still hear him. He noted that most of his instruments were now inoperative and the rumbling noises below told him water was rushing into the bowels of his ship. He was going to have to rely on his crew's on-the-scene reports from now on throughout this disaster.

"Engines stopped and flooding," came the muffled response from Saunders, the Chief Engineer. "We're still making headway at seventeen knots."

"Get your men out of there now, Fred! This doesn't look good." Will commanded. The bridge staff could then hear crewmen yelling orders to abandon ship in the engine room.

"Thank God, at least the intercom system is still working," Will called out to his men.

"Bulkheads one through seven breached and pumps out of commission!" cried the burly, thirty year old third bosun's mate, Jack Jordan.

"Electrical systems shorted, no power below decks!" The electrician shrieked into the ether. "Backup generators useless!"

"Sparks, are you still transmitting a Mayday?" Will shouted over the din of the commotion around him. He could see that despair was gripping his bridge crew.

"Aye, Captain. I still have power. But there's no response yet!"

Will was working on instinct now. Less than five minutes had passed since the torpedo attack, and all the ship's functions seemed to be failing simultaneously.

"Offshore distance, speed and list angle," he demanded.

"Fourteen kilometers off the Old Kinsale Light, Captain,

drifting at seventeen knots. The list is ten degrees to starboard and eight degrees down by the bow."

"Good God! How can we be sinking so fast?" Will cried out.

The crew had no time to answer.

"Are the passengers mustering to stations?" Will queried Jack who was trying to control the mounting passengers' hysteria on port side boat decks.

"Aye, Captain, those that can get on deck. So many are caught below in darkness with the bulkhead doors closed! Things are getting very hard to control down here."

Turner could hear the agonizing screams in the background as the bosun was talking. "What have I done?" he muttered incoherently.

The unthinkable was happening, and progressing at gut-wrenching speed. The creaking and groaning sounds coming with increasing rapidity told him that his beloved ocean liner was straining to hold itself afloat and losing the battle. Acrid smoke was now billowing up out of the torpedo rupture, and he could feel the heat of the crackling fires searing up through the deck plates. "We're out of control!" he concluded, as this sickening reality hit home.

"Jack, we're moving too fast to lower the boats yet, and we have no way to stop her quickly," he shouted into the intercom. "We need another ten minutes at least."

"Not sure we've got that much time, Captain. The bow is already awash. The port boats won't likely clear the rails. Passengers are panicked and storming those boats, and my men are powerless to stop them!"

"Then get your men to the starboard boats where you can do some good and make sure they're full up!" Will ordered. "Wait for my signal to lower away."

Claire was stalled in her climb amidst the suffocating surge of bodies crushing her in the central stairwell. She witnessed desperate fathers pressing to pull their wailing womenfolk and children up against a solid wall of other clawing men doing likewise. Claustrophobia pervaded the mob, but was the least of their fears. If they fell, they'd be crushed. If they didn't, they weren't likely to see the light of day anyway. At least the cacophony of screams and wailing prayers was drowning out the sickening grinding and groaning of the ship's metal structures she had heard earlier. The terror of being entombed alive when the ship surely sank in the cold black water frenzied them.

She had to get up and out. *Will Byron ever find me? Surely he must be right behind. Could it be that I've only climbed one deck?*

One deck to go, then. Claire risked being knocked down by turning to look down the stairs. All she saw was a mass of unfamiliar faces, like death masks already. *Where is Dor and the other ladies with their baskets?* Claire felt terribly alone in the sea of horrified humanity. *How many more seconds do we have before the end?* She became acutely aware of every putrid breath of life she was taking in that mass coffin of their prison-like stairwell. Smoke, urine and vomit odors combined to make her gag.

Painfully, step by step, like cattle being pushed to slaughter, the crowd inched upwards. She was one of them. *How many steps to go now? Ten? Five? How long had it been? It seemed like hours since I left Byron's arms, my beloved. Oh, how I long, need to have him here now.*

Suddenly a young boy blocking her upward view fell backward and got his foot lodged in the stair-riser opening. She could finally see a sliver of daylight winking down through the throng. Five steps to go she guessed.

But Claire realized she was not going to make it with this lad blocking her way. Nor with any of the frantic people pushing below her. The more the lad wriggled the more his leg wedged into the opening. His mother, on the step above, had his hand and was trying to pull him upward. That was sure to break his leg or worse.

Claire saw that she could extricate him horizontally from her position if the woman would just let go. But if she put down even one basket with a baby inside, it would likely be trampled to death in seconds.

"Let me help you," she cried thrusting one basket at the Mother. "Hold this and I'll get him out."

The woman froze, refusing to let go of her son.

"You've got to hold this baby for me while I get him out," Claire yelled.

The woman had him in a death grip and Claire could see blood spurting out of his trousers where the sharp metal grate was digging in. He was screaming. Mass murder, that's what it's going to be. And there was nothing she could do to stop it.

Claire took the risk of placing one basket on the step between her legs. The crowd below surged, and she almost toppled over onto the boy. She decided she had no choice. With her freed hand, she reached up and slapped the mother hard across the face to get her to release her grip on the boy.

At that moment, a protracted, tearing noise, like a giant's fingernails on chalkboard, reverberating through the hull and making Claire's hair stand on end. The ship appeared to have begun its death rattle.

Maybe it was the slap or maybe the ship's rending scream. The mother let go of her son's hand. Seizing the moment, Claire turned to block her from regaining her grip. Then she yanked the boy horizontally out of the riser and stood him up in front of her.

She thrust the boy's arm up into his startled mother's hand. The woman grabbed on for dear life and pulled the boy up to the next step.

"Thank you," the mother cried in a tiny voice and sorrowful eyes.

"Look out" Claire shouted, when a foot stepped up between her legs, crunching the side of one of her baskets, barely missing the baby.

Lifting the baskets once again, she turned upward. *Five more steps, four . . .*

The ship seemed to be more tilted with every step up that Claire managed.

Suddenly she was swept up in the frantic mass of wailing humanity and carried out of the main stairwell onto the port boat deck.

"Hey lady!" a man yelled nearby to her left. "Get over here with your babies! We're lowering Boat Twelve. You need to jump on board now!"

She hesitated, looking frantically back toward the stairwell for Byron. Crazed passengers tumbled down the stairs, helter-skelter, but neither her love nor Doris were anywhere to be seen. Looking back at Boat Twelve, she spied a passenger high up on the aft davit. He loosed the winch sprocket prematurely and the lifeboat tipped precariously, spilling half its contents of human cargo back onto the deck and the other half overboard.

"Look out!" The man cried. "The rope is giving way!"

Claire watched in horror as Boat Twelve flipped and crashed down off the rail onto the deck with a murderous crunch, trapping the passengers beneath it. When the fractured boat came to rest just ten feet away from her, Claire initially froze. She had seen death before but not on this scale nor this violent. This was a war zone and the nightmare was a reality.

"Gimme that baby!" A woman wrenched one of the baskets out of Claire's grasp and darted off to another boat, undoubtedly hoping to gain sanctuary because of the young child now in tow.

This jarred Claire back out of her shock. She could now see that the scene was repeating itself, boat after boat, down the port side, as untrained passengers took matters into their own hands, trying to launch life boats onto the deck or into the side of the ship on their way to the ocean below. Claire was certain that this was a

15

path to certain death as the lifeboats were destined to crash like the others had. But she was powerless to stop them.

Oh, God, she thought. Had she survived New York, the kidnapping and the many years of child labor in bondage, only to die here today, in the sea, just miles from her native Ireland? She longed for her country, for her lost mother and brother. But more than anyone else right now, she longed for Byron.

"Oh, Byron. I need you," she cried, hoping he could hear her in the main stairwell. *Why isn't he on deck yet?* Despair, that emotion she thought she had driven out of her psyche back at the orphanage, seeped back. That old nauseous weakness. Claire could feel it pounding in her chest.

No. No. I can't let that back in. I've come too far to have it end like this. Think.

Her training kicked in. She couldn't minister to all of them, but she could help at least a few of those whose limbs were partially hanging out from under Boat Twelve. Putting her attention on others always helped in trying times such as these. That would help her, too, until Byron showed up.

A scream came from a woman trapped under the lifeboat. The stump of her right arm, severed above the elbow, was reaching out beyond the boat, its disjointed forearm lying beyond it on the deck.

"Joe," the woman cried, over and over. Claire thought it such a hollow, mournful wail echoing the last plea of all the innocents. She could help at least this one victim.

"Oh, God, no." Claire gasped. There, just beyond the reach of the woman's still twitching hand, lay her son. Dried blood coagulated on his trouser leg. Claire checked and there was no pulse. Dead.

Ripping a strip off her skirt, Claire applied a tourniquet above the stump and tried to calm her patient.

16

"We're trapped, Byron," Vanderbilt exclaimed. "And we're out of time."

"You've given away your life jacket and you told me that you can't swim," Byron said.

"That won't matter if we can't get topside anyway," Vanderbilt remarked as if it were of no consequence.

They were standing waist deep in frigid water, still two decks below daylight, Byron estimated, stuck in a passageway just outside the nursery, clogged by other trapped and frightened passengers. They could only feel their way, when they could move at all. Noxious fumes spewed from the ventilators that stung their noses and throats.

Byron had seen that the stairwells that Claire would have taken were now under water—that way barred.

"People, listen to me. If you panic we are all lost!" Byron yelled. "Move aft in an orderly way to get above the waterline and maybe we'll find a dry stairwell up to the boat deck."

But the crowd was too far gone with fear. They were clawing past the masses in the darkness, knocking each other down and trampling the fallen. Some were screaming obscenities. Others were praying reverently.

"Oh, God, keep Claire safe!" Byron cried out, as he heard an ominous, thunderous crack that he correctly concluded was another bulkhead giving way. He felt the ship roll heavily to starboard, and then sucked a deep breath as a surge of cold, icy water engulfed him and dragged him under.

Claire cried out as she was yanked away from her patient by a violent roll and slammed into the port bulkhead and back out onto the cross deck. Startled, but still clutching her remaining basket, she crawled back to where the tourniquet had come loose and pulled it tight again, her mind now acutely aware of the grisly scene up and down the port side. *My God.* One of the huge smokestacks toppled onto the forward port deck. Fire and death everywhere. Some poor souls were on fire, writhing on the deck. Others were jumping overboard, preferring a quick cold death to the agony of frying alive. The stench of burning oil, wood, and flesh swept down the boat deck searing Claire's nostrils.

There was no orchestra playing. No valiant musicians like those she had read about on the *Titanic.* Just screams of agony from the deck and the water below.

Turning her attention aft again, she could see boats askew on the rails or broken against the bulkhead. Bodies were everywhere, with the many twisted, broken and hopeless moaning for help.

Jack Jordan had his hands full and then some on the starboard boat deck amidships. The captain had finally just ordered, "Lower all boats!" *Not that it mattered.* They had been forced by the passengers to start lowering the boats minutes ago. Five boats already had been launched in the melee, only partially filled. Three more had broken apart or capsized with unknown consequences.

"Jack, since that last bulkhead went, the boats are too far overboard to safely board!" one crewman yelled. "What can we do?"

"Make them jump from the rails! It's their only chance!" Jack yelled back.

He saw that the water was creeping further and further up the deck from the bow. The bridge was almost under water. What made matters worse, the fog was drifting back, starting to envelop the ship in a shroud.

Jack wondered what had happened on the port side. He glanced over his shoulder towards the main stairwell exit. No more people escaping the death trap. Must be completely flooded. He crossed himself in a silent prayer for their souls.

Through the flung-open doorway, he could make out a solitary young woman on the port side. She was kneeling by Boat Twelve. Praying?

I've got to save her, he decided, moving to action. As he emerged onto the port deck, his worst visions of the disaster were confirmed. Hopeless. That girl is not praying. She's tending to the wounded. In the midst of this disaster, he couldn't believe his eyes. She was like Florence Nightingale.

"Lady, get over here!" he shouted.

Claire didn't move. Jack ran to her side and immediately understood.

"Nothing useful can be done here," he assured her. "Come with me and save yourself and your baby."

Claire clutched at him and gazed up at his haggard face. He was a handsome enough young sailor, about her height, curly brown hair. He saw the hollow look in her eyes and realized that she had already seen too much.

"But we've got to help these people," she pleaded. "Have you seen my Byron? He'll save us."

Jack was astounded that this young woman would be thinking of others before herself at a time like this. He needed to pry her away immediately if there was a hope of saving her.

"What's your name?" he asked gently.

"Claire, my name is Claire."

"Claire, I think I heard Byron calling your name on the starboard side. Come with me and we'll find him together."

Claire's eyes brightened. "You've seen him? You've seen my Byron? Bring him here," she implored.

I have to save this woman. "I think whoever you're tending to is dead, Claire," Jack exclaimed. Her crying had ceased.

"What about these others?" Claire's arm swept down the port-side deck.

It looks like a battlefield, Jack thought.

"My God it's a battlefield," Claire shouted, standing up and starting toward the next smashed lifeboat in the line.

Uncanny, as if she'd read my mind. I've got to save this woman.

"We're going to look for Byron together," Jack yelled, grabbing her basket off the deck, rushing to her side and grabbing her by the shoulder. "There's no time to lose." With that, he forcibly turned her away from the carnage on the port deck and half carried her and her baby across to the aft starboard deck. He was sick at heart.

Captain Will had done all he could do on the bridge. He stood there alone there, with only the creaking of his wounded ship to keep him company. The water was lapping at the base of the door. Forgetting that he had already ordered his bridge crew to abandon ship, he called out, "Sparks! Any news, son?" There was no response.

He estimated that it was just fifteen minutes since the torpedo attack and that his ship was about to sink beneath his feet. How could this happen so quickly? Had he not closed the bulkhead doors? What could he have done differently, he agonized? How many were dead? How many safe in the boats? How many dying in the water? Why had that damn fog come back at this terrible moment? Had their SOS been heard? Would rescuers get here in time or at all? He had no answers to any of these questions. Shock had set in.

He could no longer communicate with Jack and had no idea whether or not the starboard boats had been launched. Clutching the ship's log and donning his bowler hat one last time, he stepped out onto the starboard bridge wing, searching for signs of life in the water. Not finding any, he headed aft to try and help the deck crew. Unable to find his crew and overcome with the weight of responsibility, he let himself slip off the catwalk and into the frigid sea.

Kapitanleutnant Schwieger had been glued to his periscope. Now, sickened by the tragedy he had wrought, he could look no more.

"*Mein Gott!*" he exclaimed to his crew. "That ship is going down already." He realized that he had gotten very lucky with that shot, but he was right about their cargo. Had to be.

"Mein Kapitan, can't we help the survivors?" asked the helmsman. "There will be great loss of life this day."

"Nein, Fritz," he countered. "Shore boats will come. They are at the mercy of their God."

And with that, he summarily turned his back on the tragic scene before him and ordered U-20 back on course for home.

"War is war," he muttered. "It's not personal."

But inwardly, he agonized.

"Come on, Claire," Jack urged, pulling her aft along the starboard boat deck. This Good Samaritan represented all that was good in this wretched world. She and her baby had to be saved.

"Jump into Boat Seventeen. *Over there.* The last one to launch."

"But what about Byron?" Claire cried as she scanned the crowd for her man. "I can't leave without him!"

"Claire, listen to me," Jack reasoned. "He's probably already on one of the boats that launched, looking for you. You must go now for the sake of your baby."

From the angle of attack and submergence of the ship and its tearing sounds and grinding vibrations, Jack guessed that the liner was within a couple of minutes of going under and would be sucking all who remained on board down with it.

When Claire did not move, Jack firmly picked her up in his arms and carried her to the waiting boat.

"Give us your baby!" cried the crewman on board Boat Seventeen, "Climb up on the railing and jump into the boat. Hurry up!"

Jack pried the basket from Claire's grasp and hoisted it into the boat. Then he lifted her up onto the rail. "Jump, Claire!" he cried.

She had to jump or fall into the sea. "Byron!" she called out as she jumped.

"Look out, Claire," Jack shouted as the on-board crewman caught the basket but dropped the bowline.

Claire saw the bow drop like a rock below her until the boat hung vertically. Passengers either fell out or clung for dear life. Then, under the strain, the aft davit pivoted inwards, sending Boat Seventeen crashing into the hull of the liner.

Claire managed to grasp the transom as she fell, holding on outside the boat. The aft rope started to play out from the damaged davit. Claire instinctively reached over the transom and grabbed the rope, but there was no way she could hold it as it singed palm and fingers. The boat careened off the hull and down towards the water.

Jack saw it first, barely, through the swirling fog. Boat Nineteen, with thirty-five aboard, was trying to maneuver away from the liner. Heading forward after successfully launching into the sea, it was directly under Boat Seventeen when it plummeted.

Horrified, Jack watched from above to see the bow of this now-deadly lifeboat cleanly slice Boat Nineteen in two. "Look out!" he yelled, too late to do any good. Then the two boats disintegrated into pieces, flinging their passengers like rag dolls into the sea. He couldn't make out the final outcome as the fog closed in around the wreckage.

With no more lifeboats to launch, Jack raced to the stern on the second class promenade. Then, when this once-thought invincible liner finally shuddered its last gasp and sliced downwards, he jumped. His last thought was that this was his only hope of salvation— if he survived the impact with the water and the enormous suction of the dying behemoth.

❀❀❀❀❀

Being above and on the outside of the transom, Claire had been somewhat shielded from the carnage below her. Although alive, the shock of the cold water almost stopped her heart. She was submerged for what seemed an eternity. Petrified, she held onto that transom that had separated from its boat, and they both eventually bobbed to the surface. There were bodies floating everywhere with only a few moaning survivors. No one was swimming. She couldn't see very far through the fog. Just when she thought she would lose all feeling in her limbs, Claire managed to pull herself up onto the floating transom.

Exhausted and numbingly cold, she lay on her back watching as the huge liner drifted away. Then suddenly, with a great hollow gurgle, the mighty ship tipped stern up and slipped under the sea.

"Oh, God!" Claire gasped as her transom life raft was dragged, like a leaf in a storm, into the cauldron where the gigantic ship had disappeared. "I'm going to be sucked under for sure!"

Then, with a mighty belch, the sea disgorged broken parts of the ship up into the air. In her weakened state, Claire thought it all seemed so unreal, reminding her of the fountain she saw one time her Ma took her to Central Park. While she was lying there contemplating the wonder of it all, something, maybe a deck chair, smashed down onto the transom and hit Claire a glancing blow on her head. That's when she saw it clearly. Just for a moment, her mind, strangely spinning in time. *"My God, he's burning, he's burning. We've got to save him!*" Looking with hollow eyes towards the hole in the sea where that fire had been raging just three minutes earlier, her brain just shut down.

Claire floated off, away from shore and the launched boats, alone in the fog. Barely alive, she was buoyed up by her salvation transom that bore the name *Lusitania, Starboard Boat Seventeen*.

Chapter Three
Warehouse Fires

"*J*e-sus, it's cold." Sam Finlay stamped his aching feet on old Geddes Wharf No. 2 at the foot of Bay Street. His old boots were fine for summer sketching trips in Muskoka but not tonight on this frozen, God-forsaken shoreline. "Sorry, Lord," he bent his head in a familiar act of penance.

His feet were going numb again. The ice shards in the cracks of the worn oak planks snapped under those boots, causing swirls of powdery snow to fly up around his ankles. *At least the blizzard has finally died.*

Sam felt the sting of residual flurries whip against his cheek. His normal cherub-like face with its sensual dimpled chin now must look more like a lopsided snowman's frozen head, with recessed eyes appearing as black as coal. Although having a some-what pointed nose, Sam was sure his protuberance did not as yet resemble a carrot. But it was cold, damn cold. He was sure that the transformation into ice-hood would be complete if he stood still much longer.

A partially frozen and foreboding Lake Ontario stretched out into the dark beyond the railings not twenty feet to Sam's left. He could hear the cracking as its rollers crunched ice spars against the pilings below him.

Shoving his vellum note pad up under his mackintosh to keep it dry, Sam was ready—willing himself to stay vigilant. Looking to his right, the giant, monolithic wooden and stone warehouses lining the wharf loomed up in the dark, their orderly symmetry now marred by the two gaping holes recently occupied by their burnt-out sisters, foreboding sentinels at their post.

A sole wharf light above and in front of Sam was dimmed from the encrustations eating away at its glass case. It cast the only pale light that this night had to offer. Flickering in the gloom of midnight, the yellow glow threatened to leave him in utter darkness.

Sam had positioned himself behind a pile of wharf crates, just outside the light's perimeter. Standing only five-foot-six, he should be completely hidden from view.

The usually prolific wharf rats were nowhere to be seen, likely forced indoors in the frigid climate. He was alone—there were no ships, and the longshoremen had long gone to the myriad of decrepit bars and brothels that infested the slums of the Ward.

Sam hoped the boss's hunch about political intrigue that had sent him down here on this god-forsaken assignment, was correct. He'd been hired as an illustrator for the *Toronto Evening Telegram*, not as a cub reporter, for heaven's sake.

In his own dimly-lit corner of the waterfront, Sam had time to reflect. He had been fortunate to be taken on by such a prestigious newspaper, as just one of many young and recently emigrated Irish lads flooding into Canada from his tortured Northern Ireland homeland. With only twenty-three years of life behind him, how could he expect more? So here he'd stand, slowly turning into an icicle, waiting for something to happen.

Sam pulled the knot in his thick Irish woolen scarf tighter around his stout neck. He wasn't portly, but he certainly had meat on his bones, which served him well on this frigid night.

The harbor in winter didn't look or feel that much different from his home city of Belfast, except for the massive Harland and Wolff ship-building yard—dirty, sooty, congested. Sam had sailed from that thriving port two years ago in his quest for love and a bright new life with his childhood sweetheart Elizabeth. Her parents, the Hefferons, had dragged their daughters to Canada a year ahead of him.

Sam had followed his love interest as quickly as he could. With the chance to develop his art in this new land of burgeoning opportunity his heart was alive at last. If he had to make some sketches for the newspaper at midnight as a starting point so be it. Ultimately, his training at the Dublin, and then London Art Institutes, would stand him in good stead in this world of rugged natural beauty. But not tonight on the grimy docks at ten below zero.

A movement in the near darkness startled Sam out of his reverie. *What was that?* Squinting through the gloom, he thought he saw two men scooting between the warehouses nearest him in the line, and then disappearing inside Warehouse Five. He stepped out from behind the crates to get a better view and waited, watching the warehouse intently.

There. They're coming back. Wait, there's only one. A big man, to be sure. Sam saw the man hesitate between the warehouses, looking toward the lake before he passed behind the building nearest the newspaperman.

Sam moved to get a closer look and froze.

Damn, the boss was right. The intrigue was on. And now, he picked up a new sensation—smoke.

Sam could see flames lighting up the window in the wall facing the wharf. It only took a few seconds for the fire to take hold in the rotten wood. Now the rats appeared, hundreds of them squealing and scurrying out in all directions from cracks in the doomed warehouse.

The flames spread fast. Sam scanned the area for help. The man was nowhere to be seen. *Was he the firebug?* Probably hightailing it from the scene, if so.

What happened to the other bloke? Was he trapped inside?

By now the burning warehouse was an inferno, blazing its way along the Lake Ontario waterfront starkly silhouetted against the cold January night sky. The fire lit up the whole line of warehouse sentinels, reflecting the leaping blue and yellow flames window by window.

"There'll be hell to pay for this, to be sure," Sam muttered, pulling out his notebook from his coat, pencil flying across a sheet of vellum in his drawing notebook as he started sketching the conflagration. "Three warehouses burned to the ground in one week can't be a coincidence."

The icy wind gusted while flames leapt higher. They'd see the blaze from the fire station up Yonge Street, Sam ventured, but the pumper wagons would arrive too late. He could feel his feet starting to tingle as the heat from the blaze radiated out across the wharf.

He stopped sketching to loosen his scarf and doffed his toque to wipe the sweat that was beading on his already receding hairline. Then he formed an open square with his two hands together, thumbs to thumbs and middle finger to middle finger, bringing it up in front of his eyes. He'd long ago been taught to use this tool to frame a picture, mentally dividing the inside space into thirds to get the proper perspective. This was all second nature to him now.

A movement caught Sam's eye and he turned his head and frame toward it, which acted like a kind of binoculars blocking out the surrounding scene. *Did he see the second man lurching into the blackness from the side door of the burning warehouse—or was the acrid smoke spewing out of the building and twitching his nostrils playing visual tricks on him?* Sam turned his focus back to recording an accurate rendition of the scene. *It wasn't his job to play detective.*

That's when he felt a blow to the back of his neck, then a searing pain shooting down his spine. The scene instantaneously flashed brilliant like an explosion in a Chinese fireworks factory as Sam dropped his notebook. That's the last thing he remembered before things went black.

The damp, frigid air roused Sam. His head felt as if it had been split in two. He hadn't had a headache like this since the morning after that Jameson's Pub farewell *cailidh* with his mates in Dublin. He tried to run his palms over his head to survey injuries but couldn't move his hands. When he turned his neck, he felt a pulling sensation on the hairs at the back of his neck. Something was matting his hair down. Then he remembered the blow and guessed it was dried blood.

The cold from the floor edged into his back. He could feel his frozen hands and feet bound behind him as he lay crumpled on his side in the dark. He could sense the bindings cutting off the circulation as he wriggled his wrists. Too damn tight. He blinked to adjust his eyes to the dimness, and could barely make out that he was lying on the floor of a warehouse. He could hear waves slapping against pilings and imagined the wharf below him.

"Just lie still, mister," came a thin, haunting, youthful male voice from out of the dark. "Lie still and keep silent, I beg ye. I beg ye."

A fellow Irishman, Sam thought. From Donegal, he guessed from the doubling. The voice was close to him and not moving. From its hollow sound Sam guessed that the building was cavernous.

"Why'd you clout me, damn it?"

"'Twasn't me that whacked you. Shut up."

"Untie me then and let's get out of here."

"I can't do that."

"So who hit me then?"

"Can't tell you that, either. You a cop?"

"No, just a newspaper illustrator doing his job. C'mon. I need to get the feeling back into my arms and legs. I'm hurt. Give me a hand here."

"I told you to fekin' shut up, damn it. You'll not be getting any help from me."

"What time is it, then?"

"I dunno. Maybe half-six. I'm not going to tell you again to plug your hole."

Sam sensed that he was in the presence of a kid and not a man—a scared kid, from the inflection in his voice. This was a dangerous mess he'd gotten himself into, possibly deadly. For the first time in his brief life, he realized his life was truly at risk and there was no one but himself to save him.

His vision for a wonderful loving life with Liz and kids and painting scenes flashed into his mind, days together at the Scarboro Bluffs with the wind sweeping down off the lake perfect for kite flying, wandering through Kew Beach Park when the tulips were finally up and brilliant in the Spring sunshine. Then he imagined Liz crying at his wake. *Stop that. Think.* He had to get free. His stomach was churning. He had to clamp his jaw to stop the chattering of his teeth. He could hear a roaring beyond the walls and wondered at the sound. The big bloke must have gotten the drop on him while he was intent on sketching. *His sketchbook, where was it? He couldn't lose that. Oh what, dear Lord, was he going to do next?*

The first dim rays of dawn came slanting through the upper windows, diffused by the cobwebs on the panes and plentiful dust particles floating in their wake. No warmth but the promise of daylight. Sam could now see that the warehouse was one of the sentinels. It was mostly filled with crates and barrels of all sizes in rows stacked six deep.

In front of him was a thirty-foot windowed wall that he knew would be on the wharf side. In its middle was a large iron double door, the kind that you could drive a lorry through. Snow had drifted through the crack underneath it and was caught in little piles by the worn slats and splinters of the wooden floor.

And there to his right, not ten feet away was his jailer, sitting on a barrel stenciled with the name Buffalo Import/Export Company and an American flag on the side. Sam's first thought was, *My God, It's Liam! Thanks be to God. He's back.* Spitting image. Sorry-looking.

About 17 or 18 years old, he guessed, not that much younger than himself, but to Sam he looked like a kid, a sad and dejected kid.

Muscular build but all hunched over. Maybe five-foot-ten, certainly less than six feet. Sam was envious of the shock of wavy black hair on his rounded Irish forehead. But it was the haunted hazel eyes peering at him dejectedly that really struck Sam—that and the jagged scar on his left cheek. What was this kid's story?

The boy absently pumped his left hand into a clenched fist while he balanced a rather large bowie knife in the palm of his right hand. He wore a campaign badge stuck on his lapel which read "Block Free Trade—Vote Borden."

Before Sam could speak again, a brawny oaf dressed head to foot in black burst open the front door. "Wake up, you lout!" He yelled at the boy.

In a flash, the man crossed to the barrel, cuffed the kid on the back of his neck with a log-like forearm and knocked him to the bare, cold floor.

"You mind me, Collin!" he cried. "Or you'll pay the price!"

The lad recoiled, and then climbed back up on the barrel, glaring defiantly.

"Piss off, Rudy," he grumbled, raising a fist to the man but then lowering it.

The oaf wheeled away from the lad and kicked Sam hard in the side. "You stay down until I figure out what to do with you," he snarled at Sam before lumbering off toward a work area on the wall to Sam's left with shelves full of foul smelling bottles and cans.

Breathing laboriously through the stabbing pain in his ribs, Sam eyed his captor. Rudy was a muscular six-foot-five, if he was an inch. He looked like he'd been hoisting fifty-five gallon barrels his whole life. A longshoreman's longshoreman. Certainly a physical challenge for a five-foot-eight artist, even if he could get the use of completely numb limbs. Probably in his fifties, Sam thought, judging by his craggy features and random tufts of hair. With his scowl and angry up-turned lip, he seemed the epitome of evil.

Sam listened for any sounds of activity out on the wharf; perhaps someone would come if he yelled for help. He heard nothing but the scurrying and occasional squeaking of a few of the rats inside the warehouse. Then he remembered. It was very early Sunday, the day of rest. *Not his final one,* he vowed.

The smells of tobacco and coffee from nearby crates permeated the heavy air. God, he wished he had his pipe. He could always think more clearly when he was drawing on his favorite Prince Albert tobacco. Normally he'd be getting ready to go to the Hefferon house for a croissant and coffee with Liz before they headed out to church.

Not this morning, and if he didn't do something soon, maybe never again on a Sunday morning. *What if he couldn't ever again feel the sizzle of their lips meeting and the warmth of their cocoon-like embrace?* The thought of his life with Liz being snuffed out because of these ruffians made Sam furious. How in hell was he going to get free from this deadly duo?

Rudy was now rummaging, banging the metal cans and sniffing their contents.

"You stayed in one piece, mister?" Collin whispered. "He sure gave you leather there."

"I'm still here."

Rudy pried open the lid of a large can and tipped it sideways, avoiding getting it on his big hands. Sam heard gurgling and splashing and could smell gasoline. The stench swamped the aroma of coffee out of his nostrils. *Dear God.* He remembered that familiar smell before the fire broke out. *Old Rudy must be the arsonist, then.*

Collin was watching Rudy, whose hands were shaking. From the cold, Sam wondered, or from fear or pent-up rage? Sam had seen the lad sneak his knife back in his waistband as soon as Rudy had appeared at the door.

Without another word, Rudy stormed out of the building

with the can as abruptly as he'd entered. The gas smell lingered. The terrible thought struck Sam that old Rudy's next job might be to torch this very warehouse. He suspected that Collin may be an unwilling conspirator, which meant he, too, could be just as easily disposed of as a lowly newspaper artist.

Sam twisted toward Collin. This sullen, quaking kid appeared to be his only hope for survival. Trusting his instincts that the boy was only following orders, Sam cleared his parched throat.

"Collin, my lad. Do you have anything for my splitting headache?"

"Do I look like a bleedin' nursemaid?"

"Just asking. Well then, how about a light for my pipe? It's here in my pocket."

"I'm not an *eejit*. I know what you're thinking. You're just trying to get me to cut you loose."

"Believe me, kid, I think that is in your best interest. It appears to me that the blaggard has forced you to do his bidding. So I hold none of this against you. You smell the gasoline? I fear that he is going to do away with both of us, likely by setting fire to this warehouse."

"No." Collin spun his head around, confirming that Rudy was gone with the gasoline.

"Let me loose and I'll protect you," Sam said. "Arson is a serious crime no matter how noble the cause."

"How would you know my cause?" Collin lashed out, grabbing and brandishing his knife.

"By looking at your lapel pin."

"What's that got to do with anything? Rudy ordered me to wear it."

"What happened to give the man control over you?"

Collin was clenching and unclenching both hands now, his eyebrows lowered, eyes darting from Sam over to the warehouse wall and back again. Trying to decide if he could trust him,

Sam guessed.

"You can tell me, lad. I'm not thinking to hurt you in any way, even if I were free."

A metal oil container clanked against the outside of the front door to the warehouse. Collin flinched and spun toward it.

"It's now or never, lad."

Finally Collin blurted out, "An American longshoreman raped and beat my Ma on this very wharf. I was there when she died."

"That's terrible. I'm so sorry," Sam said gently. "But how did that give Rudy power over you?"

"He is the longshoreman's foreman and saw it all. I was all alone after that and Rudy took me in."

"The man doesn't look like a caring sort."

"He's not. Just wanted to use me for work on the docks, and to con me into poker games with the longshoremen. Loved it, I did. But I'm no damned good at it, or anything else for that matter. So's I owe Rudy a lot of scratch."

"He threatened you for repayment, right?"

"What do you think?"

"I think he's going to kill the both of us Irish sods."

"Well, he hates our kind, that's for sure."

"There you go. So cut me loose."

"Why would he kill me when I owe him money?"

"I suspect old Rudy is working for somebody that doesn't want him to leave any loose ends, that's why."

Sam could see Collin clenching and unclenching his fists again and could sense the boy battled some inner demon. They were running out of time, so he tried another tack.

"You're from Donegal, aren't you?"

"How'd you know?"

"You said 'I beg ye' twice a while back."

"Yah, from Dungloe really."

"You want to see Dungloe again?"

"Hell, no. My Da was murdered near there. My Ma, me and my sister Claire scrammed to America."

Oh, Lord. This kid is so confused.

"I can help you out of this mess if you'll help me first. But you've got to do it now, Collin. Before Rudy comes back, if he indeed does."

Collin shook his head and toyed with the butt of his knife. Then he cried, "Shite!" jumped off the barrel and lunged toward him, his knife raised. For an awful moment Sam thought he'd misjudged the situation, until the boy dropped to his knees behind him and sliced through the rope tied his wrists.

"Undo your feet, quick," Collin whispered, pushing up and heading for the door.

Sam uncoiled, rubbing his forearms vigorously together and pumping his fists to get the feeling back. As blood flowed in, the pin-needles started. Sweet anguish. He got his fingers working and freed his feet just as Collin reached for the door handle.

"Look out, Collin!" Sam cried, seeing a telltale flicker through the lower windows. "Don't open it!"

Collin turned towards him with a puzzled, twisted look, as his hand felt for the knob and the door blew inward.

"Yeow!" The boy screamed, as the wall of flame and the in-rushing windstorm tossed him across the floor where he lay stunned.

In spite of his rubbery legs, Sam made it to the lad's side and checked him over. The boy's pulse was still strong, but his breathing seemed shallow and he moaned, obviously in pain. Sam pulled at Collin's smoldering right sleeve, where the singed material revealing a serious burn. The palm of Collin's right hand was scorched. He tried to move his head. The lad's eyes opened, but Sam could see in the firelight that the pupils were dilated. Sam's knowledge of medicine was limited, but it seemed that the kid could have sustained a concussion when the blast heaved him around.

"Wake up, Collin," Sam urged, gently shaking him. No

response. "C'mon kid, wake up." Sam heard a crackling roar and felt heat on the back of his neck.

He threw a look over his shoulder and saw that the fire had engulfed the door and half the wall. He pushed to his feet, shaking his arms to recover his strength. When he judged he could bear the boy's weight, he leaned over to gather him into his arms but was stopped short

Rudy materialized through a back door opposite the flames, crowbar in hand.

"You Mick bastards," Rudy snarled, raising the crowbar above his head, lunging at them. "You will roast in hell."

Sam saw Collin lurch up into a sitting position with his Bowie knife thrust forward, but a blow from Rudy's crowbar sent Collin's knife flying, and the crunch sounded like it broke the young man's forearm. Sam caught the brute's return swipe aimed for him and wrenched the weapon from Rudy's hand. It clattered out of reach.

Brought up on the outskirts of Belfast during the English oppression, Sam was no stranger to bullies. When Rudy charged, Sam sidestepped the attack and swung around, his back now up against the wall of flames spreading into the warehouse. He felt the inferno pressing against his shoulder blades and smelled the sharp tang of his own singed hair.

"You're a dead man, you bastard!" Rudy bellowed and charged.

Sam pivoted then stuck out his foot. In a blind rage, Rudy tripped and disappeared into the flames where a section of the burning roof had given way and come crashing down. Rudy's screams competed with the roar of the flames then suddenly ended. Sam spun around and tripped over Collin. The boy had lost consciousness again. The entire building was now engulfed in the fire, including the back door. Sam could just make out the opening through the flames. It was his only possible escape. He slung Collin over his shoulder, covered his face with his free hand, and pulling part of Collin's own shirt over the young man's eyes, dashed for the flickering gap, leaping through the solid wall of flames.

He emerged with his overcoat smoldering, just as the rest of the roof caved in and the warehouse collapsed. The whoosh of trapped air and flame threw him and Collin at least thirty feet down the back alley, where they must have rolled, Sam smothering flames on his own shirt and hair with his bare hands. Sam pulled himself up to a sitting position, checking his appendages. They still seemed to be attached, although they all resisted movement at first. He smelled like roast pig and touched his hair with fingertips—still warm. He rested a moment, then crawled to check the prone and crumpled youngster who didn't move. *Just like Liam.*

There was no telling what injuries Collin might have sustained had he been left to fend for himself. Sam felt as if he'd been scorched by a wild, fire-breathing dragon. His head pounded and seemed to want to roll off his neck at any minute. *Was there a bell clanging somewhere or was it just in his head?*

At least he wasn't cold any more. Sam could feel the heat behind him. Looking over his shoulder, he saw the contents of the warehouse still burning brightly through the windows. Only the burned-out brick façade remained standing. Windows were still popping from the heat, raining glass shards down into the alley in front of him. Even with the breeze coming in off the lake, Sam smelled roasting flesh. *Wait a minute, that's my flesh I'm smelling. And maybe someone else's.*

That brought him back to the lad. Collin was still unconscious. His arm was badly burned. He could see the imprint of the doorknob scorched into the youth's right palm . . . He may never have full use of that hand. Grabbing his wrist above the branding, he felt for the pulse. *Damn, it's almost non-existent and what I can feel is wicked fast and erratic.* The lad was in bad shape and Sam didn't feel so good himself.

An incessant clanging in his head grew louder. Sam turned to look down the alley toward Bay Street. A horse-drawn pumper wagon rounded the corner at the end of the sentinel row and came clopping down the alley. The candy apple red fire engine rolled to a halt opposite the burning ruins of Warehouse Four, steam shooting from its silver kettle boiler. Its two chestnut mares pawed the ground, snorting, their flanks twitching spasmodically and gleaming in the firelight.

Three uniformed firemen jumped off the wagon and headed toward them. *Thanks be to God.* Sam rested his forehead on his left sleeve, too exhausted to call out.

"Hell! Two warehouses in one night?" Sam heard one of the fireman shout. "These fires must have been set!"

"Over here, Hank!" Another fireman yelled. "It's too late for the building but there's a couple of blokes that need tending to. One looks to be unconscious, maybe dead."

Sam heard heavy boots coming toward him. He lifted his head and blinked at the brawny fireman kneeling next to Collin.

"Watch out for his right arm and hand. They've been burned, and I suspect the arm is broken," Sam managed to croak.

"What about you?" Hank asked. "That swelling on your neck looks ugly."

"Yeah, it's sore."

The fireman helped Sam sit up, then turned his attention to Collin. Sam swiped a hand over his eyes and saw a uniformed policeman coming toward them from the wharf behind the burning rubble, notebook in hand. The neswspaperman quickly tugged the lapel pin off of Collin's jacket and thrust the telltale symbol of trouble in his own coat pocket.

"You got a lorry? We need transport here," Hank said to the officer.

"I'm Officer Mulrooney of the Toronto Metropolitan Police," the policeman said to Sam, ignoring Hank. "What is your name and occupation?"

"Samuel Finlay, illustrator for the *Toronto Evening Telegram,* sir." Sam realized something. His notebook with all his illustrations—where had it disappeared to?

"Look here, officer," Hank butted in. "We need immediate transport to the General. This lad here is unconscious with a faint pulse and injuries."

At six-foot-two, with a burly physique and glowering demeanor, Mulrooney didn't look to Sam as if he would take any guff from the firemen, or even from his own mother for that matter.

"I need Finlay here to answer my questions."

"Do that at the hospital, officer," Hank said firmly. "Do you have transportation?"

A second fireman arrived with thick wool blankets from the pumper and wrapped one around Sam's shoulders. Sam shivered and coughed, his throat raw from smoke.

Mulroony sighed and slapped his notebook shut. "All right, all right. I'll take the two of them with me in the police car. It's out on the wharf."

"Well, get it over here on the double," Hank ordered. "Johnson will accompany you to the hospital and tend to their condition."

As Collin was being lifted into the back of the officer's car, Sam had to look away as it conjured another scene in his brain. The image of poor Liam's coffin being slid into that abominable hearse burned in his soul.

Chapter Four
The Aftermath

Afternoon, May 7, 1915
Nymphe Bank, Irish Sea

*T*adgh had been in a foul mood since his abortive meeting with the covert Society in Tenby. His requests for arms relay on behalf of the Brotherhood had been rejected, at least for the time being. Surely his Welsh compatriots could be made to see the necessity of it all. Now, sailing home to Skibbereen, he started to relax. He was in his element, alone, piloting his ship through the all-too-familiar St. George's Channel out across the Nymphe Bank. The wind whistling through the foresail soothed his anger.

God how he loved the sea! It helped to temporarily cleanse his mind from the troubles that plagued both him and his homeland. But it did nothing to permanently quench the burning hatred of the English oppressor that had been beaten into him when his parents were murdered. In his hometown alone, the potato famine had killed ten thousand inhabitants. All the while, the selfish overlords stole all foodstuffs beyond rotten potatoes to feed the masses in England and beyond. Not to mention what had been done to strip the Old Clans of their lands and brethren back in the plantation days and before. His MacCarthy ancestors had been berserker patriots to no avail. Even the fearless Romans had been no match for the barbaric Celts.

The days of reckoning were coming. There would be no quarter given and no backing down from their duty to avenge their forefathers and free Ireland!

Although the day was warm and the sea relatively calm, Tadgh knew that the stiff northerly breeze in early May could suddenly drag a fog off the south Irish coast. He reckoned that he was about thirty miles southeast of Queenstown when the dense bank started to roll in late afternoon with sixty miles west along the coast still to go. He knew this route blindfolded. The fog would typically lift at sundown and he knew all the signal lights along the shoreline to Baltimore. He had left Wales at night and would arrive home likewise. He preferred travelling in the cloak of darkness these days. It was far safer.

Be vigilant. He remembered the minor collision between his beloved Galway hooker, *The Republican,* and that garbage scow last year. No foghorns yet. Deftly tacking against the breeze, he guessed he was clipping at about ten knots.

Visibility dropped below two hundred feet. He decided to trim the lug main sail. As he reached down to un-cleat the halyard, suddenly a mammoth black shadow loomed out of the fog, bearing down on him from the west.

The German submarine, U-20 was cruising on the surface, its batteries now fully recharged after the enemy action. Kapitanleutnant Schwieger, on the conning tower, peered forward through the pea soup conditions. He was first to spy the ketch below and directly in front of him.

"Right full rudder, all back!" He immediately yelled to Fritz, his helmsman through the IMC.

U-20 swung to starboard and passed by the sailboat with only three feet to spare.

"Damn," Tadgh swore, looking up the side of the cold steel hull. It surged past, sucking the air out of his lungs and sails, its diesels hammering in his head. Then *The Republican* was hit broadside by the submarine's wash. Instinctively Tadgh had braced himself and jammed the tiller to port, which barely saved the shallow keel hooker from capsizing.

Schwieger swung the U-20 around so it was pointing at the sailboat and ordered all stop. There they sat, dead in the water, like David and Goliath before their combat, eying each other at a distance of a hundred feet. But Tadgh had no rock to throw, and the U-20 had deck guns trained on him and his little boat.

Through marine binoculars, Schwieger studied his opponent. He was a young man, apparently alone and unarmed, staring defiantly right back at him. Tall and ruggedly handsome, in his mid-twenties, Schwieger noticed. It would be a shame if he had to die.

"Kapitan, with that bluff bow, marked tumble-home, and raked transom, I think she is an Irish Galway hooker." Officer Weisbach consulted his book of ship silhouettes. "About thirty-five feet long, I'd say. She looks like a Bád Már class to me, used for commercial fishing."

Schwieger had already identified her himself. Seen them when they'd scoped Galway Bay a year back. He'd seen the dirt-red foresails before, but the dark gray lug sail was unique.

That's all the Kapitanleutnant needed to know. Irish and not English. Friend and not foe. Three days out of his home port and running low on provisions, Schwieger called out to Tadgh in English, "Have you got fresh fish?"

Tadgh was startled by this turn of events. Apparently he wasn't going to be blasted out of the water, at least not yet. He carried some fresh fish on board to give the illusion of being a fisherman. With nothing to lose and everything to gain, Tadgh simply yelled back, "Yes, to be sure!"

Schwieger admired the spirit of the man, who was standing his ground instead of trying to run. He had already decided to spare him and his craft.

"Lower the raft and prepare to board the sailboat," the Kapitan ordered in English for Tadgh's benefit.

Tadgh watched as several armed sailors appeared on deck and

lowered a raft into the water and two officers rowed over to *The Republican*. He noted that the submarine's menacing deck guns remained fixed on his chest.

Reaching the hooker, Schwieger stepped over the freeboard and onto the deck opposite the Irishman—square-cut chin, an honest face. His warm brown eyes were framed by leathered crow's feet, like his own, a squinting sailor's defense against the sun glare of the ocean. Tadgh stood tall and motionless with his bushy black hair tousled in the wind; his hairy arms folded across his barrel chest. Schwieger, by comparison, was almost three inches shorter than the Irishman, but just as fit and strong. Then, surprisingly, the U-Boat commander reached out to shake Tadgh's hand in a gesture of respect. Relieved, Tadgh shook the hand that was offered him. He knew that this man and his crew were dedicated to attacking and destroying the English, and that was good enough for him. At that moment, in the eerie fogbound ocean, Tadgh felt a bond being forged with this stalwart German captain. Tadgh offered all his fresh fish, which was thankfully accepted. Schwieger offered Tadgh his loaded German Luger as a sign of good faith. Tadgh was amazed and touched by this gesture.

"Jawohl, Weisbach," Schwieger agreed when his first officer sporke to him in German. Turning to Tadgh Schwieger said, "We sank an ocean liner two hours ago off Kinsale Head. You might want to check for survivors along your route." With that, he ordered his men back to the U-20.

Tadgh watched as they quickly closed the hatch and submerged amid the clanging of the claxton.

The fifteen-minute encounter was over, and Tadgh was left alone again in the fog with the Luger.

"Perhaps this hasn't been such a wasted day after all," he mused as he turned *The Republican* back into the wind.

Tadgh had no way of knowing where the ship had gone down, so he pressed on westward toward home. When the first piece of flotsam hit the starboard hull, it was five-thirty and the fog was not quite as thick as it had been earlier. He peered ahead and to the sides into the emerging debris field for any signs of life. Clearly this was part of the wreckage from the torpedoed ship.

There was no sign of the ship's human cargo. He tested the water temperature with his hand and decided that it was about fifty degrees Fahrenheit. That wasn't icy, but extended exposure would certainly be deadly. The debris field was thinning out.

"Hello, can anyone hear me?" Tadgh called out into the mist in case there was anyone out of sight but within earshot who could respond. No one answered. It had now been approximately three hours since the German officer said he had torpedoed the ship. Surely no one could have survived this long in the water. Tacking to starboard to stay on course, he reined in the halyard to bring *The Republican* about. This brought him back alongside the fringes of the debris field. Out of the corner of his eye, he glimpsed some gold lettering on a larger piece of debris. But it was time to tack to port, and he was late because of the U-Boat encounter. *There's no one here*, he decided as he started to bring the boom around to starboard to tack away from the debris, and that's when his curiosity got the better of him.

Suddenly the image he had seen registered, *Lus,* then a space, and then *tania*. No it couldn't be. They wouldn't . . . would they? He'd seen the behemoth ship in Queenstown harbor last year, close up. Incredible speed he'd heard, much faster than any U-Boat. It could not possibly have been sunk by a U-Boat.

Tadgh tacked back to starboard and approached the wreckage. As *The Republican* drew closer, he was startled to see the body of a woman draped over the broken-lettered structure, a transom, he surmised. Inert and ghostly pale, she appeared to be dead. Broken side spars on the plank kept her from rolling overboard. Tadgh guessed from the southeast current in the North Atlantic Drift, that the attack site must be well to the northwest where rescue efforts would certainly be underway. Surely boats would have come. They must have missed her amongst the debris.

Overcome with pity, he decided that he would bring the body back for identification. There would surely be relatives who would want to give her a decent burial.

Tadgh puzzled over how to bring about the transfer. He had tied his ship up to one of the protruding spars on the debris, but he wasn't sure if the platform was stable enough to hold his weight, let alone that of the body. The wind carrying the fog away could easily cause *The Republican* to drift and capsize this makeshift raft with him on it. The body would then likely be lost forever. He considered lassoing it from his ship but discarded that idea as ludicrous. Tadgh threw a small rope ladder over the side.

So long as his hooker remained joined to the debris, he could always climb back on board, as the sea swells rode less than three feet. Tadgh hastily scrambled down the ladder and onto the transom, lunging quickly to grab the girl in case the raft tipped over. Another wave hit, and with the bounce from Tadgh's added weight, the transom started to rock dangerously away from him and his boat.

He swept the body up into his arms just before the sea took her while bracing his legs to stabilize the transom. Another wave hit, pushing the raft hard against the boat. The transom broke loose beginning to flip vertically and drift away.

Tadgh wound one arm around the girl's waist and the other through a rung of the ladder. She was a dead weight, dragging in the sea. She didn't move but uttered a soft groan as he struggled up the ladder out of the water, pulling her behind him. She was alive!

It took ten painful minutes for Tadgh to get them both on board the boat. By then his arms and legs were numb. He could only imagine what shape the girl must be in after three and a half hours on that transom. Tadgh was ill-equipped for this emergency. With no cabin on the hooker, they were exposed to the elements, and they were still a long way from landfall. His first task was to deal with the woman's condition. She was still unconscious with a gash across her forehead. Congealed blood matted her hair and clotted down her face. Her hands and face were like ice, her breathing shallow and rapid, and her pulse faint. But there were no telltale signs of frostbite in her fingers. He'd never had to deal with a person suffering from hypothermia before.

He had heard that a person with hypothermia should be warmed up gradually, not all at once.

"Well then, lass," he soothed as he removed her cold, wet skirts and leggings. Damn the weight of them. He couldn't help but notice her beautiful quite shapely body while he undressed her. He scolded himself for having such sinful thoughts. He rubbed her vigorously with a dry towel and then gently pulled one of his extra sweaters over her head. He used the other sweater he carried onboard like a pair of pants to cover her legs and torso. Then he stripped off his own sodden clothes, wrapped the both of them in blankets and pulled her against him in the bottom of the boat. While he held her, he rubbed her hands with his to restore circulation. All the while she remained unconscious.

Within minutes Tadgh was feeling better; warmth had returned to his limbs. He felt the woman's arms and legs and realized that they were also warming up. Her pulse and breathing were improving too. These were good signs, he thought. Of course he was only treating the external symptoms. There could be multiple internal injuries.

Soon, Tadgh felt that it was safe to leave her to get up and get to work. It would be dark in a couple of hours. He wrapped himself in one of the blankets and made sure the girl was snugly wrapped in the other two. Then he cleaned and bandaged the cut on her forehead. The blow to her head had missed her temple and her right eye by a couple of inches. He took a long swig of the Jameson and he felt decidedly better.

Once the sails that he had hastily dropped were reset, they were on their way. The fog was thinning out, and the wind velocity now out of the east was freshening. With the following wind, he didn't have to tack.

Periodically he tied down the tiller and mainsail boom so that he could check on the girl. She felt warmer, some color had returned to her face, but he worried that she remained unconscious.

The sun set about nine p.m. Near midnight, *The Republican* slipped unnoticed into its berth under his home on the Ilen River at Creagh, near Skibbereen.

He staggered with the girl up the stairs, and put her, still comatose, under the covers of his own bed. Exhausted, he collapsed onto the downstairs parlor chesterfield, and he was asleep before his head hit the cushions.

Chapter Five
Resuscitation

May 8, 1916
Creagh, Ireland

*H*e thought he heard the sound of coughing; he had to be dreaming. The ghosts who peopled his solitary life made no sounds, he was sure of that. Then he heard it again and pulled himself fully awake. Yes, he remembered now—the girl he had rescued from the piteous sea in the chilling twilight. She was in his house, and still alive. He had not thought she would survive the night, but he could not have called himself a man if he had let her drift into a watery death.

It was hard to move at first, having slept hanging over both ends of the chesterfield. He rubbed his back vigorously to get the kinks out.

Ascending the stairs to his room, the image of her naked body on the boat flooded back, and it shamed him again that he had seen her that way. When he had tucked her right and proper into the bedclothes, the sweater had ridden up to where her perfectly shaped breasts with their hard raspberry nipples had been exposed. He had pulled the sweater down quickly to hide the sight, but he knew he would never forget it. He did not want to forget it, and his face burned knowing that.

Tadgh assessed the predicament quickly; he would either have to notify the authorities and get her medical attention, or he would have to care for her himself. The former option was risky, given his current endeavors, and the latter put him entirely outside his experience. But there was something about this girl that he found disquieting, yet compelling.

49

From the dresser the oil lamp's light cast a dream-like glow about the room, softening the edges of its rude furnishings. The low ceiling created a feeling of closeness, intimacy. How much the room itself had changed in the few hours that she had graced it. In his bed, her body was bedecked with his things, with his scent, with his dead dreams of loneliness.

He found her still asleep, but she had tossed about so much with her ragged coughing that the covers were now in disarray. Her breathing came raspy, and he could detect a liquid quality to her exhalations. Her face was bathed in sweat, and her dark tangled hair sparkled with crusted sea salt, that smell that kept drawing him back out onto his beloved Irish Sea. He brought himself closer to the bed and reached out his hand to touch her cheek for signs of fever. He hesitated; he thought himself too rough. He also hesitated because her face was too beautiful, even in her extremity, for the likes of him. He was shy in front of her. His hand gently covered her brow to search for the heat of illness, and he was struck by the bold beauty of her face. A warmth welled upward from his belly and coursed through his body. He knew nothing about her, had never heard her voice nor seen the color of her eyes; yet even now, as she slept, she called him to love her. Her body, the memory from last night, awoke him to care for her and bring her back to life.

Although she was still comatose, the girl seemed to frown when he touched her, an odd involuntary reaction to be sure. He quickly drew back. The vision of the bullet piercing his Mam's skull and the look on her face flashed in his mind. *God no, get a hold of yourself.*

Once in a while the girl's legs twitched as if in flight from the clutches of some sea monster, and from her lips escaped the mewing of a small animal in distress and fear. Or so it seemed. Perhaps it was just her tortured breathing. She did have a fever, and even though she was sweating, he made ready to bathe her to chase the fever away. He turned to the washstand to pour water into a china bowl, found a lump of soap and a bath sponge, and arranged everything on the bedside chair. He cursed himself because the water was cold, the soap smelled foul, and he had nothing to serve as a towel. But he could not wait. He looked quickly about the room and spied a clean linen shirt—his Sunday best!—on the wardrobe hook. That would do, as he would hardly be attending Mass anytime soon.

He had no practice with this kind of thing, no lover or wife, no child, but he was given this woman to care for, and that he would do. Since his was a rough life, handling the hooks and stinking nets and rope of the fisherman and the guns and torches of the Irish Brotherhood, he shook with anxiety as he began, gently as he could, to unwind her from the covers that could easily have served as her winding sheet had she not survived the night. He took as a good sign that her breathing did not change and she was not straining against his efforts.

He could not help it; he unwrapped her altogether. Just for a moment, his heart caught and jagged. He could never be able to put words to what he beheld; although her legs and arms bore bruises, the horrible evidence of her ordeal in the sea he saw right away on the smooth length of her body, and the room's light played along her skin with ivory and cream hues. He could not remain standing, he was so taken with her.

He could not breathe, he wanted to die with this vision his last. His sight traveled as a pilgrim to worship her, the hollow at the back her knees, the promising curve of her belly and the dip of her navel. The complete beauty of her breasts knocked him sideways—aye, this was the paradise he wanted. He slowly sank onto the bed next to her, his legs turned to water. He wanted to touch her again, to run his hands along the light down on her arms, to smooth the black ringlets that played along the back of her neck, to cradle the lush weight of her breasts. Oh, God, he was in heaven. No, he was in hell. His arousal crazed him, and now he had to bathe and clean her; now he had to touch her.

Her face had been turned slightly away from him, but now

after he rinsed and wrung out the sponge, he tilted her head towards him. He was startled to see that her eyes were open and blankly looking straight into his face. *Was she waking?* He hung his head and blushed a deep crimson. *Had she seen him all this time?* The bowl clattered to the floor and water splashed across his boots and the knees of his trousers. He raised his head to look at her; he wanted her eyes closed, he did not want her to have seen him look upon her, trapped in her most vulnerable state and him, definitely excited. What he did see was that she had green eyes, exactly the color of his beloved sea when she was at her most violent and cruel. He felt a small pressure on his wrist, and he looked down again to see that her hand rested there; perhaps she had witnessed his depravity, but she was not afraid or disgusted.

Yet there was no cognitive function, just those luminous smoky eyes and that mounting fever. He had flinched and caused the hand to move against him. He closed her eyes gently. "It's for the best, lass."

He refilled the bowl quickly and began to wash her. It seemed that his touch was lighter if he sat next to her, and he gently stroked the sponge along her neck and arms, her breasts which rose to him under his tender pressure, across the plane of her belly, the sweet darkness in the meeting of her thighs. With a clumsy rough comb he cleaned the salt rime from her hair as best he could. He wrapped her back in his linen shirt—and rolled the cleanest blanket he could find around her. When he lifted her to remove the dampened sheet and straighten the bedcovers, he was again astonished at her lightness. Light as a feather, as his Mam would say. Perhaps this lass was an angel, cloaked in feathers. No, he had seen how she was made, a full-fleshed woman to drive him from his loneliness and sorrow. His head roared with these thoughts as he turned to what he must do now, to get her to take water so she would not die from thirst. With the sorry lumps of ticking and straw that served as his pillows, he propped her up in bed so she might see something other than the rough wood ceiling if she woke up. He made a mustard plaster for her chest and covered her with the bedclothes. Then he soothed her brow with a cold compress to bring down her fever. These were things he remembered his Mam had done for him as a child.

Her breathing was becoming more even, with less coughing, but her temperature continued to climb. He worried that he could be risking her life by making the decision to tend to her on his own.

When he pulled the window curtains open, he saw that a red watery dawn had long since broken. He looked back at her as he left the room and saw that her eyes were still closed as if in sleep, but her breath was easier and her skin a little brighter.

In the kitchen below, he boiled water for tea but thought that might be too strong for her, so she would have to settle for warm water at the moment. His thick mugs would not do, so he dug into the back of the kitchen dresser to find a long-disused cup and saucer. With that and a kitchen cloth for spills, he climbed the stairs, all the while giving thanks that his room was warm and snug. Though he might be a rough man, he would give this woman his best care.

He saw that she still slept when he returned, so he sat next to her and softly ran his fingers across her hands that he had folded. She felt warmer to his touch as he pulled her to a half-seated position on the bed. This motion caused her eyelids to drift open as if she heard his sigh of relief. He poured a little of the warm water into the saucer and brought it to her mouth. *She must be so thirsty.* When he held the saucer to her lips, the water ran down her chin and across her upraised hands. Much as a shepherd would dip a cloth into warm milk and push it into the mouth of an orphaned lamb so it would not starve to death, so he did for her. A little bit at a time and with a patience he did not know he had, he got her to take most of the water. Her blank eyes were fixed on his face the entire time, and though he knew he did not cut such a fine figure of a man at the moment, he hoped he could make a more pleasant appearance when she became conscious.

Tadgh closed her eyes once more, as much to keep them from drying out as to mimic sleep for her.

After arranging her bed more comfortably, Tadgh took up the dishes and basin and quietly left her. He turned back at the door, and whispered, "Sure now, you are welcome. I'll be right back." It was plain to him that she was still in grave danger. "I'll stay close by you, and you'll never want for anything."

Tadgh spent the whole day ministering to her condition without regard for his own needs. By nightfall, she was no better. He finally took time to wash and dress himself, and then he ate a cold supper of stale leftover kippers. His only solace that night was his three fingers of Jameson.

Damn, he thought, as his originally planned tasks for the day went unfulfilled. When he returned to her bedside, she was still unconscious. Her jagged breathing had returned, and her forehead was heating the room. *My God, she's regressing*. He agonized over how to help her further beyond the cold compresses. Her countenance was grave indeed and she appeared to be struggling, but was it with her physical condition or was it something else? He was reminded of what his Mam had told him about the old man's friend. He remembered that his grandmother had died of it relatively quickly, thank the Lord. *Pneumonia, is that what she's got? The old man's friend?* Though she was still beautiful, her condition was uncannily like his grandmother's just before she passed. He changed her mustard plaster. It was causing red welts on her chest, yet it was sorely needed. He stayed up with her all that night, not wanting to leave her until either the fever broke or until she succumbed.

Chapter Six
Recuperation

May 17, 1915
Creagh, Ireland

*D*ays later her condition, although stabilized, had not significantly improved. The fever would start to come down with the cold compresses but spike back up when Tadgh took his meager, much needed rest. And still she was unconscious. During this ordeal Tadgh had a chance to evaluate the situation. The good Lord had seen fit to bring her into his life, for better or worse. There must be a purpose.

Since the time he was fourteen when his Mam and Pa had been mercilessly gunned down, five years earlier by the Royal Irish Constabulary, he had shunned the fairer sex. His parents were attacked in their home after being brutally interrogated because the RIC suspected them of being anti-English zealots he guessed. But they weren't that at all, as far as he knew, anyway. Their senseless deaths, along with his education regarding the English oppression of his Irish ancestors, had kindled an abiding hatred in Tadgh that had become his life force. There was no room in his world for romance with a woman. And anyway, this fair colleen would only get in the way of his Brotherhood mission.

He would see her sickness through to the bitter end, and then, if she survived, she could go her own way.

It bothered Tadgh that she had not regained consciousness after all this time. It was impossible for him to know if she had a brain injury. He had tried to feed her some soup, but she couldn't swallow it, although some of it drained down her throat. So he continued squeezing her water from a wet cloth. Gradually, the bruise on her forehead faded, and the purple stain started to

55

disappear. He took that as a good sign.

Finally, on the evening of May twenty-first, as he noted in a bedside journal, the fever broke. Tadgh was just starting to nod off in a chair by her bedside when he glimpsed a flicker of her eyelids and then they opened.

She had been in an underwater dream, starving for breath, chased by a huge mechanical monster with a thousand, foot-long tentacles dragging her down. Escaping long enough to push upward toward the surface, the girl burst through the veil of consciousness with a terrified and disoriented shout. Her eyes darted up and down from the ceiling to the walls, This was not some place she recognized from any memories. Her brain was thoroughly befuddled by her surroundings. She vaguely recognized someone, a shape, and then fell back into a state of sleep, not quite life, maybe not death, in some in-between place.

Tadgh jumped up, reached out and gripped her sprawled hand firmly. He had seen this happen once before, an awakening from death like this, when one of his Irish Republican Brotherhood stalwarts had been shot and lay dying in the street in Dublin. He had suddenly regained consciousness and had opened his sightless eyes, just moments before expiring.

Tadgh felt her pulse. It was steady and strong. "Well now, lass," he sighed with relief.

"C'mon back to me," he coaxed, propping her up on pillows. When she didn't respond, he sang her his favorite song "*Dear Old Skibbereen*", which ended with the refrain . . .

O father dear, the day will come, when answer to the call
All Irish men of Freedom Stern, will rally one and all
I'll be the man to lead the band, beneath the flag of green
Loud and clear, well raise a cheer, remember Skibbereen.

Perhaps it was the rhythmic canting of the poem, or the lilt to the Irish brogue in his voice that resonated with her. She opened her eyes once more. Tadgh grabbed her hand again as he spoke to her softly, "You'll be all right, you will."

She saw him for the first time, a rather menacing-looking young man with a bedraggled beard and a worried scowl on his forehead. She didn't recognize where she was, and, even more frightening, she didn't know who she was or how she had gotten there. Despite her weakness she managed to lift one hand over her face to block out this reality. "No—" she moaned.

"There now, lass, you're safe with me, to be sure," she heard. The man's baritone voice was unfamiliar—frightening.

She shrank back from the voice, so the man reached out to her freed hand, which was again trembling.

Feeling the panic of the newly blinded or of one buried alive underground, she realized that she was too weak to flee. *To where? From whom?* Sheer helplessness, but worse. She had no memory of herself, not even her own name, and she was utterly trapped. Maybe it was just a nightmare. If she could just close her eyes she might then awake on the other side, safe and remembering. Her pulse raced. But what if she fell back underwater. Maybe that would be better. Get it over with. Finish it once and for all.

But the stroking of the back of her hand was gentle and soft. The man at the end of that touch was speaking in comforting tones of encouragement. She could feel her racing heartbeat start to subside.

Moving her hand away from her eyes, she could see that she was in a rather austere bedroom, definitely masculine, but comfortable. The clock on the dresser ticked rhythmically. Windows with plain cloth drapes were dark, so it must be night. On a bedside table a lit hurricane lamp cast a soft glow around the room. She could see a basin with water and soap at her bedside and a worried look on the young man's sturdy face. Yes, and it was handsome to be sure.

She felt awful and could barely move. Her chest burned. The smell of mustard. A plaster. *I must have had breathing troubles. How did I know that?*

She could feel that she was clothed and tucked into a clean warm bed, and this hard-looking stranger was being kind and gentle with her. *I've got to get my bearings. Don't trust him.*

She suddenly realized that she was thirsty. Since she had been underwater for so long in her mind, she couldn't understand why she was so thirsty.

The man saw her licking her parched lips. Curving his arm behind her back, he slowly lifted while he fluffed the pillow behind her head. Then he handed her a cup of water.

She took the cup and tried to drink, but her hands shook so badly that the water spilled out before she got the vessel to her mouth.

He leaned forward, steadied her hands and guided the cup to her lips.

She looked up into his warm brown eyes and felt the strength in his hands as the liquid slid down her throat. She could feel her throat absorbing the water like dried, withering leaves drinking in the rain of life. Her tongue was no longer pasted to the roof of her mouth, and she was able to swallow. Slowly, she began to feel human once again.

But her head pounded and her ears rang. And she felt so hot. She tried to throw the covers off but didn't have the strength to do so.

The man used the cold compress to cool her off, and then he stroked her forehead to remove the worry lines that had formed there.

Sensing a caring touch, she reached up, shaking, and put her hand over his. This felt good to her.

Tadgh sensed the first hint of trust that came with that touch, a touch that sent shivers down his back. *What's happening? I've no time for such feelings.*

Moving to action he decided that it was time to try feeding her some soup again. As he rose from her bedside, he saw her reach out for him, her eyes imploring him to stay. He could see that he was her only tie to the living. Returning to her he asked, "What's your name, lass?" There was no response, only another anxious stare.

He soothed her brow once again and told her, softly, "I'll be right back with some soup. You need to eat, ya know."

Her hand fell back onto the bed. He could sense her eyes following him as he left the room. Her silence unnerved him. And those haunting eyes.

When Tadgh returned with the food, she was asleep again. He gently rubbed her cheek and she opened her eyes. He could see the obvious signs of relief spreading across her face. He propped her up again so that she could eat. Then he fed her the warm potato soup, spoonful by spoonful. She gagged a little at first, and then seemed to relish the warm liquid coursing down her throat. It was as if she was being brought back from the dead, he thought.

As he leaned over, carefully balancing the spoonful of soup, his locket popped free of his tunic and dangled in front of her eyes. She seemed mesmerized by the sheen of the candlelight flickering off the silver.

"Do you like this?" He dangled the bauble in front of her eyes. "It was given me by my Pa before he died. Family heirloom it is, supposedly ancient."

No response from the lass.

Once the soup was finished, Tadgh leaned her back on the pillows and turned down the lamp. For the first time she spoke to him weakly, murmuring, "Thank you for your kindness." Then she promptly fell asleep again.

It appeared to Tadgh that the crisis was over, although this woman was far from well. It was still going to take some time before she would be recovered. He recognized the newly familiar flush of attachment sweeping over him, and he didn't like it.

The following morning, the young woman awoke early. The swarthy now-shaven man with the warm brown eyes was close at hand and brought her eggs and tea, which she polished off with his help.

Picking up her empty tray, fidgeting with her egg cup, Tadgh asked, "What's your name and where are you from?"

"What's yours?"

"I'm Tadgh McCarthy, a fisherman in these Irish waters, lass. And who might ye be?"

"Where are we?"

"In my house in south western Ireland, lass, near to Cork and near the sea where the Cunard . . ." He stopped himself.

"Cunard?"

"The steamship line. The *Lusitania*, you know."

"A fine ship, so I've been told." She had no idea what he was talking about but she wasn't about to show weakness.

What's she playing at?

"I need to sleep." She rolled over and hugged the covers.

"There, lass," Tadgh said placing the tray on the bed, sitting down and feeling her brow. The fever, much lower now, still throbbed against his palm. "We'll talk later, then. Go on to sleep with ya."

The next day Tadgh had to address the issue of bathing her while she was awake. At first the girl was reluctant to have him help her, but she realized that she was in no condition to care for herself. So she succumbed to him as he washed her and then he combed her wavy black hair with the brush his Mam had given him. She kept her eyes on him as he carefully touched her. Her responses and lovely body aroused him, despite his self-admonition. When he soaped her chest she raised her hand over his to guide it gently around her breasts, never touching her aroused nipples. All the while she quivered at the cool of the cloth. Or was it his touch? He couldn't be sure. Her eyes appeared smokier than usual, hauntingly beautiful, watching him, his every move. He had to remember that he was to make her well and then to release her. She was like a wild, wounded bird.

Three days later, as he noted on the bedside journal, Tadgh could see that his patient's strength was improving. Her fever had completely subsided and mental acuity was returning. But he knew from her anxious demeanor and stoic reserve that she was in some private anguish. It was slowing down her recovery.

"Well now," he finally blurted out that evening while applying a cold compress to her worried brow. "I beg you to tell me what's troubling you so I can help you."

"I've been thinking finally. You could have taken advantage of me and you didn't. I was obviously very sick and you nursed me. So I'm going to trust you."

"Aye, lass. Thank ya."

"I can't remember anything before I woke up in your bed, not even my name," her eyes pleaded as she reached out her hand and gripped his, removing the compress.

"Well, now. I wondered. That's your problem, and a fine one

for certain." *This is certainly something I hadn't bargained on. Damn, what am I going to do now?* "At least the bump on your head is gone, girl."

"Don't you dare make fun of me. I'm scared and alone."

"There, there. Ease back a bit, lass. You're not alone, are ya now." He returned the compress to her now furrowed forehead. I'm sure it took courage for you to confide this to me, an unkempt man and you in my bed. Don't ya be frettin'. We'll find out who you are right enough." He felt the furrows relax as he stroked the side of her face with his free hand.

"I have so many questions and no answers."

"Fire away girl."

"How did I get here and what happened to me?"

"I brought you here by boat after an accident."

"What accident?" she questioned blankly.

He decided not to sugar-coat his response, eager to see how strongminded she was. "You were on an ocean liner, the *Lusitania*, the one we talked about already. You were on your way from America to England when it was torpedoed by the Germans. You ended up on a kind of raft on the ocean, where I found you. I brought you here because you had banged your head and you were very sick, to be sure." He didn't need to tell her that she had almost died.

My God. The boat sank? My family? I was in the sea? "I don't remember any of this. Was everyone saved?"

He had read in his newspaper that over a thousand had perished and that they had set up a morgue and aid station in near-by Queenstown. "No, most passengers and crew members were lost at sea, I'm sorry to say, lass," he said as gently as possible.

"And you saved me from that fate, then, didn't you?" Her eyes grew more sultry.

He didn't like where this conversation was going. "I just did what any mariner on the scene would have done, don't ya know?"

"I don't think so. You did so much more," her hands fluttered in the air.

Changing the subject, "We've got to get you well enough to travel, lass. I need your help. There's no doubt of that."

"I will get better, thanks to you, but I'm so tired now."

"There's a girl. You're still as weak as a kitten but you'll be right as rain," he assured her as he laid her back down and tucked her in.

She fought sleep as he rose from the bed. Trying to watch him her eyes were closing. They fluttered and then closed tight.

"Lord God above. Protect this woman," he murmured turning down the lamp and closing the door softly as he left her there, snug in his bedroom.

A week later on June 1st, the woman suffered her recurrent nightmare. That strapping man, who was strangely familiar to her, was caught in a burning building. There was fire everywhere. He was hurt and dazed. She couldn't recognize him but she feared for his life, and she had to save him. Her life depended on it. But the more she tried to reach him, the farther away he slipped. "No, No," she cried out in her sleep.

Her outcry brought Tadgh in to his bedroom on the run. She was sweating heavily and her heart was fluttering like a trapped bird. He could see her eyes darting back and forth behind her closed eyelids and her arched black eyebrows were now scrunched down towards her quivering eyelashes.

"There, there, colleen. It's fine, it's fine," he murmured in her ear as she held her breath. He wrapped his arms about her and gently rocked her still. Then he kissed her forehead. Her taste was exhilarating, not exactly like the salt of his sea, similar but earthy, with a hint of buttered rum. Intoxicating.

She bolted upright, almost breaking his jaw.

Tadgh cried out as he rubbed his chin.

"Oh, we've got to save him!" the woman sobbed as she reached out to hold Tadgh close.

"It's all right, lass. Who do we have to save, do ya know?"

"I don't know. But he's burning to death."

"You just had a bad dream, and you are here safe with me, so you are," Tadgh comforted her, as he stroked the hair out of her frightened eyes.

Slowly, her eyebrows relaxed as her breathing against his chest returned to normal. She nuzzled her head against his shoulder, her hard grip on him weakened, and she nodded off to sleep once more.

"There's a girl You'll be all right now," he murmured as he lay her back down and tucked her snug. "But I'm not sure that I'll be, for all that."

Chapter Seven
Collin's Plight

January 15, 1911
Toronto General Hospital

"**U**nconscious burn victim," Johnson yelled to the nurses as they pushed through the double doors at the Toronto General Hospital entryway. It was all Sam could do to carry the foot of the gurney on his aching feet. And he was wincing every time he tried to take a deep breath. *Damned policeman. Wouldn't lift a finger.* The moment they entered the building they were swarmed by attendants.

"Patient breathing weak and erratic," the fireman told the first doctor on the scene. *God, Liam . . . er, Collin looks like he's at death's door.* All the way to the hospital Sam had held the lad's good hand as it went from warm to clammy cold. An attendant had been monitoring the young man's pulse rate on the same wrist. He looked worried and announced, "Pulse faint, dropping below thirty beats per minute and it seems to be skipping beats."

"Help this man, too," Johnson pointed at Sam. "He has neck lacerations, smoke inhalation, and throw in frostbite as well as some broken ribs most likely."

Johnson removed one of Sam's boots in transit and whistled when he saw his foot. "It's frozen but not black, yet—lucky cuss."

The orderlies pulled Sam away from Collin, into an adjacent curtained-off cubicle.

"Let me up," Sam demanded.

"Not on your life," one attendant said, holding Sam down on the hospital bed.

"Watch the ribs," Sam yelped as a cinch squeezed his torso. *Just like with Liam. I can't save him.* He had been out of town studying his art when it happened. *I didn't know.*

Everything had been a blur when they arrived, but Sam remembered the illustrations he had made for the paper when the hospital had introduced its novel emergency center the previous year. *Outstanding Research Hospital* the article had read. *Most modern facilities in North America. Ten bays for simultaneous treatment of the injured. Oxygen lines and cuffs to measure blood pressure and the beds had rails to keep the patients from falling out.*

All he could see now were white curtains on both sides of his cubicle and a white ceiling with a fan above it. The attendants were dressed in white. Everything was white except for the drops of blood on the pillow where they were forcing him to lay his head. *Is that my blood?*

At first it was quiet next door, except for the occasional word from the attending staff and the faint whirring of the air circulation fans. As if he wasn't cold enough. The nurses' shoes squeaked, reminding him of the squealing mice fleeing the burning warehouse. Then a moaning—wailing, really—started up from a lady down the row of beds to his right.

A nurse came in to attend to Sam. No one checked the crying lady.

"Lie still, young man," she admonished him. "I need to examine both your feet."

"I need to check on my friend next door."

"They don't need your help. Hold still until I get that right boot off."

Sam could hear commotion from what had to be Collin's room.

"Respiratory blockage," shouted a female attendant. "Breathing has stopped."

"Tracheotomy. Scalpel, Nurse," barked a baritone voice.

"Here, Doctor."

Sam heard a gurgling sound. *What was that? Have they stabbed him?*

About a minute later he heard Baritone say, "Tube in."

"No pulse, doctor."

"External chest compression procedure," Baritone boomed.

Sam heard a series of thumping sounds with grunting. *Was that Collin?*

"Dead on arrival?" asked a female voice.

"By all rights."

"For the love of God," Sam shouted. He couldn't take this outcome. Not after Liam.

"I'm not givin' up, yet," Baritone said. "Get the machine. It's in the research lab next door."

Electric shock?" a third voice warned. "It will kill him for sure if he's not already gone. Keep at the chest compression."

"He's dead anyway if we don't try. It worked for Prevost in Geneva, didn't it?"

"On dogs. Our research here is so primitive. Our coils are untested."

"What better time to try? Nurse, bring it here and be quick about it. All right then, keep up the chest compression."

A minute later Sam saw a large generator on wheels with wires spiraling out of its machinery rolling past his cubicle and into the one next door. It looked like the contraption that he had read about in Mary Shelley's *Frankenstein*, trying a new procedure on the corpse. *Sure 'an they're not going to experiment on Liam—no, Collin?*

A few seconds later Sam could hear the words "Stand clear."

Too long, Sam thought. "The lad is going to die. Hurry up," Sam pleaded. "Why am I strapped down, for Heaven's sake? I could help." He had no idea how he could help, but after Liam, he knew he had to try.

"Lie still, will you," ordered the nurse attending Sam. "There's frostbite on your little toe, and there's no telling what you've done to your neck and ribs. I'm giving you a shot."

A bell clanged and Sam felt the *bzzzt* at the same time as the needle went into his arm. It hurt. This was accompanied by a sharp thumping sound like a sack of potatoes thrown down on the floor. *Surely Collin hasn't fallen off the bed, has he?* The air smelled electric, a kind of metallic odor. He wondered if Collin could feel it, too. He hoped to God he still could.

"Again," Baritone said.

The woman down the line wailed again.

The second shock sounded more prolonged and tortuous than the first. It made Sam's hair stand on end. His teeth ached. How long had it been since they had arrived? Time seemed a little fuzzy.

"Pulse," the female voice announced. "Faint, forty beats a minute."

"Well, now. It would seem that this cattle prod of yours works after all," the third voice announced. "Good work, Doctor. You've saved this young man's life. But you'd better get that contraption back into research. Look at the burns on his chest."

"It's not ready for general use, I'll have to agree, but at least this lad's alive."

"Not for long if we can't get him stabilized, doctor," the female voice announced. "He's still unconscious."

"Yes, but the chest compression should have helped."

"Undoubtedly. Time will tell. Administer oxygen and get me some blankets, nurse."

"What have you given me?" Sam asked as a new sensation coursed through his veins.

"A sedative. Something to make you sleep while we figure out all your injuries."

"Pulse rate, now sixty," Sam heard just before he nodded off. His last thought was, *At least there's no fireworks this time.*

Three hours later, Sam heard his name being called as he awoke to find himself in a solitary hospital room. He could see his feet at the bottom of the bed, bound in bandages. He tried wiggling his toes, moving his foot from side to side. *Must be fine. I can move them.* He wasn't so sure about his ribs. His torso was constricted by a tight wrap. He winced as he took a deep breath. He wouldn't do that again as it hurt too much.

"Mr. Finlay," a voice strangely familiar called to him. Now he remembered. It was that police officer who drove them to the hospital. "Why the hell didn't you help with the gurney?"

"Not my job," Mulrooney answered, walking into view. "And you seemed so eager to help."

"How is he?"

"Who? The lad? I dunno. They said he's under strict monitoring. Two nurses. No visitors. Can't talk right now."

"But he's alive?"

"So I'm told."

"Thank the Lord."

"So what happened down there at the warehouse? Why were you there in the dead of night?"

"My boss at the *Telegram* sent me on a hunch because of the other two warehouses that burned earlier this week."

"What kind of hunch?"

Sam saw his clothes piled neatly on the chair by his bed. "Look in my coat pocket."

"What's this? 'Block Free Trade - Vote Borden,'" the officer read, pulling the lapel pin out. "I've seen these around. Damn propaganda."

"The arsonist was wearing one of them, don't you know."

"What arsonist?"

"The one who knocked me out when he could tell I saw what he was doing."

Sam proceeded to explain what had happened, focusing on

Rudy and not Collin.

"Dead, you say."

"In the rubble. Tried to knock us out and burn us alive, he did."

"We'll search the rubble."

"You do that, officer."

"Let me get this straight," said Mulroney. "Your boss had the cockamamie idea that the warehouse fires are connected to the National Election?"

"Laurier's Liberals want economic reciprocity with the United States," Sam offered. "Borden's Conservatives want to protect Canadian industry."

"Yah. I know. They're being branded Imperialists. Situation is bloody explosive. We've had to break up brawls in the city bars over this. Damn foolishness."

"It's not foolishness. It's big business and now arson. Know whose warehouses have been torched?"

"You tell me."

"I saw United States markings on the crates in Warehouse Four. Free traders, I'd venture."

The light bulb flickered on in the officer's brain. "Damn." His hand rubbed against a cheek. "What was the lad doing there with you last night?"

While Sam was trying to decide how to respond, a doctor strode in through the open door with a young woman in tow.

"Samuel, my love," the woman cried, rushing to his bedside and scanning his condition.

"Officer, I think you need to give these two young people a minute alone," he suggested. "They're betrothed."

"Wait just a minute," the officer said.

"I call upon doctor's privilege," the medic replied. "This man needs his rest. He'll be right here for the time being."

"Don't discharge him until I finish my questioning," Mulrooney ordered. "What's the status of the other lad?"

"I don't honestly know. He's up on the third floor."

"Show me where."

"Come with me," the doctor replied, ushering him out.

Sam eyed his love, deciding how to answer the questions she had registered in her worried face. Spritely Liz, his raven-haired soul mate, was wise beyond her twenty years, with a down-to earth sense of family and heritage; she was a fine match for a jovial Belfast artist. Couldn't pull the wool over her eyes, even if he wanted to try. A real beauty—motherly, yet shapely in that pleasing way for her five-foot-five height.

"Well, it seems a fine mess you've gotten yourself into, Samuel Stevenson," she began. "You're all bandaged up and lyin' here like a mummy with a policeman askin' you questions."

Sam saw right through the false bravado. He must have looked a fright. Liz was uncharacteristically rattled. Reaching out from his partially seated position in the bed he captured her right hand.

"I love you, too," he murmured. "With this ring I thee wed . . . next August," he added, pulling her hand to his mouth and kissing the silver engagement band softly.

"Come now. There'll be none of that until you tell me the heart of it." She pulled away from his grasp and started prodding at his leg bandages.

Sam noticed that her her ample breasts were rising and falling with great rapidity.

"There was a bit of a dust up down on the docks. But I'm all right, love. Just a few scratches here and there."

"That's not what the doctor told me. Two broken ribs, who knows what kind of neck vertebrae trauma and oh, yes, the slight frostbite on three toes."

"I'm all right. Sit down on the bed beside me." He patted the coverlet gently.

"I thought you left Ireland to get away from such shenanigans."

She accepted Sam's offer, keeping a safe distance.

"I left to chase you down and marry you, don't you know," Sam replied, running his hand up her right arm brushing against her breast on the way by.

"Oh, Sam. I had hoped that an artist's life would be genteel and safe," she blurted out, tears obscuring her hazel eyes.

"And so it will be, my love. So it will be."

Her hand trembled as she cupped his dimpled chin and leaned in.

"Ouch," he grunted as her other arm encircled his body.

"Sorry." She pulled back. "Does it hurt bad?"

"Just where you grabbed me here," he pointed. "But I'll be right as rain, soon enough."

"I heard about the warehouse fires," she said tenderly exploring his bandaged torso with her free hand. "It's in the morning paper already."

"Arson it was. Bad business. But it's over now." He wasn't going to go into details. No need to worry her further.

"Who's the other lad that the officer was asking about when I arrived?"

"Well, there's the rub. He's a scruffy Irish lad who has got himself in a heap of trouble. But he helped me last night, so he did. He was badly injured, with burns and the like. He almost died this morning as they worked on him, trying to save him. He needs my help," Sam added.

"Sweet Brigid, Sam, you're pinching my fingers against my ring."

"So sorry, my love." Sam loosened his grip and twirled her ring.

"Kiss it and make it better?" he asked bringing her reddened middle finger to his lips.

"Now, Samuel, I've seen that look in your eyes before. He's not your brother Liam, don't you know."

"The spitting image, Lizzy. The spitting image."

"Now, Samuel . . . "

"He needs our help."

"It wasn't your fault. We've talked about this before at length."

"I hear you, love."

"I'm not sure you do. Liam went astray while you were away learning your trade. Your parents never told you about his situation. How could you have known?"

"But what a terrible death. I should have been there. We had been so close before I left."

"What do you know about him, this lad who's not Liam?"

"Only that he's alone in the world since his mother was raped and murdered here in Toronto."

"Why was he there last night . . . to help you? And what happened, anyway?"

Damn, the same question Mulrooney was asking. Sam filled her in on what had transpired, leaving nothing out.

"So you see, Liz, this lad Collin saved me in the end, sure enough."

"Seems to me that you saved him from the arsonist's death that he deserved."

"No one deserves death by fire, my love. Not even that black-hearted Rudy, rest his soul."

"We'll talk more of this later when you're well," Liz offered. "But I'm from Missouri. What's this about August?"

"Oh, so you picked up on that, did you now."

"Too right. Well?"

Sam's heart leapt when he saw the twinkle appear in her eye.

"You know the summer regatta at the Club is in August? The nineteenth, I think."

"So?"

"So, we could get married that day and combine our reception with the awards banquet after the regatta."

"You mean at the Club?"

"Yes, of course. With the ceremony at sunset in the pagoda on the deck. What do you think, my love?"

"Well, it certainly would save us some money."

"My thoughts precisely. And our friends will be at both functions."

"True. Could we have a band and dancing afterwards?"

"Of course, my Lizzy."

"But it's earlier that we had been thinking."

"You want to start our family as soon as possible, don't you?"

"But you want to do the things that will get that occurring as soon as possible, don't you now?"

"So it's a good idea, then?"

"Fine by me, *aroon*."

"So I'm your sweetheart again, am I?"

"That's what I said. *Aroon*."

"Splendid. I'll talk to the Commodore about it." Sam pulled Liz into him gingerly and explored her lips, tenderly.

The doctor reappeared with a stern expression on his face, gripping a medical file in his hands.

Still trembling, Liz pulled away and looked Sam in the eyes saying, "You're a scallywag, Samuel Stevenson. Our discussion about this ruffian Collin is not over."

"Could you step outside for a minute, young lady?" the doctor asked.

"If you have something to tell me, I would like to have my fiancée present," said Sam.

"Fine, then. Mister Finlay, I have some news about your condition. Your superficial injuries should heal with no long term effects."

"Why the long face, Doc?"

"We ran some routine tests and . . . found something else . . ."

"Well, that's enough time for you lovebirds," Mulrooney exclaimed bursting back through the door. "Apparently the lad is conscious, but they won't let me talk to him yet. So you're it,

Finlay."

"You'll have to leave, Officer," the doctor announced. "I'm discussing this patient's condition with him."

"I'm all ears," Mulrooney replied, rooted beside the bed.

"I'm sure you are. His injuries from whatever happened last night are superficial."

"It's all right, Doc. You can tell me what you were about to say with Mulrooney here present." Sam squeezed Liz's hand carefully avoiding her ring finger.

"Well, you ought to know that you have a heart condition, sir. Have you ever noticed that your heart skips beats? It would feel like the hiccups."

"Can't say that I have."

"Only twenty percent of the people with your condition can feel it. How about getting tired after a strenuous day?"

"Don't we all?"

"Isn't he awfully young to be havin' a heart condition?" Liz asked. Sam felt her grip tighten on him. Her ring was now digging into his ring finger. It must be hurting her, too.

"Not necessarily, young lady. Sam, do either of your parents have a heart problem?"

"My mother died several years ago. They said it was from a broken heart, from worry." He wasn't about to talk about Liam.

"Surely now, that's not related." Liz released Sam's arm.

"Can't say, Miss. We don't have all the answers about the heart, I'm afraid. It could be a valve issue or a blockage somewhere. All you can do is take it easy when you feel tired. There's a tonic I can prescribe."

"Snake oil salesman, eh, Doc?"

"Now, you listen to me, Samuel. You'll be needin' to heed this fine doctor's advice, that's for certain."

"Yes, love," Sam said. "But we're not going to let this little condition put a crimp in our planned nuptials or our family planning, make no mistake about it."

"As long as you feel up to making a family, that shouldn't be a problem," the doctor said.

"I guess I shouldn't be using the term *my heart is bursting with love for you,* anymore."

"There you go again, Samuel, making light of a serious situation."

"Exactly, Liz. Life's too short to worry."

"Don't you be usin' that term, neither."

"Enough, you two. Can I complete my questioning now?" Mulrooney interrupted.

Sam looked at the doctor for help, his arms upraised. He could see that Liz wanted to stay. He knew that determined scowl.

"Come with me, young lady," Doc said, observing Sam's body language. "I'll give you that prescription. Five minutes, Officer. Then he has to rest."

Liz started to protest, so Sam said, "I'll be fine here, Creena."

"Don't you be calling me *my heart* any more. I'm not damaged goods."

"Indeed you are not, my love. How about I call you *astore* from now on?"

"'My treasure' sounds a lot better."

"Fine then. *Astore* it is. Go check on the lad for me, *astore.* Then hurry back."

After they had left, Sam turned to the officer. "How can I help you?"

"I checked up on your story with your paper, son," Mulrooney started when the others had left the room. "Seems as though you spoke the truth there."

Sam thought he sounded more conciliatory. "What else can I help you with, Officer?"

"So why was this kid Collin there in the first place?"

Sam had decided to help Collin. He was pretty sure the Paper would go for it given the outcome of their little adventure. He'd have to take a temporary cut in salary though, to be sure. But he wasn't about to let Liam down again.

"Collin is my new assistant. First night on the job. Rudy kidnapped the both of us because we witnessed him setting fire to Warehouse Five last midnight." It was true in a sense. Collin was being emotionally tied up in knots by the fiend. And he did witness the arson.

Sam continued, "Collin was also a prisoner, but he had a knife hidden in his boot. Rudy took a can of gasoline and set fire to the warehouse from outside after spilling some gas inside. That's when Collin was able to cut me loose of my bonds. Rudy came in the back door with a crowbar to make sure we would burn up in the fire. My assistant helped me fend off the brute, but Rudy knocked him unconscious. The blaggard tripped and fell into the flames when he tried to knock me out again."

"That's quite a story. So how'd you know his name was Rudy?"

"Because the lad recognized him as a longshoreman from his time on the docks," Sam replied.

"Fair enough. That's all for now," Mulrooney concluded. "We'll check the warehouse."

"One more thing," Sam asked. "Were you on the force two years ago, Officer?"

"Yes, of course. I was a sergeant then."

"Do you remember a murder on Geddes Wharf where a young lad found his Ma just after she was raped?"

"Uh, there was a case of a laundress I remember. Let's see . . . O'Donnell case I think. Nasty business. Never found the blaggard. The boy was destitute afterwards, as I recall."

"Well, Officer, that boy is Collin. He's been through a lot in his short life, don't you know."

"There's no doubt of it." The sergeant pocketed his notebook and pencil, then looked to Sam, the lines around his mouth relaxed.

"I'll be in touch, Finlay. You take care of that heart."

"My heart's the least of my worries, don't ya know."

"That's not what I heard." With that Mulrooney took his leave.

Twenty minutes later Liz breezed in. "The doctor said you can likely go home in three days," she announced. Holding him up with one hand and plumping up his pillow with the other, she added, "into my care, love."

"I can't wait, *astore*. But first, I need you to do something for me. Do you have paper and a pencil in your purse?"

"Why yes, here." She fumbled inside her bag and found a pencil at the bottom. "What is it I should do?"

"I need you to take this note to my boss at the Paper right away," Sam replied, hastily scribbling on the notepad Liz had given him.

"What do you mean by assistant?" Liz asked, peering at the note.

"Just what it says, Liz. I've decided on helping Collin and that's final."

"But you don't know anything about him, Samuel."

"I know enough, and the rest I'll find out. I have a hunch about him. It will work out. Don't you worry."

"You're a pushover, Samuel Stevenson. And he's not Liam, remember that."

"Hurry now, love. I need that note to get to my boss before the officer contacts him again."

"If you weren't so banged up . . ."

"I know, Lizzy. But you can't live without me."

"I know that, *avorneen*. I do. I just want what's best."

"Fine, then. Your own love am I now. Give us a kiss and be off with you now."

Two days later Sam was allowed to get up and walk. He winced with every step, but it felt good to be out of bed. The cane they gave him was too short.

"Can I see the lad named Collin?" he asked when the doctor came on his rounds.

"That can be arranged if you keep it short. His heart took a beating, not to mention his head."

"But he'll recover?"

"Physically, yes." The doctor held Sam's wrist checking his pulse. "The burns are fairly localized. But he's in bad shape, if you know what I mean." He turned to capture his patient's eyes, waiting.

"Yes, I do. I'm going to work on that."

"Good. It looks like he needs a friend and you seem like the friendly type. Now come with me and we'll find your patient."

Sam had seen the *Evening Telegram*. They didn't just print Sam's partial sketch of the warehouse fire that Mulrooney had found on the wharf, but also featured Sam and Collin on the front page. *Fearless Illustrator Knocked Out Doing His Job* the headline read. They were hailed across the city as heroes for solving the mystery of the warehouse fires and stopping the Imperialist warmongers. Great press for the paper.

Sam's boss, Jim Fletcher, had stopped by the hospital to congratulate him the night before. With such notoriety by the two ,and with Sam's note about Collin, Jim told Sam he was willing to accept Collin as Sam's assistant, at least for three months. Sam would be given more significant assignments in the future, and his assistant would be a necessary and invaluable asset to the paper.

The good news came with a caution. "The lad will be on probation. If he doesn't work out, then it'll be back on the beat for you, Samuel."

"Fair enough, boss."

Jim also said that the police had just rounded up two accomplices. They had confessed that Borden's team had nothing to do with the fires. It was just corruption among the dockworkers trying to capitalize on the election hubbub. And their ringleader, old Rudy's remains, had been found in the rubble—ashes to ashes.

An orderly insisted on wheeling Sam to see Collin whose room didn't look that different from his own, but Sam noticed many more nurses and attendants buzzing around. They were trying to give Collin a sponge bath. The two girls were lookers, but Sam shook away the thoughts as he surveyed the scene. The lad, heavily bandaged on his right arm and hand, was alert and resisting.

"Can't I just have Henry here give me the bath?"

"I'd be asking the girls to bathe me, lad, to be sure," Sam joked, rolling into the room.

That solicited a guffaw from his own orderly. "Let's give this gentleman a few minutes with your patient," he said.

When they had all taken their leave, Sam saw that Collin seemed to calm down in the quiet of the room. He decided not to probe into whether the lad knew he had almost died.

"How are you feeling, lad?"

"Oh, better, better, But I have to know. What happened to Rudy? Nobody tells me nothin' around here." Collin started clenching his left hand, balling up the bed covers.

Sam answered, "Burned up with the warehouse."

"God help us." Collin went quiet and turned to stare out the window.

"Do you remember the blaggard knocking you out?" Sam asked softly.

"Sort of."

"Well, he came after me and tripped and fell into the fire. I saw him burn when the roof collapsed. He can't hurt you anymore, lad."

"What'd you tell him, that copper, I mean?" Collin turned, his eyes pleading.

"You talked to him?" Sam's eyebrows raised.

"Nah, they wouldn't let him in. But I saw him snoopin' around out there. He seemed mighty nosy." Collin pushed a lock of hair out of his eyes so he could see Sam clearly. "Well?"

"I told him the truth as I saw it. You and I were kidnapped and almost killed and you helped me escape."

"But . . ."

"No buts about it, lad. He had a hold over you." Sam stood up out of his wheelchair and crossed to the lad, grabbing him by his good left shoulder.

Collin unclenched his fist and offered it in a handshake. "You sure?" he asked. "The cop will be askin' more about it."

"It's not as if you're the villain here, Collin. More like the victim," Sam answered taking Collin's left hand in a hearty squeeze, and then patting him again on his shoulder.

"Back to my question. How are you feeling? You've had a rough go of it."

"I'll be fine. I've taken worse beatings, plenty of times."

"Is that arm broken? You took a mighty blow."

"Don't think so," he replied, bending his arm.

"You sure have good reflexes, lad."

"Street fighter training."

Sam saw him grin for the first time. "All the same, we made a good team, didn't we?"

"I dunno. I was looped most of the time."

"Nonsense. You came to my aid. That counts for a lot."

"Maybe. Self-defense."

"You could have left me tied up."

"You took care of Rudy, I guess." Collin looked away and raising his spoon he started to play with a partially consumed bowl of tapioca.

"We both did, Collin."

Collin looked up and Sam could see the relief spreading over his face. But then the frown reappeared and the boy asked, "So

81

where do we go from here?"

"Tell me some more about what happened to your Ma."

Collin hesitated, clenching again.

"I want to help you here, Collin, but I need to understand what happened when your Ma was killed." This was the critical opportunity to get the lad to open up after the trauma of their ordeal. He waited patiently, smiling.

Collin sat upright, silent.

Sam took out his pipe that Liz had brought him and tapped in some of his favorite Prince Albert. Then reaching into his robe pocket he withdrew a match and lit up. Once the bowl was glowing red he relaxed down onto the bed beside the lad, waiting. Smoke curled up towards the ceiling filling the air with that glorious woodsy scent.

Collin's nose flared up, obviously not used to pipe smoke.

"Well, lad?" He puffed again.

Finally Collin's haunted eyes locked on his.

"My Da was croaked in Donegal when I was just eight by a slugger, a gouger cop. My Ma told me later he was RIC. I should have defended him, but I froze up."

"Ease back there, lad. You were only a boy, for all that."

Sam could see Collin's knuckles go white. The veins on the back of his hands seemed to pulse as he squeezed his fists harder and harder.

"My Ma escaped with me and my younger sister Claire to New York. We didn't have nothin' when we arrived at Ellis Island. Zero. We ended up in Brooklyn, the dirty part near the Navy Yard. Ma had to do something she hated just to keep us alive."

Sam could only imagine what that might have been. But the kid was guarded in his explanation. Sam decided not to push.

"That's when my little sister was taken." Collin was wailing now and he tried to turn away. "It was all my fault, you know. I was supposed to look after her that day. "Shite, I'm a right gobdaw."

Guilt riddled the lad's face. Sam glimpsed the degree of trauma that Collin had already endured. By comparison, Sam had led a charmed life.

"How old was she at the time?"

"Twelve, I think, and I was fourteen, old enough to be in charge. But I was out brawlin' in the streets to make money for us all. A sad excuse," Collin added in disgust.

"Where was she taken?"

"We don't know. She was just gone. We looked for months, me and Ma. She wasn't just gone."

Horrible doesn't even begin to describe it, Sam thought. He hadn't gotten the answer to his original question yet. "But what happened to your Ma?"

"We escaped to Toronto, Ma and me. Lived in the Ward."

"St. John's Ward?"

"Ya, that's the one. Downtown."

Sam knew that area was a den of iniquity, certainly not a place to be caught dead in, although many were as the *Evening Telegram* often reported. He'd been there just last week to cover a multiple murder suicide.

"I saw it, but I couldn't get to her fast enough." Collin buried his head in his hands.

"Saw what, exactly?" Sam let the lad explain.

"She was a laundry woman and we was delivering clean uniforms on the docks late that night. I was getting the money from Rudy when it happened. He was the longshoremen's foreman, you may remember. The bastard rapist got away. Ma died. My whole family is gone," the lad muttered, shoulders sagging.

My God, this lad is worse off than Liam ever was. But at least he's alive.

"Hear me, Collin. Don't be so hard on yourself. It wasn't your fault, to be sure." Sam gave the young man a playful cuff on the cheek. "Don't worry. You are going to be all right."

"But I got no money and I'm homeless." Collin's eyes dropped to the bed below.

"Not any more, lad. I'm offering you a job as my assistant at the *Toronto Evening Telegram,* and I know exactly where you can live for the time being. It won't be down in the Ward, I can tell you."

This kid needed a break. It still wasn't clear if Collin had enough backbone, but with the cards he'd been dealt, he deserved another chance. And Sam was going to give it to him.

"Why would you do this for me?" Collin asked, his eyes wary.

"Let's just say that I have an old score to settle."

"I've got a few of those, too," Collin admitted, still looking down.

"So you do, lad. So you do. But let's face them together, eh?"

When Collin didn't respond, Sam wondered what he was getting himself and his darling Liz into. The boy had not said thank you. Collin sat hunched over on the bed and Sam stared at the wounded boy in front of him.

The orderly and nurses burst in on this scene insisting that they carry out their ablutions before the evening meal came. As the orderly steered him out, Sam exclaimed, "Buck up, Collin. There are better days ahead, lad."

As he travelled down the corridor he thought, *What a strange reaction to the offer of salvation.* But he could picture Liam smiling, just as he had been before Sam left for art school. And that was enough . . . for now.

Chapter Eight
Collin's Quest

May 1911
The Beaches, Toronto

*F*our months after the arsonist's warehouse fires had ravaged the downtown Toronto waterfront, Borden and his Conservatives looked like they were going to win the national election. Now Canadian industry would likely be protected from American free traders.

Sam breathed a sigh of relief as spring finally showed its color. In the waterfront cottage community called the Beaches, where Sam lived some five miles east of downtown, the multi-hued tulips were up in abundance in Kew Gardens and the cherry trees exploded in pink blossoms along the beachfront Boardwalk.

Collin had no such relief, it appeared. Oh, he'd seemed to have settled into a routine as Sam's assistant at *The Toronto Evening Telegram*, all right. It wasn't hard to tote Sam's equipment, clean his brushes and file his finished sketches. He said he appreciated the opportunity and the friendship that came with it. Lately, he'd become interested in the developing field of photography, which the paper was starting to explore, and Sam reveled in sharing that enthusiasm.

Thanks to the kindness of Reverend Dixon, Sam had found a place for Collin at St. Aidan's Anglican tent church, right there in the Beaches only two blocks from Sam's digs.

One night after work, Sam invited Collin to dinner. Liz had come over from her parents' home on Kingston Road where she lived just to make this fine meal. Sam watched him relish the beef brisket and corn, and noticed the young man had put some meat on his bones the last few months. After the meal, when they settled into their chairs and had their fill of peach pie with whipped cream for dessert, Sam handed the young man a package wrapped in brown paper.

"What's this?" Collin asked.

"It's for you," Sam said, his eyes twinkling. "Open it."

"But it's not my birthday."

"It is as far as I am concerned. Open it lad."

Collin lifted the lid of the box. "A Kodak Brownie camera!"

Sam saw tears forming in the lad's eyes. Then he said he couldn't remember the last time he'd received a gift.

"Well?" Sam prodded. "Do you like it?"

"Oh yeah, boss, I —" Collin's voice cracked. He backhanded the wooden camera box away, embarrassed. "I don't deserve such a fine thing."

"Don't tell my boss that." Sam laughed. "I talked old Fletcher into purchasing it. I told him you needed more to do. Go on, lad." Sam gave his hand a nudge. "Take it out of the box, get the feel of it. I put film in it for you."

Finally the lad smiled. He took the camera out of the box and started fiddling with it. Sam looked over his shoulder at Liz, standing at the sink. When she turned her head, he raised his eyebrows. Liz rolled her eyes and turned away.

Sam turned back to Collin. "I suspect that little box will do me out of my job one day."

"Sooner than you think," Collin said, snapping a picture of Liz as she rinsed a dish and put it on the drain board in a thousandth of the time it would have taken Sam to draw it. "See this, Liz?"

"Yes. I see it all right. Cost a pretty penny I'll wager."

"Now, *astore*. This is the way of the future," Sam grinned.

"Ours or his?"

"All of ours, my love."

"Humpf."

After Collin left, his prize in hand, Sam helped Liz finish the dishes.

"Collin's got a head on his shoulders you know. He takes direction well and picks up new information like a sponge, but he's his own worst enemy. It's a shame, but I'm not giving up on him."

"You know you're acting like a fool, don't you?"

"Not at all. Did you hear how he appreciated your cooking?"

"Cooking's one thing. But the likes of him, out of the Ward, he's going to steal you blind. Mark my words."

"Do you have any evidence of that, my love?" Sam asked, his eyebrows popping further up his forehead.

"Well, no, but I know his kind."

"And I have every faith in him to surprise you, soon enough."

Sam picked up a cup, wiped it dry and hung it on the kitchen hook. A place for everything and everything in its place.

"But you don't have the money . . ."

"Hush, my love. You worry too much."

When Collin arrived at the camp he stowed the Kodak Brownie inside the small, padlocked trunk where he kept his few belongings, and lay down on his cot among the other sleeping, homeless men.

Tonight, like every night, sleep wouldn't come. Remorse instead consumed his soul. Collin listened to the men around him mutter or snore, twenty of them in a canvas kind of circus tent. It seemed like a military bivouac, he imagined, only without the war. Except for the one that he waged nightly with himself. At least now the outside temperature was warming up.

Reverend Dixon had been kind enough to lend him one of the two pushbikes belonging to the church so that he could get together with Sam for work. Once the men around him had quieted, Collin swung out of his cot and picked up his shoes. It was just past eleven. He crept out of the tent, put his shoes on, and made his way to the bike he'd ridden to Sam's place, and he rode off into the night.

After church the next Sunday, Reverend Dixon met with Sam to discuss the stained glass windows he was designing for the new church. Once he'd approved Sam's work, the Reverend sighed. "Your boy is causing a stir. He slinks away most nights after curfew. Where he goes and what he does I have no idea. Lord have mercy, the boy is causing a big problem. Collin's nocturnal forays wake the men and they don't like it. Bad enough they can't find work. But exhausted they are—downright cantankerous."

Sam thought he knew. "Sorry for the trouble, Reverend. I'll take care of it."

"Please do it quickly, Sam."

That night, Collin took off as usual on his bike after the camp curfew went into effect at eleven. He headed due west on Queen Street.

At a safe distance, Sam tailed him on his Royal Enfield Model 160 motorcycle. With its revolutionary three-horsepower twin-v engine, two-speed gear and chain drive, the Enfield could reach unheard-of speeds of twenty-five miles per hour, but tonight Sam had it throttled back to almost idle.

The *Telegram* had recently purchased Sam the Enfield so that he could get to newsworthy locations quickly. The black enamel with green petrol tank and gold trim machine was bold and seductive. There was even a rear rack to carry his paints. He loved the freedom it gave him, the wind whipping past his already thinning hair.

As Collin pedaled past the new Simpson's store at Yonge Street at midnight, he started to feel more at home. About a half mile north of the waterfront, St. John's Ward in all its squalor played out on his right. He knew its muddy alleys cluttered with garbage, its ramshackle lean-tos and its dingy street storefronts, even in the dark. So like the Brooklyn he'd left far behind.

Even at night in May the heat was setting in, bringing with it the putrid smell of rot and waste. And overcrowded immigrants. Many were good people with nowhere to go. Young and old, fat and skinny, lying about in various states of undress, their abysmal rooms and dank cellars too stifling and cramped to tolerate.

But it was the makeshift bars and brothels on Center Street that drew Collin. Even at this hour they were jumping. At Hennesey's, where the girls plied their trade street-side, Collin was sickened. What if Claire had been forced to do this to survive, wherever she was—if she was still alive? And his Ma. All those tortured years.

His mother's last delirious words kept rattling around in his brain without answers. *Brooklyn . . . Western . . . ginger-nut . . . Betsy.* Must be a description of her murderer. He had to surface again. Big longshoreman. Red hair. *I've got to find him and kill him. But what did Western mean and who was Betsy?*

The honky-tonk pianist was playing "The Maple Leaf Rag" as Collin strode through the door. Two prostitutes were gyrating topless on the grubby bar with well-oiled sailors groping at their legs. It was hard to see with the mass of humanity and all the cigarette smoke, especially in the dingy back booths. The smell of cheap booze and sex made him gag.

No one here that's big enough, he decided after a few minutes of looking. He was propositioned three times before he could escape the hellhole.

Half an hour and five flop joints later he had come up empty-handed, again. Could he have missed him in the throng? He didn't think so. But he wasn't really sure what he was looking for, was he?

How could I have lived in that filth for so many years? He pedaled south on Bay Street, so intent upon looking for his Ma's killer he failed to notice Sam shadowing him in the darkness.

Collin pulled up in the alley behind the burned out warehouses on the waterfront. The first time he'd returned here after the fires, he'd been amazed at the level of destruction. Through the rubble of

Warehouse Four, he could see that Geddes Wharf was buzzing with lake traffic. Fifty or more longshoremen were straining to load and unload half a dozen canallers; freighters with shallow drafts needed to navigate the St. Lawrence River around Montreal on their way from the Atlantic.

"Surely this is the night," Collin muttered as he headed onto the dock. Then he peered at the dark water. *Shite. There's the New Yorker, the Saratoga. His ship to be sure.*

Sam came to a stop within feet of where they had been thrown when the warehouse collapsed. He switched off the Enfield, flipping the beast up on its kick stand and pocketed the key. Then he took off in search of Collin.

Skirting a stack of crates, Sam peered across the wharf. It was lighter now that the shipping season was in full swing. He saw a group of five longshoremen gathered around the gangplank of a ship named *The Saratoga*. They were jostling someone between them.

"Let go of me, you *eejits*," Collin demanded, shaking off the hands groping at him.

"What were you doing trying to sneak onboard our ship?" One of the longshoremen snarled, flipping open his switchblade knife. "Know what we do to snoopers?"

"I'm looking for the devil what raped and killed my Ma. He ships out on the *Saratoga* so I've been told."

"He does, does he?"

"Hold on, now, gentlemen!" Sam called out as he strolled up to the gangplank.

Collin, who had his fists balled up ready to take them on, was startled to see his boss. Two other longshoremen turned to face Sam.

"Collin, did you get what we need for our newspaper assignment?" Sam asked, flashing his *Toronto Evening Telegram* identification.

"What assignment?" The stevedore with the knife growled.

"An article about longshoremen harassing law abiding citizens," Sam said coolly.

"Not too much light, here, boss, but I think I got enough for the paper." Collin held up the Brownie camera Sam had given him. "Looks like the Yank ships are the worst."

A switchblade lunged at Collin's arm. Before Sam even saw his young friend move, Collin looped the Brownie over his wrist by its strap, disarmed the blade bearer, and dropped him to the wharf with a staggering blow to his solar plexus, followed by another to his jaw.

"Anyone else want a piece of me?" Collin taunted, not even breathing hard.

"C'mon, Collin." Sam stepped through the dock workers, praying no one else had a knife, and grabbed Collin's arm. "We've got what we need."

"Get that camera!" Switchblade yelled from the ground, grabbing his knife and slashing it across Collin's shin.

The lad stomped on his arm and Switchblade shouted, "Damn you!"

The crack of his wrist had the other four stevedores backing away.

"Say goodbye to your friends," Sam said, pulling Collin free of the pack.

"But it was just getting right exciting," Collin replied, an odd grin on his face.

The longshoremen did not give chase. They were milling around the gangway to help Switchblade, who still couldn't stand up. Sam yanked Collin out of sight into the rubble of Warehouse Four.

"Let me remind you of the way things were four months ago," Sam said hotly, as he towed Collin through the ruins. "You want to go back to that, lad?"

"Shite no, boss." Collin shook his head as they emerged into the alley where he'd left his bike, and Sam had parked the Enfield.

"Well, you could have fooled me." Sam placed a finger against Collin's forehead. "Your hard head could have gotten you knifed or worse!"

Collin ducked away and frowned. "I've survived worse donnybrooks, I can tell you."

"Well, I don't care to hear about them," Sam snapped.

He dropped to his knees to have a look at Collin's shin. Blood was oozing through the cut in his trousers. Sam ripped the bottom off the pant leg and tied the scrap over the wound.

"I think you'll live, but you're in no shape to pedal five miles home."

"Sure I can." Collin mounted his push bike. "Watch me."

"There they are!" Sam heard Switchblade's gravelly bellow. "Get 'em!"

Collin leapt off the bike. Sam spun around and saw the longshoreman heading toward them, coming through the rubble of Warehouse Four at a trot, some of his companions alongside of him now, swinging chains.

"Forget the bike. Get on the back."

Collin glanced over his shoulder, half-turned as if to engage again. Sam took him by the arm and pulled him around.

"Ease back, lad," he ordered firmly. "Let's get out of here."

Collin hesitated at first, then vaulted onto the Enfield. Sam sprang onto the saddle and gunned the throttle. Switchblade and his pack emerged from the rubble as the Enfield sped off down the alley.

"I could've handled those thugs," Collin muttered, his arms folded across his chest.

When they'd cleared the wharf, Sam stopped the Enfield and got off to retighten Collin's makeshift bandage. He finished and stepped back, wiping his hands on his trousers.

"The longshoreman with the knife," he said to Collin. "Was that your Ma's killer?"

"Nah." Collin shook his head, then ducked his chin guiltily. "How'd you know I'd come looking for him?"

"I'm not stupid, lad. It's as plain as the hangdog look on your face."

"It's none of your business what I do after work."

"Oh, yes it is," Sam retorted. "There's no doubt of that."

Collin instantaneously regretted having said that. He'd come to respect his boss and was thankful for his kindness. Sam was the one person he'd met who wasn't out for himself, but still Collin couldn't lift his head.

"I want you to come and stay with me for the time being," Sam said.

Collin looked up. "What about the church camp?"

"I think you've worn out your welcome there, lad."

"But I told you that I don't need your help."

"We'll discuss that later. Right now I want to get you fit for work this morning. We have that stockbroker murder scene to deal with. And I'm exhausted just following you around."

"Right, for tonight then," Collin relented. Then he added, "Sure and that'll be grand."

"No sarcasm, please."

"What will Liz say? She hates my guts."

"You let me take care of her," Sam replied.

Sam sure is self assured and wise, Collin thought on the ride over to Sam's place. Only a few years older, like the big brother he never had. Sam was more interested in helping others than taking the credit himself. How different from his own life experience. *But can I measure up?*

When they had arrived and settled into Sam's place at 10 Balsam, the artist sat Collin down and made tea. They had to get some things straight. "What were you trying to do out there tonight, my boy?" he started, offering the lad a shortbread from the metal can that Liz had brought over earlier in the day.

He could start, Collin decided, by being honest with Sam.

"I got to find the rapist that killed my Ma. When I do, I'm going to tear him limb from limb. It's my only hope to make a man of myself."

"It's not right to take matters into your own hands, lad," Sam chided gently. "If you find him, he should be brought to justice in a court. Killing him would just ruin your life."

"As if it's not ruined already," Collin muttered bitterly.

"You ought to leave it up to the police. Like officer Mulrooney."

"Them coppers are useless! They gave up looking a week after Ma died."

"So you want to get yourself killed, then? You almost died twice a few months back. Once right there on the spot we just left. How would you recognize the killer?"

"On that awful night, me and Ma was bringing clean laundry to the Canadian Longshoreman's Union right there on Geddes Wharf. It was mostly deserted, unlike tonight. She was attacked by a burly devil. I was a distance away collecting the money from Rudy, but I could see he was a big bastard. She fought him, but he dragged her into the nearest warehouse and had his way with her. Then, to shut her up, he beat her until she was barely conscious."

"The closest warehouse," Sam said, "would be number four."

"Yeah, the one where Rudy died."

"How fitting. That's where you turned the corner and came to my aid, Collin."

"I guess so. I heard Ma screamin' and I saw her being taken. By the time I reached her, that fekin' hardchaw was escaping. Then he turned there, not fifty yards away in the wharf light, and stared right at me and Ma. He hesitated for a moment while he rubbed his face. I thought he was going to come back after me. That's when I saw them. Those red claw marks on his cheek. Matched the color of his hair. But then Rudy showed up and the man hightailed it. He was damned big."

"Did you chase him?

Collin shook his head. "Ma was right hurt, so I dropped down to care for her."

"Good lad."

"She was crying and bleeding all over. Then she kinda fainted. I could barely hear her when she took the piece of jewelry from around her neck and whispered, 'Collin, me love, guard this—for your son!' Then I bent down to her lips and she whispered some words— 'Brooklyn . . . Western . . . ginger-nut . . . Betsy.' Them's the last words she ever spoke."

"Show me that necklace."

"It's a locket really," Collin pulled it out from under his shirt and handed it over to his boss. "See the clasp?"

"That's real silver, isn't it?" Sam turned it over carefully in his hands.

"I guess so. My Da showed it to me before he died. Said something about how he was told it was important when he got it from his own Da.

"Heart-shaped, I see," Sam said. "Intricate."

"And it's got a picture of my Ma in it, and one of my sister Claire when she was eleven."

"A valuable keepsake, I would think," Sam handed the locket back.

"That's why I keep it around my neck," Collin said. "It's all I have left of them." His voice trailed off as he looked away.

"Well, then. What do you think your Ma meant?"

"I dunno. Her attacker?"

"Likely, lad. Look at me."

Collin looked up from the kitchen table but wouldn't meet Sam's eyes. "Rudy called for a doctor. By the time they got Ma and me to the hospital, she was unconscious. She died two nights later.

Rudy asked around. His men told him an American longshoreman off the *Saratoga*."

"The canaller that you were just boarding," Sam interjected, grabbing Collin's chin and forcing the young man to look at him.

"Yeah, that's right. Rudy said that bastard was in his cups down at Hennessey's bar that night. Fit the description, burly and red headed. He boasted he was looking for some whore he'd slept with back in Brooklyn and he was going to do her good. They looked for him, but he had jumped ship and disappeared."

"Is there any chance the rapist could have followed you and your Ma from New York?"

"Nobody knew where we went. We took the train from Jersey." Collin blinked at Sam. "What are you getting at?"

"Probably nothing." Sam shrugged. "It just seems odd that he knew your Ma in New York and then he ended up here looking for her. Never underestimate the power of evil, lad."

When Collin failed to respond Sam coaxed, "Right, lad? Come on, now. The spare room is already made up. May be a little feminine for the likes of us. But no matter. It's safe and dry."

"I've been there," Collin lamented.

"Where?"

"A place where evil reigns," Collin spat out as Sam ushered him up the stairs in the dark hour of night.

Sam crossed himself. *Lord tell me he's not after talking about his own soul.*

Lying there in the frilly room with its embroidered bedspread Collin was afraid to go to sleep. He lay awake agonizing. *Why didn't I stay in our room the day Claire was taken? Why didn't I run down the demon that killed Ma?* He had already wondered if the murderer had followed them.

But he wasn't going to give up. If he did he would be completely lost. He had little to go on, but he had vowed revenge on the animal who had killed his mother. If only he could track him down. He had to come back to Toronto sometime. Collin decided that he would continue checking the waterfront shipyards and bars of the Ward, night after night until he found him.

The next evening, Collin went home again with Sam after work. Number Ten Balsam Avenue was a quaint brick and wooden two-story structure just two houses from the beach. There was a sunny office area that could be set up as a studio for Sam's artwork, some of which was already on display in a small gallery nearby. Sam was thinking how splendid a place this would be for his planned family, when Liz, who often worked on her trousseau in the third bedroom, came traipsing down the stairs.

"Hello my dear—" Liz stopped short at the sight of Collin. "Well. *Hello*, Collin."

Sam could see the fire in her eyes.

"Evening, ma'am," Collin muttered, rushing past her and leaping up the stairs.

"Really, Samuel. What's going on here, if you don't mind my asking?"

"I want the lad to live here for the time being. That way I can lead him by example and keep an eye on him at the same time."

"No, Samuel." Liz folded her arms. "He'll be after stealing you blind."

Secretly, Sam was worried Collin might slip back over the line. But he was on a crusade to help him become an honest and successful young man.

"Come now, Elizabeth. He just needs a little fathering. Please trust me."

"This is your home for now, but it will soon be ours," Liz said tartly. "I won't have him under this roof once it's mine too, and that's final."

"Liz, please. Collin reminds me so much of Liam." Sam caught her hands in his. "We've got to do everything we can to save this boy, or Liam will have died for nothing."

"Don't you be after includin' me in that *we*," Liz spat back as she headed for the front door. "Liam's dead and it wasn't your fault. Collin had nothing to do with any of it. And that's the truth of it."

Sam beat her to the door and swept her up in his arms. "I knew that you would see it my way."

He planted a kiss firmly on her lips, and felt her melt in his embrace. After a moment, her head tilted until her ear pressed against his right shoulder.

"Come back inside, *astore*."

"He can stay—but only until our wedding, Samuel. He gets out at the first sign of trouble, do you hear?"

"To be sure, my love."

At the top of the stairs Collin winced. "Better to steer clear of them skirts," he muttered.

Chapter Nine
Regatta

June 3, 1911
The Beaches, Toronto

*W*hat Collin needed, Sam decided, was a distraction, something to take his mind off his obsession with revenge, something that would also, hopefully, keep him out of the Ward. If that something included physical exercise to help work off the anger and crushing guilt the lad felt, even better. Sam thought he had just the thing. And just the place.

After breakfast on a bright, breezy Saturday morning in early June, Sam invited Collin to take a walk with him.

"Where to?" The lad asked sullenly, his head lowered. He was suspicious of every new thing Sam suggested. Understandable, considering his tragic past, but it was growing tiresome.

"Just down the beach," Sam cajoled, towing Collin out the door.

The lad kept his eyes down as they walked two blocks east along the Boardwalk. When Sam stopped at the foot of Beech Street, Collin's head came up and his eyes widened at the two-story Victorian boathouse situated on a pristine two-mile long white sand beach. "What is this place?" he asked Sam.

"'Tis the Balmy Beach Club, m'boy," Sam announced. "A paddling, tennis and curling club, as well as the hub of social life here at the Beach. Would you like a tour of the place?"

Sam, a member of the Canadian Canoe Association, had recently helped form the Club. Shortly thereafter its paddlers won the coveted "Burgee" national championship. Canoeing was a very serious endeavor with strenuous training, trials and regattas throughout the spring and summer seasons.

Collin's eyes widened a bit more. "We can go inside?"

"Sure we can," Sam said with a laugh. "Just so happens I'm a member."

Collin discovered that the upper floor of the grand old house was configured with a comfortable lounge and bar, and a dining room that also served as a meeting room. It had a sweeping verandah facing the lake, across the entire width of the one hundred-foot long edifice. At its eastern end was an outdoor pagoda that Sam explained hosted many festive gatherings.

The criss-crossed white railings on the deck were a splendid visual feature. Collin thought their open weave construction looked a bit rickety, but he didn't say so.

"I love to share a drink with friends and neighbors on this verandah," Sam said, as he and Collin settled in two of the many plush settees and rocking chairs overlooking the lake. "You can almost see Niagara Falls when the sun sets over there."

Collin squinted where Sam pointed, but couldn't see much. *I'm not sharing anything with anyone in this place. It's far too grand for the likes of me.*

"One more thing to see," Sam said, rising to his feet. "Come along." Sam led him off the verandah to the lower floor of the boathouse. This, Sam explained, was the business end of the Club where the one-, two- and four-man sprint canoes and kayaks of the paddling club were housed. There were five rollup doors facing the lake and concrete ramps from each exit down to the water.

"Those one-man canoes are right sleek," Collin said, clapping his mentor on the back. "Could I try one out?"

"I think that could be arranged," Sam replied, his eyes twinkling.

At last, something positive that interests the boy. He'd found out that Collin was nineteen, and when he managed to hold his head up, which wasn't often, he was a strapping young man of almost six feet, muscle hard.

They returned to the verandah chairs, "This is where I proposed to Liz. Sure and it was a fine moment, I can tell you. We're going to be married here at the Club on August nineteenth, in the evening after the Summer Regatta. I want you to be one of my groomsmen."

"Me?" Collin blurted, stunned. "Amblin' about in front of a crowd of people?"

"Yes, of course, with our friends and family. You are one of our friends now."

Collin could see that there was likely no way out of this obligation—still he grumbled, feeling uncomfortable, "Why bother getting married anyway?"

"It's what decent folks do before they start a family," Sam answered.

"Not where I come from. Marriages in the Ward are scarce as a swell strolling down those streets."

"Well, you don't live in the Ward anymore," Sam said sternly. "And where I come from you get married and then have your family."

"I don't know nothin' about that. I stood by while my Ma was killed, and I left Claire alone to be kidnapped. Skirts and me just don't mix. Period."

"We've been over and over that, Collin. It's terrible, but none of it was your fault," Sam said firmly. "You've got to get past that or it will destroy you."

"Listen, boss." Collin jumped to his feet. "I'm happy you got me this job as your assistant, but I've got a mind to move on if you don't stop trying to save me. Facts is facts. I stood by, useless as a lighthouse on a bog. It's shamed I am, and worthless. No colleen should throw in with me."

He turned on his heel and rushed down the stairs and out onto the beach. Sam went to the railing and watched him, head down, hands in his pockets, striding away from the Club, heading for who knew where. But Collin wasn't headed toward the Ward. *Best let him go cool off.*

He would not give up on Collin, even though the lad had given up on himself.

Through the open parlor window of Number Ten, Liz watched her best friend Kathleen O'Sullivan turn up the lilac-trimmed walk. Sam had planted the flowers the year before. They were late blooming on this sultry June morning, due to last year's severe winter. Their pungent fragrance wafting into the cottage almost made her giddy. Or was it the fact that the wedding was only a little over two months away?

Liz noted with pleasure how Kathy breezed along, her auburn curls flying as if she hadn't a care in the world. But Liz knew differently. The two of them were inseparable friends from their girlhood in Belfast. Almost sisters really. Their families had lived next to each other off the Shankill Road in the Protestant sector of the city.

Kathy's father Ryan had worked begrudgingly as a welder at Harland and Wolff shipbuilders back in Ireland, even though he was trained to be a university history professor. No professional jobs available. The horrible man treated Kathy like a five-year-old, and Ryan was the major reason both families had decided to immigrate to thriving Canada together two years ago. At least Liz would give him that.

"Hello, dear," Liz greeted her maid of honor as she bounced through the front door. Toronto could be so humid near the lake in summer, but Kathy always looked so cool and collected.

"Hello, bride to be," Kathy replied gaily. "I've come for my fitting."

"I've almost finished your dress. Come with me and let's try it on."

"Why are you working on the dresses here?"

"Because there's no room at home with my parents," Liz replied as they climbed the stairs. "Plenty of room here in the third bedroom, away from my fiancé's prying eyes."

Liz helped Kathy into her dress and stood back while her maid of honor looked in the cheval glass.

"Oh, it's gorgeous, Liz!" Kathy cooed, flashing her girlish and imp-like smile as she smoothed the flowing material around her twenty-inch waist. "I love the blue crepe material."

"Matches your eyes," Liz noted as she appraised her work.

She had always envied Kathy's penetrating cobalt eyes and her waist long auburn hair that shimmered against the radiant blue dress.

"You're just my height, five-foot-five in your bare feet. I sewed this from memory. Pretty good fit, don't you think?"

"It's just perfect." Kathy eyed her reflection, satisfied that the bodice masked her bust line. Her father incessantly drilled modesty into her head. "Can I see your wedding dress?"

"I'm having trouble with the neckline, but you can have a look," Liz replied, unfolding the tissue paper wrapped around her gown to protect it. "I hope you're enjoying your summer vacation away from that pack of ruffians you teach in that one-room schoolhouse of yours."

"Oh, I am, but you know, I actually miss them too, all thirty of them."

"Do you now? My gracious. Thirty is too many for me to handle at once."

"I love teaching them, and seeing their little minds start to work. I'm spending most of my time preparing lessons and background reading."

"All work and no play makes Kathy a dull girl," Liz joked, only half in jest. "There's a whole world of boys out there, you know."

"Oh, I know," Kathy replied, teasing back. "I've got fifteen of them in my classes."

"That's not the age I'm talking about and you know it."

"I do." Kathy's smile faded. "And you know what my father thinks about *that*, Liz."

"Really, Kathleen. You can't let that puritanical father of yours run your life. You're twenty years old and this is twentieth-century Toronto."

"I have hopes he'll soften up now that he's received tenure at Trinity College. I told you that, didn't I?"

"Yes, dear, you did. Is that why you read all the time and went into teaching? To please your father?"

"Well, I guess so, a little," Kathy replied with a shrug, "but I really like teaching."

"Thirty brats for six hours a day?" Liz shuddered. "Ugh."

"For you, perhaps, but I enjoy it," Kathy snapped. "And that's an end to this conversation. Now show me that neckline."

Liz noted that Kathy was twirling the hair behind her right ear, the way she always did when she was agitated.

"I apologize. I'm just being your annoying best friend," Liz replied, giving Kathy a big hug.

"I know you are." Kathy hugged her back. "Let's just forget about it."

As Kathy was preparing to leave just before lunch time, Collin strode through the front door, still miffed at his boss's meddling. At least the walk down the beach had done him some good. Liz caught him by the lapel as he attempted to whisk past them without speaking.

"Collin. Let me introduce you to my best friend Kathleen. Kathy is my maid of honor. She teaches elementary school up on the Kingston Road. She's from a strict Protestant family so don't you be trying to shoot her with Cupid's arrow, my lad."

Not that Liz thought he would, but she needed to make certain he wouldn't try. And she was curious to see not only Collin's reaction but also Kathy's.

With her auburn hair flowing sensuously down to her waist, Kathy didn't look like any schoolmarm Collin had ever seen, and with her piercing blue eyes she was undeniably fetching. He avoided direct eye contact with her, shrugging off an awakening desire that he had never felt before. He had to admit Kathy was a delightful lass, as lasses go. Better to stay away from them skirts, he thought to himself. *I'm bad medicine.*

"Afternoon, Miss," Collin mumbled, forcing himself to shake the hand she offered.

Was that static electricity? Collin recoiled from the contact. *Can't be. It's mighty humid out.*

Oh my, Kathy thought, as the touch of this rugged stranger made her fingers tingle. *He's very handsome and trim, in a dangerous sort of way. Those haunted hazel eyes hold a story, I'll wager.* His rolled-up sleeves revealed sizeable biceps.

"Hallo, Collin," Kathy said politely. "What part of Eire do you hail from?"

"Donegal. G'day," he muttered as he spun and walked away without doffing his cap.

"There's a queer sort," Kathy said, turning toward Liz. "A mite reclusive and moody for my liking."

"You're dead right about that. He's no swell, that's for sure, and not at all the type of man for you."

Maybe, Kathy thought, but there was something about this boy that had her curious and a little intrigued. Could it be his Heathcliff image, she wondered as she headed home, twirling her hair? Her father would never approve. And that idea seemed so frightfully wicked.

Despite his altercation with his boss, Collin immediately took to the sport of canoeing at the Beach Club and signed up to be part of the squad. Sam had been delighted to see him being enthusiastic and engaging in healthy physical activity. Collin wanted to please his mentor, up to a point. Plus, it was a great way to let off steam—and there were no girls involved.

Collin trained hard for the summer Regatta in the one-man category. After a month he had built considerable additional muscle and endurance, but with the exception of his fellow canoeists, he continued to be socially withdrawn. One afternoon after a workout on the lake, his paddle-mate invited him for a drink upstairs.

"Whoa there, Jock. Who are those skirts waving at you?" he asked as they strolled up toward the bar.

"Just my girlfriend Lacie and one of her friends. Thelma, I think. C'mon."

"No thanks, Jock. Me and skirts don't mix."

"Nonsense, lad." Jock pulled him closer so he could embrace his girl. Collin was trapped.

"Collin . . . Lacie . . . Thelma. Girls, this here is Collin. One of our fastest racers. Just look at them muscles." With that Jock squeezed Collin's right bicep.

"Let me feel," Thelma squealed, dropping her drink on the counter and stepping forward.

"Beg pardon, ladies," Collin jumped back and turned, so fast that Jock's nails drew blood through his team-mate's shirt. "I just remembered. I'd best be gone. I'm expected for supper," he explained without looking back.

"Well then, I guess you girls will both have the pleasure of my attentions this evening," Jock announced, shaking his head at the receding figure of his fellow canoeist.

"He's a *gavoon*, that one," Thelma said, gripping Jock's bicep instead.

"Hey, find your own man," Lacie countered. "What's a *gavoon*?"

"A knucklehead, boor, you name it, Lace," Thelma answered letting go of Jock.

"Seems right to me."

"He's not half bad really, just shy," Jock offered, but the girls disagreed vehemently.

When he wasn't paddling or on duty for Sam and the Paper, Collin continued to search the downtown waterfront at night. Sam accompanied him to protect his human investment. Either Collin's Ma's killer didn't surface or they missed him.

The morning of the Regatta and Sam's wedding day finally arrived. Collin was both thrilled and worried over what would occur. He felt he wasn't as skilled as everyone thought he was. The thought of the day-long competition was stressful enough. But this grand event with local and international teams from as far away as Montreal, Boston and New York, and hundreds if not thousands of spectators lining the beach, made him want to escape.

The August sun sparkled in a cloudless sky as throngs of Torontonians crowded onto the beach. Collin watched from the boat ramp. The girls in their colorful bathing costumes, which scandalously revealed their knees, were pretending to watch the practice racing heats. In fact, they were getting heated themselves by the sun and the attention of all the eligible young men.

Concession stands and kite flyers dotted the landscape, and people brought blankets, umbrellas and picnic baskets in hopes of having a raucous time. The racing lanes were festooned with color-ful streamers parallel to the beachfront. The water was as calm and as warm as Lake Ontario can get. There were great expectations for an exciting and festive competition.

Collin was in one of the first canoes out of the boathouse, and now all paddlers were warming up. The Club's Toronto Argonauts colors were double blue and white; contrasted with those of the Montreal Voyageurs, which were crimson and silver. The Boston Bruins were festooned in gold and black. The New York Knicks were dressed austerely all in black. Collin sensed the tension running high in the crews as they jostled him for practice space on the water. Finally, after some disorganized attempts, the announcer moved the sprinters for the first one-man heat up to the starting line.

From his canoe, Collin watched as the gun sounded and the lake boiled with the fervor of the paddlers straining to bring their canoes up to speed from a standing start. The combatants streaked down the one thousand meter course to the finish in mere minutes. To the delight of the crowd, the Torontonians won the first heat.

Collin was in the third heat. As he paddled to the starting line, he glanced toward the beach hoping for a glimpse of Sam. Instead, his gaze fell on Kathleen O'Sullivan, who was sitting cross-legged on a striped blanket with Liz.

When Collin's gaze locked on her, Kathy's breath caught in her throat. She'd seen Collin a few times since the dress-fitting encounter. Over those weeks, his developing tanned physique had not escaped her notice. On one occasion, when she'd been with her teaching friend Henry, she thought she detected anxiety in Collin's face when he saw them laughing together. Was there some interest in her buried beneath that hard outer skin? Kathy could see Sam also watching his protégé from up on the verandah. She gave Collin a smile and a wave.

On the line, Collin wondered what that meant. He was used to blokes giving him the finger. His heart was in his throat. He wasn't used to being accountable to a whole team for his actions. Not to mention all the people on the beach, especially Kathleen. He looked down and concentrated on counting the number of ribs inside his cedar strip canoe. Twenty, twenty one . . .

The gun sounded and Collin was momentarily startled. His heart fell when he saw the other three canoes jump out ahead of him. All the hoopla evaporated as he stood on his paddle and concentrated on the lane ahead of his canoe, picking up the stroke count. At the three-quarter pole he caught up with the leaders and began pulling ahead.

On his right a crimson canoe inched up until it was neck and neck. *Those Voyageurs sure know how to paddle.* Sweat poured down his back as he shoveled his paddle deeper into the water. Upping the stroke rate, he surged across the finish line half a boat ahead of the Montrealer.

Collin's biceps burned and twitched. His heart pulsed in his temples. Bushed, yet exhilarated, he lay across the gunnels. The crowd on the beach cheered. He looked up and saw Kathy, her hair blowing at her waist, waving and laughing and looking right at him.

Had he done this for her, for all of them, for his teammates, for Sam or for himself? He had no idea. All he knew was that it felt good. He had a sudden and unexpected desire to go to Kathy then, to share the victory only with her, but he was swept off by his teammates as they celebrated the win.

The competition progressed throughout the day. By early afternoon, the preliminary heats were completed and the score was very close. Toronto was in the lead with New York a close second. Montreal had fallen back and the Bruins were licking their wounds.

Down in the Bay Four boathouse under the Clubhouse the New York finalist, Will Owens, had been summoned with his canoe for last minute instructions by the team coach.

Walking up the concrete ramp into the now deserted bay with its empty storage racks, Will shouted out "Where are you, Hans? C'mon. I'll be late for the finals."

A hulking man with shocking orange-red hair stepped out from behind the paddle wall and slammed the boathouse door closed.

"Who the hell?"

"Relax, son." The stranger stepped forward.

"What d'ya want with me?"

"I need to borrow your boat, and your jersey and cap."

"Hell no, you won't."

"You can make this hard or even harder, son. Your choice."

Will was a big strong fellow, but the stranger, about the same size, was more than his match. After a brief scuffle Will was pinned against the boat rack framing, his jersey being pulled over his head.

"Get off me, you weasel."

"Shut up, or you'll never speak again."

"Why are you doing this?"

"I've got to whack a guy, and you're goin' to help me do it."

"No."

"Oh yes, son. They're goin' to think you whacked the guy, at least until I get away.

"You got a lotta shit which'oo."

"You'd better believe it." With that, the stranger backhanded Will in the face, knocking him out. He hesitated a minute. *It would be so easy to finish him here and now.* Then he paused. *No witnesses. Nah. Not worth it.*

Ginger-top dragged the inert canoeist into the basement one-hole bathroom and gagged him with a rag he found under the sink. Then, after tying him up with a cord from his pocket, the imposter withdrew the interior key from the bathroom lock and left the bathroom, locking the door from the outside.

As he calmly walked out of the boathouse to his beached canoe, the redhead covered his distinctive topknot with the New Yorker cap, then casually tossed the key into the lake. "That ought to hold him until I get the kid," he muttered.

The beach was packed with onlookers now, as word had gotten around that the locals were ahead. The spectators lined up to favor their teams. It seemed an extension of the National election fervor. Waiting expectantly out in the warm-up area, Collin could hear the strains of "O Canada" from the zealous crowd. Since he'd won his preliminary heats, Collin was entered in the one man finals.

When the gun sounded, he got a lightning start, bursting into the lead. Oblivious to everything except chewing through the lane ahead, he paddled faster than he ever had. He was closing on the finish line, his biceps killing him.

Suddenly, on his left off-shore side, a black canoe came charging forward. The paddler, still a blur, looked older than the other competitors and didn't seem to fit in. His canoe surged into the waves and pulled alongside, challenging Collin. *Could he hold out? Only about twenty boat lengths to go.*

The New Yorker manning the canoe was almost broadside now, a mere three feet away with Collin's canoe masking him from the shore onlookers. Looking right, Collin noticed a third canoe, closer to shore, moving up and threatening. Voyageur.

What happened next took Collin completely by surprise. The New Yorker struck Collin's canoe with his paddle to slow him down. Had the judges seen the incident, the Yank would have been disqualified.

When Collin swung to retaliate, his canoe rolled dangerously left, water sloshing in over the gunnels, threatening to swamp him.

"I'm coming for you, Mick!" the man snarled.

Shifting his weight to the right and digging his paddle deep on that side to avoid capsizing, Collin fought to regain control. *Who the hell? Shite. Focus,* he commanded himself. He looked left briefly. The sweat-slick hair on the back of his neck rose when he saw the man's red hair and American flag tattoo on his burly right forearm. The sight triggered a memory. His mother's last words rushed in—"Ginger . . . Betsy . . ."— and clicked into place.

"You killed my Ma. so I'm gonna kill you." He longed to do it now. But his team . . . He focused on the race and four strokes later he was back on course.

"It's you who's gonna die," The New Yorker momentarily continued to paddle with his left arm, but with his right he grabbed the handle of a sheathed knife and in one lightning motion hurled it at Collin's torso.

At that moment the butt of Collin's paddle in his left hand swung up in his stroke. The knife clattered off the paddle, narrowly missing Collin's chest and slicing harmlessly into the lake. That saved his life.

At the wire, the three boats seemed to cross the finish line side-by-side. Collin was livid. *I'll kill the bastard . . .* The paddler turned his face toward Collin who saw the curl of his lip and the three jagged scars on his cheek.

"You're a dead man, Mick," he hissed loud enough for only Collin to hear. Then he pivoted his canoe and sped away, blending into the throng of boats bobbing on the waves near the shore.

Collin lifted his paddle, thinking he might throw it at the man. But he stopped short, realizing the futility of that act as the paddler was yards away already, moving at quite a clip.

The crowd was going wild, the announcer calling it a first place tie between Canada and New York. Collin was in a state of shock. *It's him! Ma's killer!* But the blaggard was nowhere to be seen. Collin craned his neck, searching for him. *Bloody buggering bollocks. You've got to find him, you eejit!* He was working on pure adrenalin now, though totally spent from the race. His arms pumped the paddle with abandon as he headed into other boats. All the while his eyes were darting left and right. *Where the hell is he?*

The Toronto supporters descended on Collin and his canoe. They hoisted him up and out of the water, carried him to the beach and set him on his feet. He stumbled, off balance. Someone caught his arm. Collin turned and saw Kathy, laughing at him with sparkling eyes.

"Congratulations!" she cried. Then she gave him a big bear hug and an energetic kiss on the cheek.

A jolt of electricity shot through Collin. The scent of her, rose soap, sun and sand, momentarily left him weak, then she was gone, spinning away on her bare toes and disappearing into the crowd.

Chapter Ten
Collin's Revenge

*O*nce his mates let him go, Collin went on the hunt for the burly red-haired oarsman—convinced he was his mother's killer. He scanned the bathers in the water and the crowds on the beach, but the murderer was nowhere to be found.

The rest of the final heats played out, but Collin paid them no mind. When the Regatta ended, Toronto and New York had taken top honors, which would be recognized during the evening reception. Collin turned up the beach toward the Club.

No sign of the ginger-haired killer there, either. It was as if he'd vanished into the ethers. Collin doubled his fists in frustration. *How could he have disappeared? How could he have let him escape?*

The crowd's enthusiasm had reached a fever-pitch after Collin's win. The police kept a watchful eye on the proceedings, assisting some of the more inebriated spectators to the exits. Collin corralled one of the officers. "Have you seen a burly New York boatman with red hair come through this exit in the last half hour? He's got scratch scars on his face and a tattoo of the American flag on his right forearm."

"No sir. No one like that," the sergeant replied. "Why?"

"He's the man who murdered my ma and he tried to kill me during our race this afternoon."

"Was she murdered here today?" the sergeant blurted out.

"No . . . not today. That was, uh, on the waterfront two years ago."

"How is it you are so sure, lad? That he's the one I mean." the policeman asked raising his up-turned hands and shrugging.

Shite, this copper's useless as McGillicutty's jackass.

"My ma described him with her dying breath, that's how come."

"You sure you're not drunk, lad? But wait a minute. You're the fella what won the one-man race, aren't you, boy?"

"And the man who tied me in that race is the murderer, copper."

"Policeman, son. You mean policeman. I'm Sergeant Bentley."

"Right, Sergeant. You need to help me find him."

"I can't leave my post, lad. We've got a lot of folks to tend to. But I can get the word around and we can be on the lookout, you know."

Just like before. These eejits are useless as ditties on a spider.

"Well then, Sergeant. I've been told that there will be trophies given out at the reception later. Can you be present in case the murderer shows to collect his prize?"

"Aye, lad. That I will do."

"Thank you, sir," Collin said as he turned toward the lake, not thinking for a minute that the copper would show up.

"Congratulations on your win, lad," Sam hailed him, when Collin finally came up from the boathouse a second time.

Sam was all smiles, Collin angry and on the point of despair. He was in no mood for attending his friend's wedding. He'd failed again. Yet he couldn't spoil his boss's big day.

Sam's smile dimmed a bit. "What's wrong, Collin?"

"Nothing. Just tired."

"C'mon, then. Let's get me married. That'll perk you up."

It took Sam half an hour to get Collin dressed in the wedding suit he'd bought for him; the lad had no idea what to do with a tie until Sam showed him. Finally they were ready, and went together to the Club to await the bride's procession.

Reverend Dixon was there to officiate. The purple and white orchids were bountiful and beautiful, surrounding the family and friends gathered in the Pagoda for the wedding.

The processional hymn began, and the bridesmaids stepped

slowly down the aisle, each one beautiful in her own way. Amongst them, Collin spotted Kathy in a flowing blue dress that accentuated her lithe figure. Silken auburn hair tumbled past her shoulders to her shapely hips as she came down the aisle. She carried white and purple irises, which seemed to deepen the color of her cobalt blue eyes.

Collin was mesmerized and suddenly felt his cheek tingle where she'd kissed him. Collin couldn't help but watch her gracefully float down the aisle as she became larger in his field of view. Kathy's eyes momentarily met his as she moved past him, a hint of a smile on her lips. This vision of her blocked out all other diversions including the view of the pagoda with all its attendees and the travails of the afternoon.

Liz, resplendent in white from head to foot, was last to arrive on the arm of her father. Sam was dressed in a shiny blue tuxedo, a proud and happy gleam in his eyes as he tucked Liz's hand in the curve of his elbow and turned her to face Reverend Dixon.

The kiss at the end of the ceremony was both prolonged and suggestive. Sam bent his bride backwards almost to the floor. A whooping Irish cheer rose from the Gaelic audience. Arm in arm, Mr. and Mrs. Samuel Stevenson Finlay strolled down the aisle to the strains of "Danny Boy" under a canopy of crossed oars raised by the members of the Club. Then they were out onto the open verandah basking in the gorgeous orange-streaked sunset over Lake Ontario.

Collin paired with Kathy as they left the pagoda, her hand resting on the curve of his elbow raised the hair on his arms. He desperately wanted to tell her that she excited him, but he was afraid he might not measure up, so he remained silent. *Better stay away from those skirts.*

The reception at the Club was splendid, with more than a touch of Irish humor, pageantry. and shenanigans. An Irish melodeon playing wedding tunes in the background during dinner was almost drowned out by the boisterous participants. In deference to the regatta crews, the accordionist finally tried to play the song, "Sit Down, You're Rocking the Boat," made famous by the ever popular Billy Murray, which brought a roar of approval from the guests.

After the meal there were wedding speeches. When it came time for the best man to speak, Sam rose and addressed Collin and the guests.

"Dear friends and regatta contestants. It is with great pleasure that I introduce you to my best man and the boatman of the hour, our winner of the one-man canoe races, Collin O'Donnell."

Collin had no experience with weddings and was completely flustered. Sam had told him that this best man's speech was customary. The lad had been fretting over it throughout the meal. *How can I escape? They're all expecting me to say something, something important. All these people. And especially Sam—and Kathy.*

Collin glanced over at the wedding couple before rising. Sam's face beamed encouragement but Liz looked anxious. *I can't embarrass them. Maybe if I talk only to Sam.*

Rising slowly, Collin cleared his throat of the bite of chicken that threatened to choke him. He took a long swig of his O'Keefe Ale and stared at Sam.

Then in a raspy voice he stated the truth, "This is harder for me than paddling in the final heat this afternoon." That got a chuckle from the guests, which startled him. "I, ah, just have two things to say. First, I think that Sam and Liz are mad in lust for each other and will make a happy family together." This was a term of great affection used by his Irish folks in the Ward, so he thought it would be a clever thing to say. The comment raised an even louder chuckle from the now attentive guests.

"Second, I want you to know, Sam, that you saved me. This man is a saint, so he is."

Collin just stood there, rooted, his mind a blank. Some members of the Toronto regatta crew, picking up where the musician had left off, started to sing as a joke, "Sit down, sit down, sit down you're rocking the boat."

With that, Collin promptly plopped down and took another large gulp of ale, looking glumly at his half-eaten plate of food. *I forgot the toast.*

There was a brief silence until Kathy started clapping. Then Sam, his eyes glistening, clapped and the other guests dutifully followed. Kathy thought Collin was brave to have been so honest. Sam thought he had heard Liam speaking, telling him it was all right. And Liz, observing Collin closely, decided that there was more substance there than she had realized.

It took Sam a minute to gather himself before speaking. When he rose to give his speech, he leaned over and gave Collin a big hug. "Thank you, brother," he murmured for Collin's ears only. Liz overheard and smiled.

Collin had no idea why Sam had said that, but with the encouragement, he rose and said, "And of course, let's raise our glasses to the happy couple, Elizabeth and Samuel Stevenson Finlay."

The crowd drank and appeared satisfied now that the best man had done his duty. For a moment Collin had stepped outside himself and his problems to acknowledge his benefactor in public. It felt good to him for the first time in his life.

Once the wedding speeches were all over, the party began in earnest. As the uilleann piper started to play the first jig for the bride and groom, the crowd gathered around clanking glasses until the newlyweds stopped dancing and kissed passionately. The mood shifted from mischievous to joyous. The mandatory wedding party dance followed the first dance.

"You're going to dance with Kathy, my lad," Sam said, corralling his reclusive protégé. "It's customary."

"The hell I am," Collin declared, searching for the nearest exit.

"Nonsense. You're her escort."

"I don't know how to dance like you do."

"What kind of dancing do you know?"

"The kind that keeps you from getting knocked out in Brooklyn."

"Well, at least you're light on your feet, lad. So here you go." Sam pulled Collin across the floor to the table where Kathy sat talking to Liz. "The best man would like a dance, Kathy."

The scowl on Collin's face could have silenced the room.

He's totally out of his element, Kathy thought. *Why is Sam pushing him to dance with me?*

"Oh, I don't think he does," she objected.

"Nonsense. Of course he does." Sam turned a stern look on Collin. "Don't you, lad?"

If the dance was customary and he refused, Collin would be spoiling Sam's wedding. *I'm boxed in.*

"Sure and I would," he said with a bob of his head. "If you please, miss."

"Well. All right, then," Kathy said and rose to her feet,

"Her hand, lad," Sam muttered under his breath to Collin. "Offer your hand and lead her out onto the floor."

Collin did as Sam instructed. When Kathy's fingers touched his, his heart began to race. *I wonder if she can feel how nervous I am.* He led her out onto the dance floor, but once there, he had no idea what to do and stood awkwardly, helplessly facing Kathy.

Oh dear, he hasn't a clue what to do. Why did Sam put him up to this? "Here," Kathy said gently, lifting his hand. "Put your arm right here at my waist."

Collin did as she said. The feel of the tight curvature in the blue dress was electrifying.

The band was playing a foxtrot. Collin would have no idea where to put his feet, Kathy guessed.

"If I step forward, you step back," she told him. "Otherwise, just follow my lead."

"Aye, miss." Collin nodded. "I'll do m' best."

He did try, but he bobbed out of time with the music and wove to the side when he shouldn't have. He managed to only tread on her toes twice. By the time the song had ended, Collin's face was nearly as red as her auburn hair.

"I'm sorry, miss," he mumbled, head down, "Thank you, miss."

And then he was gone, darting off like the devil himself was behind him. One more check of the boathouse area. Under his sullen exterior, Collin had a sweet side, Kathy realized, which Sam, she feared, had taken advantage of. She felt so badly for Collin tears welled in her eyes. She blinked them away, drew a deep breath and went off in search of the bridegroom. Liz remained where Kathy had left her, at the table where they'd been talking. She'd lifted her white lace skirt a bit under the table and slipped her feet out of her fine silk pumps.

"Where is Sam?" Kathy demanded, still standing and scanning the crowd.

"Gone to fetch us some punch," Liz said. "What's the trouble, dear?"

"Collin can't dance a lick," Kathy snapped angrily. "He was embarrassed within an inch of his life. I'll know why your husband forced him into it."

"Sit down, Kathleen." Liz caught her wrist and tugged Kathy into the chair beside her. "Before you light into Sam, you should know that Collin saved Sam's life." Liz lowered her voice and told Kathy what had transpired during the warehouse fires. "The boy was badly hurt and in hospital for a week. Sam feels he owes Collin. He would never embarrass him."

"Then why did he make Collin dance with me when he can't dance at all?"

"That's the other thing." Liz sighed and leaned closer. "You remember Sam's younger brother, Liam. While Sam was away at art school, Liam fell in with a bad crowd. He was killed in a street brawl. Tragic. His ma Lia died of a broken heart. You and I were already here in Canada at that time. Sam thinks if only he'd been there for Liam he'd still be alive. Collin wasn't keeping the best company when the fires happened. He couldn't save Liam so Sam is determined to save Collin. That's why he's challenging him to be better."

"Oh, I see," Kathy said, nodding. "I think I'd like to help Sam with that."

"I hope you mean help me with this punch," Sam said, grinning as he approached the table with three dripping glass cups balanced in his hands.

"That's exactly what I mean," Kathy said, rising to take one of the cups from him.

"Thank you, Kathleen." Sam gave a cup to Liz with a kiss, then he turned to Kathy. "Remember now, my girl. Collin will be seeing you safe home tonight. I've arranged for transportation for you both at midnight."

"I'll remember, Sam. I just hope we haven't embarrassed him too much," Kathy smiled and gave him a pat on the arm. What a kind man he was, so good to Liz and, she was glad to know now, to Collin as well.

Five minutes later Collin reappeared through the verandah doors. Kathy could see that he was agitated, scanning through the crowd on the dance floor. Finally she saw him fix on Sam with Liz in the middle of *Scully's Reel* with its lively four-four beat. He waited by the door anxiously until the dance was over and then rushed over to his mentor. *Surely he's not that upset about our dance.*

Sam immediately rushed out with Collin onto the verandah, just as the jiggedy "First Night in America" was commencing. Kathy politely declined an invitation to dance from one of the boatmen and rushed to Liz's side on the dance floor. There she stood, rooted.

"What's going on?" Kathy asked gently, leading a bewildered Liz off to her table.

"Collin says he can hear noises behind the bathroom door

down in the boathouse. And the door is locked."

The women watched, and a few minutes later, Sam and Collin reappeared with a policeman at their side. He and Collin were conversing in a corner of the room when Sam rejoined his wife.

"Well?" Liz asked.

"It seems that there was a boatman from New York who was accosted and thrown into the bathroom bound and gagged earlier this afternoon. Collin found him and we had to break down the locked door."

"For Heavens' sake. Who would do such a thing and why?" Liz was clearly agitated.

Kathy could tell that Sam was measuring his words carefully as he spoke.

"Apparently there was an attempt on Collin's life earlier out on the water."

"My God," Kathy interjected. "I thought I saw a bit of a scuffle near the end of the final race, like the canoes bumped together. Couldn't quite make it out from that distance. The poor lad."

"Collin's pretty upset. He's talking to the policeman right now," Sam offered. "The attacker is still at large."

"He's probably long gone by now since he was thwarted in his attempt by Collin," Sam added. "Collin doesn't want this to interfere with our festivities."

Kathy knew that her face must be mirroring the same shock that she could see on Liz's brow.

"How can it not, Samuel?"

Sam moved to Liz's back and started to give her shoulders a gentle massage. "There, there, *astore*. The police will take care of this. Let's finish what we started."

"Yes, yes. You're right, my love," Liz replied turning her head back and placing her right hand on her husband's waist.

Kathy excused herself and crossed the room, looking for Collin. He was gone again. *My God. No wonder he was so nervous when we were dancing. I've got to find him.*

Shortly thereafter, Sam and Liz cut the traditional Irish wedding fruitcake, which was suitably doused in Jameson. As if the guests needed any more booze. Sam lecherously slid the garter down from Liz's thigh and tossed it high into the crowd of eager boatmen. Collin had reappeared at the doorway alone but stayed well away from that fracas. Before Kathy could go to him, Liz got up to throw her bouquet. Kathy made sure that she was front and center among the ladies and she snatched it, or maybe Liz threw it directly to her with one graceful backward toss.

After the wedding formalities were happily concluded, the Commodore of the Club got up and thanked everyone for coming. He then lauded the sportsmanship and prowess of the Regatta teams and handed out the trophies to the winners. When it came to the one-man canoe awards, only Collin came forward to claim his trophy. He had hoped that the American would have had the guts to show.

Kathy met him as he came down from receiving his trophy.

"Congratulations, Collin. You were wonderful out there today."

"Thank ye, miss. It wasn't easy . . ."

"I heard about what happened. That's terrible."

"I'll be fine, miss. The police say that the man is likely long gone by now. No need to worry."

"That's what Sam said. But do you believe him?"

"We looked everywhere just now. I suppose so. Just the same I want to get you home at midnight as Sam asked me to do."

"Yes. That will be nice. I would feel safer . . ."

"Yes, miss."

When Sam and Liz took their leave, Kathy and Collin cheered and applauded them with the rest of the guests. The band began packing up their instruments, signaling that the evening was at an end. The members of the Canoe Club, including Collin, had volunteered to clean up the dining room. Kathy saw him coming out of the kitchen with a stack of trays. She signaled to him and saw a blush climb up his throat as she approached.

"I'm glad to help you and your teammates clear the tables," she offered.

"Oh no, miss, we can handle it," Collin said, ducking his head to avoid her eyes. "I'll be just a bit and then I'll take you home."

"All right, then." Kathy gestured toward the open French doors. "I'll wait outside on the verandah where it's cooler."

Collin nodded and set to work clearing the tables. He was so nervous at the thought of being alone with Kathy that he kept rattling plates and dropping silverware. She was a schoolteacher; he was an apprentice. What did he have to talk about with such a fine lady?

With the whole team working, the dining room was set to rights in no time. Collin was the last to leave at about eleven-thirty. He wiped his hands on a kitchen towel, hung it up and went to collect Kathy. He'd just stepped through the French doors onto the verandah, dimly lit by the railing lamps when he heard a panicked cry that stopped him in his tracks. It sounded just like his ma's scream, and it was coming from the direction of the Pagoda.

Collin spun toward the sound. In the flicker of a single lamp still lit beneath the vaulted wooden roof, he could make out two figures struggling, one much larger than the other. On the second scream, he recognized Kathy's voice and leaped into a run.

As Collin drew closer, Kathy stumbled more fully into the light, her face tear-streaked, with her hands clawing at the huge man grasping her shoulders. The brute growled like an animal and pawed the bodice of her dress. The fabric tore, exposing Kathy's chemise and the tops of her heaving breasts. Then the lamp swung, the man lunged and Collin saw his hair—ginger red.

Collin screamed in fury and jumped on the man he was certain was the one who had killed his ma and was now trying to rape Kathy. He landed on the man's back and Collin clamped his hands around his bull neck, intending to choke the life out of him. The rapist rose up and flung Collin off of him like he was no more than a bug. Collin fell, the back of his head colliding with and cracking the front railing of the verandah. He slumped to the decking, dazed and out of breath. The killer loomed over him, a grin of pure evil on his face.

"Wait your turn, Mick," he snarled. "I knew this would bring you out here. I'll finish you, all right, like I should'a the night I killed the whore that whelped you. But first I'll have my sport."

He turned away. Collin shoved groggily up on one elbow. He saw Kathy duck behind the altar and pull her dress up to cover her breasts. The killer grasped the cloth-covered table in both hands, lifted it and flung it away. Kathy scrambled to her feet.

"Help!" she screamed, her voice ringing across the verandah. "Someone *help!*"

No one heard; no one came. *Just like the night Ma died.* Collin had failed then. He couldn't, and he wouldn't, fail again. He pushed wearily to his feet, fists doubled. He was no physical match for the burly longshoreman, but he knew how to fight.

"You'll not touch her, so long as I live!" he shouted, hoping someone was close enough to hear.

The brute wheeled on him, still grinning. "All right, you're on, little pipsqueak."

The man charged, grasping Collin and pinning his arms to his sides in a vice grip. Collin feigned falling forward, away from the rail. The Yank tightened his grip, and Collin kicked upwards with his right knee, scoring a bull's-eye to the rapist's groin. The villain collapsed, freeing Collin, and he curled into a fetal position bellowing like a gored bull.

Furious, Collin approached the groaning man, readying for the finish, but first he had to know. "Why did you kill my Ma? Why did you come back to kill me?"

" 'Cause I was ordered to. And now I'm going to finish it." The killer snarled and leapt up, grasping for Collin's throat.

Collin bent forward, hands on his knees, forcing the rapist to catapult over him. The attacker spun around off balance and crashed into the front railing. The cracked timbers rent with a splintering sound, and then gave way. The Yank lost his footing and tottered on the brink, nearly falling.

Too late, Collin reached out to grab him. The man's weight carried him through the railing and over the edge. A second later Collin heard a sickening smack. He stepped to the edge and looked over, saw the killer crumpled on the cement boat ramp, blood emanating in a pool from of his skull.

"Oh, Collin!" Kathy sobbed.

He turned and caught her as she flung herself into his arms and clung to him. She was crying and shaking. Collin was shaking, too. *I did it. I saved her. Oh, Ma.* A sob rose in his throat. He put his arms around Kathy to comfort her, and, in his memory, his Ma. It felt so good.

When Kathy lifted her head, Collin drew her back, away from the railing. He sat her down gently onto a padded settee and rested beside her. Sniffling, Kathy tucked the torn corner of her gown in her chemise and looked at Collin. Her beautiful eyes were red-rimmed, her hair a snarled tangle around her shoulders, but she was alive. And he, at last, was free.

"You're hurt." Kathy lifted her hand to the cheek she'd kissed earlier.

Collin winced, feeling the sting of a scrape beneath her fingertips. "It's nothing. Are you all right?"

Kathy nodded and bowed her head, her mouth quavering. Then she closed Collin's hands tightly in hers and looked up at his face. Her fingers were cold and trembling.

"Thank God for you, Collin. You saved my life."

"And I avenged my Ma," he said, his voice thick with tears.

"I heard him say he killed her. Oh, Collin." Kathy touched his cheek again, fresh tears welling in her eyes. "How did it happen?"

Drawing a deep breath, Collin told her. He left out the gory details of his Ma's death, and the sordid life she'd been forced to live in Brooklyn. He expected Kathy to turn away, revolted by his shame and cowardice, but she held his gaze, her eyes soft with sympathy.

"He said he was ordered to kill your Ma and to kill you," Kathy said when he finished. "What kind of monster would order such a thing?"

"I meant to get it out of him." Collin ducked his head, unable to bear her compassion. "But he fell to his death, and now I'll never know. Killing him was so satisfying, I wonder at the monster I've become."

"You tried to save him." Kathy grasped his chin and raised his head. Her gaze was fierce. "You aren't a bit like him. Don't even think it. You're a hero."

"Except . . ."

"Except what?"

"Uh . . . nothing." Kathy could see that there still was turmoil behind those haunted hazel eyes.

"What. There's something more. Tell me."

"Are you hurt, Kathy?"

She realized that he wasn't going to divulge whatever it was that was still bothering him. So Kathy took the positive, glass-half-full approach. You saved me, and you avenged your Ma. Two women saved. Not bad at settling the score, I'd say."

Collin couldn't speak. He could only gaze at Kathy, his eyes filling with tears. His heart swelled at her kindness and her beauty.

" 'Allo! You there, on the verandah! Stay where you are!"

Collin dragged the dirty, torn sleeve of the suit Sam had bought him over his eyes and turned his head. It was Sergeant Bentley with Collin's old friend, Officer Mulrooney in tow. *Just like the night Ma died*, he thought bitterly. *Too late to help.*

"It's you, O'Donnell, isn't it?" Mulrooney exclaimed when he and Bentley arrived at the pagoda. "You have a habit of turning up in the oddest places, don't you, boy?"

"He saved me from being raped," Kathy informed him, wiping away the last of her tears.

"Did he, girl? Is that a fact?"

"I'd be dead now if he hadn't," Kathy retorted, tugging up the torn front of her dress. "Just like Collin's Ma."

"You'll find the villain that attacked Miss O'Sullivan on the boat ramp," Collin said. "He fell through the rail. He's dead."

Sergeant Bentley and Mulrooney looked at each other, their eyes widening.

"We'll have a look," Bentley said gruffly. "You two wait here."

The two officers hurried toward the stairs leading down to the boat ramp. Collin took off his ruined jacket and draped it over Kathy's shoulders. He'd seen Sam do the same thing for Liz one day when they were walking in the park and a cool wind came up. Kathy smiled at him, and gathered the front of his jacket over her bosom to hide her torn dress.

"I spoke to my boss after you spoke to me this afternoon," Sergeant Bentley explained when he and Mulrooney returned from the boat ramp. "He remembered what you had told him about your Ma, son. When the boatman didn't show up for his trophy, Officer Mulrooney decided to come down and talk to you in person before the night was out."

"Right, then." Mulrooney nodded at Collin. "Tell us what happened, beginning with the race this afternoon."

Collin told them. He told them everything, just as he'd done with Kathy. While he talked she sidled closer to him on the settee and slipped her hand into his.

"Well, then." Mulrooney nodded when Collin finished. "This is clearly a case of self-defense." He held his hand out to Collin. "And heroism, O'Donnell."

Collin rose and shook hands with Mulrooney, then Bentley. When he turned back to Kathy, she was smiling, her eyes shining in the pale lamplight.

Two evenings later, Officer Mulrooney called round to the newlyweds' home, Number Ten Balsam.

"'Allo, Finlay. Do you know where I can find young O'Donnell?" he asked as Sam ushered him into the parlor. "Eve'nin', ma'am. I have some important news from our investigation."

"Do you now, Officer?" Liz replied. "Well, you've come to the right place. Collin is staying here with us for the time being until he can get his own digs, but unfortunately he is off visiting with Miss O'Sullivan at present."

"Can *I* help you?" Sam asked.

"Well, I guess you could pass this information on to him if you would, sir," Mulrooney commented. "That ugly American named George Weston was a longshoreman just as O'Donnell said. He had been convicted of rape in New York on two previous occasions, but in both circumstances he bullied his way out of the predicament. He finally paid the price for his terrible misdeeds, and we consider this case closed."

"A sordid business, to be sure," Sam exclaimed, wrapping his arm around his bride to comfort her. "We will pass this news on to Collin."

"You do that, sir," Mulrooney stated. "We have one further question for the lad, though. Does he know who might have sent Weston to kill him and his mother?"

"He and I discussed that, officer," Sam replied. "He has no idea. You can ask him if you wish. We should be at the *Toronto Evening Telegram* after eight tomorrow morning."

"That won't be necessary, sir. I'll take your word on it,"

Mulrooney stated, shaking Sam's hand and turning to leave. "You two have a good night," he added, giving them a wink.

"Really, Samuel," Liz exclaimed as the officer disappeared up Balsam Avenue. "The nerve of that man."

"I thought he'd never leave," Sam exclaimed, yanking off Liz's apron and reaching under her tunic.

In bed next to her husband an hour later, Liz confessed, "I'm proud of Collin's courageous charge to save the damsel in distress from the dragon."

"Yes, *astore*. But he's his own man. He's not Liam."

Sam snuggled up to his lovely new bride and covered her once more with kisses. Then, as they were drifting off to sleep, Sam's last conscious thought was that his crusade had reached a successful plateau. Liam would be pleased, he decided, right pleased.

Chapter Eleven
Course of Action

May 1, 1915
Toronto, Rosedale

"There he comes," Kathy giggled as Collin turned onto Elm Street. He had throttled back his beloved Enfield motorcycle, the one from the Paper that Sam had turned over to him two years ago. He always wanted to avoid attention as he approached Number 223. It had been almost four years since Liz's wedding and Kathy thrilled to think that she and Collin had been in love that whole time. He respected her Victorian insistence on chastity until marriage, although somewhat reluctantly, and that's what puzzled her. That's the one thing that her Puritanical father, Ryan, had drilled into her that she agreed with, except she wondered how long she would have to wait. Collin hadn't proposed yet and her impatience was growing.

Maybe today's the day. It will be if I have any say in the matter. Collin loves Liz's children almost as much as I do. I thought he was in agreement. Family is so important and we're not getting any younger. Is money his only problem? Why won't he talk about it?

As she was pondering her future, Collin stopped two doors short under a spreading oak tree. From her window, Kathy caught his attention. Blowing him a kiss, she motioned that she would be right down.

"I saw him out there on that contraption of his," Kathy's father barked, blocking her way as she swept down the circular staircase. "I forbid you to associate with him anymore, daughter. I know what he's after. I see his kind at the college every day."

"Nonsense, father. You're wrong about him. He loves me and I love him, and that's settled."

"Stop, Ryan, she's a grown woman now, twenty-four," Kathy's mother Fiona pleaded in the background.

"Hush, woman. You stay out of this."

"I'm going with him, father," Kathy announced. "And you can't stop me. It's a simple date, out to the amusement park, that's all."

"I should have put a stop to this sooner," her father growled.

"Collin's a good man," she added trying to push past her father, but he gripped her arm tighter. "Ouch. You're hurting me," Kathy cried as his strong hand dug into her arm.

"You listen to me, girl. If you leave here, then you're no daughter of mine. You understand me?"

"Perfectly. Now let go of my arm."

Fiona put her hand on Ryan's shoulder. "Let her be, husband."

Ryan relinquished his grip long enough to knock his wife's arm away. Kathy pushed past him and opened the front door to leave.

"Oh no, you don't," Ryan said, following her out onto the front porch gripping her wrist. "I've tolerated this illicit relationship too long and won't stand for it anymore." He tightened on her. "No decent young woman would carry on this long."

Collin came on the run. "Take your hands off her, sir."

"You mind your own business," Ryan shouted. "Come back in the house, daughter."

"I will not."

"You're coming back where you belong—with your own family."

"I believe that Kathy said 'No', sir," Collin said. "She has her own mind."

"I'm her father. I'll make that decision," Ryan shouted. He was getting red in the face now.

Kathy turned, attempting to pull her arm out of her father's grip. He tightened his grip and put his weight against it. She tried to shake him away, but cried out.

Collin stepped between them. "She doesn't deserve your ire,"

Collin stated as he quickly blocked Kathy's father from his loved one.

"Get out of my way," Ryan bellowed.

"You're wrong about this, sir. This is no way to treat someone you love," Collin warned."

Ryan stood his ground.

Collin stepped closer, raising his arm to initiate what he knew would be a blow that would set the older man off with no telling how it would end for him.

Ryan backed away, letting go of Kathy who stood by the interloper as if they were a team. He was no match for the young Irishman and he knew it.

"Let's go," Collin urged. "It will be all right, darlin'," he soothed, wrapping his arm around her shoulder.

"You'll not be welcome back," Ryan yelled as they headed down the walk. "And send someone to pick up your things tomorrow—they'll be in the street."

"You don't mean that," Fiona pleaded from the doorway.

"Get back inside, you—," he said, pushing his wife through the entrance and slamming the door, shutting her in.

Kathy mounted the motorcycle behind Collin, wrapping her arms around his waist. "Oh, God help me."

"I know he's your Da for all that. But he's a monster. I'm proud of you for standing up to him. And it's past time for doin' it."

"I know, but he means well by me, even though he's been hateful."

"He's a selfish pig." And with that Collin gunned the engine and started out, winding around the circular drive and out onto the street.

"Thank you for coming to my rescue once again, my love." Kathy pressed against Collin's back and felt the comforting vibration from the motorcycle beneath her.

"It will be all right," Collin offered, half turning and patting her hands at his waist. "But you should move out, right enough."

"What about my poor mother—?"

"You can't help her by staying there. But with you gone, they may be able to fix things between them." Collin could feel Kathy's arms tighten around him.

"But he treats her the same as me."

"Like a possession, not a person, you mean?"

"Exactly."

"You can't change that."

"You're right. But I still care about her."

"Come on, Kathy darlin'. It's half-nine already. Let's think about us, now. We had planned a day just for us, love, an' we're goin' to have it, father or no father. We're late for the park," Collin urged, pivoting on his steed and changing the subject. "It's a beautiful spring morning."

"Yes, let's just go," Kathy agreed.

As they sped down Mount Pleasant, Kathy could feel her transformation. And Collin, his black curls blowing in the wind—he had changed since Liz's wedding. She wrapped her arms more tightly about his waist as he wove in and out of traffic, deftly wheeling around a wagon pulled by a team of Clydesdales.

Leaving the bike at Collin's apartment near the edge of Kew Gardens, they strolled east on the boardwalk the four blocks to Scarboro Beach Boulevard and its amusement park. Flowers were blooming, the trees were resplendent in new apple-green foliage and the aromas of early spring filled their nostrils.

The Scarboro Beach Amusement Park was a large scale entertainment center, with carnival rides, a quarter-mile-long roller coaster, merry-go-round carousel, midway with games of chance, and much more.

Sam and Liz were waiting for them near the park entrance gate. A wicker double pram cradled their two young daughters. Kathy loved each of the little girls for their emerging qualities. The eldest, almost three-year-old Norah, with her straight black hair and staring silent eyes, was darker and more serious than her younger sister and had a mind of her own. Quietly, as if that would avoid attention, she was repeatedly trying to climb out. The other one, Dorothy, with a glowing cherub face framed in swirling chestnut locks, would soon be a year old. She was already babbling, although no one could quite translate the unique language she had chosen to speak. Kathy thought about the children she and Collin would have some day, and she smiled, daydreaming about her own future.

"Hello, you two lovebirds," Liz called out as they walked towards them.

Kathy blushed and gave Collin a squeeze.

"What's the story, Samuel?" Collin greeted his boss and friend with a newspaper salutation.

"Beautiful day for daydreaming and painting, lad."

"'Deed it is, boss. 'Deed it is."

"Get back down in the pram, Norah," Liz admonished, but Norah kept climbing until Kathy picked her up.

"Good day to you too, young Dot," answered Collin, the child's godparent, greeting the little tyke with a tweak of her nose.

"Now me," cried Norah. "Swing us round." The children giggled.

"I want to go on the Shoot the Chutes flume ride and the roller coaster," Collin said. "Come on, darlin', let's ride the wild ones."

"Right, but only if you promise to take me through the Tunnel of Love later," she said.

"We brought a lunch for us all," Liz offered. They agreed to meet in the picnic area at three p.m. "We're looking forward to the evening performance by Mattie Barr and D'Urbano's band in the bandshell after dark," she exclaimed. "Aren't you?"

"Mmm," Kathy answered.

Knowing that Liz would stay with the kids, Collin asked her to take good care of the locket he always wore. "I'm concerned it might fly off during the rides," he said.

"My pleasure, as always," Liz said as they turned and walked off toward the rides.

Hours later, after four rides on the Chutes, a similar number of punishing Bump-the-Bump adventures, and three times round on the dizzying Dips Roller Coaster, Kathy had had enough.

"Whoa there, lover. That's enough dipping and bumping for me. Let's go through the Tunnel of Love now, yes?"

Collin pulled out his silver watch on a chain, the only family heirloom he owned from his grandfather. "It's almost three," he stalled. "We'd better go find the Finlays. Aren't you starving?"

"Yes, but . . . you promised the tunnel."

"We'll go later. We will."

"Why not now? You said you had something important to tell me, remember?"

"Yes. About the Paper."

"The Paper. The Paper. It's always about the Paper. I thought it was going to be about us. Our future together. Marriage."

"It wouldn't be proper, yet. I'm needin' more time, not ready for gettin' with you permanent until I finish what I started."

"I don't understand," Kathy pouted. "You talked as if we—"

"All right. If you must know. I have to get something settled with someone first." Collin's eyes dropped. "I've sort of been meaning to talk to you about it for a long time now. Since the night you were attacked. Remember? She needs me," he whispered.

Kathy's lip started to tremble. "She?" Her heart felt raw, her cheeks hot, muscles in her face working.

"It's not what you think." Collin tried to hold Kathy, comfort her, but she would have none of it, pulling away from him.

Kathy's shock was turning into more than a desire to know. *What did he mean by telling her about another woman? Who was she? Was she making a big mistake? Was her father right about Collin?*

"Well?"

"It's hard for me to talk about."

"Fine then." Kathy turned on her heel and strode off in search of Liz and her family. At least there she was safe and loved.

"Wait up, Kathy, You don't understand." Collin followed in her wake. *Shite, I don't even understand.*

They found the Finlays in the lush, orchard-like picnic area. Sunlight filtered down through the new tree growth, heating the earth and nurturing the sprouting shoots of grass blades beneath their feet. The crocuses were up and the daffodils broke through their beds. It would have been a tranquil scene had it not been for the other twenty or so families attacking their hampers nearby. This happy clamor was punctuated by the periodic screams of Shoot the Chutes patrons in the distance.

Closing her eyes, Kathy could feel the warmth of the day and of the people around her. But it wasn't for her. The whole day had led up to this revelation by Collin and she never felt so alone. There was the tantalizing smell of fried chicken somewhere. People were having picnics, enjoying their children and loved ones. And she? Waiting for the darkness of the Tunnel of Love, derailed.

With her usual organized efficiency, Liz had found them a table and already had the picnic lunch set out on it. "Come and get it," she called.

Sam was just finishing a sketch he had made of the carousel. He had taken the artistic liberty of inserting two young girls onto the horses' backs, and he had named the piece "The Finlay Girls' First Ride."

As they sat down to eat their sandwiches of ham and tomato with Liz's homemade brown bread, they couldn't help but overhear the conversation at the next picnic table. Two women, both with infants, were agonizing over the fact that they hadn't heard anything from their men at the Front in the Great War for over three weeks.

"Max always writes me every Friday," one said grabbing her little girl and pulling her to her bosom.

"You know what they say, Madge. No news is good news."

"Yeah. I guess so, but Cynthia . . ."

"I know. Her Harold. Terrible. Flame throwers, they said. Try not to think about it."

"I heard that the Germans used a new weapon—poison gas—on our troops at Ypres last month," Sam said quietly.

"That's awful," Liz replied. "I'm glad that you two have not been sent overseas."

"We've applied for service, you know," Sam offered, looking furtively at Collin.

"Yes, we've been over it many times. You both want to go, but they won't have you; in your case, Sam, because of your heart," Liz pointed out, picking up a carrot and waving it in Sam's direction. "Don't you give it another thought, Samuel Stevenson. You're needed here at home, isn't that right, girls?" Worry wrinkles furrowed her brow.

Norah stood up in the pram and stretched her arms out to her daddy.

"They won't let Collin in because of his poor hearing," Kathy commented, trying to keep things lively, not letting on about how she felt.

"I don't understand that *shite*," Collin stated. "I can hear fine on my right side."

Liz covered up the little girls' ears and Collin blushed. "Sorry," he mumbled.

"Sam, did you see that brazen notice in our paper from the Germans yesterday?" Collin asked, changing the subject.

"What notice?" Sam replied.

"The one where the Bosch warned the passengers on ocean liners that they will attack them with submarines if they carry war supplies or military personnel from America to Europe."

"They wouldn't dare, would they?" Liz cringed.

"It was targeted for the *RMS Lusitania* that sailed today from New York," Collin answered. "There is some talk at work that it was outfitted to carry munitions."

"I did read where there are some famous people on board. For example the wealthy Mr. Vanderbilt," Kathy said.

"Really dear? I didn't think that the whereabouts of the silver spoons interested you," Liz commented, chomping down on her carrot.

They all looked sideways at Kathy for a response. She stopped cutting, her knife poised in mid-air above the banana she was slicing.

"I like to read about such things," Kathy explained and resumed her task. "Why would he be going to Europe in the middle of the World War, I wonder? Especially since the outcome is so uncertain. So risky."

"You're right. These are troubled times to be sure, dear."

"Well, I don't think that the Germans would risk sinking the *Lusitania*. It would get the United States all worked up. They might even join the war," Sam said.

"It would be a terrible loss of innocent lives," Liz lamented. "Let's hope not, for Heaven's sake."

"I have some brighter news." Sam offered, buttering another slice of bread. "I have been offered a teaching position in the Art Department of Riverdale Technical School. Liz and I have discussed it and I am going to take it starting this fall."

"Terrific," Kathy and Collin exclaimed in unison from across the picnic table.

"What goes up the chimney?" Collin said, linking little fingers with his soul mate in a feeble attempt at reconciliation.

"Smoke," she replied, thinking it was such a silly Irish custom. The touch of his fingers on hers sent a jolt through her, despite her feelings.

"It gets better," Sam continued. "I've talked to the Managing Editor at the paper, and I recommended you to take over my job as official Visual Recorder. They've agreed, particularly with your evolving skill in photography. Sketching at news events is passé now as you predicted. It's being replaced, and you are a vanguard of this change. Congratulations, lad. You've earned the promotion."

"That's wonderful!" Kathy said, glancing at Collin under her lashes.

Collin got up and clapped his friend on the back.

"Well, that's just *cla*, boss. But your decision to move to Riverdale. It's off the beaten path there isn't it, almost as far as Rosedale?"

"It is," he said.

"Are you sure that this is in your best interest? So far away?"

"Absolutely, lad, and in yours as well."

Kathy murmured under her breath, "Good. That takes care of the money, but that's not it, is it." This was going to be the day of her dreams before she heard about some mysterious woman. Now, she was pretty sure it was her worst nightmare. But she wasn't going to give up on him so soon.

"So, Collin. Now it's my turn at a little fun," Kathy said after lunch was finished. "Didn't you make me a little promise?"

"So I did. The Tunnel of Love it is, then," Collin conceded, flinging his camera over his shoulder and around his neck, the strap firmly secured.

"That is, if you are still interested." She looked away.

As they started into the long chute of the Tunnel that wound around under the base of the roller coaster, Kathy picked her words carefully. Each two-person boat in this dark waterway was isolated from the others. Privacy was a godsend, now. She wanted to bring up the subject of marriage again for the seemingly hundredth time. She wasn't getting any younger, and she wanted children early before her body gave out. But then, there was the other woman.

"This is cozy, love," she murmured.

He pulled away from her, something else pressing on his mind. "I wonder what spooky things they have in this tunnel," Collin wondered, fiddling with his camera trying to get a shot before the darkness descended upon them.

Kathy said, "Forget the photography now for a moment, love. I wanted you to share that important thing you mentioned. You know what it is." She beamed at him, put up her lips for a kiss, as they entered the darkness.

Turning in to her, he gave her cheek a peck. Then Collin picked his words carefully, " Darlin', you know the answer to the question you're after asking me again, don't you."

"But Sam just said that you are to be made head of Visual Recording. Surely now, adding in my teacher salary, we will be well off enough to . . ." she dropped off.

"Get married?" he finished her sentence, putting the camera back in its case. "Wasn't that *your* plan?" His voice took on an edge. He backed off. "That's right, our plan."

"We've been together this long . . . and I naturally thought . . . well, it's what couples are supposed to do at this point." She noticed they were nearing an opening to another tunnel and she felt a blast of cold.

"Yes, darlin'. That's true. And I love you. You know I do. It is mainly because of you that I have come as far as I have. But as I told you, *it's still no damn good.*"

"You mean *you're* still no damn good." Kathy steamed, gripping the seat harder as the boat careened around a corner.

Just then, a mechanical horse came darting out of the darkness and kicked its back legs at them. A bell rang in the distance and made Kathy jump.

"That's what I meant, I guess." Collin shifted toward the other side of the boat, rocking it a little. "I can't go through with a commitment yet until this woman . . ."

Kathy went on, "So who is this other woman who's standing between us? I have a right to know."

Collin coughed. "It's not one woman, but two." He looked at the water propelling them forward, a stream of flowing darkness. It seemed the ride was interminably long.

Kathy nearly choked. But she began to understand. The boat came to the crossroads, two tunnels, both dark.

"I want to tell you but I can't. It's too painful." The boat careened toward the wall and jolted both of them.

"All of our plans, drowned," she started, dotting her eyes with a muslin sleeve.

"I can find you somewhere near me to live, drive you to work," he added weakly. "Until we plan things out, anyway." The ride picked up speed. "I think you're still upset about your father."

"It's not because of my father, you dimwit," she sobbed.

Ahead a curtain parted and a red devil jumped out, almost into the boat, startling them both in the dark. Then, all at once, they emerged into the light and the ride was over. Blinking, Kathy sat there not moving. Collin jumped out of the boat and onto the ramp. He reached down to help Kathy up out of the boat.

She sat there, twirling her a lock of her hair with her fingers as if weaving a tapestry. The boat was moving forward again and would soon be beyond the barrier and out of the drop-off area.

"C'mon, darlin'. Take my hand before it's too late," Collin urged.

"It's already too late. I want to know where we stand, first."

"I'll think about it, dear," he offered. But she knew he wouldn't really. And he knew that she knew that.

Just before the boat passed by the entrance screen, Kathy hopped up and out onto the wooden ramp, ignoring his outstretched arm. She started to turn away.

"Let's go to the Midway. I'll win you a Kewpie doll with my wicked rifle shooting," Collin suggested, flashing her a disarming lopsided grin.

"You go if you want to," Kathy muttered, pinching her cheeks under moistening eyes. "I'm going to spend some time with Liz."

"Kathy. Let's not spoil the short time we have together. Can I take a photo of you, just like this in the light? Smile for me."

"Photographs are never as good as the real thing," she said. "Besides," she looked at him directly, "they lie."

"Maybe I won't wait for you," she said and strode off to find the Finlays, leaving Collin standing there stewing.

What the hell does that mean? So much for the Tunnel of Love. He headed off in the opposite direction to visit the building with the Disaster Exhibits. It fit his mood.

Liz saw Kathy coming back to the picnic area alone, crying. She ran out the last few feet to meet her maid of honor, and Kathy collapsed in her arms, sobbing.

"Oh dear," Liz said. "What happened?"

Kathy couldn't stop crying, her head buried in Liz's shoulder.

"What is it? I'm your best friend. You can tell me," Liz soothed.

When Kathy couldn't respond through her tears, Liz just let her cry it out on her shoulder, patting her back gingerly. "There, there, dear. It'll be all right," was all she could think to say.

Dot started crying. Liz pulled away to tend to her daughter.

Kathy had to get control of her emotions. Heavens, she didn't want to be the cause of distress to her friend and her family. "I don't know what came over me," she said as she flopped down on the blanket near the table.

Before Liz could push further in order find out why Kathy was hurt, Sam strolled up, having finished another sketch. "Where's Collin?" he said, and then caught himself up when he saw the agitated state of the females.

Kathy blurted, "He's never going to agree to marry me." She dried the sticky streaks on her cheek with a lace handkerchief pulled out of her clutch bag.

"It's Claire, isn't it," Sam stated, matter-of-factly.

"Claire? Who was she?" Kathy puzzled. But the light was coming on in the tunnel.

"His missing sister," Sam said. "Didn't he tell you all about her?"

"No, he didn't." Kathy was counting and heard Collin's voice like an echo—two women.

Sam was still talking. "He feels responsible for her disappearance." Sam saw the surprised look on Kathy's face and saw her face break into a radiant smile. He didn't think that was respectful of Collin's situation, but Sam kept that to himself.

"I could tell that avenging his Ma's death only partially cleared his misguided conscience," Sam continued.

"His ma's death?" *Could she be the second woman?*

Sam kept talking but Kathy hardly heard what he was saying, she was so ecstatic.

". . . and that makes him uncertain about taking responsibility as the head of a family. That would be my guess," Sam reasoned.

"That makes no sense to me," Liz said. "What does Claire have to do with preventing his relationship with Kathy?"

"Unfinished business I'm guessing. He needs to find her." Sam went on, "A man has to finish what he started." He frowned. "Or in Collin's case, what others started."

"But maybe my love is not enough to get him through all that." Kathy felt like she was going to cry again, but she was actually radiant inside.

"Nonsense, girl," Liz fired back. "You're the most loving person

I know. He's an idiot if he doesn't see that you are the best thing that ever happened to him. I'll bend his ear when I see him, right enough."

Maybe I can put a word in, too," Sam suggested. "Let me think about this. I'll come up with something."

Liz came up and put her arms around Sam. "You can get Collin to see it in another light, can't you?" She turned to Kathy and smiled. "It'll be all right in the end, so it will. You'll see, dear."

Kathy believed these dear people. Sam had that way about him of making things all right. And Liz was a true friend.

"There's something else wrong about today." Kathy remembered her predicament. "My father was furious with Collin this morning, and with me, and he turned me out."

"Did he now?" Liz said. "Stood up to your father, did you? I think this is cause for celebration, don't you know."

"I can't go back there now."

"You don't have to. Stay with us," Sam offered, putting his arm around his wife's friend. "The girls will love it having an auntie around."

"See, everything will be all right," Liz assured her. "Sam will see that you get to work and back, won't you, dear?" She smiled.

Kathy thought she saw a hesitation in that smile. Too perfect. Could it be that she would see me as competition for Sam's affection. *Nonsense. I'm imagining things.*

Liz was quick to add, "Collin will come around. He's crazy about you. Just has to clear his head and know what's important."

Collin had agreed to meet them all for dinner at the famous Scarboro Inn Restaurant, on the boardwalk down by the beach. It was an elegant venue. White tablecloths and fine china with fresh-cut flowers on every table. And the view of the lakefront was incredible in the gathering purple dusk. The lights on the rides and in the Midway were starting to wink on as day came to a close. Kathy thought that this made the park even more vibrant and exciting. If only Collin wasn't so insecure, ruining everything.

Collin found the Finlays and Kathy having drinks on the long outside verandah. Kathy saw that he appeared relatively normal except that his hair was disheveled—standing on end. And he was carrying a two-foot-high fuzzy pink rabbit. Maybe he had decided that he wasn't going to be the one to spoil the day.

When Collin offered the bunny to Kathy, their hands touched. Like ice cubes, he thought. She took the stuffed animal, reluctantly.

"Hello, you all," he hailed them. "I've just visited the Electroscope Building."

"We can see that from your hairdo," Kathy responded, as she passed off the stuffed animal to Norah. That action did not escape Collin's notice. The young girls, however, were delighted and they said so, each in their own fashion.

"Can a man get a Guinness, please?" Collin called to the shapely waitress weaving among the tables nearby. She smiled and waved back at him. He twirled the end of his moustache and looked sideways at Kathy. Normally, she would have made some sultry remark about that interaction. But right now, she didn't seem to have the heart for it.

They went in for dinner in muted silence. When they were seated and after they had their turtle soup, Sam decided it was time to deal with this situation head-on.

"My dear friends. You were so happy when you arrived this morning and now you are both glum. I'd like to help. Would that be okay?"

Kathy nodded, but Collin said, "I don't know what you mean, boss."

"Collin, I know you like a younger brother. And we," he motioned towards Liz, "know that you love each other very much.

146

But there is clearly a problem, so let's talk about it."

"What do you want to talk about, Sam?"

"I want to talk about Claire."

"What about her? That's ancient history." Collin clenched his fist into the tablecloth, spilling his glass of water.

Kathy hastened to set it upright.

"I don't think it is, my boy. I think that she is in your thoughts all the time."

"It was my fault what happened to her." Collin's face fell and Kathy wanted to go over and hold him, but she kept that in check merely touching his fist.

"Your fault that she was abducted?"

"Forget about it, Sam." Collin dodged. But deep down Collin knew that Sam was trying to get him to realize that it was his agony over what may have happened to Claire that was crippling and obsessing him more and more. He knew this in a deep sense, but talking about it didn't seem to help.

"No we won't forget, Collin. Tell us what happened," Kathy urged.

"Are you all gangin' up on me?"

"We love you two and want to help," Liz added.

"I know you do," Collin said. "But it's too painful to talk about."

"Don't you see that you have to deal with it, or else you will be stuck in life? Look what it's doing to you and Kathy," Sam explained.

Collin looked like he was about to get up and run. But he didn't. Deep down he knew Sam was right.

"So, what do you want to know?" he asked quietly, his head down.

"What happened the day Claire disappeared?" Sam asked for Kathy's benefit, knowing the answer.

Collin struggled to speak.

"Come on, lover," Kathy urged.

Collin looked up and into her anxious eyes. He was trapped. "All right then. Here goes. Ma asked me, as usual, to look after Claire while she went to work. She was worried that they might try and make her own daughter do what she had to do. I was busy gettin' ready for a boxin' match and I told her to stay in the flat in Brooklyn. When I came home, she was gone. We never found her after that. Don't you see? It was all my fault," Collin agonized.

"How old were you and Claire, then?" Sam asked.

"I was fifteen and Claire, thirteen," Collin answered.

"So what makes you think you could have stopped armed thugs, if you had been there?" Sam asked.

"I could have at least tried," Collin's answered. "I was learnin' how to fight."

"And gotten yourself killed in the process?" Sam responded. "So now you are alive and have a choice, Collin. You can let yourself wallow in recrimination, or you can do something about this problem, lad."

"What could I do now about that terrible thing that happened eight years ago, eh?" Collin asked.

"What would stop you from trying to investigate what happened to Claire?" Sam pulled out his pipe and tapped it against his knee out of habit.

"Ma and me tried that already, with no success," Collin stated. "For months we searched. The police were no fekin' help."

"What if you had some help, outside of the police, that is?" Sam's eyebrows arched. He gripped his empty pipe.

Kathy immediately caught on to the direction Sam was taking him.

"If it is that important to you, then I am prepared to go with you to New York during my summer break to try and trace Claire's whereabouts," Kathy offered.

"You would do that for me?" Collin asked her.

"Yes," her eyes glowed. "Don't you know I would do anything to make you happy?"

"Well, I guess we could try that. At least we would be doin' somethin'," Collin reasoned, suddenly seeing a way out. "But I don't hold out much hope after all this time. We tried, Ma and me. God help us, we tried."

"Precisely. You'll be doing something," Sam concluded, focusing on the positive in Collin's last statement. He dug his pipe into his tobacco pouch and filled it to the brim, then tapped it down.

Collin continued, "But how, how would we get there? How could we afford it?"

"All those details can be worked out," offered Liz.

The conversation, though difficult, finally seemed to break the logjam of frustration and stagnation. Sam lit his pipe and pulled on it. Liz tended to the children and Kathy went to her man.

The mood at their dinner table brightened considerably as Collin and Kathy spent a good hour planning out how they could go about it, while Sam listened. Liz watched the proceedings with great admiration for her husband. *Ever the mediator and sage counselor*, she thought. *And Kathy clearly is finally breaking free of her possessive father. Good girl.*

As darkness descended, the lights shone even more brightly throughout the park casting a festive aura over the proceedings and the participants. They all thoroughly enjoyed the music at the bandstand that balmy evening. Kathy was drawn to Sam drumming out the beat of a popular march with the bowl of his stalwart pipe on the edge of the pram while his two young daughters' heads bobbed in time. *Oh, to be as lucky as Liz and Sam with two gorgeous children and a cozy cottage by the beach*, she thought.

Later, overlooking the glittering water, Kathy snuggled next to Collin on a blanket in the grass, her arms entwined around him tightly, not letting go this time. He sat quite still, enjoying the moment, but agonizing silently over what might happen if and when they re-entered the squalor and dangers of that rats nest, Brooklyn.

Liz covered the girls from the light chill of the summer air and then settled next to her husband, drawing up her legs under her skirts to get more comfortable. Sam drew on his pipe while he watched his protégé carefully. Something he still wasn't sharing yet. Unsettling. But now was not the time. The glow from the bowl flamed up when he relit it, aromatic Prince Albert smoke wafting through their little world, joining other sea aromas and blending together.

Chapter Twelve
Needle in a Haystack

May 30, 1915
Ten Balsam Avenue, Beaches, Toronto

*I*t was Sunday. The school year had ended early due to the War, just as the humid heat of late spring set in. Children were released to their families and vacation plans were made for the lucky few. But for the majority of families, the terrible uncertainty of the fate of their fathers, husbands and brothers hung heavy on their hearts. Strapping youngsters were needed to keep the home fires burning. The war in Europe's trenches in was taking its toll.

Collin had established himself in his new role as photographer at the *Telegram*. He was able to hire a recent graduate from Northern Vocational School specializing in the new Kodak processes for photography, allowing Collin to take two weeks off with his Kathy.

"All right, you two. I'm lending you my new Model T on one condition," Sam directed the morning of their departure. "Don't leave it unlocked in New York City, and bring it back, safe and sound. By the way, that goes for you both as well. Avoid taking unnecessary chances. We care about what happens to you. And to the car."

"This car is a modern marvel," Collin said. "It doesn't need a crank, eh?"

"No. This 'Tin Lizzie's' got the new electric start. And it has electric lights that work off the magneto, too. They've done away with the need for acetylene with Prest-O-Lite tanks," Sam explained. "And this is the first year when this new closed sedan design has been offered. You should be able to travel at about forty miles per hour most of the way there. If you can keep to the main roads between here and New York City, you should have little trouble with the tires. But watch out if you get off the beaten path."

"How so?" Collin asked.

"The tires are clincher-type pneumatic. They need to be pressurized to sixty pounds per square inch to keep them properly attached to the rims at high speeds. So watch out for potholes on the roads. Fixing those tires out on the road can be near impossible."

"Got it. Thanks. We'll be careful," Collin agreed. "Are you sure that you don't need the car while we're gone?"

"We'll be fine, won't we, Liz?" Sam said. "Since it's summer, we're going to be staying here near the beach."

"That's cute," Kathy commented.

"What is?" Sam asked.

"That you named your new car after your wife. But she's not tin, you know," Kathy responded.

"No, she's the love of my life," Sam replied, smiling ear to ear.

Collin wondered whether he was referring to Liz or the Lizzie. Was that where the affectionate term for this automobile came from? Either way he knew he had to take the utmost care of the vehicle.

"Here are several lunches that I've packed in ice for you to eat along the way," Liz offered, hugging Kathy tightly and whispering in her ear. "Look after him, my dear. You're the cautious one."

Kathy gave her a big squeeze of acknowledgement.

"Time to go," Collin called out, as he fired up the Tin Lizzie for the five-hundred-mile trip. "It's half-nine and we're already late. We've got spare tires, an extra gas tank and tools, plus more clothes than you can shake a stick at. We're all set for our grand adventure."

"I'm ready if you are," Kathy confirmed. She was wearing jodhpurs and a khaki shirt, and sporting driving goggles, an outfit that her father would never approve of.

"Where's Norah?" Liz exclaimed as they were about to close the car doors.

Looking around, Kathy announced, "Here she is." Norah had climbed up into the back seat and was quietly looking very pleased with herself.

"Goin' somewhere, dear?" Collin asked politely.

"Mmmm, wif you' Unca Collie," she boldly announced.

"Get down out of there this instant," Liz commanded.

Norah reluctantly obeyed, but not without a hug from her Unca.

After they had all said their goodbyes and well wishes, including Dot who from her mother's hip gave the benediction in her native tongue, they were off.

"I pray that Collin can come to some understanding about his life, m' love," Sam remarked as the young couple drove out of sight.

"So do I, dear," Liz agreed, and she gave her man a big hug for his generosity.

After five hours of traveling around the western end of Lake Ontario, the couple reached the border at Niagara Falls.

"I think that this trip is just what we need, even if we don't find out what happened to Claire," Kathy exclaimed, pointing out the side window as they sped by. "Just look at the majesty of Horseshoe Falls. On our way back, let's stop and take the *Maid of the Mist* boat tour right up under the Falls."

Collin had to admit that it was a grand sight. "We'll see, dear," he said. But his mind was elsewhere.

"I mean it, Collin. We're coming back here. It's spectacular."

"If we live so long."

"What do you mean?"

"Nothing, just a figure of speech."

"That sounded more like a prognostication."

"Whatever that means. I am just being cautious, don't ya know."

"As long as you keep us safe, lover."

"I . . . I'll do my best, darlin'."

"That's good enough for me. You've already saved me twice."

"Twice?"

"Your ma's killer and my father."

"Once. You took care of your *eejit* father yourself."

"Only because of you, Collin. Only because of you."

"Don't be rattling on like that again. It's comin' on pitiful."

"Modesty, my dear?"

"No. Just the school of hard knocks. 'Twas all in a day's work."

"Well, let's hope that you don't need your brawn in New York."

"There's no doubt of it," Collin muttered too low for Kathy to hear over Lizzie's engine rumble.

"What was that?"

"I said I'll take good care of you darlin', and there's no doubt of that." Collin gave his girl a love tap to her shoulder.

"Well, I think that we will find Claire and all three of us will see the Falls on the way back. What do you say to that?"

"I guess one of us has to believe in miracles."

"I do, Collin. I found you, didn't I?"

"You're mistaken entirely. I'm just a common brawler put to rights."

"Not in my book." Kathy laid her hand on Collin's thigh and gave a little squeeze.

Collin knew of course that he and Kathy would be taking a big risk when they checked into a hotel in Syracuse. He was thinking fast of how he was going to pull this off; he had no "wedding band" for Kathy to slip onto her ring finger, and he did not know if she, for all her worldly pretentions, understood that they would be breaking the law if they, an unmarried couple, stayed in the same hotel room. And she was a pretty excitable gal; this might make her disastrously nervous. He took his hand from the driver's wheel and grasped her left hand. She turned her head from the landscape and caught his eye with a saucy wink. It was going to be all right, he thought, and brought her fingers to his lips. She was a brave girl, signing on with him for this—what did she call it? Oh, yes, the Great Adventure—when she had no idea what they could be in for. It was his nature to rush headlong into chancy situations, but he had to consider her reputation, and he loved her so. What if he not only failed in his responsibility for Claire, but this dear girl suffered for his impetuosity?

He felt her eyes on him again and, as if she were reading his thoughts, she leaned close to his ear so he could hear her above the whine of the car's engine and said, "Say, this is some trip we're taking, and I know we're going to make a great team, you and me, Collin, so don't worry,'" she pursed up her lips and winked again. "Just because I have an innocent face, doesn't mean I can't be a tough little cookie."

He burst into laughter at her comical expression and ingenuous words and knew he would have no fear with her at his side, and that might be for a lifetime, if only he could find Claire.

They pulled into downtown Syracuse as the sun lowered in the sky, so lights were just winking on in restaurants and hotels along the Market Street. Still buoyed by a confidence in his resourcefulness, Collin spied the elegant eleven-story Onondaga Hotel on Jefferson Street with its spanking new Annex and rooftop restaurant. "Might as well be hanged for a pound as a penny," he said as he brought Lizzie to a stop at its front curb.

Kathy clutched at her handbag, as if trying remember its contents, and commented, "Let's check out the price." She and Collin had both saved for this adventure and made a plan ahead of time.

They got out of Lizzie and gazed up at the imposing red brick structure. Kathy secured her hat to her head as she leaned back to travel her eyes to the top floor. Collin gave a low whistle as he pulled out his Brownie for a snap. They had no time to gawk as a uniformed doorman smartly opened a tall glass door under the bright green awning to usher them into the lobby.

"We'll park the car for you," he said, hand out. There was no tip.

"Don't you dare scratch Lizzie."

Apparently they passed his inspection anyway, so they must have appeared sophisticated enough for this establishment. As Collin approached the front desk, he took Kathy by the elbow and steered her to a comfortable chair.

"Sit here and compose yourself while I deal with the manager, my dear," and bending close to her, pointed to her hands and whispered, "and for God's sake, don't remove your gloves."

"I want us to stay here, please," Kathy said.

Collin could see that she had made up her mind.

"We can't be livin' the life at the Savoy this whole trip, you know."

"Yes. I agree. Just tonight."

She puzzled at his order to stay put but gave no argument and set about repairing her mussed hair and smoothing out the wrinkles from her skirt. She thought about pulling at her stockings to straighten them but folded her hands demurely in her lap. Besides, there was so much to appreciate in this lobby, the vases of hothouse flowers scattered about the occasional tables, the richly upholstered settees and wing chairs designed to offer a comfortable seat to travelers from out of town. Crystal electric chandeliers hung from tall ceilings to illuminate the polished floor and call attention to the deep mahogany hues of the hotel manager's desk. Kathy did her best not to stare at the fine gowns and evening dress of the hotel guests as they finished cocktails and made their way up to the rooftop garden dining room by means of an elevator. An elevator for heaven's sake. Took you straight up vertically.

Kathy was almost impatient when Collin returned to her with a room key in his hand and an attentive bellhop to carry their pitifully small luggage bags. Anybody could see that this young couple did not travel in the same style as most of the other guests, and the bellhop sniffed in disgust. With a finger to his lips, Collin gathered her up from the chair and escorted her to the elevator behind their attendant.

The bell hop was right; when the couple reached their room, he showed them the bathroom fitted with modern appliances, including a shower, and a beautifully appointed seating area, the gentleman gave him a ridiculously small tip for his troubles. Although he did not exactly slam the door on his way out, he did pull his mouth down into an unmistakable smirk. The girl, after all, was not half bad to look at, so he did reap some enjoyment from the encounter.

As soon as the door closed and they were alone, Kathy immediately realized that she and Collin might have to share the bed on which he had just collapsed and which was the most prominent feature of the room.

"How about some dinner?" she offered, to postpone the inevitable in her mind.

They visited the roof restaurant and dined simply on tomato soup and chicken.

When they returned to their room, Kathy opened all the doors in search of another room *en suite,* or at the least a Murphy bed. No such luck. Would Collin, now that he had her alone hundreds of miles from home, exact from her what she had been tantalizing him with all this time? Her snappy teasing and brazen manner had landed her in a real spot of trouble. How was she going to wiggle her way out of this? She shivered and rubbed her hands across her upper arms.

Collin threw his arm over his eyes as if he was confessing to a terrible sin, "Kathy, I'm sorry, but with our limited funds, it was impossible to afford separate rooms in this palatial establishment."

"So that's your ploy, Collin O'Donnell."

"Not really. This is our situation, but I will treat you with the upmost respect and courtesy."

"But I have enough money for two . . ."

"Nonsense, we'll make do. I'll take a chair for tonight. You don't have to worry."

When she heard his words, her fear melted away, and she drew a great sigh of relief. No, it was something different from relief. This man held her in such regard that he would never push her to submit to his body. She opened her eyes wide, so astonished was she to realize that Collin's love for her was greater than she imagined. Sure, their bodies could meet to satisfy their sexual desires, but Collin wanted to encounter her soul, her heart, her spirit. In the space of a minute, she resolved that she would make her place beside him. Whatever they did with one another, it was based on love, respect, and reverence for one another.

"Oh, Collin," she approached the bed and sat next to him, "What you've said, I . . . I can't tell you . . . my love for you . . ."

"Well, for a girl who always has a fast comeback, I guess I threw you a curve ball. Listen, let's take this thing slow because I know we have a long time together yet, if we both play our cards right. Besides, we have a mystery to solve and need our wits about us."

Now there's a turn of events, Kathy thought. *How comforting. But what about the Grand Adventure?*

Turning on his side to face her, Collin drew her down to slip his arms around her and hold her close. She grew warm in their embrace and pushed her body closer into him as if she wanted to climb right into his skin. Collin's body responded to her and before they knew it, before they could stop themselves, they covered each other's faces with stinging kisses and slipped tongues into mouths starving for each other's essence. Shrugging out of their outer clothes and throwing off the shirt and skirt, belt and stockings that stood in their way, they made each other mad for the other's touch.

They foolishly thought if they kept on their undergarments, they were playing it safe. They quickly discovered that their heat and sweat made Collin's long drawers and Claire's camisole and tap pants ridiculously inadequate barriers. Collin's hands glided over Claire's breasts, and he was astonished to see her nipples darken and grow rigid with the pressure of his mouth. In return, Claire could not keep her hands from him. Her whole being shook as she caressed his chest and belly and slipped her hands down to grasp and stroke his buttocks. It was no good, they had to have each other, but not yet. Not before they found Claire.

Collin tore himself from Kathy's arms and threw himself into a chair a fair distance from her. From his chest sprang a groan for he wanted her so badly he could taste it—he did taste it, on her tongue.

"We need to ease back there, girl. First things first."

"That's what I thought we were doing."

"Vixen," he moaned.

They had crossed a border and had pledged themselves to one another, not with what they had done, but the promise of what was to be their gift to one another, soon, soon.

Next day they got an early start, and fortunately there was bright sunshine for the trip. By noon they had crossed into Pennsylvania and they stopped for lunch in Scranton.

"You have been quiet most of the morning, Collin. A penny for your thoughts."

"What if we can't find out what happened to Claire? My Ma and I couldn't find her when she went missin'."

"We've got a plan and we'll stick with it," Kathy said. "We've been through all this. You told me that your Ma was working long hours at the time and you were only fifteen years old. Things are different now."

"But it's been eight years, love," Collin lamented, letting go of the steering wheel and lifting his upturned hands.

"Get hold of the wheel," Kathy shouted.

Once he re-gripped it, she offered, "Why waste your energy worrying until there is truly something to worry about?"

Collin didn't respond. Instead he just kept clenching and unclenching his right hand while he steered with his left. Kathy could see the veins on the back of his wrist bulging out.

They rolled into Jersey City, New Jersey, on schedule at five in the afternoon.

"This Ford has really worked great, hasn't it?" Kathy did her best to cheer him up.

"There's Journal Square over there," Collin pointed out. "See if you can spot the Jersey City Hotel."

"There it is on the corner. Looks like it has a gated parking area behind it," Kathy said.

"Perfect. We can leave the car here."

"See, I told you. Everything will work out for the best."

"We'll see, darlin'."

"We've discussed this before. You're not goin' with me to Brooklyn, Kathleen," Collin argued, when Kathy insisted at dinner that she was going.

"It's too dangerous for a young lady such as yourself. You can stay here and mind Lizzie."

"For the fortieth time, we need answers and I can help. So I'm going and that's that."

"You don't know what goes on there. When the terrible Five Points area was cleaned up twenty years ago, many of the poverty-stricken moved over to the area of Brooklyn that is near the

Navy Yard."

"You've never talked in detail about what happened to you there, dear.

"You don't want to know."

"I do, but I didn't want to stir up bad memories for you. I am going with you and that's final."

"I'll sleep on it."

"The train leaves the Exchange Terminal here at the Hudson North River for Penn Station in Manhattan on the hour, dear," Collin announced when he came back from the lobby with coffee at seven thirty. "It's goin' to take us a few minutes to walk there, so I suggest we get started."

"You seem more at ease this morning," Kathy observed.

"No more waiting. Let's go find Claire together."

"That's my man."

They arrived in Penn Station at 9:20 in the morning as shown on the grand four-sided clock hanging in the middle of the station. Kathy had been in Union Station in Toronto, but this was something else again. It was a huge cavernous edifice, a masterpiece of the beaux-arts style, with columns and grand arches built underground.

"This is magnificent." Kathy peered at the sights. "Look at all these people. Where are they all going, I wonder, lugging their suitcases along behind them?"

"These crowds are goin' to work here in the city or out of town to Boston or Philadelphia, or who knows where. Hundreds of thousands of them each day. And we have to find only one person." Collin sighed. "Needle in a haystack."

"And so we will, my love. Have faith."

The only faith Collin had ever had was in his knuckles, which he hoped would not fail him today as they ventured into the lion's den.

"Here, grab my hand," Collin urged as a swell with a black business case bumped Kathy sidewise into a bustling Chinaman. Looking up at the master schedule sign with its hundred or so destinations, he found what he was looking for. "Let's go," he commanded, pulling her along and threading their way through the surging river of humanity. "The Long Island Railroad train to the Atlantic terminal in Brooklyn leaves in ten minutes."

When they were aboard their train, Collin said, "You know that none of this existed when my Ma and me left New York six years ago. They were just building this station then."

"Ma and I, dear." Kathy pointed out. "None of this?"

"There were no trains goin' through tunnels under the North and East Rivers to Manhattan. We had to take a ferry from the bridge in Brooklyn to the Exchange Terminal where we boarded a train to Buffalo."

"Things are certainly changing in this world, most for the better."

"Yeah. In this case there are new techniques for boring under a river, and these advanced trains are electric. The older steam locomotives wouldn't work in tunnels. Everyone would have been choked to death from the smoke. You know, I read that twenty men died trying to build the tunnel we went through from Jersey City when the river broke through a few years ago."

"That's awful. Did you have to mention that while we are under the Hudson River?" Kathy said, thinking that this was not at all like the Tunnel of Love, red devil or not. She was starting to have a premonition of the dangers that might lurk where they were going. But she was determined to see it through. They had to find out what happened to Claire, whatever the outcome.

As they rolled into the LIRR Atlantic Terminal, Kathy noticed that it was bustling, but not as grandiose as Penn Station. In fact, it wasn't on the Atlantic Ocean at all.

Kathy thought she saw Collin shudder when they stepped out into the community. He pulled his locket out from under his waist shirt and kissed it reverently. Then he opened it and took out a small faded photograph, which he put in his breast pocket before closing the locket. He had always been reluctant to talk about his past. Not good memories, she concluded. This was the first time that she had glimpsed into the locket, and she thought that she saw a tin-type photograph of a woman's face inside.

"Who is that?" Kathy asked, pulling Collin to a stop at a shop entrance away from the crowds.

Collin took the folded photograph out of his pocket and opened it. Kathy could see the faded picture of a scrawny girl, poorly dressed with her hair all tangled. It made her sad to see the condition of the poor waif.

"This is my sister Claire when we came over from Ireland. She was eleven, then."

"She won't look like that now," Kathy noted, taking the black and white photograph and examining the girl's facial features.

"Yeah, but some of the gougers around here may remember her like that."

"Whose picture is in the locket?"

"Ma's, God rest her soul."

Kathy thought it best not to pry further. Collin was already on edge.

"C'mon, let's get this over with," Collin said, grabbing Kathy's hand firmly. "We need to check out where we lived before we left for Canada."

"What are those gigantic metal spider legs over there in the distance?"

"That's the Brooklyn US Navy Yard. It's an immense ship buildin' and refittin' base. There are about nine thousand military workers and sailors there as I remember, and they're busy twenty-four hours a day."

And so are the women down on Sands Street, he thought. So far he had avoided telling Kathy that his Ma had been forced into prostitution to earn the pittance to keep her children from starving. He wanted to keep it that way.

He guided her out onto Atlantic, crossing over to Fulton and west to Jay Street. From there they walked north to Sands Street. With this route he managed to stay as far away from the Navy Yard as possible.

"This is not a very nice neighborhood, is it?"

"I tried to tell you, darlin'. That's why I didn't want you to come."

"We're in this together all the way," she reminded him. "Where to, now?"

Sands Street was at the southern extremity of Irishtown. Looking east they could see that it dead-ended at the entrance gate to the Navy Yard. Even at this hour of the morning, uniformed sailors swaggered or staggered in and out of dirty-looking saloons that were strung out along the vice-ridden track.

And Collin knew from bitter experience that behind those establishments lurked hot-bed rooming houses, brothels, and tattoo parlors.

They noticed some reputable businesses, like the Navy YMCA, McIntire's candy store and Seeney's harness shop. Seeing Kathy's grimace, Collin commented, "As one writer put it, 'Sands is a den for cheap liquor and even cheaper women.' "

"So this is where you lived?"

"You see that broken-down rooming house over there beside Martin Connally's saloon? My Ma, Claire, and I lived up on the third floor at the back," Collin pointed to an old brownstone.

"You're joshing me, surely. How many rooms?"

"One." Trying to change the subject, "We need to go into Martin Connally's. Stick to me like glue, all right?"

He could see Kathy start twirling her hair again, like she did when she got angry or worried. *I wonder which one it is.* "We'll be all right, so we will, if we just stick together. He grabbed her twirling hand and held it tight.

In fact, Kathy was shocked by what greeted her when they pushed past the swinging doors. Through the smoky haze there were drunken sailors everywhere, gambling at the myriad of poker tables that filled the sawdust-strewn main floor. And fawning all over them were semi-clad floozies, in some cases topless, hoping for a quick trick. She counted three couples on the stairs heading to the upper rooms.

"Duck!" Collin cried, as a broken beer bottle chunk flew through the doorway and missed Kathy's ear by mere inches. A fight had erupted at a nearby table, and the combatants were reaching for their knives.

Collin sidestepped the impending brawl, pulling Kathy along behind him.

A wizened barkeep stepped from behind the bar and discharged his shotgun just above the fracas. That stopped the melee momentarily.

"Take it outside, now, O'Malley," he yelled, "or de udder barrel will cut youse bot down."

Grumbling, and still grabbing each other's collars, the two sailors beat a hasty retreat through the entrance doors.

"Anybody else wanna fight?" the barkeep challenged.

The saloon returned to normal bedlam.

"Martin Connally, you old reprobate," Collin exclaimed, crossing to the bar and pulling Kathy along with him.

"Christ, is dat you, O'Donnell? I'd know dat hooked nose anywhere. How long's it been?"

"Six yeahs, give or take, Mr. Connally," Collin answered, falling back into his old Brooklyn dialect.

"You were de best teenage boxah we had around heah," Martin quipped. "Remember dat knockout of Kennedy? You had 'im in de thoid round."

"Yah, but de Johnson fight dat went ten rounds almost killed me. Broke my nose, eh?" Collin countered.

"How could I forget it? I had to reset your schnoz," Connally remembered. "Where'd ya disappeah to? You still fightin' for a livin'?"

"Nah, woikin' foah a newspapah now," Collin said.

"Don't you dayah write me up foah shootin' up my place, Collin," the saloon operator cautioned.

"Martin, I need youah help. Do you remember my sistah, Claih?" Collin pulled the faded picture out of his pocket. "She vanished from heah when she was only twelve."

"Jeez, O'Donnell, dat's a long time ago. How old was she in dis picture? Maybe eleven?"

"About eight. Well?"

"Yah, I remember her, kind of. Scrawny kid. She used to come in wit you and your Ma. How is your Ma, son? She was a good workah, professional-like."

Collin tried to deflect the conversation. "She's dead, Martin. Have you seen Claih around?"

"Sorry, Collin. I haven't seen her heah since quite a time before you left. But you know dat young goils disappear from heah regular- like."

"Do you have any idea who the magician might be who makes the girls disappear?" Kathy asked, looking Martin straight in the eyes.

"You haven't introduced me to dis fine young lady, Collin," Martin said.

"Dis is my fiancée, Katleen." Collin didn't want to give Martin any opening to make suggestive remarks about his girl.

Kathy was astonished. This was the first time he had used that term of commitment.

"Pleased to meet you, ma'am. I dunno. You might ask Enrico dat magic question. About the magician responsible for goils disappearin'."

"Enrico. Is he still around?"

Kathy saw Collin's eyes narrow and he was clenching his right fist.

"Bolder and bigger dan evah. Usually hangs out down at Benny's Saloon nowadays. Works out of de back room dere. Likes to keep his eye on his merchandise, if youse know what I mean," Martin offered. "You want a beah or somethin?"

"Little early for us, Martin. But tanks for youah help."

Collin hurried Kathy out into the street. They saw one of the sailors lying in the gutter, still breathing, and gave him a wide berth.

"Does fiancée mean . . . ?"

Collin cut her off. "We'll see."

"Who is this Enrico character?"

Collin looked away down Sands Street towards the Navy Yard.

"Well? Who is he?"

"Enrico Salazar was a pimp for a lot of the working girls around here. Probably still is. They do a big business with the johns from the Navy Yard. He was a blowhard who used intimidation and worse to control his merchandise."

"It must have been hell living here, Collin," Kathy sympathized. This was a whole new perspective on Collin's past for her. No wonder he has been anxiety prone, she surmised, given the obvious intimidation in this environment. "I didn't know that you used to have a Brooklyn accent, dear."

"You don't know de half of it, eh?" Collin said, grabbing her hand and heading east.

Collin could feel the tension in Kathy's arm, her reluctance to head deeper into his old haunt of iniquity. His mind was energized. *Could it be that simple, that Enrico was a slave trader? If so, he and his Ma missed it—right under their noses. How could he have been so stupid?* For the first time he had some hope.

"We need to get some lunch and we need a plan," Collin announced. A thought was forming in his head and he didn't like it.

Turning right, away from the Navy Yard, back down Jay Street, they retreated from the sordid Sands Street and found the reputable Abraham and Straus seven-story department store back on Fulton Street. Collin could certainly see from her more relaxed facial features that Kathy felt safer in this respectable part of Brooklyn. Amazing. Just a few blocks apart. There in its coffee shop they settled for lunch.

"I used to come here to get away from Sands for a few minutes," Collin mused while he played with his uneaten sandwich.

"I can see why. Wait a minute. A & S, right? I read about Straus and his wife Ida. Isidor, I think he was named. Did you know that they died when the *Titanic* went down three years ago?"

"Nah. I don't know nothin' about those swells." Collin went silent and finally took a bite of his bratwurst sandwich.

"They weren't just swells, dear. They were heroes," Kathy exclaimed, pausing to sip her Twinings lemon tea.

"What do you mean, heroes?"

"It was reported that the elderly couple were offered a position in lifeboat number eight during that terrible ordeal. Isador refused since there were still women left on the *Titanic* and Ida stayed with her man saying *where you go, I go*. A memorable verse from the Book of Solomon was written on their joint tombstone, *many waters cannot quench love—neither can the floods drown it.*"

A chill ran down Collin's spine. "What an awful way to go. They were heroes for all that."

"Yes, dear. And where you go, I go."

"But not to a watery grave, hopefully."

Collin lapsed into his reverie while he downed his beer.

"Fiancée of mine, a penny for your thoughts."

Collin was toying with the idea of telling her. After all, she insisted on going where he had gone, was going. But the shame of it all. She had a right to know his whole background. To keep it from her would be tantamount to a lie. But she was so straight-laced.

"How on earth did you and your mother and Claire survive here?"

He couldn't avoid it. His hand was shaking so much that he had to drop his sandwich back onto the plate. "My Ma sold herself to feed and clothe us. Do you understand what I mean?"

"I wondered. What a brave woman." Kathy murmured, her voice cracking.

"There, there, darlin'." Collin offered his handkerchief for the tears he saw welling up in his fiancée's eyes. *What a fool I was to be so worried about telling her.*

"Thank you for being so understanding, my love. I was afraid you might not accept such a . . . stigma."

"My father would disown me for saying this, but a mother must do everything in her power to make a life for her children, any way she can, in desperate circumstances."

Collin laid his free hand over hers, steadying it on his arm and squeezed. "You got that right. They were desperate times, for all that."

"Can I see her photograph?"

Collin started to take the picture out of his pocket.

"No, I meant of your Ma."

"Oh, here." Collin offered his locket, still chained around his neck as he bent forward.

"It's real silver, isn't it. I love the clasped hands and heart design. How do you open it?"

"It's an ancient latch. Here on the side." Collin pushed the clasp and the locket finally sprang open.

"Oh, she was beautiful, Collin."

"Yes, she was." Collin looked longingly at the photograph.

"Why don't you keep that where you can see it more often?"

Collin started to close up the locket. "It's . . . too painful, you know."

"You avenged her death, Collin."

"But there is so much more. "

Kathy reached out stopped him from closing it. "Well I think that she is beautiful. Look at her again. That's how you should remember her."

"I guess so."

"What's that inscribed on the other side?"

"I dunno. Gaelic, I think."

"Maybe it's important in some way."

Collin realized that he had never given it any thought. "It's just a family trinket."

"But didn't you say that your Ma entrusted it to you when she died?"

"Yeah. That's right."

"You'd better keep it safe then."

"Yes . . . yes. Of course."

"Well, then, what do we do next?" Kathy asked.

"I don't like what I am about to say," Collin started. "But I can't think of any other way."

"Way for what?"

"We need to find out if Enrico could have been involved in Claire's disappearance."

"So, how can we do that?"

"Enrico is a shrewd operator. He controls his girls with an iron fist. They can generally never escape his clutches. All the girls are deathly afraid of him . . . and justifiably so. If they cross him in any way, they can show up with broken limbs or they might just disappear. We need to distract him long enough to check his office."

"Lover, you're not thinking what I'm thinking, are you?" Kathy winced.

"I'm afraid so, darlin'. I need a distraction. But I can't take that risk with your life."

"What other option do we have?"

"Unfortunately, I can't think of one."

"You want to find out what happened to Claire, don't you?"

Collin nodded emphatically.

"Well, then. It's got to be done. I'll be the distraction to try and lure him outside Benny's."

"In plain sight, then," Collin insisted.

From a distance Kathy could see Enrico, the man now lounging outside the saloon with a vile black cigar hanging out of his mouth. He had just back-slapped one of his girls across the face and was giving her a tongue lashing. When he was finished, he pushed her back through the entrance doors into the saloon. *What an odious little man.* Kathy observed Enrico's appearance—he was a squat fat slug of a man, maybe five-foot-two, with a shock of black hair slicked down with who knows what. He obviously thought he was finely dressed in waistcoat and spats, but their threadbare condition and disheveled, slept-in appearance made him look quite comical at best, and evil at worst. His handlebar mustache and menacing heavyset eyebrows completed the picture. He disgusted her.

"Hello, sir," she greeted him as she strolled up. The bile was rising in her throat. It was all she could do to keep it down. Can you tell me how I can get to the Brooklyn train station? I seem to have lost my way."

Kathy could see his evil black eyes ogling her breasts and then her whole body. She shifted to her left and struck a pose so that the slug would turn with his back to the saloon entrance.

As soon as he moved, Collin came around the far corner of the building and darted out of sight into the bar.

Kathy had no idea how she was going to occupy Enrico for the five minutes Collin had estimated he needed without getting herself accosted or worse. One minute was agony.

"Why don't ya come inside for a drink, dearie, and I'll point out the way?" The slug winked in a confident yet sleazy way as he preened the goo in his greasy sideburns. If he'd had a mirror he would undoubtedly be admiring himself in it. A putrid peacock, she decided.

Kathy could see Enrico start to sweat in anticipation of his next conquest. It filled her with dread but she held her emotions in check. She desperately wanted to kick him hard, somewhere where it would incapacitate him. *God, I've never had these kind of thoughts before. What's coming over me?*

"I'm in a rush. Can't you just point out the directions from here?"

Collin lost no time as he swung through Benny's doors. Kathy's safety and maybe her very life depended on his speed. Looking quickly around, he saw a drunken group of men surrounded by an equally dozy coven of brazen sluts. They were ensnared in various poses and wardrobe disarray. The smoke level was choking and Collin thought he could smell cannabis.

The only person who showed any interest in him was the bartender.

"What'll it be?" Hank asked as he looked Collin up and down.

"Give me a knickerbocker beer."

While he was pouring, Collin asked, "You got a public washroom?"

"Over dere," the barkeep pointed to the curtains at the back of the bar.

"Be right back."

The ground floor area behind the saloon was a rat's nest, literally. Collin had no intention of contracting some deadly disease by using the facilities. After passing by a storage area filled with mostly empty whiskey, wine and beer bottle cases, Collin spied a closed office. The door was locked and the sign read, 'Keep out if you Value your Life—Enrico.'

Collin took out his tools and went to work.

"Come with me, my dear," Enrico said.

Kathy flinched when he grabbed her hand. She felt as if bugs were crawling off of him and up her arm. She resisted when he tried to walk her into the saloon. This was not going well, to say the least.

"I insist on being polite to a lady," Enrico crooned as pulled her through the swinging doors.

She scanned the darkened room for her hero. He wasn't there. The inside of Benny's place looked even seedier than Connally's. *God, I hope Collin is almost finished. How many minutes has it been?*

The goon literally dragged her to the bar.

"What can I get you to drink?" Hank asked eyeing her carefully.

"I'd really like a lemonade if you have it," she answered.

Hank's eyebrows went up.

For a minute the slug disengaged from her hand in order to push the other girls to get on with their business of fleecing the patrons. Even in the men's inebriated state, Kathy could see the fear in the faces of these hookers when Enrico descended on them. The men were oblivious to the harassment.

Kathy thought of bolting for the exit. But then she remembered that Collin was in the back counting on her.

After gaining access to Enrico's office and having closed the door to minimize the potential of being discovered, Collin found pay dirt. There were ledgers in locked desk drawers dating back before 1900, in which Enrico detailed the money he had gotten from each of his girls. Despite his disheveled appearance, Enrico was apparently a miser extraordinaire, who counted and recorded every penny he brought in. There were lewd annotations written regarding the physical attributes of each girl who worked for him, as well as the method of cruelty he had inflicted to keep them in line. Collin noticed that in some cases the entries stopped, just after hateful comments about poor performance or insubordination. He imagined the worst.

It took all his willpower to look at two dates. On June 3, 1906, the date when Claire disappeared, there was no entry with her name or anything about any new girls. Nothing. But on the date of January 12, 1909 there was an entry that read, 'Fuck, fuck, fuck. Shaina's disappeared wit' de boy. I'll kill de bitch!'

The hatred he felt for Enrico welled up in him again as he realized that this fiend had likely instigated his Ma's death. He had thought as much, all these years. He ripped out and pocketed that page.

There must be more, he thought. *It can't end like this.* Scrambling through this pigsty of an office, Collin finally spied a strongbox high up on the back shelf. Taking it down, he found that it was padlocked. *Shite—harder to pick.*

Kathy saw Hank look at the beer on the bar and then glanced at his watch before staring at her intently. She was still fidgety. He approached Enrico who was grabbing one of his girls and whispered in his ear. Then he came back behind the bar.

Enrico wheeled sharply, and, passing the bar, he grabbed Kathy by the hair.

"We're goin' to go upstaiahs and chat," Enrico said. "I don't want to be distoibed."

"I'm not going anywhere with you," Kathy cried out, trying to break free of his grasp. *Oh, how her hair hurt. He was going to rip it out.*

"Who are you, bitch?" he yelled, and slapped her across the mouth. "Gimme dat pistol, Hank." Then he dragged her towards the back room.

They burst open the door to the office and Enrico saw Collin standing there with a stack of pages in his hand.

"You dere. You're a dead man!" the slug cried as he leveled the gun at Collin.

"You monster." Collin spat. "You had my Ma killed and you sold my sister into slavery. I'm goin' to wring your slimy neck!"

"O'Donnell, is dat you, you little prick?" Enrico jeered. "Damn right I took care of dem. Youah sweet sistah brought a pretty penny, too. I'd have got you too if you hadn't been fight trainin' wit' Connally at de time. Wit' dat chloroform, you wouldn't have stood a chance, you Irish turd. Youah sistah went down like a house of cards."

"These records of yours showing who, when, and to where you sold children into slavery are enough to prove that you should die," Collin hissed. "No judge and jury in the country will convict me of murder. They'll probably give me a ticker parade down Broadway, you pig."

Enrico laughed and his nostrils flared and glistened. "You seem to be ignorin' one small fact. Dere are six bullets in dis gun. De foisst one will blow away youah manhood. De second one will be in de gut and de thoid one will be right between youah scumbag eyes. And den aftah youah bitch has seen you die, I'm goin to do de same to her."

Enrico's girls usually cringed from his beatings. So he didn't anticipate Kathy's lightning fast kick to his groin just as he finished talking. It was worth the chunk of hair she lost when, with a yelp of pain, the brute ripped it out as he dropped down to his knees.

"House of cards indeed," Kathy scoffed.

Still holding the gun in one hand and his balls in the other, Enrico turned to shoot Kathy.

Collin was diving midair when the shot rang out. It barely missed his girl's head as she dove to her left. Before he could aim again, Collin's full weight came crashing down on Enrico's back.

From the front Kathy could see the Enrico's eyes bug out as his spine snapped just below the ribcage. It gave a sickening crack. The gun flew off into a corner.

Amazingly, Enrico managed to reach out and grab Kathy by the throat even as his limbs started to sag. She felt like a vise had tightened around her vocal cords as the man's lower body turned to stone. She was choking to death. Collin grabbed Enrico by the head from behind and twisted. With a splintering crunch, the head turned ninety degrees and flopped down like rag doll. Collin could see the awful vacant stare of the dead looking up at him.

And yet, even in death, his vise grip upon Kathy's neck remained. She was turning blue. While Collin propped up Enrico's body with his torso, his arms worked frantically to pull the frozen hands off his lover's throat. Finally, with one mighty tug, the wrists both broke in unison and the fingers involuntarily sprang open.

Kathy was coughing and gasping for air when Hank arrived on the scene.

"I hoid a shot," he said as he closed the office door, gun in hand. He saw what was left of Enrico in a heap on the floor between the two. "What happened here?"

"He tried to kill us both," Collin stated matter-of-factly. "He almost succeeded with my partner here, as you can see. We had to defend ourselves."

"You coppers?"

"No. We're just tryin' to find out if he sold my sister into child slavery so we can find her."

"And?"

"And he did." Collin shook his fist with pages sticking out of it.

"God in Heaven," the man exclaimed, tears in his eyes. "Show me dose pages."

"In a minute. What's your name?"

"Hank Handelman. What's youse."

"O'Donnell. And O'Sullivan."

"I taught dat you looked familiar, boy. Yes, of course. I knew your Mudder. Shaina, right?"

"Yes."

"You were dat boxin' kid, weren't youse? You was good."

"I gave it up after Hogarts's death," Collin admitted.

"I saw dat match. In '08 I tink. He was some fierce mouser. A right brawler an' a blowhard. Fair fight. It weren't youse fault. He just staggered and fell into dat block wall."

"Yah, well it was my punch that sent him there," Collin pointed out.

"Dese tings happen. Not youse fault," the barkeep reiterated.

"So what happens now?" Kathy asked. Hank's gun was still pointed in their direction.

"Sorry, bad habit," Hank said. "It comes from bein' tortured by dat weasel." He pointed at the pool of blood that was still oozing from the compound fracture in Enrico's neck. He sold my son and threatened to have him whacked if I didn't help him. All of us here owe you two a plenty for riddin' our world of dis vermin. Don't worry. I'll take care of dis mess. Enrico will just disappeah, like some of his goils."

Seeing that Kathy was breathing easier, Collin went over and slapped Hank on the shoulder. Giving him a big hug, Collin said, "Birds of a feather. Thanks for your help. What's your son's name? Bet you can find him in these records and get him back."

Hank took the sheets, and leafing through them, asked, "You found dese in here?"

"In a lock box up on that shelf," Collin pointed.

"Here he is," Hank exclaimed, crying now, as he found the record for his son on the sheets. "Oh tank you! I can look into the whereabouts of all dese kids. Dere parents will be ecstatic."

"I just need the sheet with my sister Claire on it," Collin stated, and he put it in his pocket. He noted, with disgust, that the deadbeat only got twenty dollars for Claire.

Collin went to Kathy. Swooping her up in his strong arms, he kissed her fiercely.

"You saved both our lives, my love," he exclaimed. "I guess it was a good idea that you joined me after all."

"Now we're even. He obviously had it coming," she concluded as they left Benny's.

Kathy had mixed emotions; elation over finding a record of Claire's abduction, but dread to think what a scumbag like Enrico might have done with her. It was the first time in her life that the adrenaline inside of her had been pumping uncontrollably. And the thrill of it scared her. *Father would disown me if he knew what we are up to, she thought. Wait a minute. He already did that.*

Chapter Thirteen
Providence

Brooklyn, New York

We've got a lead to find Claire, Kathy kept repeating to herself as they left Benny's behind, heading towards the Atlantic Terminal. She had to keep thinking this positive thought to drown out the dread that was creeping into her soul. This place, Collin's past, the horror of the slug, what might have happened to Claire, what might have happened to Collin if he had been home when Claire was abducted. *No. We've got a lead to find her.*

"What did you find out?" she asked, needing to know but almost afraid to ask.

She could see Collin hesitate. *Is the answer too ugly, too frightening?* That's when the enormity of what had just happened overcame her. She started to shake.

"This is all so grotesque and unnerving for me, Collin." Kathy started to cry and her breathing got shallow.

Collin led her off of Sands, then stopping, he grabbed his handkerchief from his pants pocket and dabbed her eyes. "There, there, darlin'. We're all right. The bullet missed, didn't it now. We're safe and sound you and me. Just like Sam and Liz."

"But it's so overwhelming, so . . . monstrous."

Collin put his arms around her and rocked her right there at the street corner.

"Yes, he was evil, but just a few minutes ago he was still alive and now his life is over, because of us. He's just a pile of mush."

Collin kicked the pavement of Jay Street and spun her around until her back was to the terror.

Lifting her head and gazing into those streaming blue eyes, he said, "You have got to think of it as a godsend, Kathy. We were sent there to do God's work."

"Ending a man's life is doing God's work? I don't think that's in either your Catholic or my Anglican creed."

"Listen to me. That fiend abducted Claire using chloroform and sold her to someone named Fredricson in a place called Providence. Bastard did it for just twenty dollars. It was either him or us. Self defense."

"Well, if you put it that way," Kathy said, still sniffling but now dabbing her own eyes with the handkerchief.

"You know that it's true. It's the only way to look at it, can't ya see? Plus he's the one what signed me Ma's death warrant and had that murderer try to rape you and kill me."

"*Who,* dear."

"What?"

"He's the one *who* signed your Ma's death warrant."

"I see you haven't lost your linguistic charm."

"My, what a big word that is."

"Yeah and I've learned plenty more at the Paper."

"Have you now, my love? And I suppose that I've had nothing to do with this transformation?"

"What transformation?"

Kathy gave her man a squeeze to let him know she appreciated his attempt at levity in a drastic circumstance. He returned it with a swooping backward dip and a smooch at its extremity.

"That transformation," Kathy answered, giggling for the first time since the encounter with Enrico.

"Oh, that," Collin said, bringing her back up.

She realized that her man had accomplished her transformation, at least for the time being. He was amazing.

"At least there is a lead we can follow," Kathy offered, giving back the handkerchief.

"Are you able to continue, darlin'?"

"Yes. Let's get out of this place."

Collin led her back to Fulton.

"You need to know what I found out back there," Collin cautioned, as they waited on the platform to board the train to Penn Station. "There must be over a hundred children on Enrico's list. What a devil he was. Claire was only thirteen when it happened. And there's more. There's a note beside her name with no date."

"I hate to ask."

"Fredricson says to go get her."

"What does that mean? He already had her."

"I'm not sure, but we'd better find Fredricson. And that's not all."

"What could be worse than that?"

"There are notations in his prostitutes' notebook next to his records of my Ma."

"I'm afraid to ask." Kathy frowned, but didn't break down again.

"All right. I think you need to know that, too. The first one in 1909 is—*'That bitch took her scumbag son and my money and ran. I'll get them back.'*"

"There's more?"

"Yes, I'm afraid so. At least it connects the dots. *'Finally! That dumb son-of-a bitch Weston saw her on the docks in Toronto when he was there off the Saratoga. Her regular John. Owes me big time. I'll fix them now.'*"

"There were two more entries," Collin continued, wincing. "*'Good. Shaina's dead but the boy escaped.'* and then *'Fuck! The boy killed Weston.'*"

"He really was an evil cuss, wasn't he?"

"The worst. He deserved to die. We stopped him from more evil, didn't we."

"Yes, we did."

Kathy was thinking how unbelievable it was that just ten days ago she was teaching children proper manners and today she had assisted her man in ridding the world of a monster.

"You don't think that they forced Claire into prostitution as well, do you?" Kathy cringed at the thought.

"We won't know that answer until we can confront Fredricson, will we," Collin muttered as he helped his partner up into onto the LIRR train.

Uncharacteristically, they were both silent throughout the trip back to Penn station. This wasn't a subject for public conversation. It had been a day of revelation. Not only had Kathy learned about the squalid environment that her lover had endured as a child, and the terrible persecution that his whole family had suffered at the hands of the likes of Enrico, but now she knew he had been a boxer of note, one whose opponent had inadvertently died at his hands. No wonder he had felt guilty all the time. She now understood how he came by his physical abilities as well as the reason for his reluctance to use them.

Kathy loved Collin even more because of it all. He had come so far. She grabbed hold of his hand while they sat silently swaying as the train screeched to a halt in Penn Station.

And he was certainly responding to her didactic coaching, even though he poked fun at her for trying.

They returned to the Jersey City Hotel by late afternoon.

"I'm going to take a bath, maybe two," Kathy announced, as they entered the lobby. "I may have to take a layer of skin off to get clean again."

"I'll be right up, darlin'. Just going to check on the car." Collin turned on his heel and headed back outside.

Later, as he appeared in their room, Kathy was dressing for dinner.

"Better?"

"Mmmm. Much. A bath gives a girl time to think. Hard to grasp what just happened today, isn't it."

"Yeah. Quite the dustup. You were some fierce mouser, though, darlin'."

"Wasn't I, though."

"How could I have been so stupid back then, when Claire went missing, I mean."

"Come here," Kathy coaxed holding her arms out from her half-dressed torso and then patting the bed.

Once he was sitting beside her, she pulled his head onto her shoulder. "I'm not going to repeat that it wasn't your fault, that you'd have been captured too, that you might be dead now and that I would never have met you. Think of the glass half full instead of empty. This time yesterday you probably thought that this was a wild goose chase, didn't you."

"Yeah, you're dead right there, to be sure."

Kathy turned to look him square in the eyes. "Now we know what happened to Claire in Brooklyn, we know that Enrico can't send another goon to kill you and we have a lead to follow. Not bad for a day's work, I'd say. I think that we are going to find her. How's that for finding a needle in a haystack?"

"Grand, I guess. You've a way of the positive. I give you that."

"Do I deserve another kiss?"

"You deserve a lot more than that," Collin replied, taking the cue to give his girl a hug and a warm kiss.

"All right, then. Off with you into the shower. I'm famished."

"Car's still there," Collin informed her. "I picked up a map in the lobby. Take a guess where we are goin' next." He tossed the document onto the bed as he started to take off his tunic, pulling the shower curtain around the tub in the corner.

"Providence, Rhode Island?" she said, hearing the shower start to flow.

"How'd you know?" he asked poking his head out from behind the curtain.

"I'm a teacher, aren't I? Geography is one of my favorite subjects."

Collin's shower took just a minute, but what a minute. Kathy reached in and soaped his back.

"Can you do my front now?" he asked as he started to turn towards her.

"Not on your life," she teased. "Turn back."

"Are you sure?"

"I see something rising. Shall I turn on the cold water?"

"No. I'll stay around."

During dinner they discussed their next steps.

"Tomorrow we're drivin' to Providence to find Fredricson," Collin announced, skewering a meatball and then twirling the spaghetti with his fork. "You all right with that?"

"Yes, I guess so, but should we have notified the Brooklyn police?" Kathy asked, carving off a slice of salmon and ladling on the butter sauce.

"Leave that to Hank. He said he would handle it," Collin advised, waving a roll in Kathy's direction.

"I guess he's capable of that, being a Handleman," Kathy quipped, leaning over and taking a big bite of the bread.

"More linguistic magic, darlin'?"

"No. Just trying to be *punctual.*"

"I see you are back in rare form."

"Actually, I am scared silly, Collin. The only other time I was in such danger was when I almost got raped. Linguistic magic, as you put it, is my way beating high anxiety."

"Kathy, I will protect you. Please don't worry," Collin

exclaimed, reaching across the table to hold her hand.

He knocked over the salt cellar.

"Over your left shoulder then, quickly now," Kathy said, picking up some of the spilled salt with a knife and depositing the grains in his hand.

"Why?"

"To blind the devil, of course, to avoid treachery and lies like Judas at the Last Supper."

"Honestly, Kathy. Where do you hear these wives tales."

"From my Mother, actually."

"You sure it wasn't your crazy father?""

"Absolutely not, my love."

Collin threw the salt. "Can't have them lies."

"Seriously, we need to decide on our course of action tomorrow, Collin."

"This guy Fredricson could just be a middleman, you know." Collin replied. "After nine years, he could have moved or he could be dead."

"I'll bet that the operator in this hotel could get information on how to contact any Fredricsons in Providence."

"There are three Fredricsons listed in the telephone directory for Providence," the operator said when they checked after dinner. "But I also looked up the directory from 1906. In addition to two of those three, I found two other Fredricsons that don't have current telephone numbers there," she added.

"Can you get any forwarding information for those that presumably left?" Kathy asked, gesturing to Collin from inside the telephone booth in the lobby.

"We don't have that information, ma'am. I'm sorry,"

They came back with the telephone numbers and addresses for the current Fredericson contacts. Tomorrow they would investigate in Providence, starting with the police department.

Later that night, as they lay together in bed, Kathy let Collin fondle her breasts while she lay on her back. This didn't last long. He was so tired. They both were. After he dozed off, she rolled over toward him and pressed against him until she started melting into him. Trembling, she could feel his heart beating against her breast. *Everything was going to be all right*, Kathy decided as she drifted off to sleep.

"This road in Connecticut is not as smooth as the ones in New York," Kathy announced, shifting her bottom every few minutes. But the coastal scenery from New Haven to New London near the Long Island Sound was beautiful in the morning sunshine. After six hours, she was sore and tired.

"So we're in agreement that we should ask the Providence Police department to help us find Fredricson?" Kathy asked.

"Yes, but let's not mention that Claire was abducted. With coppers we don't know who we're dealing with. And I doubt that they will help us," Collin argued. "They'll be sayin' that the trail is too cold after all these years, that's for certain."

"What did I say about half-full glasses, dear?" Kathy said.

The officer at the desk of the Providence precinct police station listened with some interest to their request to help find Collin's missing sister who may have been associated with Fredricson. They noticed that he even took notes. Kathy could see that he had written the name FREDRICSON in bold capital letters on his pad of paper. He was doodling all around it.

"Well, can you help us find the right Fredricson, Officer Stanley?" Collin asked as he finished his description of the situation.

Stanley was clearly stalling before answering. The pause was deafening.

"Just a minute," he said, and he walked into a back office.

"Officer Williams would like you to step into his office, please," Stanley informed them on his return.

"What's all this about Fredricson being associated with your sister?" Williams asked, snubbing out his cigarette in a glass ashtray bearing the inscription *Detective PPD*.

"We have reason to believe that my sister was goin' to see a man named Fredricson here in Providence when she left Brooklyn in June 1906," Collin stated. "We understand that there are at least three people named Fredricson in this town."

"What's his first name, this guy Fredricson?" Williams asked.

"We don't know anything more than what we've told you already," Kathy responded, trying to help.

"Seems odd that a young girl would take off on her own to meet a man she's never met before, doesn't it?" Williams mused.

Collin made a snap decision to open up. "Someone named Fredricson bought my sister Claire O'Donnell from a man named Enrico Salazar in Brooklyn on June 3, 1906."

He noticed that Williams and Stanley exchanged furtive glances before the detective spoke again.

"Where is this Enrico now, him?" Williams asked.

"He's dead, sir," Collin answered.

"That's convenient," the detective muttered. "Do you know who Mr. Fredricson is?"

"Would I be after askin' you if I did?" Collin exclaimed.

"You're obviously not from this neck of the woods, boy," Williams commented. "George Fredricson has been our Chief of Police nigh on to fifteen years. All the other Fredricsons are his relatives. He is a pillar of the community, him. He even set up a home for orphaned and wayward children and he pays for teaching them, finding them local employment. We can ask him if he's heard of your sister."

This time it was Collin and Kathy's turn to exchange startled glances before answering.

Collin could see from the hardened look in Kathy's eyes that she had come to the same conclusion as he had. It didn't take a genius to figure it out. *The police chief is crooked.* He was buying child slave labor, likely holding them captive and forcing them to work for his profit. *Some pillar of society!*

Collin started backpedaling. If they confronted Fredricson, he would know that they were threatening his operation. *Shite*, he thought. The police won't help us. Kathy had a searching look in her eyes.

"That won't be necessary. Don't bother your boss, sir, with our problems," Collin stated. "Maybe they'll know somethin' at the orphanage. If you can just give us the name and address, we can look into it ourselves."

"Providence Orphanage is up north in the country on the Old River Road just south of the Railroad Street junction, near the cemetery," Stanley offered.

"Thanks, officers," Collin said.

Then they beat a hasty retreat, hoping that the detective wouldn't mention their meeting to the Chief.

"We'd better set up our base of operations at an inconspicuous hotel," Collin advised.

"I think the Blackstone Hotel over there would be better than that gaudy Narragansett," Kathy suggested when they reached the center of Providence.

"Great, then we can leave the Lizzie over at the What Cheer Garage on Benefit Street," Collin agreed. "I saw it a couple of minutes ago."

After dropping Kathy and their two small leather valises off at the hotel, Collin drove back to the garage. "Can you check out the car and change the oil?" he asked the mechanic on duty "Then I need to store Lizzie here for the night. Might need it early though."

"That's a fine machine you have there, sir. Of course I can do that for you. I'll leave the key under the running board in case you get here before we open at eight."

"We've got a serious problem, Kathy," Collin announced, when they had settled down for the night in their modest room. "We've got to move fast."

"Don't I know it. And I thought that yesterday was horrifying."

"I didn't bother mentionin' it earlier, but the name Fredricson showed up for many transactions in Enrico's list. This jerk has been buying children for more than a decade. And, come to think of it, there were more boys than girls on that list. So, prostitution is less likely."

Kathy understood. "Then the Providence Orphanage could be a front for an enslaved child labor camp. We can't just show up there and ask about Claire. We might never see the light of day after that."

"Exactly, my love."

"Is it likely that those children are laboring on site at the Orphanage? What would they be making there?"

"I don't think the work is being done there," Collin reasoned. "That would blow their cover as an orphanage."

"Then they must farm them out to a business that uses children, probably nearby," Kathy concluded.

"That's a good assumption. We should go out there before dawn tomorrow and watch from a distance to see who is comin' and goin' from the place. I got a local map from the folks at the front desk of the hotel."

"And we should follow them to see where they are taking the children," Kathy suggested.

"Good idea." Collin thought for a moment. "What are the chances that the business owners are in cahoots with Fredricson?"

"I don't have any idea. But I looked up the subject of child labor practices in the United States in our library back home before we left. Typical teacher activity, you know. There's a photographer, Lewis Hine, who has been visiting businesses and poor homes all over the eastern part of the country recently to document the stories of children being forced to work in the factories. His photographs are very detailed. He is working for the National Child Labor Committee that was formed in 1904 to stop abusive use of children. They are trying to get citizens to force the government to change the laws. And for those states that have enacted laws, they want them enforced.

From the articles I have read, most of these children live in poverty with their families who depend upon the pittance that the child brings home. The business owners don't generally force these young slaves to live on their premises, but they do make them work sometimes eighteen hours a day in very dangerous circumstances."

"You sure do read a lot," Collin commented. "Sometimes it's too much information for this poor Irish brain."

"A man named John Spargo wrote a book called *The Bitter Cry of Children* that describes the poor working conditions of these children. He's a friend of Hine. Apparently children from three years of age to adulthood are used. Factories are unsanitary and typically run at very hot temperatures caused by the machinery. Tuberculosis is a commonly transmitted disease among the exhausted, ill-fed and poorly-clothed children. And, being small, these kids are forced to maintain and lubricate dangerous machines while they are operating. So there are many lost limb injuries and deaths, especially among the young ones. And, in many cases, corporal punishment is used to keep the children in line."

"My God. Poor Claire! She could be dead now," Collin exclaimed.

"Let's not jump to conclusions. I would think that the factory or factories would not be in cahoots with Fredricson. They would look at the orphanage as a home-based supplier of workers. But I could be wrong, of course."

190

"All right, but the factory managers are still not gonna be happy to have us askin' questions, are they?" Collin observed.

"We've got to find out about Claire from somebody. But from whom?" Kathy asked, twirled her hair with a pencil from the night stand.

They didn't have an answer. "We'd better head out to the orphanage early," Collin finally decided. "Need to stay ahead of Fredricson."

Sleep didn't come easily for either of them. Too many unanswered questions.

Chapter Fourteen
The Mill

June 3, 1915
Providence, Rhode Island

It was raining at three a.m. when Collin trudged the half mile to the What Cheer Garage to get the car. He cranked open the upper window and peered through the crack as he drove it to the Blackstone.

"You're soaked to the bone," Kathy exclaimed, rushing to the door of their room with a towel to greet him.

"Lizzie's a great automobile, but they should have some way to clear the windscreen of water in a drench like this.," Collin said, shaking like a drowned dog.

"Maybe we should wait a while."

"We may need a can to bail with, but we'd better get on our way. We've got to be out of Providence before Fredricson hears about our visit to his police station yesterday."

Driving north out of the city thirty minutes later, they picked up the Old River Road and got closer to the Blackstone River. With the rain, the road became a mud track. Even at their crawling speed Collin had his hands full avoiding the ditches along the route.

"At least the rain is letting up," Kathy said, as she reached through the opening to wipe a small section of the windscreen in front of Collin's face once again.

"But my feet feel like they are under water," Collin said, cranking the hand throttle open slightly. "At least Lizzie doesn't seem to mind the bath."

After two hours of tense driving, they saw the entrance to the St. James and Polish Cemeteries on their left, and a quarter mile ahead, they passed Railroad Street on their right. They could smell the river.

"Did we miss it?" Kathy puzzled.

"Must have. I'll turn around."

"There it is." Kathy pointed when she saw the sign just before they reached the cemetery. "Why do they only have signs facing one way? *Providence Orphanage, Home of Children in Need.* Now there's a prophetic statement if I ever saw one."

"It looks like it's set back into those trees at the end of this winding dirt driveway," Collin said, pulling off the road opposite the cemetery and shutting down the engine. "I'd better go in on foot. You stay here. I'll be right back."

"I'm going with you, Collin."

"I promise that I will just scout it out. You stay here."

"Be careful."

Twenty minutes later, Collin returned on a dead run. No sooner than he had jumped into the car than a set of headlights came bouncing down the driveway out of the trees. "Head down," Collin shouted as he ducked under the dashboard. The lights raked the car, temporarily blinding them.

"My God. Look at that," Kathy cried as the vehicle swept by them onto the River Road. "That old panel truck has children squeezed into the back. I saw them when one pushed the back cover aside."

Collin started the car and eased the hand throttle forward as he swung the Lizzie around.

"We're goin' to follow them with our lights off," he cautioned. "Keep your eyes peeled."

The truck was lumbering slowly, laden down with its tattered cargo. Collin caught up and settled behind it at a safe follow distance. The rain had stopped and the sun popped up over the eastern horizon.

"There are two main buildings," he explained. "The one at the end of the driveway is stone with a columned front entrance. But there is another ramshackle, wooden dormitory-like building a half mile back in the woods, down a mud track and behind a locked fence. The sign on that gate says 'Attack Dogs.' It looks like that barbed wire fence goes completely around the compound. And you can't see it from the main orphanage." Collin gripped the wheel tightly. The windshield still had droplets of water from the rain that sparkled in the sunlight.

"When I got to the gate I saw armed guards loading children into the truck. They looked completely ragamuffin and exhausted. Then the truck started off towards me."

"So there's a slave camp hidden behind the Orphanage back in the trees," Kathy said. "The Orphanage must just be a front. That is terrible!"

"You said it, darlin'."

They continued to follow the truck in silence, each imagining the worst for those poor children.

Finally Collin blurted out, "If Claire is in there, I'm goin' to kill Fredricson."

"And if she's not?"

"I'm goin' to kill Fredricson."

He instantly regretted saying it. *Shite, I've killed three men now, giving in to my animal instincts. I'm only good when I'm usin' my fists. What must Kathy think of me? I hate myself. Why can't I just find my little sister?*

"Yes, he must be stopped and the authorities won't do it since he is the highly respected Police Chief," Kathy said, rubbing the inside of the windscreen that was fogging up again. "But let's find a way without your killing him, lover."

"Right enough, darlin'. But first things first. Let's find Claire and then stay alive, in that order."

Captain Fredricson was an early riser. He'd been out at the Orphanage the previous afternoon dealing with discipline problems. One of the children had just died of consumption and had to be disposed of. When he strode into the precinct as per normal at six that morning, he was in a foul mood.

"Where's Williams?" he demanded of the front desk officer on duty.

"He's in his office, sir."

"Well, get him, man."

To his adjutant, he barked, "Bring me up to speed from yesterday."

"No news on the homicide in the student dorms at Brown, but we made an arrest in the prostitution case yesterday, sir," Williams answered, checking his notes.

"Anything else?"

"It's probably nothing, but a couple of Micks were in here yesterday looking for a lost sister, named Claire O'Donnell. They didn't file a missing person, though. Kind of an odd pair, them."

"What'cha tell them?"

"Nothing, sir. There was nothing *to* tell them."

"These people could be subversives. The Irish are known to be working with the Germans," Fredricson suggested. "Trying to undermine our American institutions."

"I hadn't thought of it that way, sir."

"Leave me for a few minutes."

Once alone, Fredricson telephoned his Head of Security at the orphanage. "Smitty, you seen anyone that shouldn't be hangin' around over there? An Irishman and his girl?"

"Nope, nothing like that. Everything's tight as a drum this morning. The early shift left on schedule at five fifteen for the Mill. Just two of the children who went are sickly today."

"Well, keep your eyes open. I may be out there again today." The Chief rang off abruptly.

Crap . . . Two more problems to take care of. Smitty would get in touch with him if they showed up there. *I'd better go to the Mill*, he decided.

When Williams returned, Fredricson told him to get Stanley. "We've got to go find these impostors."

❧❧❧❧

"Looks like more than a dozen crammed into the back of that vehicle. They're packed like sardines," Kathy noted. "Poor kids."

As they continued to follow the truck, they entered an industrialized area and saw a sign saying, "Welcome to Woonsocket, Textile Capital of the World." A few minutes later, on South Main Street, they crossed a raging river, with a thirty-foot falls on their left, and saw the placard "Blackstone, the Hardest Working River in America." The truck abruptly stopped just east of the bridge at Market Square. Collin drove on farther down Main Street and stopped as well. The street was lined with old factory buildings.

"Look behind here," Collin whispered, craning his neck to peer through the rear window. The children are gettin' out of the truck. Eleven, twelve thirteen of them."

"My God, Collin. Some of them are only about ten years old. And look at the rags they're wearing."

"But that girl in the back looks to be about eighteen or twenty, I'm thinking."

"See that thug shepherding them along with a night stick? Did you see that? He just cuffed that young boy on the head."

"What's the name on that building they're entering, darlin'?"

Kathy rolled down her side window and cautiously peered out. "The sign over the door says 'Lippitt Woolen Company'. It's a sturdy three-story brick building with a mansard roof. But I see another factory further down Main that has the same name. Must be quite a big operation."

They waited to see what would happen next.

Suddenly, a set of side doors of the factory opened and disgorged fifteen of the most bedraggled looking urchins that they had ever seen. They were all exhausted and hunched over. As a human being, Kathy was mortified. As a teacher, she was infuriated.

"Don't you get out of this automobile," Collin cautioned as Kathy reached for the door handle.

"But . . ."

"But nothing. Let them be."

"We've got to do something to help these children."

"We will. But first, Claire. It looks like she isn't among any of these groups of orphans."

"Are you sure that you'd recognize her if you saw her in such a condition?"

"I . . . I think so. Most of these urchins aren't old enough."

"How about that older girl?"

"No, I don't think so."

They watched as the same thug whipped them all up into the truck. Then it drove off, leaving Collin and Kathy sickened and angry.

"How can that man treat children like that?" Kathy cried.

"It's one thing to read about it and quite another to see it first hand," Collin said, wiping her cheek with his handkerchief.

"Uh huh."

"We have to stay strong and focused, darlin'," Collin said, leaning over and hugging her close. "I need your help."

A few minutes passed. Collin formulated a plan.

"Well, I'm ready to help. What are we going to do?" Kathy announced smoothing her hair from her face.

"We need to get inside this factory to see what is goin' on. Maybe there will be a manager that will remember Claire."

"How do you propose that we do that? Won't we just stand out like a sore thumb?"

"Not if we're customers and fellow manufacturers," Collin offered. "Look, I am Liam Magee from Donegal. You are my secretary, Colleen O'Hara. My family has been in the textile business for a hundred years. As it happens, there is such a family and I am wearing one of their herringbone tweed jackets this morning to ward off the cold."

"Where do you come up with this stuff, lover?"

"We newspaper men have all the Blarney, don't ya know."

"Do ya now?"

"There's no doubt of it," Collin joked, giving his girl a peck on the cheek. "Right enough then. That's sorted."

"I suppose that ruse is as good as any. What do you know about the textile business anyway?"

"Not a stitch, my dear."

They looked quite official, though their clothes were wrinkled and not a little damp as they strode up to the Lippitt Woolen Company front door. Kathy had been keeping records of their expenses in a notebook, which she carried under her arm. And her pencil, as usual, was tucked behind her ear.

"Look at that placard beside the door," Collin said before they rang the bell.

Embossed in scroll gold lettering on black background, it read, *Owner: Charles Warren Lippitt, former Governor of Rhode Island, 1895-1897*. And below that, on a much older plaque, was the statement *Formerly, the Harrison Mill*.

A pert secretary answered their ring and ushered them into the plush wood-paneled foyer.

"*Bonjour*. What can I do for you today?" she asked them.

Collin explained who they were and they had come from Ireland to visit textile manufacturers in America to learn about their modern ways of working.

"We understand that Mr. Lippitt's mills are among the most advanced in the world," Collin pandered. "Would it be possible to have a tour of your factory today?"

After signing the visitor register with their fictitious names, they were shown up the polished wooden staircase and into Monsieur Gauthier's office. He was introduced as the head of operations for the Mill.

"Bonjour, Monsieur Magee et Mademoiselle O'Hara," he gushed, coming around his massive desk and shaking their hands with gusto. "I hope you will excuse my poor English. Like many of our citizens in this town, I am Québécois, me. *Nous sommes tres fier, er . . . excuse moi.* We are very proud of our modern processes and productivity here at Lippitt's. I notice that you are wearing a fine jacket. Is that your product?" he asked as he stroked the coat with his fingers. "*Mais oui,* I see the label. A very nice tweed, *n'est pas?* I would be pleased to show you our factory if you will explain how you make this lovely soft fabric."

"I'd be happy to do so, sir, after we finish our tour."

"*D'accord.* Come this way, my friends." He strode to the back wall of his stately wood-paneled office to a wall-to-wall drape, and opened it.

There, through the glass window, they could see the factory floor down below.

"This is impressive," Collin observed, mentally counting. "There must be five hundred spindles working out there."

"Seven hundred and twenty-five to be exact," Gauthier corrected proudly. "And we have another seven hundred and seventy-five in the factory down the street. The water flow from the waterfall is channeled behind these buildings to give the power to operate that many at a time."

"Back home we only have a few spindles in our workshop, all manual labor. This is fascinating."

Kathy was examining the factory closely while the men talked. She could see the mass of humanity darting in and out of the whirring looms and other machines. It looked like chaos to her, a myriad of belts and pulleys and moving shuttles that could break or dismember an errant hand or arm. Several workers sweated from the heat and steam. Many were poorly dressed—children whose tattered clothing could easily get caught in the machinery. There must have been a hundred children out there, nearly half the workforce. She could also see the foremen aggressively urging the workers on with night stick prods where there was resistance.

"I'd like to go down onto the factory floor and examine the machinery more closely. Would that be all right?" Collin asked.

"*Mais oui.* Let us go." The manager was anxious to show off his modern industrial wonder. He handed Collin his business card.

They walked down out of the pleasant wood polished office area and through a door marked 'Factory Floor'. Once inside, Collin and Kathy's senses were assaulted. The beating and humming noise was deafening. The smell of the machinery and the chemicals used to treat the wool was so acrid that it burned their noses. Dense flying lint particles made them cough. And if all this wasn't enough, the heat and humidity were unbearable. Kathy felt so sorry for the workers, particularly the children.

The manager started his spiel: "What you see here is just the upper floor. Below us is another section where the dyeing and conditioning of the raw wool is done. That is also where the water wheel powers the bands that run the machines up here. Would you want to see that operation later?"

"That would be splendid."

"This floor is set up as four production lines, arranged in order," he went on. "Picking, carding and spinning are all driven by water power. Only the weaving looms over there are manual. We employ young people to oil the machinery and for other functions where their small size permits access."

"Isn't it dangerous for those children to be working among all those moving belts and spindles?" Kathy asked, pointing at one smal urchin darting under a high speed belt.

201

"They're well trained and well paid for those functions," Gauthier responded. "They get fifty cents a day which their parents need."

"And how many hours do they work a day?" Collin asked.

"Mr. Lippitt has recently reduced the time per shift as a measure to improve the working conditions for the young. They normally only work twelve hours a day now, except of course, when we have rush orders."

Kathy noticed the older girl that they had seen getting out of the truck. She had been working a weaving machine and was arguing with one of the foremen.

"Give me Claire's picture," she whispered in Collin's ear. He obliged and Gauthier, caught up in his rhetoric, didn't notice the exchange.

"Excuse me, sir. I'll be right back," she said aloud.

The men were heading off to the carding department, and Gauthier didn't notice Kathy's departure as she sauntered over near to the girl and foreman. She could hear the girl begging him to let her go to the toilet and he was ordering her to keep working. Just as he started to raise his stick to strike her, Kathy intervened.

"Cherise, I found you," she exclaimed, and tried to catch the girl's eye. "Are you bleeding again, dear?"

The girl caught on. "Yes, my period is very bad. I feel dizzy."

The foreman lowered his arm. "Who do you think you are, wench?"

"I'm the new matron that makes sure our girls don't get sick. That's who I am. You want Cherise, here, to pass out from loss of blood and damage the loom?"

"Er . . . no," the foreman admitted. "She didn't tell me she was bleedin' on her."

"Well, ask next time before you cause a big problem."

"Yes, ma'am," he stammered.

With that, Kathy grabbed the girl by the hand and pulled her away from the foreman and the machine.

"Which way to the toilet, dear?" she whispered to the confused young woman.

"That door over there," she pointed and Kathy whisked her through.

The washroom was vacant.

"Thank you, ma'am, for helping me out there. I'm burstin' with pee, me."

While she did her business, Kathy started her questioning.

"What's your real name, young lady?"

"Lucy Daggett."

"So, Lucy, tell me. Do you stay at the orphanage?"

"We're not allowed to talk about the orphanage, Ma'am. Do you really work here?"

Kathy had to make a quick decision. The foreman would be checking up soon.

As Lucy emerged from the stall, Kathy held her hand.

"No, I don't work here. My friend's sister was forced to live at the orphanage and likely to work here. I am desperately trying to find her."

She showed Lucy the photograph.

"That's Gertie. They called her Gertie. She said her real name was Claire." Lucy exclaimed. "But she doesn't look like that anymore."

"Yes, that's right, Lucy. Do you know where she is?" Kathy asked anxiously.

"No. She disappeared four months back. We think she's probably been killed like the others."

Kathy's heart sank. "The others?"

"The few girls what tried to escape before. We heard things."

"What else can you tell me, Lucy?"

"I've been captive at the orphanage for four years. Claire was there when I got there, her. She was a couple of years older than me. We were best friends and talked a lot about how we could break away and start our own lives. But they control us. It's really a prison."

Kathy realized they were back to zero. "I'm going to help you escape, Lucy. Trust me, please. Can you tell me anything more that might help me about Claire?"

"Well, when she turned eighteen she chose to stay with us instead of going to Providence to . . . you know."

"To what, Lucy?"

"To, well, to satisfy men."

"You mean, be a prostitute?"

"Yeah. They control that, too. I'll be getting that choice when I turn eighteen in a few months."

"I promise you, Lucy. That won't be necessary. What else can you tell me? Quickly, girl."

"She was like Florence Nightingale, her, ma'am."

"What do you mean?"

"Well, lots of us got sick or injured," Lucy related. "Some even died, like Frank yesterday. Claire was kind of our nurse. She had a lot of inner strength. She taught herself how to stitch a cut, set a broken leg, and all that. She looked out for us as if we were her own. We all loved her." Lucy rolled up her sleeve showing an old fracture of her forearm. "See?"

"Seems she was someone special. Can you remember anything abnormal that happened at the orphanage when she disappeared? Anything at all?"

"It was just this March. But it was here, not at the orphanage. One of the boys that worked here, Marty, he got his leg mangled in a carding machine. Usual like, Claire rushed to help him. There was a young stranger visiting the factory that morning, must have been a doctor or something. He jumped in to help and they let Claire help Marty outside with him I heard them say he would take Marty to hospital. It was quite confusing with blood spurting everywhere. We heard later that day that Marty had died and Claire had run away. Last we ever saw of her. We are real upset. We loved and needed her so."

"I see," said Kathy at this possible lead. "We'd better get back out there now, before you're missed."

Then she gave the girl a hug and promised, "I will get you and your friends freed somehow soon."

Lucy started crying and gave her a big hug back. "Thank you," she sobbed through her tears.

When they returned to the factory floor the foreman was heading their way. He grabbed Lucy by the arm and half-dragged her back to her machine, glowering at Kathy. Kathy looked around for Collin. He was just coming up stairs from the lower level, with Gauthier at his heels. Kathy walked quickly over to them and said, "You about done, sir? It's time that we're on our way." She gave Collin a knowing nod. He looked puzzled.

"Well, that about does the tour, Monsieur. Can we go to my office now so you can tell me about your operation in Donegal?" Gauthier asked.

"Certainly, sir," Collin replied, giving Kathy the eye roll warning flag.

In return, Kathy gave him a 'we've-got-to-go' gesture with her head.

They exited into the lower level office complex just in time to see Detective Williams and an angry looking giant of a man starting down the stairs from the front foyer with the pert secretary. Williams pointed towards them.

Damn, Collin thought. *That must be Fredricson. We're trapped.*

"Stop them, they're Irish imposters, probably German spies!" Fredricson yelled, jumping down the stairs two at a time.

Gauthier looked stunned and he froze in position.

Collin grabbed Kathy's hand and yanked her back through the factory door. He spied a mop standing in a receptacle by the door. Collin jammed it through the looped door handle. "C'mon," he urged Kathy as he moved to the outside service door the children had been forced through and opened it. He could see Stanley and another officer sitting in a police car at the end of the alley on Main Street. "Not that way," he whispered, turning back into the factory to seek a different path. The windows were too high up. The thought of escaping through the giant waterwheel on the lower level crossed his mind.

Collin saw the wild look in Kathy's eyes. *Shite. What a mess I've gotten us into. Another woman in my life in deadly trouble because of me.*

A banging started on the barricaded door and one foreman rushed towards it.

"Back through the door, Kathy. Keep moving," Collin urged as he turned and slipped through the tradesman's door into the alley, softly closing the door behind him.

Crouching low, he half dragged his girl away from the main street towards the river.

The alley was bounded on both sides by the adjacent factories towering above them. Looking skyward he saw that it was still cloudy, looking like rain again. Glancing backward he was thankful that the officers weren't looking in their direction . . . yet. Collin's elbow thudded into a solid obstruction. Scaffolding. The next door factory wall was starting to crack. At least he hadn't knocked any planks off the scaffold. He rubbed his arm to stop the tingling. The officers were still oblivious to their whereabouts.

The alley ended abruptly at a metal railing between the back walls of the buildings. Beyond the railing, Collin and Kathy could see the river channel boiling past them along the plunging factory back wall. Downstream, Collin could make out the monstrous water wheel thrashing in its counter-rotation against the current. The width of the water channel was about ten feet, just enough room for the wheel, with a brick wall on the other side of the channel topping out at approximately the same height as the alley-way. In no way would Kathy be able to jump it, and it was certain death if they fell into the cauldron.

"We've got to find a way across this," Collin exclaimed, looking around for some form of bridging.

"You can't be serious!" Kathy cried above the din of the torrent.

"It will be suicide not to," Collin assured her grimly. "There's no other way out. Fredricson's not gonna' let us go, knowin' what we know. We'll disappear, just like many of those kids have likely gone."

"Can't you overpower the policemen?"

"No telling how many are out there and sure it is they've got guns," Collin decided. "No, we've got to cross this."

"What about that scaffolding?" she asked, pointing backwards up the alley.

"There's a girl," Collin exclaimed, rushing back to the metal structure. "This wooden plank might barely do," he guessed, estimating its length. Looked like about twelve feet. "Let's try it. Quiet now."

They slid the plank out of the framework. Kathy could barely lift one end. "You all right doing this?" Collin asked as she hefted the weight.

"It's got to be done," Kathy grunted.

"To be sure, darlin'."

After a struggle, they managed to get it to the railing. But then Collin realized they had another problem. The three-inch thick board would just span the channel but how were they going to support it horizontally to get it out to the other side. It must weigh at least fifty pounds.

He knew that Fredricson could burst through the side door at any moment.

Shite, this is all I can think of at the moment and we are out of time. "Kathy, let's line the board up to cross the channel with the closest end up over the bottom rung of the railing."

"What are you going to do? We can't just push it across."

"Yes, we can. I want you to push it towards the other side from the back end slowly," Collin instructed.

"I won't be able to keep it from falling in."

"Don't you be after worrying. I will be helping you," Collin assured her, stepping up and over the railing and grasping on to the top rung from the water side.

"Oh, God no, Collin," Kathy cried. "You're going to fall in."

"Not if I can help it. I am going to hold on with one hand and guide the board with the other," he exclaimed. "Let's go, darlin'."

"I'm afraid."

"So am I, but we can do this. We have to. We promised Sam we'd bring Lizzie back safe."

"Don't you be joking. Not now. It isn't funny," Kathy chided. "Be careful."

"Yes, push and try to hold your end down," Collin ordered, reaching out behind him as far as he dared with his free hand and lifting the board as it started sliding across the divide.

"How far is it?" he groaned a minute later when his arm started to go numb.

"About two thirds of the way, I think," Kathy answered, not wanting to lose her grip by looking around him. "But I can't hold it down much longer."

Collin realized his arm was not going to hold out much longer either. The weight was killing him.

"I want you to give one big push on your end," he said. "Down and out. Hard as you can. Now."

He braced himself for what would come next.

Kathy pushed with all her might and cried. "I can't hold it down."

The board slid through his outstretched hand and sagged downward. With all his remaining strength, Collin gripped the board, pulling it up flinging it outboard at the same time.

"Look out!" Kathy cried, as he lost his grip on the board and swung outward, his other hand slipping on the rail.

The outboard end of the board clattered on the brick on the other side. Collin lost his grip on the upper rung and started to fall, hitting the top of the board on his way down. That gave him a second to jab his arm out and he grabbed the lower rung. The end of the board bounced and slipped over the lower rung beside him. It was going to fall into the channel. Collin grabbed it with his other hand and held on for dear life. He was now hanging down below the level of the alleyway and the end of the board was down around his feet. The torrent pounded below him and the creaking wheel and mist swirled up around his torso. He couldn't hold the wet wood much longer. His left arm felt like it would come out of its socket.

At that moment, Kathy was at the rail with her arm reaching down and her hand locking on the bicep of his left arm. "I won't let you go," she exclaimed. "Can you raise the board up?"

Collin nodded and squeezed his shoulder blades. Slowly the end of the board started to rise until it was at waist level. Now his right bicep felt like it was on fire. Kathy's support was saving his shoulder socket, but his grip on the board was slipping as he squeezed it tighter and tighter.

With one last effort, Collin pulled and then pushed the board upward until it was at head level, about even with the alleyway.

"Can you grab the end and pull it back under the rung onto the alley?" he cried, not knowing how much longer he could hold it and the rung. "You can let go of me for a moment."

When Kathy refused to let go he added, "Do it now. I can't hold it much longer."

Kathy obeyed and was able to pull the board onto dry land.

"Not too far or it will come off the other side," Collin cried in alarm.

A moment later the board came to rest, safely supported on both sides of the abyss, but only by about a foot at either end.

Moments later, Kathy reapplied her grip on her love, averting her eyes from the cauldron below.

"Give us a hand, darlin'," Collin urged as his arm was about to give out.

He groaned upward until he had both hands on the lower rung. Then he let go with his left hand and Kathy pulled up on his arm until he could grasp the upper rung. A minute later he was up and over the railing and sitting on the alleyway rubbing his left shoulder.

"Oh, Collin. I was so scared," Kathy cried, flinging her arms around him and holding tight.

"You and me both," Collin admitted. "We'd best be going, darlin'," he urged, standing up and pulling her up with him. He knew that every second counted.

"You need to follow me across our bridge. Watch," he said, as he stepped once more over the railing, this time onto the board. Testing it, he found it somewhat wobbly, since it wasn't completely flat on the other side. Stepping cautiously and raising his arms horizontally for balance, he traversed the span in a couple of seconds until he was standing on the other side.

"See. It's easy. Don't rush your fences and you'll get the right of it."

"I don't think . . ."

"That's right, darlin'. Don't think and don't look down. Just do it with your arms outstretched to balance you. I'll catch you on this side." Collin put all his weight on his end to the board to help stabilize it.

Jodhpur breeches enabled Kathy to climb unencumbered up onto the railing. But there she sat looking down at the torrent below.

"Kathleen, you can do this. I need you to do this now," Collin ordered.

Slowly, Kathy turned and lowered herself onto the ten-inch-wide plank. She was looking back at the alleyway and holding the upper rung fiercely.

"You need to turn around and look at me, Kathleen. Look only at me."

Collin thought that he was going to have to cross over and carry her back.

Kathy turned around and faced him, still holding the rung behind her.

Her wild blue eyes were riveted on his. *God help her,* he prayed, crossing himself.

"Just remember when our eyes locked at the regatta," Collin suggested, hoping it would calm her down.

He thought he saw a flicker of recognition in that penetrating stare, and the scowl started to lift. "You need to let go and raise your arms while you walk to me, darlin'. You can do this, just like I did."

Collin could see that she was too frightened to speak or even to breathe.

Then, all at once, she let go and raised her arms. Before she took her first step she swayed sidewise until she got the feel of her arms for balance. Then she stepped out. One, two, three steps.

She was mid-span when it happened. Her right foot shifted slightly and caught the edge of the board. Her right knee started to buckle.

"Push off with your left leg," Collin cried and he started to step forward out onto the board to meet her. The board rocked precariously to the right, but she did as he had commanded. There was only about five feet to go, less than her height. So as she lurched forward, she met him just at the edge of the wall. Her forward momentum pushed them both backwards as he sought to grasp her firmly. Collin felt the shock of pain in his left shoulder, but he held on and pulled her to safety on the ground just as the board fell out from under him.

Down it went into the cauldron and was swept away in an instant. Moments later there was a grinding crash as the plank hit the waterwheel. The wheel shuddered but then resumed its motion, forced by the incredible power of the torrent. Collin could see the gouge of the paddles as it rose up out of the depths.

"Quick. Over here," Collin whispered. The ground fell away from the wall on the other side down a grassy slope. Collin dove over the edge, pulling Kathy along with him. Although it had seemed like an eternity, their crossing had taken only eight minutes since they had left the Mill.

Collin and Kathy lay together on the slope behind the wall completely spent, but alive. The water continued its rush to the sea, oblivious to how close to death the two had come due to the water's power and treachery.

Chapter Fifteen
The Chase

Woonsockott, Rhode Island

*F*rom down the alleyway, Collin heard the factory metal side door slam open. He dared not look. "Keep your head down," he whispered, holding his finger across his moustache. Kathy nodded. They heard voices nearby.

"Stanley, get over here. Leave Timmins there," someone bellowed. It sounded hollow echoing down the alleyway.

"They go your way?" the voice barked.

"No, boss. Nobody came our way."

"You sure, you?"

"Yes, sir."

"The workers heard a crash out back," the voice yelled, getting closer.

"I heard it too when we were down by the dyeing room."

That voice sounded like Williams, Collin thought.

"Back this way, men," the first voice commanded. 'Must be Fredricson', Collin decided.

"Look. By the rail here. Scuff marks in the dirt," Williams yelled, his voice quite close now.

"They could never have jumped this," Fredricson announced. "The rail would have stopped them from taking a run at it."

"Can't see any marks on the far side, boss. Wait. Look at the wheel. See that chunk out of that paddle?"

"Damn. It would have been suicide to try. But German spies would be ordered to face death before capture if trapped."

"Are there logs in this river?" Stanley asked.

"I would think they would trap any debris upstream."

"How can we get across to the other side of this channel?"

"You said it yourself, boss. There's no way."

"Detective?" Fredricson yelled.

"The bridge upstream to the right at the end of Main Street," Williams answered.

"Back to the street," the Chief ordered.

Collin heard them running back down the alley. A minute later he heard Fredricson shout, "You stay with the car, Stanley. You come with me, Williams."

"Now it's our turn to skedaddle," Collin said, standing up cautiously to confirm that the coppers had left the alley. He could barely see the police car in the distance, so he ducked again and led Kathy down the grass embankment past the waterwheel and away from the Main Street Bridge. He checked that they had not disturbed the soil or clodded the grass.

There was a stand of trees at the bottom of the embankment, so they slipped down among them and headed downstream. In about a quarter mile they came to another bridge at the other end of Main Street. Up and over brought them back into the town on the far end of the street, beyond the textile mills.

"Quick, out of sight," Collin urged, pulling Kathy across Main Street and darting amongst the stores on the far side.

They circled around behind the stores to where they could observe the front of the factory without being seen. Lizzie was where they had left her, exposed. Stanley was guarding the front entrance of Lippitt's Mill, gun in hand. And the other copper was sitting in the police car only fifty feet or so to the right of Lizzie, seemingly asleep.

Suddenly Fredricson and Williams emerged onto Main Street down to the left of where they had come, and started running past the mills towards the police car.

"Stanley, you and Timmins. Seen anyone?"

"No, boss. No one came out of the Mill."

"I mean down this street," Fredricson bellowed.

"Nobody suspicious," Stanley groveled.

"Well, we're not sure, but the grass back there was matted down," Williams announced, wheezing and out of breath.

"Is it possible they escaped that way?" Stanley asked, trying to divert his boss's attention.

"We don't know," Williams answered. "I still don't think they could have jumped that river."

"Stanley, you check the Mill again with me. Those guards are no damned good. I'm going to interrogate Gauthier." Fredricson's large frame shook as he roared orders. "Timmins, Williams. You search all the buildings on this street. If they're not in the factory then maybe they're hiding somewhere else."

They split up and each one darted into a building nearby. Stanley disappeared through the front door into the Mill.

"This is our chance," Collin whispered. They scurried down between the buildings until they were opposite Sam's car. Then they sauntered toward the Ford.

"Duck," ordered Collin, as he saw Williams come out of one building and go into another near their location.

"Kathy, stay down while I get us outta here," he said as he started the car and put it into first gear. They drove slowly down Main Street without the police reappearing. Turning right, they crossed the Blackstone River on Court Street heading for Providence.

"We're damn unlucky that the police came when they did. I think I could have got some information about Claire outta Gauthier," Collin grumbled as he opened the hand throttle.

"All is not lost. I have news," Kathy told him, placing her hand on his right leg. "We've been so busy that I couldn't tell you until now."

After she relayed what she had obtained from Lucy, Collin pulled the car over to the curb and gave her a big smooch. "My turn to thank you," he laughed. "How'd you do it?"

"Just a little woman-to-woman chit chat, my love. Out of your league, really. By the way, I promised Lucy that I would help her and the others escape from the orphanage."

"That's precisely what we're after doin' for the rest of the day," Collin jibed, putting his right hand over hers and squeezing.

"What? That water torture must have addled your brain. Don't you think we've had enough excitement for one day?"

"You'll see."

Minutes later the four officers returned to their police car empty-handed. Williams was sure someone was going to get fired, or worse.

"Say, what happened to that new Ford that was out here on Main Street?" Timmins exclaimed.

"What Ford?" Fredricson shouted.

"The one that had the Canada license plates."

"Did you get the plate number?" Fredricson demanded.

"Yes, boss. "Finlay4RT. It's a new black Ford Model T Sedan."

"Damn. "Why didn't you tell me about this sooner?"

Timmins cringed.

"Wait a minute. Didn't Gauthier say they asked where the Governor lived?"

"Yes, Chief. Said that he gave them one of the Governor's business cards from the front desk."

"Quick, boys. Back in the car. Let's go. Down Old River Road to the mansion."

"Hey, we just passed the orphanage," Kathy pointed out as they flashed by the cemetery. Collin had the hand crank throttle pulled wide open.

"I know. Get out the map, dear. We're gonna make an important house call."

"You're joking. They'll be chasing after us, you know. And with this new sedan, we'll be hard to miss."

"Probably. Here, find this location on the map," Collin asked, as he took the business card out of his pocket.

"Who's this?" Kathy stared at the card, holding it near the window to see the name. "The factory owner and a former Governor of this fine State, darlin'. I hope he's home." Collin's real hope was that former Governor Charles Warren Lippitt would be an honorable man.

"I see the Lippitt Memorial Park on Hope Street. This card shows the Governor Henry Lippitt mansion to be at 199 Hope. Well now. There are two of them."

"Two of what?"

"Former Governors named Lippitt. It says so on the map's legend."

"Well, I sure hope that one of them is home."

"The mansion must be right near the memorial park," Kathy craned her neck toward the glass.

"Good. How do we get there?"

"When we reach the south end of the Old River Road, we need to turn left on Front Street to go to Valley Falls. Then we can turn right on Broad Street heading south through Pawtucket. It eventually becomes Hope Street.

"How long, do you think?"

"I'd say thirty minutes give or take."

"Let's make it in twenty," Collin exclaimed urging Lizzie onward.

Twenty-two minutes later they were on Hope Street leaving Pawtucket behind them.

"There, up ahead," Collin pointed. "Where a road splits off to the right."

"That's Blackstone Boulevard." Kathy peered at the map. "This should be the place."

"I see a park but there's no mansion here," Collin said, slowing down to a crawl. "What's the number of that house on the right?"

"The address is 1020 Hope Street," Kathy answered, squinting to read the number on the front door.

"Shite, we're too far north. Keep a look out for something looking like a mansion," Collin requested, gunning the Lizzie.

Soon after, the house numbers were in the three hundreds. "Look there's Hope Street High School on the right. There it is—324."

"Getting close," Collin said, navigating Lizzie through a curve to the right.

That's when he heard it, faint at first.

"Look behind us," Collin shouted, not wanting to take his eyes off the road.

"Car with a flashing light back there. Police?"

"You can bet on it," Collin barked, pulling the throttle wide open. "To hell with other traffic."

Cross-streets flashed by with no mansion of any kind. At one intersection Collin had to swerve to miss a horse and buggy that threatened his flank.

"It *is* the police," Kathy announced. "I think it's the same car that was outside the Mill. They're only two streets back now."

"*Shite.* Fredricson." Lizzie was straining on her blocks. "How the hell did he know where we were going?"

Passing the next street, he spied an opulent three-story brownstone Victorian ahead on the left. "We're coming up to Angell Street. I think I see it. It's got to be it. Hope and Angell. The circular drive is on Angell. Hold on."

Entering the intersection at high speed, Collin misjudged the turn. Lizzie groaned up on two right wheels and the dinged front one popped.

"Look out!" Collin cried as Lizzie swerved to the right crashing into the first driveway entrance pillar and metal fencing.

The police car was bearing down on the Angell Street intersection, its siren almost deafening now.

"Get out my side," Collin ordered, seeing the damage to the passenger side of the vehicle. "Hurry now."

"My foot is stuck. Help me."

Glancing back he could see the cop car come to rest behind them. The doors were opening.

He reached down and yanked on Kathy's ankle.

"Ouch," she cried as her foot ripped out of her pinned boot.

"Come on," Collin urged, pulling her across the driver's side and out onto the cobblestones.

Kathy stood up as if to run, but her ankle couldn't support her weight.

"Stop in the name of the law, you German spies," Fredricson yelled bringing his gun up to level.

Swooping Kathy up in a fireman's carry, Collin left the car door open as a shield while he made his way into the short circular drive and darted under the arched stucco portico. Lowering Kathy gently to the ground, he reached for the doorbell.

Several guns were trained on them.

"Don't you dare push that button, you imposter," Fredricson hissed as he stepped to the edge of the porch. "You are both under arrest."

At that moment, the front door of the mansion opened. A well-dressed elderly gentleman, with a bristling moustache and a penetrating stare, surveyed the scene and demanded, "What's going on here, Fredricson?"

Fredricson knew Governor Charles Lippitt well. He had had run-ins with him on several occasions. Lippitt was always interfering, siding with the workers at the Mill. He had been the instigator of curbing child abuse in his state and its factories to the extent that good business would allow. The Chief hated the man. His interference cut down on revenue.

"Just a routine police matter, sir. No need to trouble yourself with it."

"With all those guns pointed at me, it looks like anything but routine," the Governor countered.

"Put your guns down," Fredricson ordered. He lowered his own weapon, but he did not put the safety on nor did he holster it.

Collin sat Kathy down on the steps.

"What police business?" Lippitt pressed.

"These two Irish imposters misrepresented themselves at your Woonsocket factory this morning. We think they are spies for the Germans. I am going to take them in for questioning."

Governor Lippitt looked Collin and Kathy up and down with a suspicious eye.

"Well, what do you have to say for yourself?" he asked Collin.

Fredricson cut him off. "These are fugitives from the law and under my jurisdiction, not yours. Come on, you two. We're going down to the precinct."

Collin stood his ground and looked Governor Lippitt square in the face.

He opened his mouth to speak, but before he could say a word, Fredricson stepped forward and jammed his gun to Collin's throat. He whispered in his ear, "Don't talk or you are a dead man."

In the twinkling of an eye, with one deft jab with his right hand, Collin grabbed the gun and broke the Chief's trigger finger. Then he calmly handed the gun to Governor Lippitt, butt first. The officers immediately redrew their side-arms in support of their boss.

Governor Lippitt defused the volatile situation. "Stand down your weapons. I'm going to hear from this man. Go on, son."

The officers once again lowered their handguns and Fredricson started looking around for a way out.

"Sir, we've come to see you today to expose a corrupt business going on in your State, in fact in Providence." He chose to avoid implicating the Mill. "My twelve-year-old sister was abducted in Brooklyn and sold into slavery. The purchaser was Mr. Fredricson here. He bought her for twenty dollars. We found out today that she, and many other girls and young women, have been held prisoner in Mr. Fredricson's Providence Orphanage. He does this so that he can sell slave labor to the factories around here, including your Lippitt Woolen Company in Woonsocket. We have reason to believe that many if not all of the inmates at the orphanage are purchased slaves. Also, with the cruel treatment imposed at the orphanage, we think that some of the child injuries, and deaths, including damage to a girl named Frankie yesterday, were caused by Mr. Fredricson's actions."

"And what makes matters worse, is that many of the young women have been forced into a prostitution ring that Mr. Fredricson controls in downtown Providence," Kathy added.

"What hogwash," the Chief screamed, frantically looking to his men for help. "These misfits are concocting an absurd story to mask their real purpose here; that is espionage for the Germans. Let me take 'em downtown. I'll get the truth out of 'em."

Governor Lippitt ignored Fredricson's ranting. "This man doesn't sound Irish to me. New York accent if anything," Turning to Collin, "What proof do you have of your assertions in this matter?"

Collin took Enrico's sheet of records out of his pocket and handed it to the Governor.

"We obtained this two days ago in Brooklyn from the despicable man who sold all those children into slavery. This is only one of several such record pages. The total amounts to over one hundred slaves over the years. You will note that my sister, Claire O'Donnell, was sold on June third 1906 to Mr. Fredricson here."

"It could be any Fredricson," the Chief protested.

"You will notice it refers to Fredricson, Providence. Also you will note that there are twenty-one slaves who were purchased by

Fredricson of Providence on this sheet alone. I bet that an inspection of the orphanage would show that these slaves all ended up there. As an example, we met one girl, Lucy, today, an orphanage inmate who works at your factory. She says she was brought there as a slave four years ago."

"Can anyone else, other than your lady friend here, vouch for this evidence and what you say?" the Governor pressed.

"Yes, a Mr. Hank Handelman, the bartender at the establishment where these records were kept was present when they were recovered. He is in possession of the rest of these records. He was forced to work for the seller because his own son had been abducted by that fiend."

"Detective," the Governor addressed Williams. "Take Mr. Fredricson into custody until we can confirm all of these charges. I will speak to the Mayor this evening. Pending his decision, you are now temporary Chief of Police. Immediately begin an investigation into the operations of the Providence Orphanage. Get a search warrant from Judge Archer and raid the place tonight. The Mayor and I want a full report in the morning."

Williams and the other officers were stunned by these revelations. But they followed orders.

Drawing his weapon, Williams said, "Boss, er . . . Mr. Fredricson, you are under arrest."

Then as Williams went to handcuff the prisoner, Fredricson grabbed Williams' gun. Before any of the officers could react, Fredricson rushed up under the portico and put the gun to Governor Lippitt's head.

"Everybody move to the side. Put your guns away. The Governor is going to come with me as my guest."

In a flash, Collin's right palm caught Fredricson in the left shoulder temporarily paralyzing his arm. The gun fell to the ground. Collin's left jab hit the former Chief in the midsection, doubling him over. Collin grabbed him by the hair and put the head lock on him. *It would be so easy to snap his neck.* Instead, Collin hit him with a right cross to the jaw and knocked him unconscious.

"Where'd you learn to fight like that, son?" the Governor inquired.

"On the streets of Brooklyn, sir."

After the officers had taken their prisoner and left for the precinct, Collin and Kathy were left alone with the Governor.

"You folks look like you have been put through the ringer today," the Governor observed. "Why don't you come in and have something to eat?"

They didn't need to be given a second invitation. They both accepted with gratitude. Once they had been given a chance to freshen up and had eaten a hearty supper, they felt much better.

At the Governor's request, Collin related a blow-by-blow account of their adventures since they entered the United States, leaving out no details.

"Both of you have performed a great service for our community today," Governor Lippitt said when they had finished. "What can I do for you in return? Just name it."

"Sir, we started this venture to find out what happened to my sister. We now know that she was an inmate of the orphanage from 1906 to just three months ago. We also know that she disappeared the day that a boy named Marty was critically injured at the Mill. One of the inmates told us that they think she was killed for trying to escape. We would appreciate any assistance you could give to help us find her whereabouts, sir."

"I will have our office check into what might have happened the day your sister disappeared. Our receptionist keeps a record of visitors for my use and we have records of all serious accidents in the factory."

"Is there anything else I can do for you?"

"Well, you've seen the condition of our Tin Lizzie," Collin replied. "It would help to get 'er patched up, especially since she's not even mine." He coughed. "I'm sorry about your pillar and fence, sir."

"It's not a problem, son. I'll have your automobile towed and fixed. Now, I'm going to insist that you remain here as my guests until you feel better and until your car is repaired. I won't take no for an answer."

They both had no objection to that suggestion.

And Collin realized that his hope had come true. Here was a very reputable and decent man, the true pillar of Rhode Island society. And they had found him at the intersection of Angell and Hope Streets.

Governor Charles Lippitt was more than true to his word. On Saturday morning, Lizzie was brought to the mansion in pristine condition by a mechanic from the What Cheer Garage. They couldn't see a scratch on her.

"I've had a report on the situation at the orphanage," the Governor told them. "The conditions there are appalling. I got the Brooklyn police to get a copy of the other record sheets from Mr. Handelman. When we compared all of them to the real names of the inmates at the orphanage, we found that about a quarter of the hundred and twenty names from Brooklyn were brought in by Fredricson and his henchmen over the years, all girls just reaching puberty.

They forced the children to adopt new names when they got there, by the way. At least fifteen have died or disappeared while in residence there, including Frankie Bocello just five days ago. Fredricson and his guards have been brought up on murder charges, and the former Chief has been arraigned on thirty-three charges of illegal trafficking in human slavery."

"We're very happy to see that Fredricson and his cronies are behind bars," Collin assured him.

"Do you happen to know where Enrico Salazar is? The

Brooklyn Police want him for all these same charges and more."

I guess that Hank did take care of things. "Enrico can go to hell," he answered. "He's already there, I suspect. Now there's a picture to savor, sir."

The Governor continued. "All the residents of the false section of the orphanage are being placed temporarily in good foster homes, as we speak. In some cases we are able to contact the real relatives to get them reunited as soon as possible. Lucy says thank you so much, Kathy. She says that all the girls want you to know that you have saved their lives. And I heard from the Brooklyn Police that Mr. Handelman already has his son back with him."

"This is great news for all of them," Kathy said, looking over at Collin. "But what about Claire?"

"I saved the best for last," the Governor smiled. "We found two records at the office. On February fourteenth Marty Feldman was injured badly by a carding machine and subsequently died. Very regrettable, to be sure. There was a young man who signed in as Byron Harrison that morning. Did you notice the plaques at the front door of our factory today?" the Governor asked.

"Formerly Harrison Mills," Kathy replied.

"Yes, that's right. You've got a bright young lady with you, son."

"I questioned the receptionist myself. The young man present-ed himself as a descendent of the Harris family that sold the Mill to my father Henry many years ago. Said he lived in New York City and worked at Beth Israel hospital, which explains why he provided medical support for the lad. It seems he was tracing his roots. He did as Lucy told you, and he and your sister left with the injured lad. The receptionist said there was a great hue and cry to find Claire. She hasn't ever seen her again."

Collin couldn't believe it. Claire was alive three months ago. *Maybe Byron Harrison helped her get away.* He crossed himself and bowed his head.

"I think you're right," the Governor offered, noting Collin's gesture. "I called the police in Brooklyn. They said someone claiming to be your sister came to them with a young man about three months ago with a crazy story."

"She is alive," Collin cried.

"What did the police do about it?" Kathy asked.

"They said they discounted it. It was too long ago with no leads to work on."

"What about contacting authorities here?"

"They said they did. Providence Police force."

"Fredricson. No wonder. Claire probably didn't know that he was the police chief."

"That notation in Enrico's notebook opposite Claire," Collin said.

"What notation?" the Governor asked, perking up on the conversation.

"Fredricson says to go get her."

The Governor's forehead creased as he raised his eyebrows.

"Beg pardon, what?"

"It looks like Fredricson warned Enrico your sister had escaped. He must have known that Byron lived in New York City."

"But that means . . ." Kathy started twirling her hair.

Collin filled in the blanks. "That Enrico might have been after Claire."

"It would seem so, my boy. If I were you two, I would check with Beth Israel Hospital when their personnel office opens on Monday."

"That's all that we could have hoped for. This is great news, sir. But we have to get back to New York City immediately. Thank you so much!" Collin shook the Governor's hand with vigor.

"Not at all, my boy. Least I could do under the circumstances."

Kathy gave the Governor a big hug. His face turned beet red. "Try to get that work day down to ten hours, sir," she whispered in his ear. "And how about schooling on site at the Mill as well?"

"I'll give that some thought, young lady," the Mill owner answered, stroking his ample chin. "All in good time."

As the young couple bid their farewells and drove off in the Lizzie, Governor Lippitt waved, and then strode back into his mansion.

His butler met him at the door. "I checked and they haven't seen Byron Harrison for a month or more at Beth Israel Hospital. I fear the worst."

"Well then, Stuart, make sure Collin and Kathy are taken care of in New York. They're special people."

Chapter Sixteen
Discovery

Saturday, June 5, 1915
Jersey City, New Jersey

*T*hey arrived back at the Jersey City Hotel in time for supper. The implications from Enrico's note weighed heavy on their hearts. Time was of the essence.

"I should have questioned him before he died. Just like Weston. Shite, I'm too quick with my fists."

Kathy had been hearing this all the way back from Rhode Island. She was tired of telling him over and over that he did what he had to do to save their lives.

"I'm sure that Claire would have been able to stay safely away from Enrico. Otherwise he would have said something to you about it when he was gloating."

"Maybe. Maybe not. I'm still worried until we find her."

"From a glass half full perspective, at least we're alive, and we saved an orphanage full of girls and boys," Kathy mused.

"I'll grant you that, but we still don't know how to contact this Byron Harrison, do we now?"

"Tomorrow we will go to the hospital even if their personnel office is closed on Sunday. We'll find him and then Claire. You'll see, my love."

After supper they went out on the roof terrace and viewed the majestic skyline of New York across the East River.

Hugging Collin, Kathy said ruefully, "It is tragic that such terrible things can happen in a city that is so beautiful."

Collin leaned over and kissed her on the cheek, saying, "Amen to that, darlin'."

"Tomorrow we will find her, dear. I can feel it."

"We'll see," said the man who still saw the glass as half-empty.

Sunday dawned with radiant sunshine. They went into the city mid-morning, excited to have traced Claire's whereabouts from 1906 to a few weeks ago, yet worried.

"How ironic," Kathy said, when they reached Stuyvesant Square in Lower Manhattan.

"How so?"

"That Claire returned to the city from which she was abducted."

"But this is an entirely different New York City from the world that I was brought up in."

They had brought a picnic basket with them, so they sprawled on the grass of a nearby public park under the stately English elm and little-leaf Linden trees and ate a romantic lunch.

Kathy had read up about Stuyvesant and the Square in a book entitled *Manhattan 1900,* which she had found in the Governor's library. Assuming her role as the educator, she explained to Collin, "Did you know that Pieter Stuyvesant was the Director-General for the Dutch Colony of New Netherlands back in the mid-1600s? In those days the Dutch claimed what is now much of the States of New York, New Jersey, Connecticut, and Rhode Island where we were the last few days. And the Capital of this Dutch Province was the southern tip of what is now Manhattan, which they called . . ."

"You know what we talked about, darlin'," Collin interrupted.

"But I thought you might like to hear about the history."

"I don't need to know anything except whether Claire is safe," Collin stated. "We lived in Brooklyn."

"Sure then," Kathy pouted.

"I just want you to know that I love you even if you are not an expert on every subject in life."

"We're not going to talk about my father again, surely."

"Not today, of all days.

"All right, then, smarty pants, what's that big tall building on the east side of the square?" Collin asked.

"That's why we're here. I read up on that, too," she said. "That's the Beth Israel Teaching Hospital. It was built fifteen years ago to treat the Jews from the lower east side of Queens. And, what might be interesting to us is that it runs the Phillips Beth Israel School of Nursing some six blocks north of here."

"Do you think that Claire could have studied here?"

"Definitely a possibility. Claire was obviously interested in nursing, according to Lucy."

After lunch, they went to the triage center at the hospital to try and find Byron. The nurse on duty was annoyingly officious. "Yes, Byron Harrison works here as an orderly, but I haven't seen him in over a month," she said.

"Can't you tell us any more about him than that?" Kathy asked flashing the woman a broad smile.

Maybe it was because a woman asked her. The nurse opened up. "Well, I dated him once about a year ago. He lived in a flat nearby. Kind of a swell boy, but he has a new girl now."

"Really. Is she here at the hospital?"

"I dunno. I never saw her. Came from somewhere else, I heard."

Collin looked at Kathy.

"Do you know where we might find Byron?"

"His address is on Lexington, just north of Gramercy Park, not far from here. A walkup tenement." She gave them the number from her personal address book.

"Have you ever heard of Claire O'Donnell?" Collin asked.

"There's a Claire Swanson that's been a nurse here for about ten years, but no one named O'Donnell, I'm afraid, far as I know. Come back tomorrow. My supervisor will be here in the morning."

They thanked her for her time and headed north for Gramercy Square hoping they would mercifully find Byron at home.

"These are kind of chancy digs," Kathy said, as they approached the address they had been given by the nurse. Byron was definitely not a man of means.

"C'mon. Let's try the door."

Standing on the rickety front stoop, Collin rang the bell. Three times.

"That's disappointing. No one at home."

"What's this?" Kathy pointed. "Collin, look at this window."

"Looks like three bullet holes to me," Collin commented running his finger over the jagged holes in the glass. "Pretty large caliber bullets. Maybe a 45."

An ugly thought dawned on him, "Fredricson would have had access to the same records that the Governor got. Shite. The nurse said she hadn't seen Byron in a month."

"Don't jump to conclusions," Kathy stated, grabbing Collin's hand and pulling it back from the window. "These holes may be years old."

"It was probably Enrico. His gun was a 45. I shouldn't have killed him. He could have told us what happened here."

"Not that again. Now you're going off the deep end," Kathy chided. "You had no choice. It was him or us."

"We've got to get in there," Collin growled, rattling the doorknob.

"We're not going to break in, surely."

"What if they're both dead inside and have been for a month?"

"Everything looks in order," Kathy said looking into the parlor through the window.

"Doesn't look like the door's been forced," Collin admitted. "But I've got a very bad feeling all of a sudden."

"There's no point in worrying about something you can't do anything about. We'll find out where Claire is tomorrow. I can feel it."

Pulling Collin down off the porch, Kathy changed the subject.

"C'mon let's explore the city on this fine sunny afternoon. Since we have to wait anyway to speak to the Nurse's supervisor, how 'bout we see what the lights of Broadway have to offer."

"Why don't we just go back to the Jersey City Hotel and wait for tomorrow?" Collin argued.

"Because we've come all this way, and I want to see some of the glitter of New York," she insisted. "Who knows if we'll ever get a chance to come back here."

Begrudgingly, Collin allowed himself to be led west to Broadway Avenue. They arrived at Union Square, so named for the union with the Bowery Road, and were faced with an enormous bronze statue of General Washington on horseback in its center. *How serendipitous*, Kathy thought.

"That reminds me," Kathy said. "I've always wanted to take a carriage ride in New York City. There's a carriage over there on the corner of Fourth Avenue. Can we take it, please?"

"If you insist."

When they were clip-clopping in a splendid white coach pulled by a chestnut mare, the coachman asked, "Where can I take you two lovebirds?"

"How about Ireland," Collin suggested facetiously.

"We'd like a tour of the south end of Central Park and then please return to the Knickerbocker Hotel in Times Square," Kathy chirped.

"What's goin' on here? Am I being set up?"

"Well, I admit it," Kathy murmured coyly. "I planned all this last night. I know that I'm taking my life into my own hands here, but I've organized a romantic evening for the two of us. You're not to ask any questions, and you're to do what I ask. Is that acceptable?"

"You've got my interest, darlin'. But won't this be quite costly?"

"It's fine, dear. I have saved some of my teaching money just for this occasion. When I mentioned it to the Governor, he insisted on helping out. You'll see."

The rest of the carriage ride was relaxing, with the sun streaming through the tree-lined streets in the late afternoon. Kathy settled into the crook of Collin's arm and they talked of their future together.

The cab driver enjoyed the young couple's animated conversation as he drove them back to the Knickerbocker. He told himself they must be newlyweds, they appeared so young and fresh, but they had an unusual ease of manner which bespoke a deep understanding and respect for one another. The young lady's sparkling laughter recalled to him the days when he danced attendance on his own wife because they found the world in each other's eye, and young bodies as well.

By the time they reached the Knickerbocker Hotel, Collin was more focused on Kathy than on Claire. Her long auburn hair flowing down onto his shoulders smelled so good.

As the young man handed his lady from the cab, the driver noticed that she pressed some bills, the fare for their ride, into his hand. She seemed to be at home with the customs of the New York fine nightlife, and he chuckled a little to see the way she guided him so seamlessly into the role of a gentleman who appreciated the electrified sights of Times Square.

"The Governor made the reservation for me at this wonderful hotel," Kathy explained as she took his arm. "Isn't it gorgeous?"

The fourteen-floor Beaux Arts style hotel, sporting its red brick façade with terra cotta details, was glowing in the setting sunlight. Even Collin was impressed by the grandeur of the building, and he stopped to take a photograph.

When they entered the hotel lobby, Collin smiled down at Kathy and winked; he could not believe that he was in this elegant place with a woman on his arm whose beauty surpassed any other present. He wanted to pinch himself; he had never imagined he would find himself here, a boy who had rough and tumbled through boyhood in the squalid neighborhoods of this same city.

"Just look at this elegant three-story restaurant right off the lobby," Kathy gushed.

"Stay here, my love. I'll be after getting us our room like before, although, Sweet Jesus, I don't have any idea how we'll pay for it."

"That won't be necessary dear. As I told you, Charles has taken care of everything."

Collin was unsure so Kathy pulled him up to the front desk.

The clerk behind the desk looked like he was about to go to a fancy dress ball. Looking them up and down, he asked, "May I help you?"

"I believe you have a reservation for Collin O'Donnell," Kathy said.

"Oh, yes, Mr. and Mrs. O'Donnell. We've been expecting you. Welcome to the Knickerbocker. Governor Lippitt has instructed us to take very good care of you. Apparently you are very very special people in his eyes. Here is an envelope from him for you. Please let us know if we can be of any assistance."

He rang a bell and an attendant immediately accompanied them onto the elevator. He pressed the button labeled 'P' and up they went, to the top.

Collin gave Kathy the raised eyebrow one-two when the attendant showed them into the Penthouse suite.

"I had nothing to do with this hotel selection," Kathy chortled. "It was all Charles's doing." She was giggling now like one of her schoolgirls. "I've never seen, much less been in, such a splendid suite of rooms! And it has a fancy living room as well as a gorgeous huge bedroom."

"This is unbelievable, to be sure," Collin agreed. "The Governor must carry some swell weight around here. Look at the size of that bed."

Trying to change the subject, Kathy directed his attention to the assortments of flowers throughout the suite. She sniffed the air. "Don't they smell lovely?"

Collin was over at the corner windows and he opened one of the curtains. "You've got to see this," he beckoned. "You wanted to see the Great White Way."

From their perch at the top of the world they stood overlooking Times Square and beyond that, the theatres of 42nd Street. The lights of the City were blinking on in the gathering twilight, and the streets were filled with bustling Hansom Cabs and the odd Taximeter Cars hurrying their passengers to the theatres and restaurants. Words initially escaped them as they stood entwined together in awe of the sight below them, taking it all in.

Finally, Collin said, "If I'd known for sure what dangers awaited us, I would never have subjected you to all these risks. There's no doubt of it. But you have been incredible throughout this ordeal. I agree that it has strengthened our bond, and I want you to know how much I love you, darlin'."

"Enough to marry me?"

"After we find Claire."

There it was again. The elephant in the room.

Kathy leaned further in by the window and planted her most sensuous and prolonged kiss on her beau, while the sea of well-dressed humanity passed hurriedly on the streets far below. *No you don't lover. Not tonight. It's just me and you now.*

Coming to his senses, Collin asked, "What's in the envelope, my love?"

"I have no idea," she replied impishly. "Open it!"

Collin ripped open the side, careful not to tear interior contents, and blew on the envelope. His eyes lit up. "Box seats to the Ziegfield Blue Follies at the New Amsterdam Theatre for this evening at nine, and a voucher for dress clothing at the shop off the lobby," he announced, waving the tickets in the air like flags.

"What a wonderful surprise!" Kathy clapped her hands. "Thank you, Gov'nor!"

It took an hour to choose their attire for the evening. After bathing sequentially in the immense, clawfoot bathtub of the grandiose bathroom, they dressed for the theatre.

"You look mighty dapper in that blue evening suit with matching silk cravat and spats, dear."

Collin was left speechless when Kathy appeared in a floor length, strapless, gold sequined gown, with matching pumps and handbag.

As if on cue, there was a knock on the door, and a bellman delivered a wrist corsage of roses for Kathy and a matching boutonniere for Collin.

She read the appended note. "To my new good friends. Thank you so much on behalf of my state, my business, myself and all the children whom you have saved. Hope you enjoy your evening in New York. You are very welcome in my humble home any time you are in Rhode Island. With highest regards, Charles."

"What a grand touch of the swank, I'm thinking."

"Wait. There's more. Postscript: Dear Kathy, I am changing the rules at the Woolen Company. From now on the workday for minors under the age of eighteen will be ten hours maximum. Further I will require that they have weekly schooling in the three Rs, which I will provide on-site. They can take the time off work for these studies. And, I am raising their wage so that they won't lose any salary. Thank you kindly for your wise counsel. Charles Lippitt."

By the end of her reading, Kathy was crying openly.

"It's wonderful, my dear." He comforted her and dried her cheeks with the ends of his cravat.

They could see the New Amsterdam from the window of their penthouse suite, so it only took a few minutes to walk there. But when they stepped out of the Knickerbocker near curtain time, they were overwhelmed by the mass of people trying to get to the theatres.

"I've never seen anything like this in Toronto," Kathy

exclaimed, as they darted in and out of the throng.

"Hold my hand, dear, so we won't get separated," Collin cautioned as they crossed busy Seventh Avenue.

Their destination was just half a block away. The New Amsterdam was a very tall Art Nouveau edifice, "This entrance looks more like the west entrance of a European cathedral than a Manhattan theatre," Kathy said, as they walked under the figured and columned arch.

"Maybe it's meant to," Collin remarked. "These people worship the singers and dancers who perform here, don't they now?"

A sign in the lobby informed them it was the biggest theatre in New York.

As they walked through the entrance corridor they were met with wall portraits of the famous entertainers, including many of the showgirls and comedians who had performed there.

"There's Mr. Ziegfeld," Kathy noted, stopping to gaze at the handsome man posing with his most notorious diva, Lillian Lorraine. "I heard that they are together."

"What do you mean? Tangled or married?"

"Tangled, as you put it. But he's married, too."

"Lucky swell to be mad in lust for that one."

It was Kathy's turn to give her man the old eye one-two.

"Just spoofin' you, darlin'. Don't you look the diva yourself, this evenin'." Collin took Kathy's hand and led her through the vaulted archways into the theatre proper.

Kathy caught her breath as the opulence of the three-tiered theatre came into view. Plaster figurines and motifs, frescoed paintings adorned the walls and over the huge stage. The semicircular floral-decorated boxes ran floor to ceiling on each side of the theatre.

"Leave it to the Governor. We've got the front box seats on the mezzanine," Kathy announced as they started up the sweeping marble stairs. "Just look at this beautiful green and pink floral carpet."

"Yes, it's grand, for all that," Collin agreed, running his hand over one of the metal figurine heads which constituted the massive newel post of the staircase.

Once in their seats, they could see out into the audience. The theatre was full of swells and dames dressed in their finest, all talking at once. Kathy thought it was marvelous. Her gaze turned towards the stage with its pendulous gold curtain. "I wonder what those three women in the painting over the stage represent," she asked, turning Collin's head to look.

"Moolah," was his immediate response. "I see plenty of moolah in here."

The lights went down, the curtain went up and the orchestra started to play. Kathy was entranced.

The Ziegfeld Follies show was modeled on the Folies Bergère from the Moulin Rouge in Paris, the program said. And they both thought that the show lived up to its billing.

Kathy marveled at the opening number called 'The Gates of Elysium', which simulated underwater effects featuring water spouting elephants. High-stepping showgirls in flimsy feathered outfits no bigger than their derrières strutted and preened their way through twenty or so numbers meant to excite the men in the audience. The female lead dancers were Ina Claire and Ann Pennington. They were knockouts, Kathy had to admit. The catcalls from the cheap seats attested to the fact that their exposed antics were having the desired effect. Many of the ladies in the theatre appeared happy when their men got excited, perhaps because of their expectations for the rest of the evening. She wondered what effect this was having on Collin, who seemed mesmerized by it all.

"I've never seen this much bare female anatomy before," Collin whispered. "But, you are the most beautiful person in the theatre, on or off stage," he added, smiling broadly.

"But you've never seen me in feathers." Kathy blushed, winking at him. She realized that he meant it, so she gave his arm a squeeze.

W.C. Fields who had recently traded in his juggling act was juggling punch lines instead. Ed Wynn also provided gut-splitting comic relief by directing a spoof film from the audience.

When they left the theater, they were truly excited.

"And now for my surprise," Kathy announced as they crossed Seventh Avenue.

Re-entering the Knickerbocker, she wheeled Collin into the restaurant that they had seen earlier.

"This restaurant could seat more people than the New Amsterdam Theatre," Collin observed.

"After theatre crowd, darling. Do we fit in, do you think?" Kathy, all shimmering and golden, struck a pose.

"Now there's *my* diva," Collin exclaimed, leaning in and giving her a big smooch.

The Maitre'd seated them immediately at a private table by the window, looking out towards Times Square. The table was laid out with gold plated silverware and fine floral china.

"Would you both like a martini?" their waiter Franz asked. "It was invented here, you know." They obliged and then decided on a bottle of Bordeaux for the main meal.

Collin turned his eyes to Kathy as she picked up the menu and decided she had much more knowledge of how to maneuver in this environment, so he asked her what she would like to order and closely followed her lead.

Collin and Kathy soon found their appetites and gave themselves to the pleasure of a well-grilled steak and lobster, complemented by the wine, Kathy's recommendation, of course, and salad. Throughout their repast they talked of the theatre and the lovely hotel, and Kathy made sure that she steered the conversation away from Claire.

When she sensed Collin's thoughts were drifting, potentially in

Claire's direction, she said, "Did you know that Enrico Caruso lives in this hotel full-time with his wife and takes all his meals in this restaurant? I can prove it to you. There he is over there."

Collin saw that Caruso was packing away a sizeable meal with apparent gusto. "If he eats here every night, he'll soon look like Ole King Cole over there."

Kathy's eyes followed Collin's pointing arm to where a thirty-foot-wide mural of the merry old soul himself adorned the wall. It all seemed to add joviality to the festivities of their evening together.

When they finished their meal with cake and small cups of strong black coffee, Collin was sorely tempted to lean back and rub his hands across his stomach, but he knew better and again followed Kathy's lead in table decorum. She dabbed her lips delicately and as he interpreted that she was well content, Collin reached across the table to take her hands in his and began a speech that he hoped was not too unpolished.

"Kathy, dearest girl, what we have experienced together has been incredible. I cannot believe how you have thrown your lot in with me, leaving home and safety, to help me find what happened to my sister. When we began this enterprise, I thought you would be a liability if we got into a dangerous situation, and I dreaded the possibility of being the cause of injury to you or worse. How could I live with myself? I was wrong, I misjudged you, and I am sorry."

Kathy closed her eyes and tightened her hold on Collin. He felt their connection grow stronger, and when she opened her eyes, tears dazzled their blueness, and a smile lit up her face.

"Oh, please, Collin, please know I love you so much, I am drowning in this happiness. You are the man that completes me, and I want to stay with you—always. How can I make you understand what I mean to say—drat, the words cannot begin to . . . "

"Shush, dear heart, I can tell from the way you look at me, and I am crazy for you—no, wait, loving you is the most sensible thing I know I have ever done. We are meant for each other."

Beneath their passionate conversation ran that current of anticipation. They were pledging themselves to one another and would find the way to seal that pledge before the next morning. They were not teasing one another now, and Kathy had lost her fear of making love, of how polite society could judge them for their rash behavior and the possible consequences. This was her challenge, to make a decision that would bind her for life to this man she wanted at her side. Of one thing she was certain, whatever the future brought to them, Kathy would never forgive herself if she did not open her arms to him. "Now it's time to go to our next surprise," she announced, nervously.

Collin and Kathy left the table and made their way to the exit, keenly aware that they must not let on their intentions for the coming night. Kathy felt sure that every woman in that room knew what she and Collin were up to, and the rims of her ears burned a hotter pink than usual. Indeed, other men in the room may have felt that tension exuded by a female that signals her taking a mate, and a few shook their heads slightly in disappointment that they would not enjoy that type of union with this lovely woman dressed in gold sequins who passed so quickly from the room.

When they reached their suite, Collin dug around clumsily for the door key, and Kathy nearly broke out in laughter at the way they were both acting—like puppies or kittens rushing headlong into unknown territory. They possessed an innocence that many wiser heads would condemn as foolishness, and just as many others would say is the greatest gift a man and woman give in their love. When, at last, the door opened and then closed behind them, they hesitated. Although their bodies hummed with unbearable need, both wanted to mark every moment of their sweet possession of one another.

"Kathy, are you sure?"

"I've reconsidered my beliefs during this last week and I cannot think of a more romantic place and time for us to make love for the first time than here and now."

"But I thought you were keeping yourself chaste until marriage . . ."

"To hell with my father."

"I am not actually prepared . . ."

"Shhh . . . I know that we are soul mates for life. We both want to be married, right? It is the time of month where I shouldn't get pregnant, and most of all I need you . . . now. So, please, please love me tonight."

With their senses wide open, they began the exquisite dance of union.

With measured, slow movements, Collin gently drew the narrow straps of Kathy's gown down her arms to reveal her lovely shoulders and the deep curve of her bosom. He gasped when he saw that she wore no corset under the thinnest silk camisole; every time he had touched her that evening, he was touching *her*, not a female shaped contraption. He became dizzy with lust, he felt trapped in his own clothing, but forced himself to pay attention to every movement they made in this intense experience.

For her part, Kathy brought his fingers to her lips and then drew them to her breasts, her nipples springing up erect, and showed him how to caress them. Her breath became deeper and stronger; they were torturing each other. How long could they stay themselves, they had no experience with this tidal wave of passion. Their hearts were in danger of collapsing, and they opened their lips wider in their kisses so they could breathe in the scent of one another. They kept stripping clothes from each other's bodies so they could lick sweet salted flesh and crush themselves close, closer—they wanted to fill the same space. They lost the ability to stand, so they sank into the bedclothes as they turned themselves inside out for one another.

Freed in their nakedness, Kathy frankly gazed at the beauty of Collin's body and knew the way that her own body longed to be joined to him. His member leered blindly, looking for its home, and without a pause she reached out to take it, to feel its full hot strength in her hands. Collin drew back quickly out of her way and jumped from the bed to wash himself hurriedly at the sink. His erection diminished as the cold water poured over it, but would return quickly with Kathy's massaging attention. Kathy pushed back the bedclothes; she was bathed in a heat that suffused her and would know no coolness until Collin moved within her. His surprise at her eagerness and shamelessness utterly delighted him, and he cried out when she grasped his now-erect member and teased it with her fingers to coax it fully from its hood.

He was nearing the end of his sexual patience, so he rolled to her and made his way into her body as gently as he could possibly bear to do. And then he could not help himself; he slipped his hands beneath her hips and lifted her body so he could move more deeply into her. She gasped, opened to him and matched his rocking movements. As their passion increased, they echoed each other perfectly; their hands caressed and then pulled closer. Collin's shudder at his release matched her cry at the pain that bloomed within her and mixed with his fluids. He spilled into her, it was endless.

He did not want to leave the shelter of her body when his climax had passed. He covered her hair and neck and sweet, sweet shoulders with kisses. When he did withdraw, he saw that her face was wet, whether it was a sheen of perspiration or from tears, he did not immediately know. He rolled from her and then saw on the sheet the watery blush of blood that had issued from her. It shocked him and he gathered her in his arms, angry with his selfishness that hurt her. He showered the tenderest of kisses on her, wanting only that she forgive him the brutality with which he had taken her. Kathy's arms came up, and she stroked his face and amazed him that she did not recoil from him. The wonders of this woman! He would never, ever hurt her again in word or deed. Kathy clearly saw the pain in his face and guessed its source when she saw the stain on the sheet.

"Aye, laddie, it is only my initiation into womanhood. You will not see it again, and the next time we meet this way, it will be a most pleasurable time for us both," she pulled his face to her breast and fiercely kissed the crown of his head.

With that, she turned into the curve of his body and fell into a most luxuriant sleep.

Again, he puzzled at her wisdom and love—how could he have been so worthy of this most excellent of creatures?

Some hours later, Collin awoke to a peculiar sensation; a most pleasant thrill of heat coursed through his body and summoned an ardent desire to be satisfied. Startled to find this arousal came not from a nighttime fantasy, but from a mysterious seducer right there within the shelter of his arm was stroking him, teasing him with her lips, bringing him to an urgency he could not ignore.

Kathy whispered into his ear, "So now, my love, you are me and I am you—together. Come into me again, and I will match your desire with my own."

As he moved her hips so that she would this time be above him, she pinned his arms down with her own and swallowed him in a thrill of pleasure. This time, they rode each other as equals and when they reached their plateau, they did so together. Such completeness, such total joining.

There was no morning-after remorse. They went down for breakfast in the packed elevator holding hands and exchanging knowing glances. Each touch was electric and each thought delicious. They couldn't wait to be alone together again. But that would have to wait. Today was the day when they would find Claire. *Refocus.*

They went back to the hospital at ten and proceeded directly to the personnel office.

Collin waited his turn and then asked the receptionist at the desk, "We would like to find one of your orderlies—Mr. Byron Harrison. A nurse on duty in triage yesterday said she had not seen him in over a month. We need to see him urgently."

"Wait here a minute," the receptionist said and she disappeared through a doorway.

"Can I help you?" a matronly woman asked when she poked her head through the same doorway moments later. "Come this way."

Collin explained their need to this Personnel Manager and waited anxiously for her response.

"Are either of you relatives of Mr. Harrison?" she asked.

"No, but Claire is my sister," Collin answered.

"I am not sure if this will help you find your sister, but I can clear up the mystery of Mr. Harrison's whereabouts. Byron accompanied one of our doctors, Dr. Gilroy, who had assembled a small team of nurses to go with him to Europe to practice a new triage technique we have developed for the battlefield. Unfortunately, the ship they sailed on was sunk by the Germans. As far as we know from the Cunard Steamship Lines, none of this team survived."

"Not the *Lusitania*, surely?" Claire exclaimed.

"Yes, the very same."

"I told you I had a bad feeling," Collin moaned, turning to Kathy for support.

"Just because Mr. Harrison went on that trip doesn't mean that Claire did," Kathy stated, taking his hand and stopping it from fisting.

"Do you have the names of all the members of Dr. Gilroy's team?" Collin asked.

"All who were employed with us, yes. But I heard there was a late addition. Don't know the name though."

"Do you have any suggestions on how we can find my sister

Claire O'Donnell?"

"Well, Claire O'Donnell was not one of our employees," the manager stated after checking her list. But I do recall that Mr. Harrison brought a young woman in here three months ago asking if she could be admitted for training. I sent them off to our sister organization, the Phillips Beth Israel Nursing School. Maybe you'll find her there."

"I see," said Kathy. "We want to thank you for taking the time to talk with us today." She could see that Collin was crestfallen.

"I'll bet that it wasn't her," she said as they headed north up First Avenue towards the Nursing School. "Stop worrying."

But when they got there, they were informed that Claire had enrolled three months earlier and then, after two months, she had withdrawn from the program. The school did not know why, or where she was.

Even Kathy had a premonition.

They found out that the Cunard New York Office was adjacent to Pier 54 on the west shore of Manhattan on the North River. They walked the fourteen blocks to the pier at the end of Jane Street in sick anticipation.

"They'll have the passenger manifest at the Cunard office. She probably wasn't on board," Kathy hoped.

"I should have come earlier," Collin kept muttering. Kathy decided not to try to be optimistic this once. No point in raising false hopes.

When they finally arrived at the Cunard office, they met with the operations manager, Anthony Fry. His assistant had told them that his boss had been working around the clock since the tragedy. He had been through the wringer with relatives of the passengers on board that fateful day. Yet he maintained his professional and supportive demeanor despite the calamity.

"Yes, Mr. O'Donnell," he stated after looking at the manifest list. "I'm sorry to inform you that Ms. Claire O'Donnell, nurse's aide and Mr. Harrison, orderly, were both passengers on the *Lusitania* in the company of Doctor Gilroy of New York City. None of these persons survived the sinking as far as we know, and their bodies have not been recovered."

"Oh God, no!" Collin wailed, burying his head in his hands.

Kathy asked Mr. Fry, "Is it possible that she survived?" She gripped Collin's arm.

"We have a team assembled in Queenstown, the nearest port to the disaster. They are combing the countryside for potential survivors. Relatives have gone there to try to find their loved ones, dead or alive. So far, your sister has not shown up, according to the Queenstown team."

"It's been two months. What are the chances that Claire could still show up?" Collin mumbled.

"Slim to none, I'm afraid," Mr. Fry answered honestly.

After consulting the record again he added, "If it is any consolation to you both, Mr. Harrison and Nurse O'Donnell, along with Mr. Vanderbilt and Mr. Frohman, were known to be helping out in the children's nursery at the time of the attack."

"Did any of these children survive?" Kathy asked.

"I'm afraid not, ma'am," came the brutal answer. "The ship sank just eighteen minutes after being torpedoed."

"I can't accept this fate for her unless you find the body," Collin snapped.

"We will do everything in our power to do so, sir. But you must come to grips with the likelihood that she will not be found at this point. There were 1,198 out of 1,959 souls lost, as far as we can determine."

"That leaves 761 people who survived," Collin said after rapidly making the subtraction in his head.

"But all those people have been identified, sir," Fry responded.

"Well, don't stop looking." Then Collin added, "*Please,*" as an attempt to be civil though his heart was breaking.

In a state of shock, they gave the official contact information for Collin, Kathy and Sam to be used in the event that there would be positive news. But the Operations Manager said that he wasn't hopeful of that outcome. He told them he was sorry on behalf of the Steamship Company for their loss.

As they turned to leave, Kathy put her arm around a sagging Collin and led him out. He was mumbling, "Many waters cannot quench love–neither can the floods drown it."

"Well said, my love. Well said."

Chapter Seventeen
Despondence

June 8, 1915
Somewhere in New York State

*T*he drive back to Toronto was somber at best. The shiny black Ford seemed like a hearse, albeit an empty one. They couldn't get the horror of drowning at sea out of their minds. There was no interest in going on the "Maid of the Mist." The deluge of water over the Falls seemed to further choke Collin's spirit. The word "morose" didn't half cover it.

He repeated, "If I had been abducted, too, I could have found a way out sooner. And if I had gone looking just two months ago . . ."

Kathy could see that her objective of receiving a marriage proposal was slipping further and further away. *Maybe it would have been better to have let things be, to have never come on this trip.* Then she realized just how selfish that thought was.

"I feel so awful about Claire," Kathy said when she couldn't dissipate Collin's sorrow. When he didn't respond, she said, "If we hadn't come on this trip all those children in Rhode Island and the others Enrico abducted would still be in bondage. And Enrico would still be at large perpetrating evil."

"But poor Claire . . ."

"She was a Florence Nightingale and she rose above her captors. That must count for something special. Many people live their long lives without accomplishing half of what Claire did."

"I see that, but she might still have been alive today."

"You are determined to find some way to blame yourself, aren't you. To be the martyr. How is that going to help Claire, or us?"

After a long silence, Collin admitted, "I am proud of Claire.

251

She came a long way, to be sure."

"And so have you, my love. And so have you."

As they drove down Balsam Avenue at the end of their trip, Kathy said, "I've been thinking. I believe that we should name our first daughter Claire."

For the first time in two days she saw Collin smile.

Collin returned to work at the Paper the following Monday. He had been gone two weeks and there was a backlog of stories and photographs to be processed. Work seemed to be the only thing that could mask the hurt that he was feeling for Claire and himself.

Kathy was still on summer vacation as were Sam and Liz. They tried everything they could think of to raise Collin's spirits.

Finally, two evenings later, when Kathy came over herself out of frustration, Sam came up with an idea.

"I think that Collin needs to grieve but he also needs a way to end this chapter in his life," he suggested to the two women. "Normally, when someone dies, the family holds a funeral to remember the person and to provide closure. What if we were to have a service for Claire and a burial?"

"With no body?"

"They do that with soldiers who die in foreign lands sometimes. I think they call it missing in action," Sam offered, drawing on his pipe and waiting for Kathy's input.

"And all the people lost off the *Lusitania* are war casualties," Liz added, nodding her head in acceptance of the idea.

Kathy twirled her hair in silence. Then she finally said, "I don't know if he'd go for it, but I can ask Collin about it."

"We could invite people that you both know from the Paper, Sam, and people from your school that Collin knows, Kathy," Liz suggested.

"How about inviting some of his rowing buddies from the Club?" Sam added, picking up on his wife's enthusiasm. "That way all the people who care for him can show their support. I am sure that Reverend Dixon at St. Aidan's would officiate. He knows Collin from when he lived in the tent city there."

The next night, Sam and Liz invited Collin and Kathy for dinner at Ten Balsam. Liz was making Irish stew, Collin's favorite. Kathy arrived after school, alone. Liz could see her from the kitchen window. Her normal perky step was missing as she trudged up the walkway, stopping to smell the star jasmine flowers blooming near the porch. The window was open to catch the afternoon breeze and the sweet smell filled the kitchen.

"C'mon in, Kathy. I'm in the kitchen."

As she entered, Kathy dropped her books on the sideboard with a thump and started twirling her hair. "Collin here, yet?"

"No dear, but Sam is if you'd like to talk to him."

"This idea of a remembrance service is growing on me. But what if Collin doesn't come around?"

Sam poked his head in from his art studio and said, "Why the long face? This is going to work."

"I don't know. He wants to be the martyr, you know."

"I don't think so," Liz chimed in, chopping onions and wiping her streaming eyes with her apron. "He's too smart a lad to throw your life together out the window. He'll come around, you'll see. Now could you be a dear and get the girls up from their nap?"

After Kathy had ascended the stairs, Sam came over and kissed his wife's neck. "That's why I love you. You sure know how to calm down a tempest."

"So do you, dear. So do you."

Twenty minutes later Collin opened the front door. "What a disastrous day," he lamented, throwing his hat at the hat rack and missing it by a mile. "I just seem to be going through the motions. Hard to get focused anymore."

The Finlays grabbed the girls and retired to the kitchen to finish fixing dinner, leaving Kathy to greet her man.

"Hello, darling. I love you even if you are a grump."

Kathy handed him an O'Keefe's Old Vienna. He drank it down in one long gulp and plopped down in Sam's favorite chair, legs sprawled out in front of him. She picked his hat up off the floor and placed it on the rack. Then she came over to the chair and gave the top of his head a kiss. "Collin dear, what do you think about having a memorial service for Claire? She turned around to face him. "I think it would be a wonderful idea."

"What good would that do? She's dead and gone and there's no body to bury."

Sam and Liz, who had heard the exchange from the kitchen doorway, joined Kathy. The giggling girls dashed in, each one grabbing one of Collin's legs, then he leaned over and gathered them up into his arms on his lap.

"Don't be sad, Unca Collie," Norah coaxed. "We love you."

Dot tugged at his sleeve.

"I know you do, girls. I love you, too." Collin gave each one a kiss on her forehead.

"Your friends are also grieving for Claire, as well as for you," Kathy continued. "They want to show their support for you both."

"Having a burial would be symbolic. It would be a place where you can go in future to remember her and talk with her. It would be like she was really there," Sam said.

"I still don't see the point," Collin sighed. "But I will think about it." He started bouncing the girls up and down on his knees. Kathy could see a little color returning to his cheeks.

"We should do this as soon as we can arrange it with everyone. It will depend on the availability of Governor Lippitt who wants to attend." Kathy soothed. "Thanks for considering our suggestion."

"You already contacted him?"

"Yes. He's all for it."

"So you're all after gangin' up on me again, then."

"No. We're just trying to help you. Help all of us, really," Kathy said, holding his gaze intently.

"I said I'd think about it."

"Now let's eat," Liz invited.

At the announcement of dinner, the girls jumped down. Grabbing Collin by the hands, they pulled him up out of the chair and led him to the dining room table.

That weekend Collin got a reprieve from the overload at the Paper. On Saturday, Kathy convinced him to do some rowing at the Club. She knew that the physical exertion could help reduce the tensions that he felt. As she watched him from the front verandah, she could see that he was taking out his frustration on the canoe and the lake. He was passing every other canoe like it was standing still and leaving a churned up wake in the lake. After an hour, he suddenly slowed his pace and brought the canoe to the ramp.

Kathy could see the sweat glistening off his face and arms, and his rowing shirt was soaking wet, his chest heaving.

"How'd it go out there?" Kathy called to him.

"I guess I scared the fish," he fired back, between gulps of air.

Good, she said to herself. *He can come out of these doldrums.*

"Why don't you have a shower and then we'll have a drink out here and watch the sunset," Kathy suggested, calling down from the verandah.

Half an hour later, they were drinking martinis. They had instructed the bartender how to make them.

The summer sun was setting beyond the lake, somewhere near Niagara Falls they thought. There was a cooling breeze, and the purple tinge of twilight was lighting up the cloud formation just above the horizon.

Collin sat, sipping his drink, silent for the longest time. Then, taking Kathy's hand and kissing it softly, he said, "I think you all are right about havin' a remembrance service. Claire would have liked it. She would have had one for me if our roles had been reversed. I'm thinkin' that it's the least we can do for her now, darlin'."

Kathy encircled his neck with her arm and leaned in, hugging him tight. "And it's the most we can do for her. She will be there with us, you'll see, lover," she whispered, as the last rays of light faded into night.

Chapter Eighteen
Aidan's Plight

Sunday, June 20, 1915
Creagh, Ireland

"*T*adgh. I've got to find out who I am," the girl announced when he brought up her breakfast of coddled eggs and toast. "I really appreciate your hospitality, but it's time for me to go. I have a life somewhere."

In the three weeks since her burning man nightmare, the woman had been constantly making this request. He could understand her obsession. It must be terribly frightening not to have any clue who you were. But she was still too weak to travel.

"In due time, lass, when you're well and able."

"But I am ready, now. See?" She moved the tray aside and swung her hips out over the edge of the bed.

Tadgh tried to look away as the nightshirt she was wearing rode up her thighs. Her feet hit the floor, and her knees began to buckle.

"Oh," she cried and Tadgh turned to see her falling. With a deft lunge of a swordsman, he swooped her up in his arms and raised her back up onto the bed.

"Ease back there, girl. It'll take time to get your sea legs back. You're barely able to get down to the bathroom without my help, and it's only thirty feet down the hall."

"It's not sea legs I'm needing but land legs, surely. I think I've had enough of the sea, thank you very much."

"Point well taken, lass. But in my books you can never get enough of the sea. Though I'll grant you, she's a cruel mistress at times. Later we'll try the stairs and maybe a walk in the garden, if you'd like."

Before the girl could respond to the suggestion, there was a banging on the door below.

"Open up, Tadgh! It's me, The RIC are after me!"

"Not Aidan," Tadgh groaned, racing to the top of the stairs. He shouted through the door, "Go down into the boathouse lad, and I will meet you there!"

"Righto," Aidan yelled back, and Tadgh stepped back into the bedroom.

"Who is Aidan?" his patient asked with a worried look on her face. "And what is the RIC?"

Tadgh knew that he had to tell her something.

"He is my younger brother. Lives alone in Cork City, about forty miles from here. The RIC stands for the Royal Irish Constabulary, who make up the occupational police in our country doing England's bidding for the time being. They are our enemy because they have done some very bad things to our people and our country. I will explain everything, I will, when you are completely well. Meanwhile you will be safe as a church mouse with me here, my dear."

This wasn't the moment to divulge that he, himself, was on the RIC hit list. He could tell from her broadening smile that she indeed felt safe with him there.

"I'll be all right, Tadgh. Go and meet with Aidan."

Yet Tadgh could see the uncertainty, and a little trepidation, in the furrow of her eyebrows. He gave her a lot of credit for letting him off the hook so that he could deal with his problem immediately.

"I'll be back shortly."

Tadgh bounded down the stairway and out the door. The boathouse was empty except for *The Republican*, but Tadgh quickly surmised that Aidan was likely waiting behind the wall.

He moved an old unused oil lantern, which was sitting on the side table near the back wall, just a few inches to its right. A lever clicked in place and a panel, hidden in a section of the barn's wooden wall, cracked open. Tadgh put his shoulder to it and the panel rotated open to reveal an operations center room that had been hewn out under the house. It was a large enclosure about thirty feet wide and deep. A sturdy underground roof and wall structure held up a low ceiling.

Chairs and tables were assembled in the center of the room, and it was there that Tadgh found a frantic Aidan. As if looking in a mirror, Tadgh realized his brother seemed the spitting image of himself, only a younger version—a strapping young fellow his own height with bushy black hair and eyebrows. He had a split lip and a shiner around his right eye, and his shirt was ripped and bloody.

Tadgh embraced his brother, as much to check his condition as a show of brotherly love. He didn't appear to be too badly injured.

"Aidan. What happened, lad? Are you safe? Were you followed?"

Tadgh's big brother protective nature kicked in. The memory of their family tragedy flooded over him.

"Jeez, Tadgh, I was in Clancy's last night, minding me own business, when these two RIC coppers came in lookin' for a fight. Me and Andy O'Henry tried to ignore them, but then one of them started pushing poor Andy around, he did. He said that Andy was a member of the Volunteers, which isn't true. They started to haul him out of the pub, and I couldn't let that happen. Andy yelled out my name, and the little copper's head snapped around. He came after me, calling out *You McCarthy bastard*. So I punched the bugger in the face. He roughed me up pretty good, but I got my licks in, too. He wasn't the one that killed Mam, but he was there that night, I think.

We ran like hell out of there and the RIC gave chase. But we gave them the slip down by Cogan's Mill by hiding out in the grain bins. I waited until dawn to start out for Skibbereen. I don't think that I was followed here, but I'm scared that they know me now and will hunt me down."

"They're the bastards! Calm down, brother. You are safe here with me," Tadgh countered. "Wait while I check something."

Tadgh rushed up to the main room and peered out of the barred windows. He did this on all four sides of the house. Thankful that he saw nothing suspicious, he rejoined Aidan.

"The coast is clear at this point. Aidan, you've got to stop picking fights, or you're going to go to *gaol* or worse. Get that through your thick skull once and for all," Tadgh glowered.

"Yah, I know," Aidan muttered, averting his eyes.

"You're not hearing me, dammit. Don't ya know, you've already compromised me and my work. You picked a fight with RIC men. You know about our safe house, and you're here now."

"Yah, I guess so," Sean conceded.

"We've been over this so many times, brother. The senseless deaths of Mam and Pa at the hands of the murderous RIC five years ago was a travesty, to be sure, but we've got to use our anger to liberate our country, not waste away hiding in the boozer, langers all the time. That's why I joined the IRB, and that's why I made this safe house that you helped me with. I'll give you that."

"So?"

"So if you keep acting the maggot, you're goin' to get me and you killed."

"By the RIC?"

"Yes. Or by the IRB. They won't let you compromise our operations."

"But why you?"

"Listen. They bankrolled me to modify this home as a safe house for the coming revolution. And they're paying the mortgage. I didn't have much money left from my playwriting days in Dublin, and I'm a wanted man myself because of what I wrote. Why do you think I wear disguises when I'm in Cork?

"But I'm not you."

"No, you're a crazy with a screw loose. If you don't straighten up, the IRB will kill you."

"No they wouldn't, surely."

"Yes, surely, you bleedin' git."

"That's no way to talk to your younger brother, Tadgh."

"Would you rather I just show up at your funeral then, lad?"

"No . . . of course not."

"Well then, you'll stay here with me for the time bein' until I know if the RIC can trace you to me. It is not safe for you to leave this room at this point. Right?"

"If you say so."

"Damn. I mean it, Aidan."

"Get some sleep, brother. There's food on the shelves. I will check on you tonight, I will."

With that, Tadgh left the operations center and moved the lantern back, which closed the hidden barn door. Tadgh could feel his heart as heavy as his footsteps sounded as he mounted the stairs. If Aidan continued to be a problem, the Brotherhood would kill him, since dead men tell no tales. He couldn't let that happen, and he couldn't abandon the Brotherhood, either. They might kill *him,* too.

But things were getting very complicated. He now had a woman with amnesia in his bed and an out-of-control brother on the run from the RIC hiding in his boathouse. And he had been completely neglecting his role in the planning for the upcoming war for independence. His IRB leader, Padraig Pearse, would be wondering whether the Sea Serpent's Society would play ball in helping the Germans deliver armament.

He was trying to figure out his next steps as he ascended the stairs to his patient. The only thing that he knew for sure was that Jameson would be an important part of his deliberations. He stopped in the kitchen for a drink. He could just drop the girl off on the doorstep of Cunard in Queenstown and be rid of this distraction. Yet she was already becoming a voice in his head that he had to admit he didn't want to drown out, at least not yet.

He had been dismayed the day she took the sponge and towel from him so she could bathe herself. She had not turned from him in modesty, but he felt she had thus established some border that separated them. His hands and heart felt empty, and he ached to touch her. Her body had taught him the strength of gentleness and kindness of touch, and he wanted her to continue teaching him.

A tension had come between them, a change in their meaning to one another. As she grew more able to take care of herself, he had to adjust his own understanding of her. Of course, he would have been happy that she remained under his care, but then that thought shocked him—it would have made him into a keeper, a guard. He knew what prompted this feeling: he did not want her to leave him. More than the body that drove him to distraction, she was quickly becoming the shelter that allowed him to rest, to forgive himself, and find his measure of goodness.

Chapter Nineteen
Awakening

June 20, 1915
Creagh, Ireland

*T*he colleen was sitting by the window when he returned, gazing out at the meandering river in back of Tadgh's home. At least it looked peaceful in the afternoon sun

There were so many questions unanswered. *Who am I and where do I come from? Is this river flowing towards my homeland? I must have come from America if I was on the Lusitania. Do I have family there? Children? Were they with me and now they're dead? Why can't I remember the sinking itself, then? It must have been terrible.*

Their eyes met and locked for a moment. She was clad in one of his work shirts she must have found in his drawer, which only covered her down to mid-thigh. It tugged on her breasts so that their tantalizing shape was silhouetted. She looked rather fetching in that attire, Tadgh mused, distracted. Clearly she was feeling somewhat better, or pretending to be, and the vision of her loveliness instantly cheered him up.

He wondered what was going on in her mind. Was she doing this on purpose to signal that she did not want to be discarded by him like a rag doll? He realized that his brother's arrival would have raised many questions for her, which would put their budding relationship to the test. *What relationship?*

This was the first time that his manhood had overcome the haunting memory of his Mother's fate, and it was unnerving. He had heard that often a patient will have affection for her caregiver, but was the converse also true? He knew that he had brought her through a tough time and he could see that she was a fighter, which he liked about her. He crossed to her and touched her shoulder

263

gently. She twitched and lifted her chin, eyes questioning.

"How's your brother Aidan?"

"He'll live." Just a few cuts and bruises from a donnybrook at the bar. He's downstairs recuperatin'. You can meet him later. A penny for your thoughts, lass." He rubbed her shoulder and neck, so knotted.

"You'd need a bag of pennies for my thoughts right now. Confused mostly."

"I can imagine. Why don't you get back in bed?" He tried to pull her up unsuccessfully.

"No. It's at least one positive step to be up at last."

He knelt by her side. "You must be afraid not knowing who you are."

"Yes, that's a big part of my angst." She turned and looked out the window again, murmuring, "How would you feel?"

God, it would be awful. "Devastated to be sure, lass."

"You've been more than kind, Tadgh. Saving my life." She turned to face him and stroked his hair. He could feel her fingers trembling.

"But I don't know you, really. You seem to be in such danger. And who are the RIC? Are they here?"

"They're nowhere to be seen, thank God. And you're safe here with me, lass. Believe that."

"I'd like to believe you, but . . ." She started brushing her silken hair with a brush Tadgh had lent her, a masculine one with prickly bristles.

It must be stinging her scalp. Tadgh hunted for a comb in his night table drawer. Finding a suitable one, he offered it to her. She thanked him with her smoky eyes drawing him in. Tadgh realized that she needed more information. Either he had to decide to keep her in the dark and let her go into Queenstown, or if he wanted her to stay, he would have to take her into his confidence. He was starting to see that she was a lass of substance, albeit one whose mind may not be fully functioning yet. He wasn't schooled in the effects of amnesia, so he wasn't sure when, or if, her memory could return.

Standing up, Tadgh looked away, staring past her out the window at the Ilen River, and avoiding her gaze. Those smoky green eyes. Even at the young age of twenty-one, he felt the river of life was passing him by.

Damn. Aidan is uncontrollable. I've tried. Oh how I've tried. The boy needs you, Mam, and you're dead, rest your soul. The floozies that he hangs around with are imbeciles, dragging him into sin and depravity. And I'm no role model, to be sure. But now he's risking my life and safe house. Maybe we need a good woman's voice, and touch, despite the risk to her life. Mam, what should I do?

A punt came into view upstream from around the bend. A couple out for an afternoon row, laughing. No, a family, with a baby on a woman's breast.

Tadgh decided that he wasn't ready to let the woman go and wanted to trust her. But she was right. They were in danger, and the risks were going to get much higher.

Turning back into the room, their room, he said, "Heaven help me . . . and you. Look you, now. There is a lot about me that you don't know. I need to tell you some of it. The rest will have to wait. Right?"

"All right, Tadgh. What can you tell me?" She fixed her gaze once more, and he could feel himself melting into her sultry green eyes as he took her trembling hand.

"Well, now. For centuries, England has subjugated Ireland harshly," he started, kneeling back down like a suppliant to be eye to eye. "Like all the Irish clans, my family members were driven out of their homes and off their land. This was partially for religious beliefs but mostly for conquest." With his free hand, he flipped one of her black curls behind her ear so he could see both of those mesmerizing eyes clearly. It was unnerving, to say the least. He needed to break free from that captivity.

"This story would go well with a glass of Jameson, so it would. Do you think you could manage the stairs with my assistance? We can talk while I prepare dinner."

"Oh yes, I'm able, you'll see. And I'd love a glass of whiskey."

"How'd you know that Jameson is whiskey?"

"I dunno, just came to me."

"Aha. Your memory's coming back."

"Just silly little things. Nothing important as yet."

"Give it time, lass. Give it time. Now what can we find for you to wear on your legs?"

The girl sat at the kitchen table, whiskey glass in hand, while Tadgh chopped vegetables.

"I love your kitchen, Tadgh, so homey. That stove must be a hundred years old."

"I don't have any of my parents' belongings, I'm afraid. It's pretty roughshod in here."

"It's lovely. What are you cooking?"

"Irish stew, of course. You get it every other night."

"I remembered the taste from my girlhood the first time you gave it to me."

"Did you, now. And where might that have been?"

"I have no idea. My brain's a fuzzy ball. And this Jameson's not helping. It stings my throat," she added, taking another sip.

"But it's damned good for what ails ya."

"Of that I have no doubt. So go on with your history."

"Well now, it's a sad tale to be sure. For two hundred years, the English have stripped us of our dignity and, in millions of cases, our lives. Irishmen of our Roman Catholic faith have been persecuted and systematically killed. Our rights to own land and to vote were taken away for many years."

He could see moisture gathering in inner corners of those eyes, and her eyebrows were knitted. But the gaze was still strong.

"When the potato blight came in the middle of the last century, we were vassals to tyrannical overlords who were living high on the hog in England. They had murderous henchmen managing their estates in Ireland—our ancient homeland. Irish families were treated like cattle. They were beasts of burden to be whipped until they became useless, and then they were put out of their misery."

Tadgh's knife was slicing the carrots with a vengeance.

"Mind what you're doing or you'll cut your finger off."

Tadgh smiled, ignored the warning, and continued his story, slicing away. "The wheat and corn that we produced could have saved our people from starvation. But it was shipped back to England and abroad by them, leaving only rotten potatoes to feed us. Millions died or emigrated away from the country that they loved. Here in Skibbereen, we were hard hit with ten thousand killed."

The tears were flowing now and the young woman's lip was quivering. Her grip on her glass tightened fiercely. "My God, Tadgh. How could they?"

Tadgh pulled his coarse handkerchief from his back pocket and came to her, dabbed her eyes.

"It gets worse, I'm afraid. That was when the RIC was established by the English to enforce the brutal evictions of those who were sick or who could not pay crushing taxes to the overlords. They continue today to do their bidding and to stamp out any of our efforts to regain independence for our people."

"It is terribly tragic." The girl took a larger swig of the amber liquid.

"You have no idea."

Tadgh put his thumb and forefinger to his forehead and pinched the bridge of his nose, averting his eyes downward for the first time. His trembling voice was barely a murmur. "It got personal. My Mam and Pa were senselessly murdered by RIC executioners five years ago in our family home nearby. My brother and I witnessed the killings."

"Oh no!" she cried.

"Our parents knew it was coming, and they pleaded for their lives to no avail. It was horrible. From a crack in our bedroom door, we watched as our parents got shot in the head."

Her grip had strengthened, and she pulled him to her and cradled his head on her breast. "What happened to you then?" She whispered.

"We had a good look at their executioner standing not thirty feet away. He was an evil-looking English thug, and I'll never forget his tattoo and the missing finger on his right hand. I watched him repeatedly squeeze the trigger of his Webley revolver. He was screaming obscenities, that monster."

"God, Tadgh. What did you do?" She started to stroke his hair.

"That's the shame of it all. I did nothing to save them."

"You were just so young then, surely," she said raising his head to recapture his gaze. "What could you children have done to stop it?"

"We were sleeping and it all happened so fast," Tadgh remembered, wincing. "They burst into our home with guns drawn. That thug beat up my Pa while his henchman threatened my Ma. He was trying to get some information."

"You were trapped with no one to help you," she remembered her own underwater monster.

"I could have done something," he lamented. "I don't even know why they did it. Senseless." He got up, finished chopping the vegetables, and let the knife lay there on the cutting board, glinting in the light.

"How did you get away?"

"We hid under our beds when the constables stormed into our room. Those devils doused our beds with kerosene as well as the rest of the house. Then they rushed out after setting it ablaze. We managed to break the window of our back bedroom and escape with only our hair singed. When we reached the woods at the back of the property by crawling through the dark in the stubbled field, we could see the constables standing at the road, laughing and shooting from rifles into the house. There must have been five or more of them. From that moment, we hated the RIC. That very night, Aidan and I made a pledge to exact revenge, not only on the evil English in general, but on our parents' executioners."

"But Aidan, then . . . how was he affected?"

"My brother has fallen by the wayside, I'm afraid. I can't seem to influence him much."

"At some point we cannot be our brother's keeper, Tadgh," she said clear-eyed now.

"If I can't get him under control, then my bosses will have him exterminated, don't ya know."

"Surely not. Why?"

"Surely yes, lass. He knows too much, about me, this place, them."

"Who are *them*, Tadgh?"

Putting his arm around her shoulders, turning her to face him he said, "Well then, lass I'll tell ya. The time has come to rise up and fight for our independence. Since England is embroiled in war with Germany, my comrades think we have an excellent opportunity to strike a blow for freedom here at home. I am a member of the Irish Republican Brotherhood, the IRB, that, with other organizations, is planning a revolution. That's *them*."

He hadn't meant to name his covert organization, but at that moment, uncharacteristically, he decided to take the risk of bringing her completely into his confidence.

"My God, it isn't just your family. You're all going to war and potentially going to kill each other. This is a lot to take in for a girl who doesn't even know her own name."

"Aye, lass, to be sure." He realized that he had gone too far, too soon, sensing how she must feel. He pulled her up from the chair and gave her a gentle bear hug, being careful to judge her reaction, to not offend her.

Initially she stiffened but then relaxed into his shoulder. "I am beginning to understand your hurt and your passion for your country," she said. "But I need to find out who I am."

For the first time the electricity of body and soul flashed between them.

Tadgh was shocked by her response. He had expected her to recoil from his news. He had never needed feminine comfort, except as a child from his Mam. Yet here, with this woman in his arms, he somehow felt safer than when he was alone. This was the opposite reaction that he would have expected of himself.

Tadgh disengaged from the embrace. He immediately regretted his response, as he was suddenly separated from her warmth.

Returning to his task and scraping the vegetables from the cutting board into his iron pot simmering on the Stanley solid fuel stove, he said, "I've been thinking about that problem. You are not quite ready to venture out into the world at large yet. But you can stay here by yourself for a day if I leave food and drink for you. I will go to Queenstown where they are accounting for the passengers at the Cunard office in Queenstown, so I can see if I can find out who you are, lass." He wasn't going to tell her about the temporary morgue that he'd read had been set up dockside.

"Oh, would you please?"

"Yes, and after that we will see where we stand."

"Fair enough," she agreed looking up into his amber eyes with a broad smile.

Tadgh kissed her forehead. "We'll figure it out then, lass."

The next day, after checking on Aiden to make sure he would stay put, Tadgh took his motorcycle and rode to Queenstown. This was a risk that he would have to take. He dressed casually, with his

Irish tweed cap pulled down over his eyes. But it was his full, curly black beard that he had grown during that long period of recuperation of this girl that he hoped would truly mask his identity. He avoided the checkpoints where the authorities might recognize him.

The scene he found on the docks and in the transit warehouse in Queenstown was one of abject horror and anguish. Some foreigners were wailing in grief as they claimed remains of their relatives. Others were consoling each other while they awaited news which was unlikely to come at this point, Tadgh thought. Cunard officials with passenger lists were checking off the names as relatives arrived and as bodies were claimed. In the makeshift morgue, the smell was revolting. It was, indeed, the aftermath of war.

Tadgh pretended to be a relative to blend in with the crowd. There was a copy of the passenger manifest hanging on the wall of morgue. Perusing it, he realized that there were over 900 women aboard, of which only a hundred or so had been identified by a check mark in the margin. Further, the ages of the passengers were not given. Sadly there were no photographs taken of the passengers to identify them, either.

This is hopeless. I've got to bring the lass here to Queenstown to see if anyone can recognize her. He hoped that her memory would return to her by then.

Tadgh arrived back mid-afternoon and went straight up to his bedroom. The colleen was sleeping. He noticed, with satisfaction, that she had consumed all of the food and drink that he had left for her. As he touched her brow, which was much cooler now, she woke up.

Reaching up to hold his hand, she smiled and kissed it gently. This was definitely not a good development.

"Well, did you find out who I am?" she blurted out.

"Unfortunately no, lass," he responded gently. "They don't have photograph records or ages listed. And there are so many missing.

Unless you regain your memory, the only way to identify you will be if a relative or friend claims you there, don't ya see?"

Tadgh could see that she was crestfallen. Her cheeks sank and eyes dropped, her lashes moist, so he took a different tack.

"Well then. I've decided that you need a name that I can call you by. What do you think of Morgan? It is a Welsh name derived from "mor"—"sea" and "gan"— from "the". I think it suits you, so I do, lady who came from the sea," he smiled.

"It seems fitting if I am to have a new name," she exclaimed. "It will work until I remember who I really am. It's certainly better than 'Hallo, Colleen, you there.' "

"I know you are concerned about your past," he said. "I'm not trying to make light of it. We will keep trying to find out your identity. Trust me."

"I do trust you, Tadgh. You saved me. Thank you for trying to understand my nightmare."

"You are most welcome, Morgan," Tadgh replied, being careful to use her new name.

"What do you have there in that package?" Morgan asked.

"Well, although you look terrific in my shirt, I thought that you might need some new clothes. The ones you were wearing when I found you were completely destroyed."

She started to smile, and her sultry green eyes twinkled for the first time since he had returned. He found her smile infectious, especially when her cheeks dimpled like that.

"Show me what you brought," she coaxed him.

"All right, then. Don't blame me if these clothes don't fit. I don't know anything about corsets and the like."

"I should hope not, with your upbringing." Then ripping open the package, she cooed, "Oh, Tadgh, these short skirts are delightful. And the blouses match. You amaze me. I think that purple is my favorite color. Maybe it wasn't before, but it is now. But how did you know they would fit . . . ?"

"Don't give me any credit. I contacted an associate of mine in Dublin two weeks ago when I realized that you would need these clothes. I gave her my guess at your height, beam and girth. She did the rest. They were waiting for me at the Post Office in Cork."

"Beam and girth, really, Tadgh?"

"Well, those are the fisherman's nautical terms for it."

"So I'm a fish now."

"I like fish, and boats."

"You have a girlfriend, Tadgh?" she asked, her eyes lowered.

"Constance Markievicz isn't a girlfriend. She's a business associate, a Countess who performed in a play that I was involved in at the Abbey Theatre two years ago. She's a friend of W.B. Yeats, one of the greatest writers of our time."

"Really?"

"Absolutely. With regards to the clothes she chose, all I can say is that I heard her once say, *Dress suitably in short skirts and strong boots, leave your jewelry in the bank and buy a revolver.*"

"What jewelry might that be?"

"We'll have to see about that, I suppose."

"You are a most mysterious man. A play at the Abbey Theatre?"

"Yes, that's right. Got me into big trouble in Dublin, I can tell you. But I think you are much more mysterious than I."

"That's how it should be for the woman. Turn around," Morgan asked. "And don't you peek."

"Wouldn't think of it," Tadgh replied, turning but positioning himself in front of the wardrobe mirror.

"They fit fine. Oh, they make me feel like a girl again," Morgan giggled after she had donned one of the outfits. "I don't think I'll wear the corset just yet. The countess has good taste in clothes, and in men."

"She's just an associate, really."

"Of course she is. Oh, thank you, Tadgh." She laughed as she threw her arms around him.

"Don't mention it," he responded, taking a step backward. Her outburst had unnerved him. But he couldn't take his eyes off her. The purple skirt and jumper accentuated her full figure. All in all, she was dazzling.

"Does this mean that I won't see you in my shirt anymore?"

Morgan's eyebrows went up at that remark, and her dimples deepened as she handed him his shirt. He sniffed in her scent from it, and his knees felt weak.

"You clean up right good, lass."

"Thank you, kind sir. Oh, Tadgh, I met your brother."

"Damn. I told him to stay put."

"Well, he came up here and looked like he was checking me out, drinking from a bottle he called his Jameson elixir."

"Were you still dressed only in my shirt?"

"Yes, but he was a perfect gentleman. He just looked and sounded like a boy in serious trouble."

"That's Aidan."

"It seemed to me that he was agonizing over what to do as he started back downstairs. You'd better look in on him."

"I'll be back in a few minutes."

Morgan was adjusting her skirt in the mirror when Tadgh bounded back up the stairs not three minutes later.

"That eejit's gone," Tadgh fumed. "Aidan can't be trusted to stay still for long."

Tadgh had checked his liquor cabinet. "Three of my four bottles of Jameson are missing. That figures. He never could hold his liquor, and when he's drunk he's a mean son-of-a-bitch."

"I know that you're concerned for Aidan's welfare, Tadgh, but there must be more to it than that, isn't there?"

"You're right, lass. There is a lot more going on here than meets the eye. Let me give you a complete tour of my home, and maybe you'll understand."

"My home is set back about one hundred feet from the Baltimore Road at Creagh, about three miles southwest of Skibbereen center, right on the headwaters of the Ilen River," he explained. "Being just two miles from the open sea at Baltimore, and off the beaten path, away from the Cork Road, it's a perfect spot for covert operations."

"Covert operations?"

"Yes. I'll explain later. This was the area where the Irish settled after the Barbary pirates attacked Baltimore in 1631."

"I thought Barbary Corsairs just fought in the Mediterranean."

"Another silly little thing?"

"Yes, I suppose so. They came to Ireland then?"

"Just the once, I'm told. Took over a hundred Irish slaves back to North Africa."

"How barbaric."

"Not all that different than how the English have been treating us now, is it."

"I suppose not. Can we go outside for a brief walk? It looks sunny."

"Yes, I think it would be a grand idea after I turn off the stove."

For the first time, Tadgh took Morgan out for a walk in the garden. Looking back at the house from the road, she could see that it was an old, two-story fishing shanty typical of the west Cork seaside communities of the seventeenth century. Yet it was built on a stone foundation that was obviously much older. The steeply pitched roof was of thatch, and the walls were whitewashed clay brick with exposed oak beams that separated the floors.

"If you look closely, you can see chips in the walls where my old house stopped bullets during a raid in the past. See? Here." He pointed. "It's close to three hundred years old, I think," Tadgh offered, seeing Morgan's quizzical look as she ran her fingers over the old brick. "It's a wonder that the English overlords left it standing during the evictions of the potato famine."

"Yes. I can feel it."

"Feel what? Its age?"

"No. Its history. There's something powerful here . . . damn. It won't come to me."

"You've been here before?"

"No. Of course not. But I have this feeling when I touch the brick."

"Feeling?"

"Yes . . . of déjà vu. This is a strange house, Tadgh."

"It is that, to be sure. That's why I bought it. But I think that your brain is a might jumbled at the minute."

"Aye. I think that's an understatement."

Continuing their walk towards the river, Tadgh pointed out the top floor with gabled windows containing the one big bedroom and a small workroom, plus a retrofitted indoor bathroom. The pipes to it ran external in a cross-cross fashion on the ivy covered wall.

"So that's where I've been living for the last month and a half. It looks different from the outside, especially in the sunshine," Morgan commented, throwing her arms up outstretched to the sky. The radiant smile on her face cheered Tadgh enormously.

From the outside, Morgan could see how the ground floor's expansive, homey kitchen and eating area, and its more civilized parlor were packaged together. All in all a very charming, though rustic home.

On the river side, the land dropped off just behind the house, with a massive windowless boathouse some 25 feet high, just at the water level. This was where Tadgh housed *The Republican*. Sturdy, bolted boathouse doors closed out the world and its weather. The house was built on the edge of the hill with only the adjacent boathouse to shore it up. Tadgh had built a roof deck on top of the boathouse, and you could step out of the parlor directly onto it through modern French doors.

"Your home is quite lovely," Morgan said, admiring how the garden shrubs and trees integrated the building with its rural surroundings.

"It's our home, now," Tadgh commented. "At least for the time being."

"Certainly, and I thank you for it, my dear."

Dear what? Tadgh thought.

They descended the long staircase on the outside wall of the boathouse until they were standing on Tadgh's dock, which spanned that side of the boathouse. Tadgh unlocked the side door. The couple Tadgh had seen earlier from the bedroom window rowed by, the man now straining to make headway against the current. The woman waved the baby's hand in her own, and Morgan gleefully waved back.

"I'd like to do that, go for a boat ride sometime."

"I'm sure we'll be after doin' just that, sooner than you'd think." The rescue had been his last chance to sail, and he longed to get back to the sea.

He ushered her inside where *The Republican* lay in its berth in the river. The boathouse's wall-mounted tables and platforms were covered with a hundred years of fishing and nautical paraphernalia, including gaffing hooks and nets of all shapes and sizes. Much of it was rusted beyond repair. The back wall was paneled in old barn wood and adorned with pictures of *The Republican* and other older boats hauling in large catches of fish. This added to the aura that this was, indeed, a fisherman's home. It was all a good ruse to hide the current function of this fortification.

When Morgan turned to go up the inside stairs to the house, Tadgh asked nonchalantly, "Can you see anything amiss, lassie?"

"Nope. It looks like a well-used boathouse to me. Why? Should I?"

"Just wondered," Tadgh replied as he moved the oil lantern to his right.

"Cripes." Morgan jumped back as the hidden door cracked open. "What is this?" she asked as she pushed the door open and stepped across the threshold.

"This is my operations center," Tadgh switched on the light. He looked closely to see her reaction. There were no dimples now.

Morgan scanned the cavernous room. Two walls were lined with triple-high bunk beds, enough to house up to 30 men. On one half of a third wall, floor-to-ceiling shelves were crammed with storable foodstuffs. Large gun lockers occupied the other half of this wall along with a new-fangled telephone. There was a rough sink of sorts and a spigot that brought fresh water from the underground cistern that had collected rain water. A toilet was housed in a corner enclosure. Maps, charts and personnel and schedule boards filled the fourth wall. All self-contained. He still marveled at how equipped he was for any operation.

"Where does this room go?"

"Dug it out of the hillside underground, me and Aidan. Did it all from the river side to avoid notice. It took quite a while to dig and haul the dirt away, I can tell you."

"What's its purpose, Tadgh?"

"My home is the Cork West fortified safe house for the Irish Republican Brotherhood in the southwest part of Ireland. So far, the war is only in the secret planning stages, but we are going to liberate our country very soon.

"I am in charge of communications, transportation and armament for the Cork-West brigade of the IRB," he went on. "I often wear a disguise when out in public because the RIC have me on their hit list, at least in Dublin."

Morgan took a step back. "Oh, really. Are those lockers full of guns?"

"I wish they were. Not yet. I was trying to negotiate to get some the day that I found you."

"Saved me, you mean."

"If you'd like to call it that . . ."

"What disguise?"

"My new beard, a false moustache, thick glasses. It depends. I can show you."

"You didn't used to have that beard?"

"Not before I found you. You've seen it grow fuller."

Morgan leaned in and stroked his curly chin. "It makes you look right handsome, almost regal, so it does."

"Does it really—regal indeed?"

"When can I see the fully-disguised Tadgh?"

"You will, soon enough, lass. My motorcycle can get me away fast, if need be."

He stopped at this point to let the grim, yet glorious reality of his situation and mission sink in for her. If she didn't reject him now, she never would.

"Like I told you yesterday, this is more that a bit overwhelming, especially for someone who doesn't even know her own name," she said, turning to leave the operations center.

"I'm sure it is. Your name is Morgan, now."

"You know what I meant."

"Yes, of course. Let's go on up. There's still stew in the pot."

"Good. I'm famished. Give me a hand, please."

Tadgh had hoped for some positive affirmation of his home and cause during dinner, but Morgan seemed to be avoiding those subjects.

"What am I going to do to find out who I am?" she asked finally, picking at a piece of mutton on her plate and avoiding Tadgh's gaze.

"We're going to have to go to Cork, Queenstown really, when you're able."

"I'm able now."

"I must admit that a walk in the afternoon air seems to have done wonders for you, lass."

"Yes, I think that it's cleared away the cobwebs, no longer cooped up in your bedroom. Not that there's anything wrong with your bedroom."

"But not the mental ones."

"Not yet."

"All right, then. How about if we look for Aidan in Cork and then go to the Cunard office to try and find your name?"

"When?"

"Tomorrow." He knew he couldn't postpone his search for his brother.

"Yes, please. I'd better get my beauty rest then, hadn't I," Morgan said turning to go up the stairs to bed.

"About my work . . ."

"Can we talk about it tomorrow?"

"Of course."

Standing halfway up the sturdy spiral staircase, Morgan paused to examine the ancient wooden banister. "Have you seen the engravings in this old rail? Initials and some nautical remarks."

"Yeah, I think that thing has been here since the house was built. Never gave those hen scratchings much consideration, though."

"Just another curiosity. Did you know that they feel warm to my touch?"

"Do they, now. Must be the fire in the hearth."

"I don't think so. This house is strange."

"That it is, lass, and so are you."

It was midnight and Tadgh couldn't sleep. He had to find Aidan before the RIC did, and then he had to get him under control . . . his breach of security never happened before, not at this level, jeopardizing everything. And after more than a month of sleeping on the chesterfield, it was getting more and more uncomfortable. He needed his sleep. He needed to be sleeping in his own bed.

He heard her restless turnings in the room above him, and he could find no peace. Even a tumbler, aye, a whole fifth of the Jameson could not take away his longing for her. He ground his teeth, fearful that she would not want him, that she would see him for a brute that imprisoned her for his own designs. Now his defense crumbled, he could no longer pass another moment without her touch. He was turned around inside and wild for her. He could not stay away, the devil take him.

He did not need to creep up the stairs; she was quite accustomed to his looking in on her throughout the night. He pushed the door open, and the low lamplight revealed her small movements as if she could not settle. He approached her and, as was his habit, touched her forehead and stroked her cheek to assure himself that she was not too warm.

It was her habit to submit to his touch and grow quiet almost immediately. This time though, she reached up her hand to take his and guide to it to her mouth so she might kiss his fingers. Then her eyes opened and she held him with her steady clear gaze as she opened her lips to take in his fingers and taste him. Her movement, so sudden that he nearly pulled away, caused him to lose all sense of anything other than the feel of her tongue licking the length of his fingers. She then kissed the palm of his hand, a hand roughened by the sea and revolution and sorrow, and he was lost. He closed his eyes, his breath drew in; this moment defined him. What they did now would change them and their place with one another forever, so they hesitated. For only a moment.

He went to her and removed her coverings, just as he had done before. This time, when she looked at him, she rose to meet him so he could take away her nightdress—it slid to the floor— and unbind her hair. The raven bounty fell over her shoulders and tumbled down her back. He caught the heavy tresses and buried his face in them, breathing in their perfume.

Every movement was charged with a delicious, luxuriant anticipation that slowed time and fed their desire. They lingered, teasing, in their desire for this union of their bodies.

But then, suddenly, the girl shrank back, pulling the covers up around her neck.

"What's wrong, lass?" Tadgh managed to croak out. *God in heaven, I've gone too far.*

"What if I made another family?" she murmured, trying to get control of her heart rate.

"Yes, yes. I see. You need the truth of it. I'll go back down."

"No, Tadgh. Don't go. Can we share without . . . ?"

"You felt us. We're tangled, no doubt. That's a tall order, girl."

"Well? Can you, for now?"

"Can you?"

"Yes, for now. Stay, please."

Tadgh lay down outside the covers. He was still quivering. "We'll give it a go. But we've got to put this family question to rest, sure enough."

"Yes, let's."

Tadgh laid there sleepless 'til almost dawn. He noted that she seemed to sleep much more soundly than on nights gone by.

Whatever waited outside that room could never make them forget the gift of each other's body that they had started to share. In her, he found solace and renewal; she anchored him and gave his troubled soul a space to work his way from the chaos and loss he had experienced in his youth. His political commitment would not change, but he might be able to lay the ghosts of his parents to rest. He desperately hoped that she, in turn, would lay down her sorrow for what she had lost and rebuild her life, with him.

Chapter Twenty
Search for Aidan

June 22, 1915
Cork City, Ireland

*H*ead Constable Darcy Boyle always got to his office at the RIC Union Quay Headquarters before sun-up. It wasn't that he was diligent in his duties. He just needed to catch his subordinates and the bloody Irish off-guard. And he couldn't sleep anyway.

"Intimidation is the most important skill that our ancestors possessed to rid our lands of these degenerate vermin," his father had drummed into him. Since Darcy was muscular and six foot two, that part was dead easy for him.

It was the other character trait that his Pa demanded of him that confounded the bejesus out of him. Deception. *Now how in hell can I be deceptive if I'm intimidating the shite out of some sodder?"*

The regrettable truth was that Darcy just didn't have the intellect, and, after centuries of Boyle in-breeding, he wondered whether his capacities were diminished over time. In those early morning introspections, he would often recogitate what happened that fateful night, back at the turn of the century when he was just a pup. His Pa had brought him along to teach him, hoping this time to finally hit pay dirt.

The shame of it. We had Fergus McCarthy alone, dead to rights, but Pa underestimated the bugger. Pa let his guard down, just when he thought he had him subdued. McCarthy killed the ole fella and severed my little finger with a rusty sword hanging over his mantle-piece. At least I finally overpowered him, beheading the bastard with his own weapon. But I almost died from the blood poisoning, Darcy remembered, looking down to where the phantom digit should have been.

It still ached when it rained. *There was nothing I could do. Pa was dying right there in McCarthy's parlor. I couldn't carry him out.* "I'll go get help, Pa," he had cried out, but his father caught his ankle with his arm and held fast.

"There's no time for that. I am already dead. You are the last Boyle in the line. You must not fail in our family's ancient quest. Never show weakness, lad. Be ever ruthless. It is now your destiny to finally seize the spoils of our conquest from the heathens. Promise me, son." Though his voice was faint, his tone was ferocious.

"Well, lad?" *It seemed his pa was holding on to the last vestiges of life until he got the commitment.*

What could he say? "Of course, Pa, I will not fail you. I promise."

Pa's grip eased, but his dying eyes were fixed on his. He bent down. "There's a pact in my safe."

Those were his last words.

Darcy understood the family obsession, sure enough. It was due his family, the spoils of victory. The McCarthy gold, they called it. His ancestors had worked hard for it, died for it, under Oliver the Roundhead. Now *there* was a soldier who epitomized his father's methodology. *Slash and burn. Pillage and rape. Exterminate the vermin.*

And his father had told him where to find the proof of existence. Not just the McCarthys in the south but also the O'Donnells in the north. But where were these treasures buried? That was the unanswered question that had haunted fifteen generations of Boyles before him, and led to the premature death of many of the Irish bloodline at the hands of his forefathers with no revelation of the hiding places. Now he was the remaining Boyle, the prodigal son, charged with the ancient family quest, or curse, depending upon one's point of view. Like his father before him, he wasn't going to let the family down. He had kept his subordinates in line five years ago when they confronted Fergus' son and his wife in their home near Skibbereen. They had it coming in retribution for his Pa's murder.

Claimed they didn't know anything about gold. Served them right. *He didn't let his guard down that night.*

But as much as his Pa's strident voice always rang in his ears, there was his Ma's emotional plea in the background trying desperately to keep what was left of her warmongering family intact. How odd that she had been the first Boyle of her generation to pass before she could convince her only son to seek a wife. Oh, there had been conquests to satisfy the flesh, but they had all ended badly, sometimes fatally. Now at age forty-eight, he feared it was too late. Darcy had to find the treasure or the age-old secret would die with him. He'd make sure if it came to that.

And now, he couldn't believe his luck. Here was another McCarthy, who may be in the bloodline, to hunt down, interrogate, and kill in the ways of the ancients.

How could that son-of-a-bitch be so dumb as to pick a fight with the RIC? Maybe this one will talk before he croaks.

"Gordo, how the hell did you find out this guy is a McCarthy?" Boyle yelled at his underling as the man strode into the office.

"We questioned the sods in the Pub. He is a regular at Clancy's," Constable Gordon James piped up. He was still nursing his bruised ribs from the incident. "Seems his pa and ma died during an eviction by the RIC five years ago over in Hollyhill, according to Clancy himself. We forced that much out of him."

"Why didn't we find him during the eviction, then?" Boyle.

"Beats me, boss." You'll remember that we torched the place immediately after the shootings. I don't think anyone could have gotten out alive."

Boyle thought for a minute. "Get a couple of the constables on our payroll and have them watch Clancy's, out of uniform. When he gets thirsty enough, he'll show up. When he does, don't stop him. Follow him and report back to me immediately."

"Right, boss," the short, stocky constable answered, turning on his heel without giving his master the opportunity to criticize him once again.

When Tadgh awoke first, he was on his back, in his own bed at last. He found Morgan seemingly asleep, sprawled diagonally with her arm draped across his chest. Apparently, she wasn't alarmed that he was sharing the bed. He lay quite still for some time, drinking in the intimacy of the moment and feeling rejuvenated. *Don't get used to this. She could remember who she really is. Then what would he do?*

When he finally went to gingerly move her arm to get up, Morgan grabbed him. "I wondered when you'd finally wake up," she murmured, snuggling closer.

"Got to go and find Aidan," Tadgh replied, jumping out of bed as if the previous night never happened. "I need to go to Cork, but with Aidan's indiscretion, I don't want to leave you here alone. Are you up to accompanying me?"

"Yes, I think so. I want to be with you. Can we go to Cunard like you promised, so I can try to find out who I am?"

Tadgh had been thinking about that. "Are you sure that you want to know, lass? Aren't you content here with me and your new life?"

"Yes. But wouldn't you want to know, if it happened to you?"

"Probably. But there might be anguish if you knew. I'm thinkin' of my own Mam and Pa." He returned to the bed and sat next to her as she rose, kneeling to meet him.

"What about the anguish of not knowing? The emptiness." She reached her arm around his waist, holding him firm. Her emerald eyes were searching his for the answers that he couldn't possibly give.

In the depth of them, behind that frown framing them on the surface, below the smoke that swirled within them, he suddenly caught a brief glimpse of her soul. Amazing, the strength of this girl. She was not crumbling from being in this total void of knowledge like he might have done. She had not withdrawn when told of his gruesome history and perilous mission. Not yet anyway. *I am not letting her go.*

"I see it in your eyes, Morgan, in your soul. Yes, we can certainly go to the Cunard offices in Queenstown after we search for Aidan in Cork City."

"Good. Let's be off, then."

After breakfast, Tadgh and Morgan set out on his motorcycle. They tooled along the bumpy Cork Road at high speed.

"This is quite a machine," Morgan yelled over the whine of the engine and whoosh of the wind. "Where'd you get it?"

"Isn't it great? It's a *Kerry* 670 cc sv V twin built by Abingdon, and you're sitting in its Watsonian wickerwork sidecar," Tadgh explained. "It was provided by the Brotherhood for my transportation and communications assignments. It can travel off the road at high speeds of thirty-five miles per hour to elude the RIC when necessary."

Morgan kept a hand on his right thigh for stability, so she could feel his strong muscles flex each time he shifted through the gears. They both felt a charge of excitement.

Tadgh was wearing his laborer's disguise with motorcycle goggles and a moustache, and he kept a wary eye open for constables. Fortunately, none materialized. When they neared Cork City, Tadgh kept off the main roads and arrived undetected at Aidan's tenement house.

Morgan noticed the gun tucked into the side waistband of Tadgh's trousers, but she didn't say anything.

"There it is," Tadgh pointed, as they rounded the hill under Fort Elizabeth on Barrack Street.

Mindful of the possibility that Aidan's apartment could be watched, Tadgh parked out of sight off the main street.

"Morgan, I want you to stay put in the sidecar and protect the Kerry."

"I want to go with you."

"Listen, lass. Twenty-four hours ago you had not yet ventured outside my home."

"But I feel fine. The brisk air has done wonders."

"Has it, now? You stay here and rest up. I can't afford to lose you, Aidan, and the Kerry all in the span of a day."

Tadgh tucked the blanket around Morgan's waist. She leaned toward him and gave him a kiss.

"All right then. You hurry back to me."

"Back in a bit."

Tadgh approached the flat from the rear. Although there were plenty of people bustling by, and beggars looking for handouts on Barrack Street, the back alley was deserted. Tadgh found the key Sean usually left on the ledge above the door and silently entered the hovel. With all the dust, it was obvious that the place had not been searched. *That's a good sign.*

Tadgh could see that Aidan slept on the floor whenever he was there. The debris in the living area and dirty sink was appalling. Somewhere in the dim past, he must have eaten fish. The rancid stench was sickening. How could his brother have stooped so low? Tadgh had heard that Aidan often slept it off at one of the many dingy pubs in the neighborhood. Clancy's was just one of his favorite haunts.

"Aidan's not come back here," Tadgh announced, as he returned to Morgan. "At least he has that much good sense."

"So where do we go from here?" Morgan asked, stepping up and out of the sidecar to stretch her legs.

"Aidan works at Beamish and Crawfords, just over there across the South Gate Bridge; at least when he's working, that is. Maybe they've seen him."

"What's Beamish and Crawfords?" Morgan asked.

"It's that huge stout brewery factory over there on the other side of the Lee River. It's been there since the 1700s—third largest in the country." Tadgh pointed to the extensive brickworks with its very tall chimney and the walled-in loading docks backing onto the river. "Can't you smell the yeast and the hops?"

"I wondered what that was."

"Fermentation, my dear. I worked there just after my parents were killed. Half of Corkers are associated with it in one way or another."

After chaining the front wheel to a street sign, they left the motorcycle and crossed South Gate Bridge. Three minutes later, turning left off South Main Street, they arrived at the Counting House of B & C, with its formidable three-story Tudor facade. They mounted the steep steps and entered under the large clock just as it struck the noon hour.

Tadgh moved quickly through the front office as if he owned the place. Just as a pert receptionist acknowledged his request to see the manager in charge, a portly, balding man with a ruddy round face strode out of his office.

"Mr. Henderson, sir," Tadgh addressed his former boss.

"Is that you, Tadgh McCarthy?" Alex Henderson exclaimed. "You in trouble, boy?"

"Yes sir," Tadgh responded. *I must be slacking. My disguise didn't fool old Henderson, not even the real beard.*

"What brings you back here, my boy, and with such a lovely lady? I presume you don't want your old job back."

"No, sir. This is my friend Morgan."

"Pleased to meet you." Morgan met Henderson's handshake with gusto.

"I'm looking for my brother, Aidan. Has he been at work this week?"

The manager scowled. "Night and day, my boy."

"Meaning . . . ?" Tadgh prompted.

"Meaning you was exemplary, dear boy. Your brother is a slacker and a drunkard. He hasn't been at work for two weeks now. If you find him, tell him he's fired."

"I'll tell him that when I find him." *No chance that Aidan's job can be salvaged. Old Henderson is adamant.*

He thanked his former boss. As they left the brewery, Tadgh could tell from the frown lines on Morgan's brow that she was starting to see the depth of the problem that he had with his brother. "So, let's check Clancy's Pub where the fight occurred. We can get lunch there."

Clancy's was just a staggering distance from Aidan's place and B & C, east along the river and north up Princes Street. It was a cozy enough pub, with a grand old floor-to-ceiling mirrored bar and plenty of cubbyholes where cloistered groups of patrons were chatting while they ate their midday meal. It was dark and smoky—the kind of place where a lad could get lost in a hurry.

Tadgh picked an unoccupied cubby near the door, one from which he could see anyone entering or leaving the establishment. They sat down and Morgan said, "Oh, our first lunch out together." She looked radiant.

While she read the menu, Tadgh scanned the faces looking for any sign of trouble. Aidan was nowhere to be seen. With the exception of a tall fellow in a longshoreman's uniform near the end of the bar, the patrons looked harmless enough. Tadgh watched the longshoreman carefully and wondered why he wasn't eating or drinking. He seemed to be disinterested in his surroundings. Tadgh was now concerned with his disguise. So he waited in semi-darkness the few minutes until the proprietor, Tom Clancy, joined them at their cubby.

"Have ya seen Aidan here since Wednesday, Tom?" Tadgh asked in a low voice.

"Tadgh McCarthy, is that you? Who's the gorgeous lady, then?"

"Yes, it's me." Tadgh wasn't about to introduce Morgan. "Keep your boomin' baritone down, mate."

"Sorry, Tadgh. I haven't seen your brother here since that night. He was in a foul mood, and he got into a hell of a fight with some RIC goons that was harassing poor Andy, don't ya know. Word is, they're after him now."

"Yes, thanks for lettin' me know, Tom. Give us two pints of Beamish stout and some mutton sandwiches, would you?"

Tom returned a few minutes later with their lunch. "How come I don't see you around here no more, Tadgh? Where you keeping yourself?"

"I'm around and about. Been kind of busy of late."

"How can I contact you if I see Aidan?"

"I'll have someone stay in touch with you." Tadgh bit into his sandwich, and a large hunk of it slid off the bread.

While they ate, Morgan kept quiet. The Beamish looked foul but tasted great. Tadgh was absorbed by a second longshoreman who had just entered the Pub and joined the one at the bar. The two men were in an animated conversation, and once or twice they looked over in his direction.

Could he have overheard Tom referring to Tadgh and Aidan as his brother? At least he hadn't had time to call it in if he did.

"Damn," Tadgh muttered under his breath.

Morgan heard that and looked up with questioning eyes.

"Don't look now and don't worry, Morgan, but there are two men at the bar that could be RIC. Act normal. Finish your sandwich and we will leave quietly."

Dropping three bob onto the table, Tadgh led Morgan, still chewing, out the door and down Princes Street towards the river. They wove in and out of the substantial foot traffic for a couple of blocks. When Tadgh glanced over his shoulder, he saw the two longshoremen following them, but keeping their distance.

Clearly, these were RIC constables in plain clothes, and they were tracking their every move. They needed to be dealt with before they could report to headquarters just across the river. At least that would provide him some payback for what happened to his parents.

He wasn't going to let Morgan out of his sight. She would have to be part of whatever was going to happen next. But what about her stamina? Only yesterday she was just getting her legs under her. Tadgh knew this part of Cork City like the back of his hand. Undoubtedly, they did, too. Quickly, he decided to lure them into the loading area at the back of B & C. He could deal with them there, among friends if need be, he hoped.

"Come on, Morgan," he urged. "We're being followed by the two men from the bar. Let's speed up. Maybe we can lose them."

With that, he whisked her away down the South Mall to the Grand Parade and ducked down Old Post Office Lane. They were running at this point with their pursuers keeping pace. Emerging onto South Main Street, they could see the Counting House ahead.

"Hurry, Morgan," Tadgh urged. "Run for that open door on the left."

Tadgh knew he was asking a lot of the lass who had been so ill, but it couldn't be helped. *Should have left her home.*

They reached the door just as a B & C lorry was driving out. They jumped around behind it and ducked through the doorway as the RIC constables emerged from the lane.

"Maybe they didn't see where we went," Morgan offered, breathlessly.

Peering around the corner of the partially-open door, Tadgh saw them coming from across the street with their Webleys drawn. RIC for sure, probably with orders to bring him in dead or alive. They had the run of the city, and no one would dare stop them or question their authority.

He quickly looked around the yard for a defensible position. Stout barrels were stacked along the wharf to his left some thirty yards away, near the aft end of a cargo ship moored at the dock. A moveable wharf crane amidships lined up to hoist the barrels.

The loading yard was deserted, with the workers presumably inside at their noontime meal. The main brewery buildings were at least seventy five yards away to his right—too far.

"Run for those standing barrels and hide behind them," he ordered Morgan. "Don't come out no matter what happens. It's me they're after. I'll lead them away." While he was saying this, he had whipped out the Luger, and flicked off the safety.

Morgan raced to the stack of barrels and disappeared out of sight just before the constables burst through the doorway into the yard.

Tadgh had covered most of the ground to reach the crane, but he was caught exposed in flight.

The first constable they'd seen yelled out, "Tadgh McCarthy, stop and surrender. This is the RIC. You are under arrest."

The other constable fired twice, and Tadgh felt the bullets whiz past his head as he dove behind the wheels of the crane.

"Stop firing, George, you idiot. The boss'll kill us if we don't take him alive!" yelled the first constable on the run.

"Like hell, Ken! They're getting away."

Tadgh rolled right and came up shooting. The first bullet found George's right knee, and blew it away. The second hit at the bridge of his nose as he fell. George was dead by the time his body hit the ground.

Seeing Tadgh was armed, Ken dashed for the protection of the barrels, right where Morgan was hiding.

Tadgh knew which barrel the Constable had darted behind. But he couldn't take the chance of shooting Morgan since he wasn't sure where she was. The crane only provided partial cover, so he'd have to act quickly. A moment later, Morgan's hand emerged from behind a barrel a row behind and to the left of the constable.

Tadgh saw the signal and realized Morgan had moved out of the line of fire. *Good lass.* He took a chance and fired one bullet right through the constable's barrel at stomach height. The bullet must have caught the constable, as he yowled. Stout gushed out of the oaken barrel onto the wharf. "Damn you, McCarthy!" Ken shouted as he took aim and fired.

Tadgh felt the bullet burn through his left shoulder just below his clavicle as he fell behind the crane. "Damn," he cursed. The pain seared him, yet he was strangely numb.

Ken shifted right between two barrels and crouched down. He fired two rounds at the crane. They ricocheted harmlessly off the boom arm. Tadgh saw his chance and took aim at the dodging constable. His bullet winged the officer on his left hip, but he didn't go down. He instinctively fired again, and the last bullet misfired with a loud click.

Ken realized then that Tadgh was done. The constable stood up, his Webley pointed at his adversary's chest.

Tadgh knew the man was going to savor the moment. No one would blame him, given his wounds, if the rebel died in the gun battle. Tadgh had killed the constable's partner. He staggered on his bad leg as he stepped forward, knocking over the now half-empty barrel.

Tadgh needed him to approach. He tried to minimize his exposure profile by standing up behind the boom arm. He put up his fighting arms, knuckles tensed and hard, with a little help from some metal.

"You Limey bastard. Come here and fight like a man," Tadgh taunted Ken.

The constable hobbled forward until he was about fifteen feet from Tadgh's position. At this range he couldn't miss. "McCarthy, you're not long for this world," Ken sneered, as he slowly took a bead on his head. Suddenly, the overturned barrel careened forward hitting the constable's legs from behind. A perfect strike; he went down, sprawling forward like a bowling pin. Before he could recover and get a shot off, Tadgh reached up and yanked the lynch pin out of the crane's arm. The free end of the boom crashed down on the constable's head, crushing his skull and then his windpipe before coming to rest beside his body.

Morgan, who had kicked the barrel forward, stood up and ran to Tadgh.

He knew now that Morgan would be more than moral support to him. She had just saved his life. But she had killed an officer of the law. Her involvement in the movement was now clinched, and she would be a fugitive. It seemed as if the world had disappeared for an instant as they came together.

"You're hurt," Morgan blurted, as Tadgh winced from his shoulder wound when they embraced. "Let me look at it."

"In a minute you can," Tadgh said. "Come on, help me." He grabbed the dead constable's arm and tried to drag him to the edge of the wharf. Morgan showed no squeamishness as she grabbed the other arm and pulled. Together, they dragged and then dumped the body into the water between the wharf and the ship. Then they quickly repeated the grim task for the other constable, hoping the bodies would be crushed beyond recognition by the wave action of the ship against the wharf.

They ran and ducked under one of the loading ramps at the back of the brewery just before workers swarmed out into the loading yard, having heard the shots. The Beamish boys looked puzzled since nothing appeared amiss and went back to work.

"You're bleeding. Let me take care of it." Morgan ripped open Tadgh's coat and found the damage. He had a serious wound, oozing quite a lot of blood. Checking his upper back, she was relieved to find that the bullet had gone clear through him, just missing his shoulder blade. Morgan ripped off two patches of her own blouse under her coat and used them to apply direct pressure into the wound at both the entry and exit points. This stopped the bleeding for the moment. Then, shedding her coat, she removed her blouse completely, tearing it into two strips. With the first, she held the two pads over the wounds by binding from his left shoulder to his neck tightly. With the other she strapped his left arm to his side just above the elbow and around his torso.

That should hold it until we can get out of here," Morgan said as she donned her coat.

Tadgh was amazed. "Where did you learn to do that?"

"I dunno," she replied honestly. "It just came to me."

Tadgh was trying to figure out their next move. The RIC might be waiting for them outside the confines of the B & C loading yard. He was in no shape for another encounter, and Morgan was looking pale from the ordeal. The empty Luger was of no use at this point.

At that moment, a B & C delivery lorry appeared from nowhere and backed up to the loading ramp, hemming them in.

"Damn," Tadgh exclaimed.

From inside the lorry, Tadgh heard a voice call out, "Get in, you two, for heaven's sake!"

Preparing for a fistfight with his one good arm, he peered up into the cab.

"Wiggins, lad, is that you?" Tadgh couldn't believe it.

"In the flesh, McCarthy. You wanna jabber or what." He motioned them to join him. "Can I give you folks a lift?" he asked, as Morgan helped Tadgh up into the cab and then hopped up herself. Tadgh ordered them to lower their heads as Wiggins maneuvered the truck out of the yard and into South Main Street.

"You need a doctor, Tadgh. I'll take you to our new Bon Secours Hospital. It just opened a week ago. They'll help you."

"No hospitals, no authorities, Jeff," Tadgh cut in. "Morgan has done a fine job. Head right across South Gate Bridge."

"But it's a dangerous wound," Morgan cautioned.

"No hospitals, No authorities. Our transportation is up this alley to your left. Do ya see? There."

"The coast is clear," Wiggins announced, pulling alongside the motorcycle.

Morgan had a questioning look.

"Jeffrey, here, was a fine mate of mine when we were budding Beamish Boys five years ago, weren't we, lad?"

"Aye. Best mates 'til you decided to go to Dublin. Now look at ye. Shot an' bleedin'. I'm transportation leader now, Tadgh. Henderson rewards his best Beamish boys, don't ya know. You shoulda stayed."

"Couldn't be helped after I joined the volunteers, Jeff. Higher cause now."

"Like killing RIC?"

"That couldn't be helped, either."

"Ya, I saw from my operations shed. Self defense." Turning to Morgan, he said, "We could use you out on the docks. You roll a mean barrel, lass."

Morgan blushed, and turned to examine Tadgh's crude bandage.

"Why?" Tadgh looked at his friend for answers.

"I despise RIC goons maybe more than most folks because of what they have done to my brother. Terrible incarceration. We have no idea . . ." Wiggins stopped, unable to continue.

Tadgh consoled him. "They killed my Mam and Pa."

"So your brother said."

"You've seen him, Jeff, recent-like?"

"Not for about three weeks. Not very reliable, Aidan, is he now."

"Shamed I am," was all that Tadgh could think of to say.

"Don't you dare," Morgan piped up." You're not your brother's keeper."

But both men knew they had brother problems.

"Listen, Tadgh. If you're fightin' the RIC, you can count me in. If ever you need help, call. I have assets that could help here and can be borrowed, if need be."

"How so, lad?"

"I can drive or just manage, if you know what I mean."

"I do, indeed. The company would never . . ."

"Never you mind. They wouldn't know, lad."

"What about Martin Murphy, Jeff?"

"Martin's on our side. He can be trusted."

"I thought so. Good, Jeff. We may take you up on that offer." Tadgh said clasping his friend's hand across the cab. You saved us today, lad."

"Once a Beamish boy, always . . ."

". . . a Beamish boy."

Morgan leaned over and kissed Wiggins on the cheek. "We are forever in your debt, kind sir," she said. He blushed.

With that Morgan helped Tadgh down from the cab.

Jeff announced, "Your secret is safe with me."

Having said their farewells, Wiggins drove off towards his beloved brewery.

After they mounted the motorcycle, Morgan insisted on checking her triage. The bandage was holding with little evidence of further bleeding.

"Looks like you're going to live," she announced. "How I knew how to do this is beyond understanding. Are you able to drive this contraption?"

"Of course. Never better, still have my right arm. We'll go and see Tomas." Tadgh fired up the Kerry.

"Who's Tomas?"

"My Cork boss. Tomas MacCurtain. He has a home here."

It took all of fifteen minutes to maneuver the back streets to MacCurtain's safe house.

"Go ring the bell, lass," Tadgh requested as he brought the Kerry to a wobbly stop.

"There's no answer," Morgan announced after several attempts to rouse Tomas.

"Damn. Lives alone. He spends a lot of time in Dublin with

the Brotherhood these days."

"So what do we do now?" Morgan could see that Tadgh's condition was deteriorating.

"We drive home, lass. There's no other way for it."

"But . . ."

"I'm sorry, Morgan. I'm in no shape to go to Queenstown today."

"No, of course not. What I was going to say is that I don't think you will make the trip home in your condition."

"You'll be surprised what I can do when I put my mind to it." He grinned at her.

"Keep talking," she told him repeatedly as the two-hour trip stretched into three. He had been pretty drowsy and they were weaving all over the road since his left arm was partially immobilized. At one point when he was almost incoherent, she thought of stopping him and taking over the driving even though she had no idea how to do so. He kept muttering, "I'm fine, just fine." But she knew better. *He's lost a lot of blood. We could crash. He could easily die.* He was her only lifeline to reality. But what a life, full of danger and mayhem. "God help us," she blurted out. It must have been God's grace, aided by her verbal coaxing, that got them home safely.

Morgan half-dragged Tadgh into the kitchen and propped him up on a chair. Then she ripped open his coat and examined the wound. Her blouse bandage was sodden red on his shoulder. She had to adjust his sagging posture to keep him from falling onto the floor. *How did you get us home? You've just about passed out.*

Remembering where Tadgh stashed his liquor, she took the chance and let go long enough to get a partial bottle of Jameson off the shelf. Grabbing a facecloth off the sink, she lurched back to the table. That's when she realized that she was in bad shape herself.

She opened the bandage and was strangely fascinated and recognized the damage. Had seen something like it somewhere before. Exposing the wounds, she poured in the alcohol. Then, dousing the cloth with the stuff, she jammed the rag down into the shoulder wound. That revived the patient. Tadgh winced and then sniffed the air like a bloodhound on the scent.

"Pour us two fingers, lass," he murmured, a bit of a twinkle returning to his amber eyes.

"You've lost a lot of blood, Tadgh. You look mighty pale," Morgan cautioned as she held a shot glass to his lips.

"Drink this." She found that she had to guide and steady his arms if there was any hope of the Jameson's finding his throat. She checked his back and found that her makeshift bandage had held, with little loss of blood. *Thank God he's not coughing up blood*, she thought. *Likely no lung puncture. Now how would she know that?* "First aid?"

"In the Ops Center. Cabinet above the sink," Tadgh stammered, reaching for the bottle of Jameson's on the table in front of him. "You remember?"

"Yes, the oil lantern on the right."

By the time she returned with bandages, she realized her mistake. The kitchen table was awash with Jameson's, and Tadgh was lapping it up like a dog.

"Stop," she commanded, righting the bottle and sopping up the liquid. "How am I going to get you to bed?"

"I've been wondering that myself for a week or more."

"You're incorrigible."

"So you like me then, lass, do ya now?"

"Leave off now. I've got to tend to your gunshot wound before you bleed to death." Morgan applied fresh bandages after cleaning the wound with lather from a pink bar of carbolic soap she'd found in a Red Cross tin. *How did she know it would disinfect the wound?*

After applying a tight sling for the left arm and shoulder, she announced, "You got lucky there, you. The bullet went clear through. How does it feel?"

"G-good as n-new . . ." Tadgh stammered. But Morgan knew

differently. He had restricted range of motion. She surmised his muscle and joint capsule were badly damaged.

Looking up from the table with inquisitive eyes, Tadgh mumbled, "Followed?"

"No. I don't think so. Can you help me get you to the chesterfield?

Tadgh nodded weakly. Together they staggered to the parlor couch and collapsed onto it. Tadgh was instantly asleep, snuggled in the crook of Morgan's right arm. But she was wide awake. *What had she gotten herself into?*

Gordo entered his boss's office the next morning, not wanting to tell him the grim news.

"What's happened, man? Out with it."

"You're not going to like it, Darcy." James cowered in the corner wondering what Boyle was going to do to him.

"Spit it out, man."

"One of our men, George O'Roarke, was found face down in South Channel an hour ago. He was shot up and pretty mangled. He and Ken were on the stakeout at Clancy's yesterday when they disappeared. Ken hasn't shown up yet."

"Fuck, James." Boyle screamed, pounding his letter opener repeatedly into his desk, gouging the surface. "Have you interrogated Clancy and his customers about what happened?"

"I'm on my way over there right now. I'll beat it out of them if necessary, boss," Gordo answered pulling the door open and starting to step through it. He had seen Darcy throw that letter opener more than once before.

"You'd better, or I'll beat you senseless myself," Boyle threatened.

A half-hour later, Gordo and two more uniformed constables

strode through the front door of Clancy's Bar.

"What happened yesterday when my men dressed like long-shoremen were in here?" James demanded.

"What do you mean, Constable?" Clancy answered nonchalantly. "I remember them in here at noon, but they left together a short while later."

"Who else was in here then? Who left at the same time?"

"Jeez, Constable. I had about thirty customers in here at that time. I don't remember who left when."

James tried the incentive approach. "Here's a bob if you can remember."

Clancy made no attempt to pocket the cash. "Sorry, I just didn't notice."

Without a care for what customers would think, Gordo grabbed Clancy's arms from behind the bar and dragged him over the bar. Glasses shattered, crashed to the floor. Clancy landed on the broken glass.

Then, with the help of the other RIC officers, they carried Tom forcefully to the back room. After they tied him to a chair, the two constables started pounding him around the head and in the stomach with their fists.

No one from the bar came to Tom's aid.

Old Tom defiantly took the blows without speaking, but they were having a brutal effect. After several minutes of beating, Gordo spoke in a quiet, but venomous tone, almost hissing. "Stop boys. Maybe old Tom, here, can remember now, can't you, me boyo."

Tom had seen Tadgh and his girl leave, followed rapidly by the RIC men. But he hated these goons and wasn't about to tell them anything.

Through bleeding split lips he murmured, "It was dark and smoky. I was serving at the far end of the bar. I saw your men leave, but I don't know if anyone else left at the same time."

"Have you seen McCarthy in here since last Monday?" Gordo

took a different tack.

"Aidan hasn't been here since you ran him out," Tom answered feebly.

"You sure?" Gordo asked, as he smashed Tom across the face.

Tom just faintly mouthed, "I'm sure," then passed out.

They splashed water on Clancy's face. It was enough to bring him around. Another round of beatings knocked him and the chair over, but he didn't talk.

They left him, barely conscious, in a pool of his own blood.

When they returned to the pub, Gordo took out his Webley and discharged it into the ceiling. That got the patrons' attention.

"All right, you people. Who was here yesterday at noon?"

No one offered to admit they were there.

"I know some of you were here. Who saw the two longshore-men leave? And who left at the same time? Speak up."

Again, there was silence.

James went over to one of the cubbies that he recognized housed a group of regulars. He lifted one old-timer out of his seat and held the Webley to his temple.

"Speak up, or I'll shoot this boozer," he yelled out for all to hear.

From the back of the pub came a faint voice. "I saw them leave in a hurry, right after a laddie and his girl left."

"What did this laddie look like?" Gordo demanded, waving his weapon."

"I don't have the foggiest. You can see how smoky it is in here."

Gordo cocked the Webley and ordered, "On your knees, geezer."

Another voice in the back blurted out, "Don't kill Jimmie. Barkeep called him McCarthy."

"Aidan McCarthy?"

"No. Tadgh. Tadgh McCarthy."

"Well, I'll be," Gordo exclaimed shouldering his Webley.

Turning on his heel, he summoned his contingent out into the street. They had gotten what they came for and more. Far more. *Two McCarthys. They must be related. Could they be the long lost grandsons of Fergus? Tadgh, the renegade playwright from Dublin and his hotheaded brother.*

When he brought the news to his boss, Darcy told him, "We need to find them, alive, mind you."

"Yes, boss," his underling replied, knowing full well that the trail was already cold.

In the days that followed, they found the bullet lodged in George's brain and determined that it was a nine-millimeter slug, fired from a German Luger. This confused the investigation even further. Constable Ken's body was never found.

Boyle was livid. "Why are we always one step behind these bastards?"

Chapter Twenty-One
Morgan's Quest

July 15, 1915
Creagh, Ireland

*T*adgh's shoulder wound was much worse than Morgan had initially thought. Infection had set in during the ride home. He had torn muscles and he almost dislocated his clavicle. For the first week and a half his fever was continuous. Morgan made do with limited medical supplies.

After three weeks when his fever subsided and his shoulder pain was manageable, he was starting to become an impatient patient. "Damn, this joint is so tight I can hardly raise my Jameson glass."

"Don't you dare take that sling off again," Morgan chided, when Tadgh tried to hurry his recovery.

That evening at dinnertime even Morgan had had enough of his griping. "I think it's time for me to finally go to the Cunard offices. Is there a train that could take me there tomorrow?"

"Well now, if you could get to Skibbereen, which is six miles yonder, there is a train to Cork City. You'd have to change trains to go to the Port of Queenstown."

"I could do that in a day, right?"

"I suppose so. I don't know the schedules since I don't travel in the open like that."

"I think I'll do that then. I need to find out."

"I know, Morgan. You have been very considerate, focusing on my health, especially since we planned to go the day I was shot, but . . ."

"But what?"

"I worry about your safety, lass. It's a dangerous world out there." He stopped short of telling her what he was thinking. Those damn RICs could have found out about her involvement at B & C to add her to their wanted list.

"But relatives may be there and may give up waiting. I could have a husband and children, don't you see?"

"How much longer until I can travel by my motorbike, do you think?"

"Another week or so, I suppose. But that might be too late."

"I think it best that you wait until I can take you. It's been more than two months since the accident."

He liked to use that term to soften the traumatic impact. But it had been no accident. And he had already come to realize that his saving her was no accident either. The Lord had intervened, and he didn't want her to leave him. She might never come back. He got up from the kitchen table, crossed to the stove where she was working, and brushed the tousled hair from her eyes.

"Another week probably won't matter. I'd feel better if I was there to protect you." He put his good arm around her waist.

Morgan took a step back, her eyes blazing. "Who says I need protecting? I saved *your* life, didn't I?"

"Aye, Morgan, you did. And I'll be forever grateful and beholdin' to you for it."

"Let's just say we're square on that account, then."

"Agreed, girl. So we're a good team then, don't ya think?" He stepped forward to her once again.

"I can't say that there's no such feeling on my part, but you're becoming a bother, you know." She waved a ladle from the vegetable soup she was cooking, spattering him in the eye with the warm mixture.

"Ouch." Tadgh wiped his eye.

"Did I burn you?" Morgan cried, rushing to his aid and dabbing his eye with her apron.

306

"I'll live," Tadgh announced, blinking. He grabbed her by the waist again, holding tight this time. "And the soup smells delicious." He smiled impishly and planted a kiss on her cheek, leaving his lips firmly in place. "As do you, my dear."

There was a slight tug at his arm, but she yielded to him, hesitating there, at his lips.

"I suppose I could wait another week."

"Right, then," Tadgh wheeled, and grabbing the Jameson bottle from the table, he liberally doused the soup with his own elixir. "The soup's ready. I'll cut the bread. Let's eat."

A week later on Thursday evening, the sling came off for good. Morgan helped him wash his back. The thought of his brother nagged at him. "I'm so worried about Aidan. Damn fool could be dead by now."

"No point in worrying about it 'til you know more," Morgan offered, massaging the recovering shoulder vigorously.

Tadgh pulled her arm over and down onto his chest, brushing his nipple as he did so. Her hair tumbled down over his face and her head rested against his cheek. This had happened before, and it sent shock waves through him now.

"You're feeling better, I can see."

"You have a way about you that relieves what ails me, girl," Tadgh said, taking in her fragrance.

Looking down into the bath water, Morgan said, "I can see that you're ready to salute and stand at attention, so I think we can stand down the revolution for tonight."

"But the troops are ready to advance, my dear."

"Are they, now. On what military objective?"

"First I would take these two hills." Tadgh spun her around and grabbed both breasts through her tunic. She almost fell into the tub.

"Whoa there, commandant. These hills are not enemy territory, you know. More like neutral ground. No man's land, I think they call it." She gently pried free from his grip. "So I think we should just hunker down in our own foxholes for the night." She went to the rack and returned with his towel.

"But I want to advance the troops."

"This may cool you off." Morgan dumped the entire bathing pitcher of cold water down his front and threw in the towel.

Early the following morning, when he was luxuriating in the platonic bed they shared, he listened to Morgan breathing beside him, and then he heard a ring in the distance. This was a rare occurrence in the McCarthy residence. He bolted down the stairs, opened a special cupboard door in the kitchen, and picked up the receiver just in time to make the connection.

He said hello and on the other end of the line, a familiar voice said, "Mackerel and cod schools have been sighted. Need your boat next Thursday at one. Should be a good catch. Transport to the normal place. I'll contact you later with specifics."

Tadgh said, "Understood. We need to talk personally."

Then he hung up. The call took only twenty seconds. But the phone could have been tapped. There was always the connecting operator if she stayed on the line.

Tadgh was reflecting on the orders he had just been given by Padraig Pearse as he made the coffee.

Suddenly and silently, Morgan grabbed him from behind. He whirled around, his arm twisting her wrist behind her back.

"Ouch," she squealed, in fright.

Tadgh released his grip and kissed her on the forehead. "Sorry, Morgan, automatic defensive action. Hope I didn't hurt you. I just got a phone message regarding our cause, and I was thinking about what I have to do about it. My warrior training kicked in."

"But I am not a threat to you."

"I know, but you came at me from behind. I didn't know it

was you."

"But we're the only ones here."

This put a whole new light on Tadgh's personality, and Morgan didn't like it. It conjured up another painful feeling of déjà vu that she couldn't put her finger on.

Tadgh could see that there was more to her reaction than the physical effect of jerking her wrist. She must have been physically attacked in the past. He did not want to frighten her by explaining that he was constantly at risk of being apprehended. The painful memory of the suddenness of the attack on his parents in their own home momentarily flooded his thoughts. And what if Aidan had already been captured and tortured or killed? "I just have to be really careful," was all he could say.

"As if I didn't know that."

The mood was chilly as they sat to have coffee in the kitchen.

"I didn't know you had a telephone way out here in the country," Morgan commented, to break the silence.

"They put it in a few months ago when they laid the line from Skibbereen to Baltimore. Cost the IRB a pretty penny as they say. We talk in code in case the RIC are listening in. On the other end they phone from a public telephone booth, and we keep the communications short. I do the reverse from Skibbereen if I need to call them, except in an emergency."

"So what orders did you get?" She was testing him again, he thought. She's all in, he decided.

"There is a shipment coming in on Wednesday, including human cargo. I'm to take it to the usual place in Dublin. They will contact me later this week about specifics."

"How do they code the messages?"

"A lot of my transportation starts with my hooker at sea. So the orders for sea pickup and delivery refer to fishing expeditions. My cover is that I am a fisherman."

"I see. But what is a hooker? That boat in the boathouse

I suspect."

"That's my boat, a Galway hooker, named *The Republican*. It's the one I used when I found you at sea."

"You mean when you saved my life. How do you know that it is people you will be transporting?"

"It's mackerel for people, cod for guns and ammunition, and salmon for other goods," Tadgh carefully explained. "And 'the fish are running' refers to an off shore delivery, and 'schools have been sighted' refers to a pickup at sea."

"And how do you know when to act?" Morgan asked.

"The message always states a day and time. The real need is earlier than stated by the number of days equal to the time. In this case, one day earlier because they specified one."

Morgan smiled, and Tadgh realized she was pleased to be entrusted with this information. She was already becoming a key partner in his life, in more ways than one.

Tadgh now knew that Morgan could receive and translate a message if she had to and if the sender would give it to her. They would do so after they got to know her—that is if they accepted her.

"Who was it that called?"

Tadgh decided she didn't need to know. "One of the leaders of our organization," was all he said.

"Can I come with you on this trip?"

Tadgh was still concerned that their safe house may not be safe much longer. On the other hand, he didn't want to put her in harm's way on a mission. He felt she would be safer with him than alone in the house.

"If my boss approves of it when he comes here in a few days, then you can come with me."

"This will be exciting," Morgan said with a smile of satisfaction.

After breakfast, Morgan announced, "While we are waiting for your boss to decide my fate, I want to go to that Cunard office to see if I can find someone who knows me."

Tadgh wasn't sure that he wanted her to rediscover her past life at this point. But he realized that she had a right to know the truth about herself. He couldn't postpone it any longer.

"Yes, then, we'll go today but I need to stay incognito."

"Of course, dear."

They arrived by motorcycle at the Cunard dockside offices two hours later. Along the way Morgan leaned over repeatedly to massage the knot in his shoulder.

As they rolled up to the edge of the main dock, Tadgh turned off the engine and slid the bar lock over the front wheel. Morgan was encouraged to see that a few of the mourning family members were still there, waiting.

"Morgan, I'll show you where to go, but I need to be inconspicuous. Please don't tell them who found you or where I live."

"Of course," she replied, flashing him a smile.

Morgan went up to look at the *Lusitania*'s passenger manifest at the records official's desk. In order to protect Tadgh, she decided not to divulge that she had been a passenger.

She saw the lack of passenger specifics and the fact that over four hundred women and girls had not been found and identified. She didn't recognize any names on the passenger list. Which one, she wondered, was hers? Was she Sally Swanson, Holly Anderson, Claire O'Donnell, or Margaret Simpson, to name a few? She had no clue.

She circulated past all the people present on the wharf, but nobody showed any recognition of her. Then she rejoined Tadgh just outside a viewing tent that had replaced the makeshift morgue Tadgh had seen a month earlier.

"No luck then?"

"None. I was so hopeful that I'd remember if I saw my name in print."

"Maybe you were travelling with someone who could jog your memory. Are you strong enough to go in here?"

"Let's just get it over with," she answered flatly and strode inside.

She was surprised to find that there were no bodies to be seen. There was a sign that explained they had used a new Kodak process to photograph the corpses before they had been embalmed and put on ice. Officials had identified some of the corpses by what they had been wearing or what they had in their pockets.

It took an hour to examine all the photographs.

"This photographic process leaves a lot to be desired," Tadgh observed. "Many of these reproductions are out of focus."

"I don't recognize any of these poor people," Morgan observed, wincing at the photograph of a particularly bloated corpse.

She thought that after exposure in the ocean, they probably didn't look much like they had in life anyway.

"This is how I would have looked if you hadn't saved me." She shivered as she said it. "Or worse if no one found me."

Coming out of the viewing tent onto the wharf, Tadgh said, "I'm sorry that this has been a wild goose chase for you, Morgan. Can we go now?"

Morgan persisted. "I'm going to tell them I was on board."

Tadgh grabbed her arm. She could see worry in his amber eyes. "Do you think that is wise?"

"I've got to try."

"If you must." He let go.

She strode off in the direction of the records official leaving Tadgh in the shadow of the viewing tent.

"Excuse me, sir," Morgan addressed the uniformed officer standing outside the office with the clipboard. "I was a passenger on the *Lusitania,* saved at sea, and I now have amnesia. I am trying to regain my memory and find out my name."

The official stuttered, taken aback. "Did you check the

passenger list? Maybe that would jog your memory."

"Yes, I checked the list. But I can't remember anything."

"How do you know that you were on our ship, young lady?"

"The man who found me told me so. I was in desperate shape and he nursed me back to health. It took all this time."

"Who is this man, and how did you get here today? Where can we reach you?" he questioned.

Morgan realized she was perilously close to compromising Tadgh if she went any further.

"I'm not at liberty to say, sir."

"Not at liberty? Really? I don't understand why."

She turned to leave.

The official scratched his head and seemed unsure. Then he reached out and grabbed her hand."Well then, let me take your picture and make some inquiries," he finally suggested.

Morgan was trapped. "All right then."

He hurriedly took the photo with a camera he had on the podium beside him. She had her back to the sun.

"How can I contact *you*?" she countered.

He scribbled down his name and business address for her. Then he started asking more questions, those that she didn't want to answer. *Maybe this wasn't such a good idea. It's probably a waste of time at this point anyway.*

"Come with me. I'll introduce you to my manager. He'll want to talk to you."

Morgan resisted.

"Suit yourself. Wait here." He opened the office door and stepped inside.

She hurried off to where Tadgh was waiting and listening. They ducked behind the visitor's tent.

"I think we'd better go," Morgan urged, pulling Tadgh towards the motorcycle. "They're asking too many questions that I can't answer."

"You don't have to ask me twice. You were a pretty cool customer with that agent. I heard you."

"I didn't want to lie," she said, leaping into the sidecar in one supple move.

"Of course not." Tadgh jumped into the saddle and gunned the engine.

At that moment, the new office manager for Cunard followed his agent out onto the wharf. As the motorcycle flashed off the wharf, he thought he recognized the girl with her long black ringleted hair flying in the wind. Then he remembered. It looked like Claire, the woman who insisted on trying to save the dying passengers on the port deck. If it was the same person. Amazing! She'd survived.

"Claire!" He called out to her, but she was gone. As he spun his wheelchair around, Jack Jordan vowed that he would find this woman, even if he never walked again.

Chapter Twenty-Two
A Hero Comes Home

July 26, 1915
Creagh, Ireland

*T*hree days later, there came an expected knock on the door. Tadgh went to the peephole and confirmed it was school Headmaster Padraig Pearse before letting him in.

"Welcome, sir." Although he was a close associate with Padraig, Tadgh usually addressed him as if he were still a Gaelic student at the Headmaster's military-oriented school at Rathfarnham.

Pearse stepped into the parlor and asked knowingly, "And who might this fair colleen be, Tadgh?"

"This is my partner Morgan, sir." In introducing Morgan to Pearse, Tadgh spoke of her rescue at sea, how she saved his life in the RIC encounter in Cork City, and pointed out her excellent medic skills.

He left out that she had amnesia. At the end, he explained, "Morgan has become an important partner for me in pursuit of our cause for independence. I hope you will accept her as a valued member of our IRB."

Morgan could tell that Padraig Pearse was a learned man, charming, clean-shaven and ruggedly handsome, probably in his thirties. She noted his familiarity with the place while Tadgh talked.

"Well now, Morgan, Mr. Pearse is a leader of our IRB, and one of its most eloquent proponents. I met him when I was his student, and he helped me linguistically when I was a failing playwright in Dublin in 1913. We work together on many aspects for our cause, including speeches, documents, and military planning and armament," Tadgh explained. "Padraig is a strong supporter of education for our youth in our native language, so he is."

With Padraig's ramrod military bearing, Morgan thought it odd that he was an important educator.

"Your play *A Call to Arms* was actually excellent for our cause, Tadgh, but poorly timed in its presentation. I am surprised that Yeats and company authorized its exposure at the Abbey Theatre. Some day you must take up your quill again—after we successfully take up arms, of course. Perhaps a play titled *A Call for Peace.*"

"My only interest now is our revolution, sir."

Turning towards Morgan, Padraig said, "We have become aware of you, young lady."

"Really? Do you know who I am?"

"Only that a woman of your description was seen leaving Clancy's pub with Tadgh here a month ago, I'm afraid."

"The RIC, boss?"

"Yes. As you know, Tomas monitors RIC communications in Cork for us. I'm surprised that he didn't get the message to you out here. It was in the *Cork Examiner.* They are looking for you both as being those responsible for the death of two of their forces. You've got to be more careful, Tadgh. Now is not the time for notoriety."

Tadgh and Morgan locked eyes. Strangely, she could tell what he was thinking, the dear boy. For a moment she saw into his soul through those sorrowful eyes. He was in anguish for getting her involved in his problems at the risk of her life.

He went to her and put his arm around her waist. She squeezed his hand.

"Tell me, Morgan, why do you want to join our dangerous movement?" Padraig asked, stepping forward to shake her free right hand.

"I believe in Tadgh, Mr. Pearse. And he believes in you and freedom for the Irish people. Something in my past resonates with this cause, sir. I can feel it, and I want to be a part of it with Tadgh."

"What part of your past resonates, then?"

"I don't know, sir, since I have had amnesia since the sinking."

Pearse looked askance at them both. "Amnesia, young lady?"

"Yes, sir, but whether I regain my memory or not, I know that I want to follow Tadgh and support this cause with all my heart."

"So how do you know your name, then?"

"My new name is Morgan. Tadgh named me since I don't know my old name."

"From the *Lusitania*, you say?" Padraig asked seemingly satisfied that she was therefore not a security risk to the organization. "Then you must be a lucky woman."

"I think so, definitely, sir," Morgan answered, looking up into Tadgh's amber eyes.

Tadgh was beaming. His Morgan was holding her own with one of the finest literary minds in the world.

After inspecting Tadgh's shoulder and Morgan's triage work, Pearse said, "I presume that you don't know where you acquired this expert skill in nursing, young lady. Am I right?"

"Yes, sir."

Morgan could see Pearse hesitate before continuing.

"Lass, you appear to be a remarkable woman and you dress like Constance, so you can't be all bad. If Tadgh believes in you, then I do, too."

Morgan felt relieved and honored.

"Tell me more about the condition of your brother, Aidan," Padraig asked, turning his attention to his reasons to be there.

Morgan could see from Tadgh's expression that he had known that this line of questioning was coming. He had shared with her that Padraig knew Aidan had helped with the construction of the safe house.

"You already know, he's never really recovered since he saw our parents killed. Now it seems that he has been recognized by the RIC after he fought with them in Clancy's Pub in Cork City a month ago. We were looking for him when the RIC goons attacked us."

"I see. Admirable. We're counting on you in this part of the country, Tadgh. We can't have Aidan compromising us."

The message was only too clear to Morgan. Find and control Aidan, or he would be found and eliminated by the Brotherhood.

"I'll find him and keep him safe, so I will."

"You've got two weeks."

Morgan noted that Tadgh was visibly shaken by the conversation.

"Now then," Padraig continued. "Did you know that O'Donovan Rossa's dead?"

"Yes, I read that in the *Irish Freedom* this month, in an article by McGarrity I believe. Died on Staten Island about a month ago, sir, so he did."

"He was a great leader for our cause, the unrepentant Feinian. The Clan na Gael and Tom want to make a big show by having him buried at Glasnevin."

"How's that possible, Padraig?"

"McGarrity and Devoy have arranged to have his body shipped back home on ice. It's en route and will be arriving Wednesday on the freighter *Talmooth*. We have some intelligence that the RIC or the British Navy may try to stop the shipment when it reaches Liverpool to prevent the funeral service. So we have fifty Irish Volunteers lined up to meet the shipment and carry our hero on their backs the two miles on the Liverpool docks to the ship for Dublin. That ship will land on North Wall where we will take over and get him to City Hall to lie in state."

"Grand. How can we help?"

"I need you to meet the freighter at sea, Tadgh, before it gets to Liverpool."

"I don't understand."

"They've decided to deliver us arms and munitions as part of the shipment. We badly need them."

"Why take the risk when Mr. Rossa's funeral is so important?"

Morgan asked, engaging in the conversation.

"That's exactly the point, Morgan. The British will be focused on O'Donovan and the funeral. They won't be expecting an arms shipment. Not to mention the fact that it is very difficult to arrange such a delivery, and it is easiest if it is included as a part of a bona fide shipment. The risk seems low compared to what we have ahead of us, right, Tadgh?"

"We can be sure of it, sir."

"We don't get many chances like this, and we have to seize them when they appear," Padraig went on.

"And when we pick the arms up off the southwest coast, we decouple the two deliveries," Tadgh offered. "At night, presumably."

"Precisely. Too many British warships and German U-Boats around."

"What are the rendezvous coordinates and time?"

"51 deg 39 min. N latitude, 8 deg 52 min. W longitude, 3 a.m. Wednesday."

"Two days from now. That's ten miles south of Glen West, Cape Clear Island, isn't it? Close to home and still dark."

"That's right. They will give you a light signal with the Morse code name 'Clan'. You must respond with 'Gael'. Then you can approach them."

"Why can't we rendezvous in the Irish Sea closer to Dublin?"

"The owners will not allow the ship to deviate on its way to Liverpool. There are more English ships in the Cork to Dublin corridor and the owners want to minimize the chance for an international incident. McGarrity paid big money to get them to carry this cargo. And there will be a trusted Clan na Gael member named Henry Driscoll accompanying the shipment. It's your job, Tadgh, to get Henry and the munitions to our rendezvous point in Dublin by the safest means, undetected. I will be expecting delivery by 6 p.m. Wednesday."

"So soon?"

"Yes, while the British are presumably focused on what is happening on the Liverpool docks. Mind me, Tadgh. Mr. Rossa's safety is our main objective, but he does present a grand diversion."

"That he does, sir. But I don't like the plan. It puts Morgan and me at risk over a large distance."

Padraig just stared him down.

"When is the funeral, Mr. Pearse?"

"Next Sunday, August first. I'd like you two to be there."

Morgan was pleased to be included.

"There's one more thing, Tadgh. Tom has asked me to give the eulogy as a bugle call for revolution. I would appreciate it if you would look over this draft with me before I leave."

The two men spent three hours discussing the principles of their cause and the contents of the eulogy while Morgan fixed them tea. Then Padraig Pearse set off by car to his beloved school and home at Rathfarnham in the environs of Dublin.

Tadgh closed the door to keep out the blustery night. Then in the cheery warmth of the kitchen where Morgan was washing up, he threw his arms around her aproned waist from behind. "You were wonderful with him, my dear."

Morgan spun within his encircling arms, setting down a dripping frying pan in the process. Then she encircled his neck with her arms and pulled him in, planting a sensuous kiss on his startled mouth. "I'm so happy right now," she said, obviously thrilled to belong to something so grand and powerful.

The kitchen fireplace crackled and sizzled. Morgan was full of questions, as usual.

"What are we going to do to find and protect Aidan?"

Tadgh was impressed that her first concern was for his brother. He had tried to control Aidan so many times since their parents' death. The problem seemed insurmountable. And they had spent a day, at the peril of their lives, looking for him in Cork, and all that did was get him shot and Morgan put on the wanted list. The one comfort he felt was that now, he had a partner who also cared what happened to him.

Morgan jumped in. "At least we know that he was alive and at large as of a month ago. And he's probably not in Cork or they would have found him. So come on, Tadgh, where would he be if he was hiding out?"

He thought for a moment and then it came to him. "Well, now, Aidan had a girlfriend, Aileen Mahoney, who lives in Dublin. She has a Da who's a member of the Irish Volunteers. Maybe he went to see her, do ya think?"

"Maybe. What are the Irish Volunteers?"

"They are a brother revolutionary organization led by Eion MacNeill."

"Aren't we going to Dublin with this shipment, and isn't Aileen likely to go to the funeral?"

"Good thinking, Morgan."

"So why is Mr. Rossa so important to our cause?"

"O'Donovan Rossa was an early crusader for our freedom just after the potato famine. His father died from it and the rest of his family emigrated. He lived here in West Cork, I believe, where the famine was severe. He connected with our people and their plight like no one before him."

"But why did he die in America?"

"He was put in jail in England and treated despicably for several years. In 1871 Queen Victoria agreed to release him along with four other freedom fighters if they agreed to leave the British Isles and our Ireland forever. They went to America where Mr. Rossa continued to be a leader for our cause as part of the Clan na Gael."

"Clan na Gael?"

"It is a Republican organization of Irish immigrants in America who fuel our revolution. In fact they are the financiers and organizers that support us from other countries, including the United States. One of its leaders, John Devoy, whom we deal with these days, was one of the five exiled in '71."

"I remember Mr. Pearse mentioning his name."

"O'Donovan masterminded many dynamite bombings in England in the 1880s from America. England tried to have him extradited but failed. Without his leadership we would not be able to muster a revolutionary army today."

"I see. Then we had better make damn sure that we don't get caught and jeopardize his triumphant return to his native soil!" exclaimed Morgan, brandishing a soup ladle.

Tadgh was inspired by Morgan's growing commitment to the cause. She was going all in.

After dinner Tadgh was perplexed as to how they would be able to get the weapons and their guard to Dublin undetected on the same day as the rendezvous at sea. By boat in *The Republican*, it would take at least twenty hours, depending on the wind conditions. And there were significant risks at sea from naval patrols. The Howth arms delivery had been difficult enough back in 1914 before the authorities had been warned. In that instance, the gun runners barely escaped being caught, and the subsequent killings at Bachelor's Walk in Dublin showed the menace of the British authorities.

As if she had been reading his mind, Morgan asked, "How can we get to Dublin by six?"

Tadgh felt the hairs on the back of his neck bristle. It was uncanny that they were so aligned in their thinking.

"*The Republican's* too slow. Train travel is out of the question with munitions."

"Do you have a truck stashed some place?"

"No, just the motorcycle and my hooker."

Morgan paced the kitchen, deep in thought.

"What about Wiggins? He was willing to risk his life for us. He seems to have transportation assets at his disposal."

"That's a great idea, Morgan. The rendezvous in Dublin is at the *An Stad*, a famous pub and hotel we use. There couldn't be a better cover than a beer truck delivery. I'll visit him tomorrow and see if he will cooperate. You should stay here in case Aidan returns."

"You're just trying to protect me now that we know I am also being hunted."

"No sense both of us risking capture, Morgan."

"You're a sweet man, Tadgh McCarthy." Morgan threw her arms around him and kissed his lips lovingly.

He pulled back long enough to say, "Well, I'm not going to save you from drowning only to lose you to an RIC bullet, am I now." Then Tadgh leaned in and slipped his tongue between her lips. "The sweetness is all you," he said, coming up for air.

"I, I, I . . ." Morgan's face reddened and her green eyes moistened.

". . . think we should get some sleep," Tadgh finished her stutter, leading her to the stairs. "We have a critical mission at last, and there's work needs doing."

An hour later, on their shared bed, with palpable sexual tension between them, Tadgh leaned over and gave her a peck on the cheek, "I'll be leaving early, so I won't wake you."

"That's considerate. I've got a lot to think about. It's been a revealing day."

"Yes, to be sure. Unfortunately there's no good news about your identity, lass."

"I've been thinking about that. I know that it is dangerous for either you or me to go back to the Cunard office. Probably wouldn't help anyway. But could we place a notice in a New York City newspaper explaining my circumstance with a response requested to a private post box in Skibbereen?"

"I suppose we could, but not Skibbereen. It's too close to home. Cork perhaps. But I don't think it would do any good. What would you say, anyway?"

Morgan, still wearing Tadgh's shirt, jumped out of bed and opened the bureau drawer. "Here. I've written it down."

"I see, just giving a physical description of you, stating that you have amnesia and the post office box number. But you've got it all wrong."

"Wrong, Tadgh? What do you mean?"

"You're not a normal 5-foot-7-inch athletic, young, black-haired woman. You're the most beautiful woman I've ever met, with a perfect hour-glass figure, and smoky green eyes that I could lose myself in."

"Nonsense. You've just had too much Jameson again." Tadgh could see that she was blushing, and her nipples had hardened under her nightshirt.

Sitting back on the bed, Morgan grabbed Tadgh's hand and kissed it softly. "Well?"

I was just thinking that, as they say, a picture's worth a thousand words."

"What do you mean?"

"I'm sure that Cunard is in the process of circulating that picture they took of you to their New York office. They'll have a better description of you from that than any word description we would write. If you have any living relatives then they will surely be in touch with either that office or the one here in Queenstown."

"Then do you think that Mr. Wiggins could go to Cunard and see if they were able to get any response with my picture?"

"It's a legal matter, Morgan. To some extent Cunard is account-able for the loss of lives. There's money involved, I expect. Big money, I'm thinking."

"So if he goes, then they will question him as to where I am, right?"

"Yes, and the officers would call in the authorities. I can't put Jeffrey in that position."

"So how will I know?"

"I'll call in anonymously from the central pay phone in Cork and ask Cunard without divulging anything."

"Oh, thank you, Tadgh." Morgan all but knocked him to the floor as she leaped to hug him close. "That's all we can do, right?"

"Yes, my dear. But I have to focus on our mission for Padraig."

"Yes. Yes, of course. But it's a chance, right?"

"Right. Now give us a kiss and let's get some sleep."

When they had settled in as usual with a pillow separating them on the bed, sleep wouldn't come to either. Morgan now knew she had a life with Tadgh and a plan to check up on progress of finding her identity at Cunard, and he knew she had been accepted into the IRB as his partner and they had a plan to find Aidan in Dublin. The pillow was no longer an acceptable barrier. Morgan reached across it to hold his hand, saying, "You mind that shoulder."

The next morning Tadgh left before dawn, arriving in Cork City just as the workday at B & C was commencing. He parked the motorcycle just behind Aidan's place again and checked to confirm that no one had been there.

Jeffrey Wiggins was in the loading area, having just finished organizing a three-lorry delivery. Situated behind some crates near the Brewery dockside entrance, Tadgh waited until the lorries had departed before he emerged and grabbed his friend's arm.

"Tadgh, my boy, there must be a very good reason for you to return here and risk being apprehended. The *Examiner* had an article about them finding a constable dead in the South Channel. They suspect that you and your lady friend killed him and his companion. The RIC is still madder than a hornet's nest."

"I've heard." Tadgh drew Jeff back into seclusion behind the crates and got right to the point. "I have to take that risk, Jeff, because I need your help. I got the feeling that you would do anything to support a group that would attempt to overthrow the English. Am I right?"

"What do you mean, Tadgh?"

"You helped us when you could have turned us in to the RIC. We're against those bastards, and we are going to set Ireland free of them. Can I count on your continued support, lad?"

Wiggins answered his fellow Beamish Boy without flinching. "Tell me what you need, Tadgh."

After their rendezvous had been planned and agreed upon, Tadgh stepped into the office and asked to use their business telephone for a call to Cunard. Being the former fair-haired Beamish boy, his request was granted with gusto. Alex Henderson, manager of B&C, even let him use his office for privacy. The call rang through.

"This is Jack Jordan. Cunard Operations Manager here. What can I do for you, sir?"

"A young woman approached one of your officers four days ago claiming to have amnesia. I was wondering whether the photo taken of her has yielded any results as to her identity."

"And who might you be, sir?"

Using his best British accent, Tadgh answered, "I'm Sir Neville Chamberlain, Inspector General of the RIC. We have reason to suspect she's a fraud looking to collect compensation from you."

"I see, sir. This request is very unusual coming over the telephone like this."

"Get on with it, man. Did the photo yield results?"

When Jordan hesitated, Tadgh jumped in, "Well?"

"Unfortunately the photograph was smeared with too much light in the background. The image was unrecognizable."

"Where I'm from we call that incompetence, son."

"But I was on the *Lusitania*, sir. As she was riding away in the wicker sidecar of a motorcycle driven by a young Irishman, I caught a glimpse of her. I could swear it was a girl named Claire whom I helped into a lifeboat."

"Really. And her last name?"

"I don't know."

"Just a glimpse, you say. How far away?"

"Maybe 100 yards."

"You could easily have been mistaken at that distance. Why would you have remembered her, of all the passengers?"

"Because while everyone else was trying to jump ship, Claire was tending to the injured on the port deck. A saint, I tell you."

"It may be wishful thinking on your part."

"Perhaps, but I think it was her."

"Didn't you run after and call out to her?"

"I called, sir, but I'm confined to a wheelchair at present."

"War injury lad?"

"In a matter speaking, sir."

"I see, the *Lusitania*."

"Precisely."

"How about the Irishman?"

"Just a blur, sir, probably under 30 years. But I checked up on his motorcycle, an Ablinger. Not too many registered in Ireland, I can tell you."

"If it is registered. I'll send a constable around to collect your statement. We'll follow up from here."

With that they both rang off.

On the way home Tadgh had plenty of time to consider what he had just heard. *Damn, he saw us. But he could have mistaken the woman. Yet it sounds like Morgan, nursing the injured even in a dire situation. Brave girl, whoever she was.*

That Jordan was probably mistaken. He seemed so agitated on the telephone. After the trauma he must have gone through, he's just looking for any port in the storm.

I'm not going to bother Morgan with this or tell her that her photograph was damaged. She probably has no relatives left, and if she were to find out that she lost some in the sinking, it would only upset her more.

Yet he knew down deep that he was just rationalizing that he couldn't bear the thought of losing Morgan, not after the way his Mam had been taken from him and his brother.

It was a glorious July day in southwestern Ireland, the kind that made the larks sing and the heart soar. At least it would if the bloody British were finally gone. Tadgh found Morgan waiting for his return in their vegetable garden. To relieve the periods of boredom waiting for orders to come early in the year, Tadgh had set his mind and body to the task of planting a sustainable garden—one like his Mam and Pa had grown for all those young and happy years of his life. Until that travesty.

Now, as physical and mental therapy, Morgan was tending to the plants as they were speedily maturing. Tadgh needed to teach her. This wasn't one of those skills that broke through the amnesia.

Morgan looked up as he rode into the drive. "Well? What did you find out?" she cried. "Come over here."

There were no neighboring houses for half a mile around so they were, as usual, together alone.

"I see that the nasturtiums are up. They're edible you know, Morgan."

"Don't you keep me waiting, Tadgh McCarthy," Morgan scolded, doffing her gardening gloves and wiping her hands and perspiring forehead on her apron. "You tell me right away, do you hear?"

"Jeffrey's agreed to help us get our shipment to Dublin."

"That's important, but that's not what I meant."

Tadgh had decided not to lie.

"I spoke to the Operations Manager at Cunard, man named Jack Jordan." He looked for a flicker of recognition in those sultry eyes that were glued on him. There was none. "He says that there is no information obtained from the photograph of you that they took. They are still trying to find out who you are."

Morgan looked crestfallen.

"There now, Morgan. It's not as bad as all that surely. There's tomorrow, and there's still our cause for all that. It's only been four days."

"But did they send the photograph to New York?"

"I don't honestly know for certain. I would think that it would be the logical thing to do as we talked about. Give it time, girl."

Tadgh felt the sudden pangs of guilt and hoped that they weren't obvious. This was for the best for Morgan. They both had a critical job to do, and needed their wits about them.

Morgan returned to her task of weeding the carrots, whose tops were now prominent, with a vengeance. Tadgh could see that this was her main outlet for frustration and disappointment.

It was one a.m. on Wednesday morning when Tadgh and his first mate, Morgan, set sail into a clear but moonless night. They were wearing black, nondescript clothing.

"*The Republican* is a unique Bád Mór class hooker," Tadgh explained. "At 35 feet she's one of the bigger varieties. She is decked fore of the mainmast, with plenty of storage space for fish and other cargo, as you can see." Tadgh had covered over the name.

The wind was freshening. Tadgh easily navigated down the Ilen River past Baltimore harbor, a trip he had made in the dark many times.

He was not sure how Morgan would handle being on the open sea once more. But she showed no sign of anxiety as he plotted his course to the rendezvous. Pretty soon they were passing Cape Clear Island on their starboard side and heading out into the Celtic Sea.

"Tadgh, I can see why you love the ocean so much," Morgan sighed. "It's the solitude."

Many people don't get it, but Morgan instinctively does, even after the ordeal she went through. Of course she doesn't remember any of it anyway.

"There ya go, dear. Here I can temporarily forget the troubles at home and be myself."

Morgan came to him as he worked the tiller and Tadgh threw his free arm around her shoulders. She now felt safe in his strong arms.

The stars were brilliant. The kind of night for romance, Morgan dreamed, but not tonight.

"What's that you're looking through?"

"It's a sextant, my dear. With it and the stars I can figure out where we are. Why don't you take the helm, while I do some calculations?"

"Me?" Morgan looked shocked. "How do you work this thing?"

Tadgh explained how the tiller operated. The sails were set, and with a following wind, there was no immediate need to tack.

"You see that star ahead of us? The one that looks kind of orange."

"Yes."

"Well, that's actually the planet Venus. Just keep us pointed towards it, yes?"

"Will do, my Captain." Morgan saluted him.

Inwardly, for some reason, she remembered that Venus was the goddess of love. Let's go there, she mused, as they sailed on.

Tadgh reckoned that they had reached the rendezvous point at a quarter to three. He noted that the sea swells were about two feet. That would make the transfer easier. Then he thought he heard the faint sound of diesel engines pounding. He looked in the direction of the sound but at first saw nothing but black.

"I thought I saw a flash of light out there," Morgan cried.

"Yes, I just saw that, too," Tadgh replied, spinning around to get a better look. They're signaling us."

"How do they do that?"

"See how the flashes are either short or longer. Each unique sequence is a letter of the alphabet. It's called Morse code."

"The pattern seems to be repeating. What are they saying?"

"They're flashing the word 'Clan' over and over."

Tadgh pulled one of the new-fangled tungsten filament pocket torches from under his sweater and proceeded to turn it on and off rapidly with the push switch as he pointed it at the light.

"Gael, Gael, Gael, I bet," smiled Morgan.

"Exactly right, dear lass."

Tadgh brought *The Republican* into the wind and maneuvered it towards the flashing light. As they approached the stopped freighter, its superstructure loomed ominously high above them, shrouded in darkness.

"Tadgh, let's do this quickly and get out of here. I have a sinking feeling, cold and foreboding." She wondered if this was some of her memory of the sinking coming back to her in this critical situation.

"Let's not use the term sinking tonight, girl. Come on, Morgan. Help me lower the main sail and swing the jib out of the way," Tadgh coaxed. Then he showed her how. He was pleased that she was a quick and avid study. "Good," he remarked when they had completed the task.

"What's good?"

"You're good, my dear. We'll make a mariner out of you yet."

"Ahoy there," yelled someone from way up on the freighter's deck. "Come alongside amidships and we will tie you off."

"At least they speak English," Tadgh said.

"Can the man accompanying the shipment identify himself," Tadgh yelled back.

"Driscoll, here," an Irish voice replied.

They coasted to a stop there, just nudging the barnacle encrusted and rusted hull. A light panned down over *The Republican*, temporarily blinding them.

"Turn off that damn light," Tadgh yelled. A few seconds later the blinding beam was doused, leaving them in darkness except for the weak light shining on their Panamanian flag high above. A rope tumbled down, and Tadgh tied up. He could barely see the tiny figures above silhouetted against the starry sky as someone walked the rope aft and tied it to the rail. This process was repeated and he walked a second one forward. It was strange that there were no other lights to illuminate the operation. And Tadgh had his running lights covered. It was impossible that they could see us down here on the black sea very well, Tadgh realized.

"We have one big pallet for you." Driscoll shouted. "I'll ride it down."

After a couple of minutes, a derrick boom swung out over the freighter's rail. Tadgh could barely make it out, as well as the pallet hanging horizontally from it.

"Lower away," bellowed a scruffier voice from above.

Suddenly they were blinded by a tungsten spotlight from above again. As the pallet came closer, Tadgh could see that it measured at least 4 feet wide by 10 feet long. But it was not lined up right! He was going to have to move *The Republican* aft or the shipment would smash into the transom and tiller, capsizing or sinking his boat. If he moved it too far aft, it would break off the main mast.

"Whoa, stop!" he yelled repeatedly, but they didn't appear to hear him. The pallet kept coming. He quickly untied the fore line and let it go, calling out, "Morgan, quick, help me. From the bow, use that paddle to push us backward along the hull. Hurry."

Looking up, Morgan reacted swiftly. She started frantically pumping the paddle forward against the freighter's hull. *The Republican* started to inch backward.

Tadgh noticed that the pallet had cleared the top of the main mast, and the descent seemed to be accelerating. *Why weren't they asking him for a status on proximity to his ship?*

"Driscoll, you up there?" Silence except for the creaking of the ropes holding the pallet.

He couldn't see anything. This was not an accident. Tadgh pulled his Luger from his back waistband and niftily shot out the light with his last bullet. It took several seconds for his eyes to adjust to the minimal ambient light. By then the pallet was a mere six feet above the gunnels. Tadgh yelled, "Keep pushing, Morgan."

One more foot aft for the hooker and the package would clear the transom. But *The Republican* had begun to swing away from the freighter by the bow. *God, no.* Tadgh's arm scraped the freighter and a large patch of barnacle material disintegrated taking along with it some of his skin and flesh. At this rate of descent, Tadgh gauged that the package would hit the port gunnels aft of the main mast and shear it off. "Damn." He looked quickly over at Morgan who was losing the battle of keeping the hooker close to the freighter's hull.

"My God, Tadgh," she screamed. "Look out!"

Tadgh only had one option. He leaned out toward the freighter, hooking his feet securely on the inside of the gunnels. At the same time, he reached up and grabbed the outboard edge of the pallet and pulled with all his might. The hooker moved back towards the freighter and the pallet swung slightly inboard towards the hooker. The pain in his left shoulder was intense.

Just when he thought his arms would give out, *The Republican* hit the freighter with a jarring thud, shaking the deck like an earthquake. Tadgh ducked under the descending pallet, swiveled, and jumped up on top of it. At that moment, the pallet cleared the transom and the port gunnels by no more than an inch, crashing onto the deck on the port side with a sickening splintering sound. But he was relieved that the deck held. "He yelled, "We're sunk."

In the next instant, the heavy aft rope from the freighter

tumbled down striking Tadgh's head. Dazed, he began to topple overboard. He thought he heard a cry and then a loud splash aft. A hand came from nowhere and grabbed his left ankle. Then all went a numbing black.

The Republican was rebounding off the freighter, sidewise into the night, listing badly to port due to the imbalance of the heavy pallet. Tadgh was hanging overboard, limp and silent with his head, shoulders, and torso underwater.

Morgan's right arm felt like it would be pulled out of its socket. The black menacing sea was trying to drag Tadgh overboard. For a moment, a portal to her soul opened up and the paralyzing shock of the cold, wet darkness that Tadgh must be feeling enveloped her. She had been there before. *God, the Lusitania.* The recollection lasted an instant and then thankfully the portal closed, returning her to the present. If she let go, Tadgh would drown. She'd never find him in the dark.

As she started to call out to him, another light flashed nearer the bow of the freighter now some 100 yards away. The beam swung down and illuminated the edge of the freighter where the hooker had been. She saw it sweep the ocean nearby, narrowly missing *The Republican* as it drifted away. Somehow, despite her petrified fear, she realized that silence was essential if they were to survive.

Morgan braced her feet against the port gunnels bringing her left hand to join her right. Then, with strength that she didn't know she possessed, she painfully started to drag Tadgh back into the boat. She could see now that his head was out of the water as she pulled with all her might.

She heard a Satanic-like voice call out, "I think we sank them. Their sails were furled." The light winked out, leaving only darkness. Morgan heard the mighty turbines of the freighter come to life and felt *The Republican* buck in the swell of its wake. There was the sea trying to take Tadgh again. Her grasp slipped and Tadgh's head went back underwater. Just as his foot was about to step out over the gunnels, she heard an inner voice. *Act now.*

Her body was not her own. The force of God must have propelled her exhausted upper body from over the gunnels. She caught Teague's foot mid-air. It almost pulled her overboard. It was as if the evil sea was determined to take its due, both the *Lusitania* near-victim and her savior. Although her feet were still planted on the hooker's deck at the gunnels, her body from the waist up angled precariously overboard. Tadgh's body slammed against the outside of the hull and still Morgan held on. The terrible tentacles of the black abyss reached up, slapping her. They tried to pull her out. Her nose and eyes burned. And the utter blackness roared. *We are not going to die tonight.*

The fact that she had wedged her right foot between the pallet and the gunnels saved both their lives. It seemed an eternity, but slowly she managed to drag herself and Tadgh back into the boat. At first, as he lay on the deck on his back, he was limp and lifeless. *God, grant me the power to save my worldly savior. He isn't breathing!*

Seconds later, he started choking and gagging. Morgan quickly checked his mouth for obstructions and moved his tongue, which seemed to be blocking his airway. The choking sound turned to unproductive coughing. There was still water in his throat, so Morgan started breathing into his mouth. Then, Tadgh emitted one huge watery cough. Then he stopped coughing altogether. She could tell that he was exhausted, but he had a pulse.

Mindful of her own recent trauma, Morgan thought, *Oh Lord, what if he hit his head against the hull.* She couldn't find any contusions except for the scraped arm, which was minor.

Morgan looked around for help. There was none. The freighter was nowhere to be seen in the darkness. She could hear the thumping of its engines receding into the distance. The swells were lapping to within a few inches of the top of the gunnels on the port side. *What am I going to do out here on the sea at night with a boat that is floundering and Tadgh unconscious?* Stripping off his wet clothes, she wrapped Tadgh up in blankets from the storage locker. She sat on the deck and held him to her for warmth. He was so cold.

To keep her mind from panicking, Morgan forced herself to take stock of her situation. Tadgh had taught her how to steer the boat but not how to work the sails, which were now furled. Useless like that. Maybe in daylight. She could just imagine what would happen if an English ship found her like this.

She couldn't possibly move the cargo to the centerline of the boat by herself. Worst of all, in the dark she couldn't even tell which way to go to reach shore. Tadgh stirred in her arms.

"Darling, wake up. I need you!" His eyes fluttered, and then opened them, gazing into Morgan's pleading face.

"What happened?" he murmured. "You safe?" He instinctively reached for his Luger. Morgan could see his vexation when he found it missing. "I saw it on the deck over behind the pallet."

"Thank God."

"Oh, Tadgh, you're back," Morgan rejoiced. "Thank you, God."

"I'll be damned. They tried to sink us, didn't they now?"

"That's what I thought, too. That's why I kept quiet while they were still near."

"Where are they, then?" Tadgh looked out into the blackness, darting his head from side to side.

"Gone. I heard their engines start up then recede into the distance."

"Good. What's the status of *The Republican,* do ya know?" Tadgh asked, as he tried to sit up.

Morgan saw how wobbly he was and his eyes appeared glossed over. "Well, the cargo is off center. That's all I know. But the good news is, it's inside the boat and we aren't sinking yet."

Tadgh pulled himself to his feet, holding a presumably throbbing head.

"You look a little wobbly. Let me help you," she said as she propped him up. Then it just came out. "I was panicking, Tadgh.

You're my savior. I don't know what I'd do without you." She threw her arms around his blanketed body.

"It was your hand on my left ankle wasn't it, and here I am. So you are my savior for all that. Don't you ever leave me. Not even if you regain your memory and have a life somewhere else. That would panic me."

She kissed him fiercely. "No, never."

"All right then, *aroon*. Can I call you that, Morgan? It means sweetheart."

"Yes, by all means do, my love."

"Right then. That's settled. Could you get me that spare set of clothes from the locker, please?

When he was clothed, Tadgh appeared alert. They returned to business.

"I thought I heard a scream and a loud splashing noise just before I went under. Did you hear it, too?"

"Yes, it was a strange sound."

"Damn, I'll bet they threw Driscoll overboard. Quick, give me the torch over there under my sweater."

They spent the next several minutes sweeping the sea around them with their light and calling out Henry's name, but could not find him in the water. Tadgh realized that a fall from that height, even if he was conscious at the outset, would have most certainly been fatal. Eventually they had to abandon their search. "First thing we need to do is center the cargo," he explained. "Let's see if we can drag it over." Try as they might, they couldn't move the whole pallet.

"Probably weighs about five hundred pounds," Tadgh guessed.

"First, let's cut those straps and move the crated munitions and pallet separately." Tadgh produced a pocketknife and severed the cords. Together, using the paddle for leverage, they shoved the three crates to the centerline.

"They didn't need such a huge and heavy pallet for this

shipment, did they, Tadgh?"

"It wasn't so much a pallet as a projectile lass, meant to sink us."

The decking under the pallet was splintered and broken through in a few places. "Stout old hooker," Tadgh commented. "A lesser boat would have sunk." They heaved the heavy pallet up and overboard. With *The Republican* now balanced, Tadgh set the sails and turned for home. "We have lost about an hour and we've gotta get back before daylight."

They made good time. The wind had again turned in their favor. The full moon came up behind them and Morgan was struck by its size and beauty near the horizon.

While *en route* they talked about what had happened. Until Tadgh needed her to do something to manage the boat, Morgan stayed close to him.

"Now then, *aroon*, did you call out right after the cargo hit the deck? Tadgh asked.

"No, I almost did but then I realized that the enemy would hear me." Morgan went on to describe what happened after Tadgh was in the water.

"So they think they sank us, do they?"

"That's what they said before they turned off their light."

"Good."

"Do you think that the RIC are behind this, Tadgh?"

"That or the British themselves, likely," Tadgh answered. "If we were sunk then the freighter's crew could say there was an accident during transfer, in the dark. That way, they get their money, the munitions disappear, the transporter is eliminated, the ship owner is in the clear and no one's the wiser," Tadgh speculated. "They could probably have seen the top of our mast to set up the derrick to sink us."

"If they knew about the transfer at sea, do you think they will know that you were the transporter?"

338

"No, I don't think so. Padraig is the only one who knows what I do, and I trust him explicitly." Morgan breathed a sigh of relief and as they rounded the final turn of the Ilen at Creagh, the first rays of dawn were breaking over the horizon. They had made up half the time that they'd lost. They still had a long day ahead of them, even though they felt like they'd already been up a fortnight.

"I'm relieved that we have the arms, and our hero, O'Donovan Rossa, will shortly be back on his native soil for good, after forty-four years in exile. That counts for something, to be sure."

"To be sure."

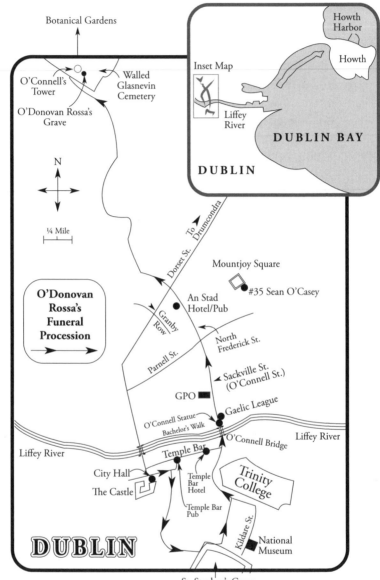

Botanical Gardens

O'Connell's
Tower

Walled
Glasnevin
Cemetery

O'Donovan Rossa's
Grave

N

¼ Mile

O'Donovan
Rossa's
Funeral
Procession

To Drumcondra

Dorset St.

Mountjoy Square

An Stad
Hotel/Pub

#35 Sean O'Casey

Granby Row

North
Frederick St.

Parnell St.

Sackville St.
(O'Connell St.)

GPO

Gaelic League

O'Connell Statue
Bachelor's Walk

O'Connell Bridge

Liffey River

Liffey River

Temple Bar

City Hall

The Castle

Temple
Bar
Hotel

Temple Bar
Pub

Trinity College

Kildare St.

National
Museum

DUBLIN

St. Stephen's Green

Inset Map

Liffey
River

DUBLIN

DUBLIN BAY

Howth
Harbor

Howth

Chapter Twenty-Three
Down to Dublin

Wednesday, July 28, 1915
Creagh, Ireland

*W*iggins **was waiting** for them, as promised. His staked B & C lorry was parked at the shore end of Tadgh's lane, at the top of the staircase that wound down 25 feet to the end of Tadgh's dock. As requested, the vehicle was laden with twenty-gallon charged stout barrels. Tadgh brought *The Republican* neatly alongside the dock that ran down one side of the boathouse where shrubbery allowed privacy from the road and prying river traffic.

"Tadgh, I'm really glad to see you and Morgan back safe and sound."

"Not half as glad as I am to see you," Tadgh responded. "Thanks for being on time, Jeff. And speaking of safe and sound, do you think you could get your Martin to repair the cockpit decking on my hooker? I may need it shortly."

"Consider it done."

"Introduce me properly to Morgan here. Looks like we're going to spend some time together."

"She's my partner. A goddess that I plucked from the sea."

"Beg pardon?"

"Off the *Lusitania,* she was."

"You don't look the worse for wear, young lady."

"Thanks to Tadgh. You show remarkable courage, Jeff."

"It's my country, too," was all he said.

Morgan wondered if it had been her country, too, before the sinking. It didn't matter now, she decided.

Tadgh had already tied up the hooker and was busy in the boat loft. He opened a door on the dock side of the boathouse at the roof level and extended the swinging arm derrick boom that he used to transfer his fishing catch to the shore.

"Grab the ropes that are coiled on the boathouse wall please, Morgan. I want to get on the road and away from here as soon as possible."

It took the three of them almost an hour to remove the barrels, swing transfer the munitions crates onto the lorry bed, cover it with tarps, and then completely cover the truck bed with the barrels.

"There, now it looks like any other beer delivery," Jeff said, cinching down the last tie-rope.

Even Tadgh was satisfied. After he moved *The Republican* into the boathouse, Tadgh locked the doors, and showed Jeff where he hid the key just in case. Then they set off for Dublin, taking back roads all the way to Cork.

"Where in Dublin are we headed, Tadgh?"

"Do you know the *An Stad* hotel and pub in Dublin?"

"Know it well. We've delivered many a pint to them over the years, I can tell you."

"Well, that's where we're after goin'."

Morgan was curious. "Why a pub for a rendezvous, anyway? I've been wondering 'bout that."

"Well now, that pub and guesthouse has been a meeting point for great literary minds interested in nationalism and independence since Cathal McGarvey opened it in the 1860s," Tadgh explained. "Great *craic* there, I'll tell you. Many of our IRB and Irish Citizen Army leaders pass through its doors. And what better destination for a B & C beer lorry delivery, don't you think?"

"Makes sense to me."

"There's just one catch," Tadgh added. "Our leader, Padraig, hates the place, so he does. His flavor of our Catholic religion doesn't approve of alcohol and tobacco. But he'll understand, in this situation. Anyway, he's off at the Dundalk conference of the Gaelic League today."

"Doing what, may I ask?" Now Wiggins was interested.

"As you probably already know, Jeff, up until now the League, of which I am a member, has focused on national literature in the Irish language. Douglas Hyde, its chief spokesman, formed it way back in the 1880s. Many Irish literary geniuses, such as William Butler Yeats, James Joyce, and the budding Sean O'Casey are, or have been, active members. Now, we need this League to support our political cause. Hyde objects. So Padraig Pearse intends to have the Irish Volunteers take over leadership and change the League's charter."

"Will the members agree to this?"

"I hope so. Many of our most staunch Republican supporters are poets and writers. It's the idealists who ache to restore the Gaelic life with spiritual and literary freedom . . . "

"Which has been brutally suppressed by the English tyrants over the last few centuries," Morgan added.

"We will know the outcome by Sunday at the funeral."

"Whose, Tadgh?"

"Why, the one who accompanied those three crates back there until we met them at sea this morning, O'Donovan Rossa," Morgan threw out nonchalantly.

"You're funnin' me, right? He's still in America, isn't he?"

"Not as of today. He arrives in Dublin later this afternoon. The funeral procession will be grand this Sunday, I can assure you."

"What's in the crates, if you don't mind my asking?"

"Rifles and ammunition for our cause." Jeffrey went very quiet from there on out. They wound their way up through the Irish countryside taking the back roads. Around mid-morning they passed through Tipperary and then Cashel. Tadgh acted as tour guide. "Well now, I don't suppose you know, Morgan, that my ancestors settled here in Cashel when they came here in the fifth century from Wales."

"I hear tell that the MacCarthy Clan were the rulers in these parts and then later in Munster up into the 17th century," Wiggins added, winking at Tadgh.

"So you are Irish royalty, then." Morgan pushed her nose up with her finger.

"Someday perhaps, when we're free," Tadgh quipped back, smiling.

Morgan thought she had struck a nerve because of the twinkle in Tadgh's eyes when he said that. Not the time to broach that subject, Morgan thought, and certainly not with his pal Wiggins present.

Tadgh wasn't going to continue with that conversation.

"This lorry rattles my teeth but nothing as jarring as the Kerry," Morgan exclaimed as they bounced along. She asked questions about every hamlet that they passed through. In almost every locale Tadgh told her a tale about some ancient or recent connection to the struggle for freedom from the English. He wondered whether this thirst for knowledge was common for those with complete amnesia, or whether it was just Morgan's nature.

About noon, Jeff asked, "Does anyone fancy a sandwich and some Beamish?" He had had the foresight to bring the former and they had a lorry-full of the latter.

"Wonderful, thanks," they both said. They had been so focused on the mission that they had forgotten about food. Wiggins found a particularly isolated part of the road and pulled over to eat lunch.

Jeff was turning out to be a valuable compatriot, Tadgh decided. What if they hadn't ended up in the B & C loading yard the other day?

"What compels you to help us at the risk of losing your job at Beamish and Crawfords?" Morgan asked while they chomped down on their mutton and swigged their stout.

"What makes you think I could lose my job?"

"Borrowing company vehicles to support the cause of freedom?" Morgan answered, looking him square in the eyes.

"Yes. That. I can handle the logistics. Don't worry. Old Henderson thinks I'm one of his best Beamish Boys, just like your partner here."

That fortuitous turn of events demonstrated that there was support for their cause in many corners of his country. The show of force by this small band of three encouraged Tadgh immensely. "My friends, it's time to be most vigilant from here to our destination," he cautioned as they passed through Portarlington and into the environs of Dublin mid-afternoon.

"Unless they think we were sunk this morning, then they can likely guess that the arms will be coming to Dublin."

"You're obviously referring to the possibility of ambush and detention—or worse, aren't you," Morgan surmised, glancing quickly over at her partner.

"Sunk this morning?" Wiggins picked up on that.

Tadgh briefly explained what had happened, which appeared to make his friend more nervous. "They probably think we're dead," he said in an effort to allay Jeff's fears, but the man's expression told him otherwise.

Tadgh immediately realized that this would only raise the level of the transportation manager's anxiety. If they were stopped, his former colleague would be a dead giveaway.

Morgan jumped into the conversation. "Look, Jeffrey, it was probably a rogue sailor wanting to dump his dangerous cargo and get out of there. We haven't been stopped so far. I have great confidence in Tadgh to get us through safely."

That seemed to work and Tadgh saw Wiggins' anxiety level drop appreciably as he drove on.

"Cool as a cucumber," Tadgh teased, to laud his partner.

He had been prescient. As they passed through Clane on the north side of the Liffey River, just twenty miles from Dublin

Center, they could see a slowdown ahead. Vehicles were being stopped at a police checkpoint. "How fitting that this was the site of the start of the 1798 Jacobite war," Tadgh blurted out.

"What if they are searching for munitions?" Jeff asked, gripping the steering wheel with white knuckles.

"More than likely they are just checking the myriad of Irishmen coming for the funeral."

"You mean outlaw ones like you two?"

Tadgh realized that he'd said the wrong thing again.

They had already planned what to do if they were stopped by the police, including Tadgh's disguise. As soon as they pulled behind a dozen or so vehicles back, Tadgh got out of the lorry to assess the situation. Three RIC constables at the checkpoint were focused on the car they were examining. They were in the middle of town with parallel streets and plenty of homes for cover.

"All right, Morgan. Now." She was out of the lorry and halfway to the nearest house by the time Tadgh had finished his remark. Tadgh pulled the B & C workers tunic that Wiggins had given him up around his ears and pulled down his cap. Then he crossed over and took his position in the driver's seat as Jeffrey shifted across to the passenger's side.

All of this took less than a minute, just time enough to move forward in the line. They crept forward slowly, until finally they were second in line to the checkpoint.

"It's going to be fine," Tadgh coached "Just take it easy. I'll do the talking."

"Oh, the Saints preserve us," Wiggins exclaimed, when a Constable yanked the driver ahead of them out of his cab. They had the boot of his vehicle open and had found something they didn't like, Tadgh speculated. Then they knocked the driver down, cuffed his ears, and dragged him off to their vehicle.

Tadgh's left hand was grasping the Luger in his pocket. Little use it would do him. The one round that had jammed in his Luger at B&C had taken out the ship's light, but now he was devoid of bullets. He wished he had checked the armament crates for nine millimeter bullets before they left home. Not a likely caliber.

One of the constables swaggered up to driver's window, and Tadgh lowered it. This is what Tadgh had been counting on.

"Hey, you two blokes. Where you headed with that beer?" The constable started to look around the cab.

"Several of the pubs in town, gov'nor. Our usual rounds," answered Tadgh smartly.

"Which ones?" the constable pressed for an answer.

Being very familiar with Dublin, Tadgh rhymed them off, being careful to exclude *An Stad*.

"Need to wet your whistle, gov'nor?" Tadgh coaxed, starting to open the driver's door. "We can spare a brew or two."

"Now, you wouldn't be trying to bribe an officer would you?"

Tadgh could see behind him that another constable was starting to nose around the truck bed of the lorry. Tadgh's hand tightened on the gun butt.

Damn, he thought. *I've got to bring this to an end right now.*

"Excuse me, gov'nor," Tadgh said as he stepped out of the cab. "There's going to be hell to pay for how late we is already." With that he walked quickly to the back of the lorry, jumped up on top of the stacks of barrels, and threw one down to the first constable, being careful not to expose the tarp.

"Best stout in the land, Beamish is," he announced with gusto. Then he hopped down and slapped the Constable on the back, adding, "Take it for you and your men, gov'nor, and let us be on our way. I'll find a way to cover the missing keg, so I will." He was counting on the fraternity of thieves. It worked.

"Move along then," the Constable ordered.

Tadgh lost no time in climbing back in the cab and leaving the checkpoint.

Wiggins was white with apoplexy, but managed to stutter,

"T-That was a c-close one, to be s-sure, to be s-sure."

"All in a day's work, Jeffrey, my lad. We're fine, now, don't ya know."

About a quarter mile ahead, Morgan was waiting by the side of the road.

"Going my way?" she called out as they pulled up. She had hiked up her skirt so you could clearly see her knees.

"Don't think we'd have made it with you on board, dear. You don't look like a barrel-toting bloke."

"Oh yah. I can roll them with the best of them," Morgan joked, pulling herself up and in.

"Oh yes you can, and did," Tadgh exclaimed.

Wiggins nodded his remembrance and the color started to return to his pudgy face.

They pulled up to the loading dock in the alley behind the An Stad pub at 35 North Frederick Street an hour later. Tom Clarke, the senior leader of the IRB, came out to greet them with open arms. Tadgh made the introductions. Tom took him aside.

"You know that B & C is not sympathetic to our cause, don't you, Tadgh." He looked worried.

"But Jeffrey here, a close friend and colleague of mine when I worked there five years ago, has a brother unfairly incarcerated. He is transportation leader with the freedom to make deliveries as often as he organizes them. He is definitely in our camp, sir."

"Be careful, Tadgh."

"Always, sir."

"That's not what I hear. Where's Henry Driscoll?"

"I'm sorry to tell you, sir, that there has been foul play. We believe that he was thrown overboard and drowned." Tadgh recounted the dangerous transfer at sea and the incident at the checkpoint.

"Damnation!" Tom exclaimed. "So we were right to worry. They may know we've got arms today."

"They think they sank us, sir," Morgan offered, stepping over to where the men were talking.

"It may not have been the English. Could just have been the foreign shipping company getting cold feet."

"We'll know soon enough. So come in, come in and rest awhile, my friends. You've done a great service for our cause and our country. My men will offload your lorry." With that they entered the hallowed *An Stad* pub and hotel.

"Well if it isn't Mollie Gleeson," Tadgh cried out, giving the proprietress a peck on the cheek. "How are you, my dear?"

He could see that Morgan was taken aback by this show of affection.

"Tadgh McCarthy, you scallywag. It's a shame I don't see you around here no more, ever since your play—"

Tadgh cut her off. "Out-of-towners these days, Mollie."

When it came to arranging the accommodations for her guests, Mollie Gleeson said not a word when it was clear that Tadgh and Morgan would share a room that evening. Bless her soul, she enjoyed having a poke at the sanctimonious priests of Holy Mother Church with their mealy-mouthed hypocrisy; she would turn a blind eye to lovers who lived outside the ridiculous matrimonial laws. That gave her as much pleasure as making it no secret that she welcomed those who might from time to time lean over their pints and "talk a little treason" in the pub.

Mollie chuckled quietly when she addressed Tadgh and Morgan as "Mr. and Mrs." She was only sorry that the room she gave the couple did not match the evident quality of Tadgh's lady; she wasn't just a bit of skirt, of that she was sure. Mollie sighed and wished herself twenty years younger; she would never have let Tadgh sleep in the arms of another if she were as handsome as that lass.

Then, while Jeffrey rested from the ordeal in his own room, Tadgh and Morgan debriefed Tom fully on the events of the last few days.

"Padraig told me about your encounter with the RIC in Cork, Tadgh. Unfortunate. Good work though, Morgan. Any sign of your brother Aidan, Tadgh?"

"We hope he's here in Dublin, sir. We'll find him, so we will," Tadgh frowned.

"Time is short, lad."

"I think you have an informant high up in the organization, sir. They definitely intended to sink us today. He may be in the Clan na Gael organization in America. I suggest you talk to McGarrity and Devoy about this."

"Point noted, Tadgh. Do you think your safe house might have been compromised?"

"No sir, I don't. We covered our tracks."

"I certainly hope so. Tadgh, we are treating this as a State funeral. O'Donovan is already on his way to City Hall. He will lie in state there starting tomorrow morning for the people to pay their respects. There will be an Irish Volunteers honor guard at his side. We are expecting a very large turnout. I've asked Padraig to give the eulogy. He is a powerful orator. This is not only fitting for our hero, but will motivate our cause."

"Yes, I know, sir. Padraig shared some of his thoughts for the tribute with me when he came to the safe house on Monday. It is going to be a very inspirational speech, I'd venture to say," Tadgh said.

"Is there any nine-millimeter ammunition in the shipment, Tom?" Tadgh asked.

"Ask MacDonagh. He's the munitions man," Tom answered. And then he added, "We don't want any more bloodshed this weekend, Tadgh. Won't help our cause."

"Of course, sir. Understood."

In the pub, Tadgh introduced Morgan to Thomas MacDonagh, who was assigned as Chief Marshal and to Terence MacSwiney from Cork, and who had produced a pamphlet on the life of Rossa.

Both were thankful that O'Donovan had finally been returned to his friends and his homeland.

"Why do you want nine-millimeter ammunition, Tadgh? It's German, isn't it?"

"The weapons we just received are Enfield Mk 1 rifles, with .303 ammunition."

Tadgh showed him the Luger and explained where he had got it.

"Leave it with me. I'll see what I can do."

MacSwiney piped up, offering a handshake, "I'm glad you are with us in West Cork, Tadgh. And I understand that you are a writer of note for our cause."

"Well, now. Just some work I did at the Abbey Theater early last year. Nothing really important," Tadgh replied.

"That's not what I hear, son. The *Sinn Fein* newspaper printed that it was the best play they had seen to stir up our Gaelic spirit; so good that the authorities shut it down after less than a week. It had crowds outside every night, some not so friendly, I understand."

"That's why the RIC and the Dublin Metropolitan Police still have me on their capture list, don't ye know." Then Tadgh saw young Michael Collins enter the pub and pointed him out to Morgan.

"He's certainly a fine-looking man in that khaki uniform, Tadgh," she said.

"Better'n me?"

"He's a soldier. You're a fisherman. Apples and oranges."

"We're the same, him and me. C'mon over."

"Well, Mick, how long has it been?" Tadgh slapped Collins on the back.

"McCarthy, is that you? I haven't seen you since Lisavaird. It must be fifteen years since we were in school together in Woodford. We sure learned a lot from Headmaster Lyons and Santry, the old blacksmith."

"They taught us so much about what it means to be Gaelic, didn't they?"

"Cornerstone of my beliefs, Tadgh. I remember that your main goal was to prove your lineage, wasn't it?"

"Not the most important thing these days, Mick, is it? Let me introduce my partner Morgan."

"Pleased to meet you, ma'am. You and Constance sure dress alike."

"So I've been told, Mr. Collins."

"This is going to be quite a show, which should boost our support. And, of course, it will be a fitting tribute to our first generation Fenian leader. He really resonated with our people, more so than anyone since Wolfe Tone, I think. I'm in charge of organizing the recording of the funeral for posterity."

"There is a very extensive funeral committee, isn't there," Morgan announced as she and Tadgh sat down to have dinner and a drink.

"I expect so, *aroon*. It has taken a lot of planning, I am sure."

"Why did they wait so long to give you orders when this is so important?"

"That's how we operate—on a need to know basis. There are small circles of responsibility and knowledge. Very few know much about the overall plan."

"Wouldn't it be better for communications if more people knew what was going to happen?"

"All it takes is one traitor to put lives at risk. You saw what happened this morning."

"I see your point."

After dinner they checked on the condition of Wiggins who had retired to his room. They found him propped up in a stuffed chair.

He hailed them: "Tadgh, my boy, we did a marvelous thing today, didn't we?"

Tadgh noted his now-ruddy cheeks and the five empty Beamish bottles by his night stand. *Liquid courage after the fact.*

"I'd love to stay for the funeral, but I've got to get back to my business tomorrow. I left Olson in charge, and I can't trust him to keep on schedule for more than a couple of days. Can you both find your own way home?"

"We'll take the train back, Jeffrey. Thank you for all your help. We couldn't have done this without you. I saw that the checkpoint was only for traffic coming into Dublin today. So you should not be stopped on your way out, especially if you take the southern route. You know how important it is to keep all of these activities secret, don't you?"

"Of course, my boy. I know what the authorities can do to people like us."

"Good."

Morgan gave him a big hug and said, "Safe passage home," clasping his hands in parting. They left him to sleep it off. Exhaustion showed in both their faces as they climbed to the third landing and waited for the little chambermaid to open the door to their room. The girl dipped a curtsey to them; she was in awe of all the brave young men of the Brotherhood and murmured that she would be bringing up the bathwater as soon as it boiled.

When they stepped into the room, they were greeted with a peaceful quiet afforded by the double windows that faced North Frederick Street with its narrow sidewalk still full of workaday residents on their way to a pub or stumbling home from one.

The room seemed cozy enough to Morgan with its lace curtains of Irish respectability and high feather bed. Even a framed picture of the Sacred Heart picked out in violent colors seemed fitting in its place on the wall, but the startling orange fire that haloed the figure of Jesus disturbed her. Fragmented nightmares of fire and the figure of an unknown man engulfed in those flames still plagued her dreams. Since their trauma with the RIC on the B & C wharf, this searing vision was sometimes triggered into conscious daytime thought, if only for a minute. So it was tonight, but like always, she forced it out of mind. *But who was that burning man?*

Sure enough, a chamber pot beneath the bed and the washstand with mirror, ewer, and basin were evidence that indoor plumbing had not yet reached this establishment. A thought nagged at the corner of her mind, a memory of a room so much like this one—a room from her girlhood? Before she could catch it, the memory slipped away and she was again left frustrated. It seemed as though the veil of secrecy that her mind imposed was close to being parted right after times of great stress. Like a name maddeningly just out of reach.

At a timid knock minutes later, Tadgh opened the door and ushered in the chambermaid. She carried steaming kettles to fill a copper tub discreetly hidden behind a screen in a corner of the room. This heavy work colored her cheeks, and perspiration glowed on her neck and arms, but she went about filling the tub without a sound or a wasted movement. She didn't dare look at either the gorgeous man or his lady, but scurried across the threshold, kettles ringing as they knocked together, and closed the door after herself.

Though they both craved sleep because of the day's events and what still lay ahead of them, Morgan and Tadgh did not want to waste the moments of time they could steal from the rigors of their mission.

They used very few words with one another so they could let the language of their bodies speak for them. It was as though their mouths, so full of questions, could only be satisfied with kisses that parted and opened their lips. They had found their rhythm and as they began to undress one another, it was with sweet slow movements that would soon become strong and powerful as their tongues found all the folds and curves of their exposed flesh. Morgan brought Tadgh to the tub and guided him into the water, just as she would, at the point when they could no longer bear to be separate, guide him into her body.

She knelt behind him to massage his knotted shoulder muscles and could not help burying her face in the crown of unruly curls that tumbled over his ears and down his neck. She heard the pattern of his breath lengthen and deepen as she teased his ears and jaw with kisses. She ran her hands along his arms and paid special attention to the scar left from the bullet wound he had suffered, his body's only blemish. Its rumpled edge reminded her once more of the mastery of her work making him whole again. She only wished she knew from where the ability to attend to him had come; but no matter now, she had further care for this man at the moment.

Her breath also began to lengthen and deepen, matching her touch on his neck, shoulders and arms. Then Tadgh turned his head to kiss her fingers as they fluttered across his skin, and she felt a tingling pressure at the meeting of her thighs, and a sweet liquid wave moved within her. The steam continued to rise and envelop Tadgh's face and shoulders; droplets of moisture smoothed the signs of weariness from his forehead, and his teeth shone as pearls from the thick forest of his beard.

He took her hands in his, and with the deep sigh of his surrender to her, drew Morgan into the water with him. Her back easily slipped to meet his chest and loins and, as he caressed her breasts and stomach; they began to breathe with more force and their hearts set to pounding. If the water was beginning to cool, they did not know; perhaps the heat of their hungry kisses and increasing movement together forced the water to churn with their hot intensity. They teased each other with sighs and moans that revealed their mounting excitement, and Morgan slowly turned to face him so her eyes could delight in the sight of his erect, thrusting member.

Sucking and licking, Tadgh bruised her breasts and nipples, and she urged him on. As if in answer to the question in his smoldering amber eyes, she pulled him over unto herself and opened so he could enter and plunge into her farthest reaches. He buried his face in her neck and pressed more deeply into her. Again and again, he pulled and returned, as her breath quickened and water splashed over the sides of the tub. Above her, he felt himself begin to explode and spill into her, and the look in her eyes—the emerald sea green of them—urged him on; she was there with him, no need to slow.

Again they found the point of their recklessness. They were helpless in the throes of their need for each other's exquisite vulnerability, and their cries wound around them as they reached the place of completeness. This time Tadgh and Morgan met their climax together. In the turbulent pleasure of their joining, they were pledged to one another. Just as much as they pleasured themselves with a wild abandon, they were also the place of solace in each other's arms.

As their breathing began to slow, they were loathe to draw apart; Tadgh would not leave her body, and Morgan wound her legs about his hips to keep him tucked within her. They sealed their pledge with tender kisses and caresses. He brushed the hair that covered her face and continued to rock her slowly with him. When their heat had cooled, Morgan began to shiver. Rising from the water, they hastily toweled water from each other, and laughed when they saw the water that had rushed from the tub in the face of their stormy lovemaking.

They climbed into the high feather bed, exquisitely spent. They were hungry for one another, wanting to make love again, but sleep called to them. Tadgh and Morgan contented themselves with curling tightly into one another, so they could continue to touch and kiss. And this they did until their eyes closed. They fell into dreamless slumber that meant a rest for Morgan from visions of fire and cries of babies to torment her, and for Tadgh that night, no nightmare of his parents' senseless murder.

Chapter Twenty-Four
Saving Aidan

Thursday, July 29 1915
En Route from Cork City to Dublin

*I*n his car that morning, Darcy Boyle was gloating. The Inspector General of the RIC, Sir Neville Chamberlain, had requested his services to help control the expected civil unrest at the funeral of the bastard Rossa. Boyle hated the Irishman for his leadership of the dynamite bombings in England in the eighties. He gave no credence to the report that O'Donovan had been cruelly mistreated, along with many of his countrymen, while erroneously detained in Chatham prison in England. Nor did he acknowledge that England had been oppressing the Irish as if they were vermin for centuries. He reveled in his country's superiority. How could it be otherwise? He had been taught that concept from infancy by his father. His poor Mother, on the other hand, what had she thought?

Chamberlain had bypassed the Cork District Inspector in charge, Dean Maloney, a fact that delighted Boyle. *Maloney is such an ass. I can do whatever I want with Irishmen, and he is oblivious.*

"Gordo, what's the latest news?" Boyle barked as they rode north into Dublin.

"Rossa's body made it to Dublin and is now lying in state at the City Hall. Thousands are filing past it to pay their respects. And it is being guarded by the Irish Volunteers. Looks like this will be a major propaganda coup for The Republicans."

"Damn, I thought they were going to intercept Rossa and avoid this nonsense," Boyle cursed, scowling over at his subordinate who, as usual, was driving.

"Even in death he seems to be able to slip through our grasp,"

Gordo lamented, avoiding his boss's stare by focusing on the road ahead.

"How many sub-constables do we have under our thumb?"

"Six, all told, but only two on this trip today, boss."

"Officially, we're to keep the peace outside the City Hall and on Sunday along the funeral procession route. We will be stationed out of Dublin Castle, which is conveniently next door to the Hall. Fine, but I want to find that McCarthy kid and possibly his brother and his girl who killed George. Since they're expecting half of Ireland to show up, I'm guessing those boys will probably be attending this funeral and its wake."

"But Darcy, that's like looking for a needle in a haystack. They're expecting over thirty thousand people in the streets."

"Yah, but there's only a finite number of drinking establishments, and the young drunkard's bound to be in one of them."

"Why would he bother coming all the way to Dublin if he's just going to be in a pub?"

"I've been tracking his friend Andy. I know that he's going to be staying at the Temple Bar Hotel. There are quite a few pubs there. It's likely that we'll find our Aidan not far from his friend sometime during this weekend."

"That's why you're the boss, Darcy," Gordo groveled just as he wheeled their paddy wagon into the south entrance of the castle grounds.

"Tadgh, I love Dublin," Morgan exclaimed as they left the *An Stad* heading south for the City Hall that morning. "Oh good grief. Your moustache!" She started to laugh, the kind that would send a man rolling on the ground in apoplexy.

"Why? What's the matter?"

Morgan produced a small mirror from her handbag and lifted

it up for Tadgh to see. Passersby started to gawk as they hurried down North Frederick Street toward the Liffey River.

"Can't you feel it? It looks so silly."

Tadgh saw that the false moustache was only gummed down on one side, and it drooped diagonally down over his lip, lodging in his curly black beard.

"It wasn't that way when we finished breakfast a few minutes ago," he griped as he attempted to fasten it properly. "Looks like I had other things on my mind this morning when we were getting ready." He let one hand free to pat her bottom. "Not much of a disguise without these face fins of mine." He had grown his beard since his Dublin days and he added the false handlebar moustache as a finishing touch.

"That looks better now if it'll hold," Morgan announced putting away her mirror.

"Well, now, lass. Are you sure that it's Dublin you love and not what happened last night?"

"What happened last night?"

"I dunno. I got a good night's sleep."

"Like hell you did, love." Morgan laughed, heaving her breasts against the silk blouse Tadgh had bought for her.

"This new clothing line Madam Chanel has introduced, to free us women from the confines of painful corsets and the like, is a godsend. If there's one good thing that has come out of the terrible World War, that's it."

"There's no doubt of it." Tadgh eyed Morgan's chest. "Let's go back, and I'll show you how we slept."

"Later. Don't we have a brother to find?"

"Yes, yes of course. But we should go and pay our respects to Mr. Rossa first."

Morgan grabbed his arm and pressed her body to his for a fleeting kiss just before they hopped up into the passing tram, heading south on Sackville Street.

"Shhh, lass. They don't know you yet, but they sure as hell know me." Tadgh pointed towards two Dublin Metropolitan Policemen conversing on the other side of the tram as they sat down. These DMP fortunately were self absorbed.

When they reached Dame Street, the line of people waiting to see their hero, stretched three blocks from the City Hall. Those who were streaming out after seeing him were congregating outside the building, and most of them seemed to be in animated conversation.

"Isn't this encouraging?" Tadgh exclaimed. "This is exactly what we need. The people will follow our lead, to be sure."

"There must be thousands here already. I've never seen anything like it."

Tadgh marched right up to the Irish Volunteer guarding the entrance, spoke softly in his ear and he and Morgan were given a place in line at the doorway. No one seemed to mind the intrusion.

Inside the splendid rotunda of the City Hall, the line of mourners passed up one side to the mahogany casket and down the other. There lay O'Donovan Rossa, in his open casket mounted on a low black catafalque and draped ceremonially with the tricolor flag, green for Catholic south, orange for Protestant north flanking white for purity and unity. The message in this Republican flag was obvious and intended. Three faceless statues looked down on the scene and four yellow candles shone light on a lone crucifix. More guards were stationed near the body, both for its protection and to help guide the mourners as they filed past. Morgan could see that many of the citizens were overcome with emotion as they left the rotunda.

After a few minutes, they were finally at the coffin. Morgan whispered, "He almost looks regal with his white beard. Mr. O'Donovan looks quite natural and at peace, despite his advanced age of eighty-three."

Tadgh leaned down close to the patriot's head and recited a portion of his ancestor, Denis Florence MacCarthy's, poem,

"Ireland's Vow" by heart.

> *On went the fight through the cycle of ages,*
> *Never our battle-cry ceasing the while;*
> *Forward, ye valiant ones! Onward, battalioned ones!*
> *Strike for your Erin, your own darling isle!*
>
> *Still in the ranks are we, struggling with eagerness,*
> *Still in the battle for Freedom are we!*
> *Words may avail in it—swords if they fail in it,*
> *What matters the weapon, if only we're free?*
>
> *Oh! we are pledged in the face of the universe,*
> *Never to falter and never to swerve;*
> *Toil for it!—bleed for it!—if there be need for it,*
> *Stretch every sinew and strain every nerve!*
>
> *Nourish it, treasure it deep in your inner heart—*
> *Think of it ever by night and by day;*
> *Pray for it!—sigh for it!—work for it!—die for it!—*
> *What is this life and dear freedom away?*
>
> *Irishmen! Irishmen! think what is Liberty,*
> *Fountain of all that is valued and dear,*
> *Peace and security, knowledge and purity,*
> *Hope for hereafter and happiness here.*

An Irish Volunteer guard was asking Morgan to move on. She grabbed Tadgh's shoulder and helped him to his feet. Tears welled up in his eyes that he had to wipe away with his handkerchief. She began to understand the depth of feelings that Republicans felt for their country and for all the people who had suffered so much over the ages. It was so personal for all of them, as it should be.

As they left City Hall, the congregation had grown considerably in size. Morgan spotted several DMP officers dressed in distinctive dark blue uniforms with their custodian-style peaked helmets. The officers were watching the crowd intently from their perch at Dublin Castle.

"Let's get out of here," Tadgh urged. He tried to give the DMP and the Castle as wide a berth as possible by heading north on Parliament Street.

Then, as luck would have it, when they rounded the corner from Parliament to East Essex Street, he collided with a DMP officer coming the other way. His moustache flew off.

"Excuse me, sir," the officer said. Then he spied the moustache and turned to scrutinize the face. There was a moment of confusion and then it dawned on him. "You're McCarthy, the playwright, aren't you," he blurted out and he reached for his night stick.

They were opposite Crane Lane. In one motion, Tadgh brought a right arm blow down onto the officer's neck, finishing with a powerful dragging motion that launched him down the stone lane. He was unconscious when he hit the cobblestones. Tadgh looked quickly around for witnesses.

Morgan was stunned by the swiftness of Tadgh's response to this threat. She rushed over and checked the assaulted officer's pulse. "My God, Tadgh, are you that well known by the police everywhere?"

Tadgh, who had been blocking the view of the lane at its entrance, said, "Obviously here in Dublin, and now in Cork, I think. Is he dead?"

"No, at least not yet, anyway. We need to get him some help, Tadgh."

"That would get us incarcerated. He'll be found soon enough."

"Let's get out of here, then," she said, scooping up and dusting off the moustache. "Put this back on for good, won't you?"

Sticking it back on, Tadgh said, "Aileen's working as a waitress at the Temple Bar Pub. It's only a few blocks from here. Let's head there."

As they turned east on Essex which turned into Temple Bar, Morgan said, "You go on ahead. I'll catch up in a minute."

Tadgh saw her engage with a passing woman for a moment and then move on.

"She'll get the DMP officer some help," Morgan said, when she rejoined her beau.

"What'd you tell her?"

"Just that we saw him there, but we are in a hurry to meet a sick brother."

"Well, at least that's partly true, isn't it, now."

Within ten minutes they had arrived at the Temple Bar Pub on the corner of Temple Lane. Tadgh had been on the lookout and didn't think they were being pursued. It was hard to miss this pub with its fire engine red, first-floor façade. Being bright and inviting even on a cloudy summer day before noontime, its large windows on each street, with a wide, well-laden bar in view, beckoned the weary and thirsty traveler. But this formidable establishment was far more than a first-class pub-eatery. In the tradition of many such businesses which had sprung up in the 1800s along the south wall of the Liffey River, Temple Bar Pub was also a grocery. The brick façaded second and third floor above the pub were offices and the personal dwelling of the pub's proprietor.

As soon as they came through the pub doors, he heard a familiar voice ring out, "For the love of God, is that you, Brother McCarthy?" The girl behind that loud voice gave Tadgh a big hug.

He couldn't help but notice the shapely young figure and provocative waitress uniform.

"Hello, Aileen lass. Still selling your wares, I see," Tadgh kidded, and he took a step backward. Glancing around the cheery, half-filled room, he was satisfied that there were no authorities present.

"Aileen, this is my partner Morgan. We're tryin' to find Aidan. Have you seen him in the last few days?"

"I heard from him yesterday, Tadgh, but I haven't seen him yet. Is he in trouble again?"

"To be sure. Serious trouble. If we don't find him soon he will be arrested or killed."

"Where was he when he called?" Morgan asked, giving this waitress the evil eye one-two.

"He was with Andy, I think." Aileen brushed something off her apron, apparently not concerned.

"And where might that be, do ya know?" Tadgh leaned closer.

"I don't know. He mentioned that he and Andy came down to see the Rossa funeral. He would drop by sometime he said. Listen, I gotta get back to my customers, Tadgh. You two want anything?" Aileen gave a wink.

"Not right now, Aileen. Don't ya be tellin' anyone except Aidan that you saw us, okay? If you see him, tell him I'm lookin' for him and find out where we can reach him. Tell him that he's in grave danger."

"Surely will, Tadgh," said Aileen, who then disappeared back towards what looked like the kitchen.

"I suggest that we wait for Aidan here," Morgan reasoned, concerned Tadgh might be recognized again out on the street. "How about that dark booth in the back?"

"It's better to be near an exit facing any entrances," Tadgh replied, scanning the room. "How about over there near the kitchen door."

They sat down and waited in a dark booth where they could see the main entrance and could still leave in a hurry, through the kitchen if necessary.

Gordo and Boyle started up the stairs of the Temple Bar Hotel. They had extracted the number of Andy O'Henry's second floor room from the front office clerk without having to resort to force. Darcy could actually be quite charming when it suited his purpose.

"Where would Andy get the money for a swanky place like this?" James asked, looking at the expensive wall coverings.

"His father's a barrister in Cork. I looked him up." He had already decided that this would be valuable information for a later extortion opportunity.

When they reached the landing, Darcy ordered, "Gordo, you guard the stairs here and don't let anyone by. I'll break into Andy's room and see if we can get lucky."

Inside Andy's room, Aidan had finally awakened. He was, at that moment, contemplating what to do. Where was Andy, he wondered? He was hungry but had no money, as usual. He wanted to see Aileen. It had been a few months and he was horny as hell for her. But he was still afraid of being recognized and arrested. Better to hole up here until Andy returns, he decided.

There was a knock at the door. Aidan did not want to answer it. After a few seconds he heard the sound of someone trying a key in the lock. Then from the scratching noises it sounded like someone was trying to pick the lock.

"Shit."

Suddenly, there was a loud thud and the door to the room vibrated and groaned. At least at the first assault, the lock, although loosened, held.

Aidan already had the window open and was outside on the platform, lowering the fire escape ladder.

On the next try, the lock gave as the door frame splintered. Boyle burst into the room and found it empty. Then he spied the open window. McCarthy was halfway down the ladder when Darcy saw him through the open window. He drew his Webley and fired off a shot, winging Aidan in the upper arm, who fell the rest of the way to the ground.

Darcy rushed to the door and yelled, "Gordo, I shot McCarthy. He's escaping down the fire escape. Get out front."

Then he bounded out the window and down the ladder in hot pursuit. He met Gordo at the foot of the ladder. By that time, they could see Aidan running west down the busy Fleet Street heading for Temple Bar. He was half a block away already.

"Run!" Boyle, screamed and they hoofed off after him.

Aidan was frantic and running for his life. *Why the hell are they shooting at me? Aileen's pub is six blocks away. She'll hide me.*

James and Boyle kept losing sight of their prey momentarily as he darted in and out of the crowd on the street.

"Damn, he's fast," Boyle shouted as they pushed people out of their way.

Aidan finally reached the Temple Bar Pub and staggered inside. He was panting, breathless and bleeding.

"Damn. There he is," Tadgh exclaimed, recognizing it was his brother in trouble. He rushed out of the smoky haze and grabbed hold of him.

"Aidan, it's me, Tadgh," he called out, as he pulled him into a dark corner of the pub. In the same moment he glanced out the doorway and saw the blur of two men, a block away, running towards them. RIC for sure.

"Gordo, I think I saw him go into that pub over there," Boyle shouted. "We've got him trapped."

"Tadgh, is that you, brother?" Aidan wheezed, as he tried to catch his breath. "They're right behind me. I'm shot."

Morgan pulled Aileen over. "Where can we hide?" she whispered urgently.

Just as Aileen was struggling to understand the situation, the bartender rushed over to the group.

"What's going on here?" she demanded quietly.

"RIC bastards are tryin' to kill my brother here," Tadgh answered, hoping she was sympathetic to the cause.

"Follow me," she commanded, and they ducked through the door into the kitchen and into a large cold storage pantry, closing the door behind them.

"There's a hole in that back wall that leads down to the storage cellar," the bartender said. "I'd better get back out front."

"Thanks, lass," Tadgh said as he pulled the bin out of the way.

They scrambled through the hole, and Tadgh pulled the bin back in place after them. It was cold, damp and pitch black.

On her way back to the pub, the bartender opened the alleyway door and cautioned her cook, "Derek, if you're questioned, one man ran out through this door. Got it?"

"Got it, Deirdre." Derek Slocum had a strong allegiance to his boss, the owner of the Temple Bar.

Deidre reentered the pub just as Darcy and Gordo burst through the front door. She grabbed Aileen and pulled her behind the bar, as much to muzzle her as to protect them both.

"Don't you dare say a word," she whispered to her waitress.

"Why?" said Aileen, and Deirdre shot her a dirty look.

Out of their jurisdiction, Boyle decided not to use his normal brute force tactics.

"We're RIC. Where is the man who just ran in here?" he asked of Deirdre.

"Strange young man in a hurry. He rushed back into the kitchen through that door."

Boyle went back into the kitchen while Gordo surveyed the patrons and empty booths.

"What happened to the man who came through this doorway a minute ago?" the constable asked of the cook.

"At first I thought that he was a disgruntled customer coming to complain about the food. But then he just ran through the kitchen and out the delivery door back there," Derek answered.

Boyle rushed to the now open back door and looked out down the alley. It was empty.

"Missed him," he grunted.

On his way back into the pub, he examined the kitchen. Then he opened a cold storage pantry door. In the dim light, he failed to see the drops of blood on the floor.

Back in the pub, Gordo announced that no one had confessed to seeing what happened to the man.

"Come on," Boyle ordered his deputy. They raced out the back door and down the alley onto an adjacent busy Temple Lane.

Derek slammed the door after them and muttered, "Good riddance."

Waiting five minutes to make sure the Constables weren't coming back, Deirdre moved the potato bin that had been hiding the fugitives out of the way.

"All clear, for now," she signaled and Tadgh, Aidan and Morgan emerged from the dark hole.

"I'm Deidre, owner of this establishment. What's this all about then, may I ask?"

"A case of mistaken identity, to be sure," Tadgh replied, and then he introduced them. "You saved our bacon, so you did. Thank you, lass."

"You're welcome," Deirdre returned. "In my line of work the police are not always my friends."

"Bartender and clerk?"

"And owner."

Tadgh took stock of their benefactor. Deidre was a fetching Irish colleen, about his own age and height. Uniquely blond for an Irish woman, statuesque, with closely-cropped bob hair. And muscular arms protruded from under her short sleeved blouse. She looked as if she could handle herself as well in the boudoir as in a pub brawl. *A formidable young woman*, Tadgh thought.

Morgan had already been examining Aidan's arm in the dark cellar. "Deirdre, can you spare some first aid supplies, please?"

"Coming up. I keep them handy behind the bar."

"The bullet is still in your arm and it has fractured your humerus bone. You're lucky that it's not a compound fracture. I'm going to have to get the bullet out and set your arm in a sling," Morgan told Aidan.

"It doesn't seem funny to me," he responded. "Those guys wanted to kill me."

"RIC uniforms, brother. I'd guess they came all the way from Cork to find you," Tadgh speculated.

Derek brought hot water, linens, knife and tweezers, while Deidre brought supplies and whiskey.

Aidan looked worried. "Does she know what she's doing?"

"Absolutely, brother. Take it from me." Tadgh pulled open the collar of his shirt to his shoulder showing the now-healed bullet hole wound. "Morgan sewed me up pretty good when I took a bullet looking for you a month ago in Cork City."

"Really, Tadgh?"

"You have no idea."

Morgan smiled in admiration for the one brother and swallowed her disgust for the other.

After they had gotten Aidan suitably drunk, she set to work, removing the bullet and dressing his wound. Derek had scrounged up two long handled wooden spoons for a splint. She reset the broken arm, secured the splint and improvised a sling.

"Morgan, you're a marvel of modern medicine," Tadgh kissed her cheek.

"Now, don't flirt with the nurse."

Aileen sauntered into the pantry. "I see he's drunk again," was all she could think of saying. Then she left to get back to her work.

"That woman is so scatterbrained. What could Aidan see in her?" Morgan shook her head.

Deirdre brought them some food and drink and a blanket to wrap around the patient who was now shaking from the cold and loss of blood.

"Why don't you folks stay overnight in my lodgings above the pub," she offered. "Your brother doesn't seem to be in any shape to travel."

Tadgh did not want to have to lug him all the way to the *An Stad* in his inebriated state. And he was not going to let Aidan out of his sight until he decided what to do with him. Tadgh looked at Morgan who was already one step ahead of him again.

"That would be much appreciated, Deidre. You have saved us today and we are very grateful to you," Morgan responded for all three of them.

"That's settled then, for sure." Deidre seemed genuinely pleased that they had accepted her invitation. Her relief bartender had just come on duty.

"Let me show you to your room."

"First, do you have any bloody meat?" Tadgh asked, returning from wiping up the spots of blood in the pantry.

"Whatever for?"

"To leave a trail in case those goons come back again."

Derek provided a bloody sheep shank, and Tadgh sprinkled blood across the kitchen from the pub entrance, as well as down the back lane to the busy street.

"That ought to lead them astray if they come back."

"So where are you from, Morgan?" Deidre asked as she led them upstairs.

"I haven't a clue, Deidre," she responded truthfully. "I was apparently on board the *Lusitania* when she sank. I bumped my head. Tadgh here saved me. I've had amnesia ever since."

"My God. The *Lusitania*. I'm so sorry to hear that. But I'd develop amnesia if Tadgh would save me too," Deidre quipped, as she winked at Morgan.

These two women seem to be hitting it off very well, he surmised.

That night they all slept in Deidre's one spare room; cozy but certainly not intimate. Aidan snored like a buzz saw.

"Tadgh, get some sleep, for heaven's sake," implored Morgan, curling her arm around his waist and pulling him in. "It's three in the morning."

"I'm trying to figure out what to do with Aidan, so I am."

"You are too close to the problem again. I think this last episode has scared him. Was he close to his ma?"

"We both were, but him particularly."

"I thought as much. He's not likely to listen to a big brother. Let me have a crack at him today."

"Go ahead. You know that they are going to be on the lookout for both of us from now on?"

"Look on the bright side. Maybe they can figure out my true identity," Morgan joked.

Tadgh was not amused.

In the morning Deidre had prepared a traditional Irish breakfast for them. "Aidan, eat up those pancakes and syrup. It'll cut that hangover," she offered.

"I guess a bartender ought to know these things," Morgan said, digging into the sausage and eggs. "How does that arm feel?"

"Hurts like hell, but less than the pounding in my head. What did you give me to drink yesterday?"

"Mainly scotch. Believe me, you didn't want to be fully awake when I operated on you." Morgan smiled at him.

Aidan smiled back. "Thanks for fixing me up. I was really lucky to run into you folks, wasn't I?"

Morgan nodded with satisfaction. She was going to get through to him.

Suddenly, they heard a commotion downstairs in the pub. Derek was arguing with someone.

"Stay here," Deidre ordered, picking up a clean carving knife and tucking it in her belt beneath her apron. "I'll find out what's going on down there. The pub isn't even open yet." With that, she disappeared. The group could hear her arguing with men in the pub below.

Tadgh went to the head of the stairs where he had a vantage point through the stair-rail balusters without being seen. He saw and heard them plainly. Two uniformed RIC Constables were facing Deidre who wasn't giving any ground. The bigger of the two, had his hand raised as if he was going to strike her. His little finger was missing.

"I'm Boyle and this here is Constable James with the Cork RIC. You are interfering with an official police investigation. Stand aside or I will have to make you comply."

Constable James was examining the floor from the front door of the pub to the kitchen entrance. "He went through here, Darcy," Gordo announced.

Clearly they were following the trail of blood. Then it dawned on Tadgh. Anger seethed up. There, below him stood two of the butchers that killed his parents—years ago. The larger man called Boyle had pulled the trigger.

Tadgh started down the stairs to kill these murderers, but stopped short of being detected. He was unarmed and they undoubtedly were carrying their Webleys. An impetuous move on his part would threaten the lives of those he loved, as well as Deidre and Derek. He throttled his emotions and decided to wait for another opportunity to seek revenge when he had the advantage. Justice would be served, he vowed.

Tadgh could see Deidre reluctantly allowing the Constables to pass her into the kitchen area. Derek was hovering nearby, in case she needed help, a loyal employee and friend, Tadgh concluded.

Then they were outside Tadgh's field of view. He heard a few minutes of muffled voices and then the back door to the establishment slammed.

When Deidre reappeared in her quarters, she eyed Tadgh and said, "You're a crafty one, Tadgh McCarthy. How did you know that they would come back on the trail of blood? They're off down the alley convinced that your brother just passed through the building."

"Well now, in the words of Conan Doyle, that's elementary, my dear Deidre."

Chapter Twenty-Five
Meeting of the Clans

Friday, July 30, 1915

*A*fter thanking Deidre and Derek profusely for all their assistance and promising to return soon, the three Republicans set off for the *An Stad* on foot. Tadgh had fashioned crude disguises from some materials Deidre had given him. All the same, he was very careful to ensure that those two bullies he had seen were nowhere in sight. *At least now I know their names. I'll get them soon enough.*

"Look how much more crowded the streets are today. It's a madhouse downtown," Morgan said as they pushed their way through traffic on Fleet Street.

The crowds helped to keep them undetected and they arrived at their hotel at about noon. Aidan needed no coaxing to avoid going back to the Temple Bar Hotel.

Thomas MacDonagh noticed their return with an injured young man in tow. It was his job to be observant. Tadgh could tell he had seen through his disguise immediately.

"Tadgh, is that your brother there?" he asked, calling them to attention. "Good thing you found him before we did. Was he in the hands of the RIC?"

"No, Thomas. But he was shot by them. We got away."

"There was a DMP officer badly injured down on Crane Lane. You wouldn't have been involved with that would you?"

"Yes, sir, he recognized me. I had to act." Tadgh stepped forward until he was in Thomas's face. He did not tell him that Morgan had also been identified.

"Honestly, Tadgh. You're leaving quite a trail of debris in your wake. We don't want to be aggressive until the time comes.

Let me remind you that, at this point, the IRB is a clandestine organization."

Morgan chimed in. "They're bringing the fight to us, sir, and not the other way around. Tadgh is doing his job as directed by your council. And he's trying to protect his family."

Tadgh did not need to respond. Morgan had said it just right. *Spunky girl*, he thought to himself, and he gave her hand a squeeze.

"I presume that you're going to control your brother from now on," Thomas said.

"To be sure," he responded not having a clue how he was going to accomplish this. "Not to press a point, sir, but did you find any nine-millimeter ammunition?"

"Yes, we have some from the Howth delivery, which I can provide if you promise not to use that Luger of yours this weekend in Dublin."

"Agreed, sir."

With that, Thomas left them alone in the front lobby.

"I'd like to lie down for a while. My arm is very sore," Aidan announced, plopping down into a lobby chair. He had been a trooper on the walk and tram ride, but now he looked gaunt and shaky.

"I'll take you up to our room," Morgan offered, pulling him up out of the chair by his good arm. "If you sit there too long you might never get up, and I should check that wound for infection anyway."

"I'll get us a table for lunch," Tadgh offered, stepping into the bar from the lobby.

On entering the Pub, Tadgh noticed his friend Sean O'Casey seated in a corner booth. Tadgh saw that he was holding forth with a group of younger lads who appeared engrossed in whatever he was saying, so he headed over to pay his respects.

"Well if it isn't Tadgh McCarthy," Sean exclaimed. "I thought that they ran you out of Dublin on a rail last year. Your play at the

Abbey caused quite a stir, let me tell you."

"Good day to you, Sean," responded Tadgh, clapping him on the back. "You should know why for certain. You helped me with it and suggested the title *A Call to Arms*. I was a bit idealistic and naive, I'll have to admit."

"I've left the organization, Tadgh," Sean commented." I can't support a group that considers Larkin's Irish Citizens Army's fight for syndicalism here in poverty-stricken Dublin to be a shortsighted local effort. The trade union movement is as important a national priority as is Republicanism."

"The government leaves us no choice, Sean."

"We'll see, my boy. I still believe that the pen is mightier than the sword. I thought that you believed that, too."

"I guess that you are filling these boys' heads with nonsense, Sean. Right, lads?"

"Well, actually, by coincidence, I was just starting to quote your great uncle's poem. You know the one, "The Voice and Pen":

Oh! The orator's voice is a mighty power,
As it echoes from shore to shore,
And the fearless pen has more sway o'er men
Than the murderous cannon's roar!
What burst the chain far over the main,
And brighten'd the captive's den?
'Twas the fearless pen and the voice of power,
Hurrah! for the Voice and Pen!
Hurrah!
Hurrah! for the Voice and Pen!

The tyrant knaves who deny man's rights,
And the cowards who blanch with fear,
Exclaim with glee: "No arms have ye,
Nor cannon, nor sword, nor spear!

377

Your hills are our—with our forts and towers
We are masters of mount and glen!"
Tyrants, beware! for the arms we bear
Are the Voice and the fearless Pen!
Hurrah!
Hurrah! for the Voice and Pen!

"Don't ya be throwing Denis McCarthy's words back at me, Sean," Tadgh protested. "Parnell tried the pen, and the British bastards spoke with forked tongue. Look what's happening to the Home Rule Bill to finally integrate our homeland. Those demons are allowing the buildup of arms for the Ulster Volunteers to stop the bill by force if necessary."

"On the contrary, Mr. O'Casey makes perfect sense. The social order of the common Irishman must be restored through bargaining with equality for all," piped up one of the senior lads who looked to be Tadgh's age.

"I couldn't agree more with you, Mr.—" said Tadgh. "It's how we go about it that's crucial for success, don't ya know."

"Peader O'Donnell is my name," the young man said. "The boys and I is attending St. Patrick's College in Drumcondra up the road to become teachers. I have strong beliefs about liberating our nation from the tyranny of our foreign government."

"Are you from Donegal, then, Mr. O'Donnell?" Tadgh asked.

"Aye, yes I is, Dungloe actually, and proud of it, to be sure," Peader answered.

They all talked for a few minutes about the plight of the common Irishman.

Morgan waltzed in to the Pub and over to Tadgh, silk blouse bobbing. The whole table of gentlemen stood up to greet her.

"Well, now, fair colleen, and who might ya be?" Sean, who was older than the rest, greeted her with a mischievous grin.

"I'm Morgan, Tadgh's partner, gentlemen, and very happy

about it," Morgan shot back with an equally jocular twinkle in her eyes. She grabbed Tadgh's arm and gave him a squeeze for emphasis. "And who might ya be, sir?"

"Morgan, let me introduce you to Mr. Sean O'Casey. He is one of the literary luminaries that haunt this establishment. He helped me with my play that I wrote last year here in Dublin."

"The short-lived play that fueled a revolution," Sean quipped. "Your partner is quite a writer, don't ya know."

"I have aspirations to write, also," Peader added, stepping forward to shake Tadgh's hand. "I should like to talk to you about that."

"Then why don't you join us for lunch, Mr. O'Donnell? That is fine with you, Morgan?"

"Mmmm," she nodded.

"We'll look you up when we're back in Dublin, Sean," Tadgh said.

"Fair enough, Tadgh. Be safe, my boy."

"Nice to meet you all," Morgan said as they took their leave. *Sean senses that Tadgh is in trouble.*

Before they sat down to eat Morgan took Tadgh aside.

"Aidan's running a fever. He may have lost more blood than I thought. I had some soup sent up for him. He needs to rest for a couple of days."

"At least that will tie him down for now," Tadgh said.

"I'll keep an eye on him. It will give me a chance to talk to him," she added.

They lunched on Irish lamb stew and Guinness for a change.

"Although we are farmers, I've been told that I have strong roots in Donegal that go back to the times of the Clans. I am quite interested in tracing my lineage back to them," Peader commented.

"My Ma and my aunt are Larkinists, supporting the emerging trade unions. I have been following James Connolly's trade union efforts with the Irish Citizens Army here in Dublin. I like his socialist ideas."

Morgan did not understand any of this, so she coaxed them to bring her up to speed.

"Well now, Dublin is in terrible shape, to be sure," Tadgh explained. "Many of those poor Irishmen who survived the horrors of the famine ended up here, eking out an existence in and around this choked city. The English tyrants continued to treat them like slaves, while the overlords became more wealthy at their expense. There are slums and sickness everywhere, with thousands dying of tuberculosis every year.

So, Mr. Larkin formed the Irish Transport and General Workers Union to fight this problem. They were getting nowhere a few years ago and one of their members, James Connolly, pushed for armed force. There was a major confrontation in the last half of 1913 where ten thousand workers went on strike and three hundred employers fought them with scab labor. Some workers were tortured or killed by the police. So he and Larkin established the Irish Citizens Army here in Dublin to protect the workers. Like us, they are fighting for their rights today." He added, "It was more of a secret society than the ITGWU," and slammed his tankard on the oak table.

"I see," said Morgan, forking in another slice of lamb. "But what's that organization that you said Mr. O'Casey dropped out of?"

"He used to be the General Secretary of the ICA. A part of the Larkin/Connolly creed is a belief in a socialist philosophy whereby the people are governed by many co-operative trade unions. We considered Mr. Larkin's movement too regional and did not support his general strike. Sean did not agree with this."

"I am a Larkinist at this point," Peader chimed in, hailing the bar maid for another pint.

"Are ya now? Not all that surprising, is it now. I am a Republican, focused on restoring our complete country to independence with the Gaelic way of life, by force if necessary. Now Connolly is starting to join with us to break us free from the British."

"To each his own, Peader, as long as we are united against the English."

"Definitely." The men clinked their tankards together and Guinness sprayed all over the table and Morgan's wrist.

All this was hurting Morgan's head, but she was becoming more and more convinced that the English had ruined Ireland and its people, with one person in particular that she already loved.

"Tadgh, that's a very interesting locket you wear on a chain around your neck, sure it is," said Peader.

"Isn't it now? It is an ancient family heirloom," Tadgh said, fingering the talisman around his neck. "My father gave it to me just before he was killed by the RIC a few years ago. I think he knew he was in danger. He told me to guard it and to wear it always. Finally he instructed me to pass it down to my eldest son when the time comes. Apparently this has been a family tradition handed down since the time of the Clans. I don't think he knew why it was important, and I certainly don't know either. It's just a pretty keepsake with tradition for our family."

Peader looked at it closely, remarking that it was old silver, very old. "That's the Claddagh design on the front, isn't it, two hands holding a heart, surmounted by a crown. I wonder how far back that pattern was designed?"

"I've researched it. There are a few myths. One states that a woman received it as a recognition gift for doing good deeds with her money. Apparently an eagle dropped it in her lap just after she married the Mayor of Galway in 1596. The hands symbolize lasting friendship. The heart is for love and the crown is for loyalty."

Morgan had a perplexed look on her face.

"What's wrong, Morgan?"

"I'm having that déjà vu feeling again, and I can't bring it to mind. I remember seeing that locket around your neck when you were nursing me back to health."

"Well now. It's curious that you said you were interested in the heritage of your family, Peader. I've a mind to find out my place in the heritage of the McCarthy Clan, make no mistake. My father often told me that I was descended from the Clan Chieftain. I always thought that it was wishful thinking on a working man's part. This locket is one of two family heirlooms that I was given."

Now Morgan was interested. "What's the other one, Tadgh?"

"The family Bible. Again, I've done research on that. It is one of the original Douay-Rheims versions; the first full English translation of the Latin vulgate, consistent with our Roman Catholic faith. It has three books, and they are dated 1582, 1609 and 1610. There is a handwritten family tree in the front in Gaelic. It appears to go back to 1630 with an entry for Our Clan Chief, Cormac Mac Carthaigh Reagh. The tree is mildewed and faded in many places, but the entry in 1630 is discernible, so it is."

"Wouldn't that prove your lineage back to the Clan leaders, Tadgh?" Morgan asked.

"It certainly helps, but with the smudges there are gaps in the information. Also, anyone could have written this down. It really isn't proof of anything."

"What's that on the back of the locket?" Peader ran his fingers over the imprint of it.

"The red stag crest of the McCarthy Clan."

"It really looks authentic, doesn't it," Morgan said, hefting the weight of it. Doesn't it hurt your neck? Wearing it all the time, I mean. It's almost the size of an egg."

"My Pa instructed me to keep it close. This is as close as it gets. I like the locket because of what's inside," Tadgh added, and paused for effect.

"Well, aren't you going to open it and show us?" Morgan finally demanded.

"Oh, to be sure. I thought you'd never ask."

The clasp was worn down, but Tadgh, with some manipulation, was able to spring the mechanism and the locket opened.

"Who's the cameo of? She is beautiful."

"That's my Mam, Morgan. You would have loved her as I still do. Our family tradition is to replace this cameo with one showing the next generation matriarch once a first son is born. I have my grandmother's and great-grandmother's cameos at home as well. This is why this locket is a treasured keepsake, I think."

"There must be more to it than that," Peader said. "What's that engraving say on the other inside half of the clamshell?"

"As you can see, it's in Gaelic. Fine scrollwork isn't it? The English translation is 'Seek ye the battler's box.' It's meaningless as far as I can tell."

"It's a riddle," Morgan said, "and an important one I'll wager."

"A centuries-old one by the look of it," Peader said.

Tadgh closed up the locket, slipping it inside his tunic.

"I've got to get back to my mates," Peader announced after checking his watch.

"And we'd better go check on Aidan," Morgan suggested. "It was nice to meet you, Peader. Maybe we'll see you at the funeral."

"I'll look forward to it, Morgan. I would still like to discuss your philosophy about writing, Tadgh."

"Happy to do it anytime, Peader, me lad."

Chapter Twenty-Six
Morgan's Counsel

Friday, July 30, 1915
An Stad Hotel Pub, Dublin

*M*organ and Tadgh spent the rest of the day and evening cloistered in their room and focused on Aidan. He slept soundly in the tub where Morgan had laid out sheets and blankets. His snores resonated with the metal of the tub, filling the room with rasping rumbles.

"I'm concerned about your brother, Tadgh. His color is very pale, and he is quite weak. We may have to take him to a hospital."

"No hospital, Morgan. They'll be looking for him there."

"I'll have to watch him very closely then."

"Please do whatever needs to be done. He's the only brother I've got, such as he is."

"Of course," Morgan replied. "I've been thinking, dear. Didn't you say that Mr. Pearse is involved with education in the Gaelic language?"

"Yes, that's right, *aroon.*

"I like my nickname, *aroon.* I want one to call you."

"How about *mavorneen?* It means 'my own love' in Gaelic."

"That's exactly right." Morgan played with the sound. "*Mavorneen.*"

"Why did you ask about Padraig's school? He is the headmaster at the St. Edna's School at Rathfarnham close to Dublin. There students learn our rich Gaelic history, language and accomplishments. I was there for two semesters."

"How old are the students when they graduate?" Morgan asked.

"Nineteen or twenty, I'd guess. Are you thinking what I'm

385

thinking?"

"Precisely, dear."

"That's a wonderful idea, Morgan. But would he stay or bolt, do ya think?"

"Is it a disciplined, military type environment with controls over access?"

"Yes, disciplined with controls. I wouldn't exactly say it's military."

"It sounds perfect to me. I think that Aidan is really crying out for the structured life that he didn't get after your parents were killed. He probably never dealt with his grief over that horrendous loss either."

"But as his older brother, I worked hard to provide that family guidance. Lord, you don't know how much effort I put into trying to get Aidan to join me in our cause."

Morgan could tell Tadgh blamed himself for not being able to help Aidan become a trustworthy man. She realized that what she would say next would be critical to their future relationship.

"Come, here, *mavorneen,*" she cooed and she pulled him down onto the bed with her.

While they snuggled, Morgan could feel the tension in his body start to drain away. The furrows that etched his forehead started to dissipate. And, as a result, he was fighting back tears that were welling up in his eyes. *Could it be that Tadgh, also, had not dealt with his own grief?*

"Tadgh, none of this is your fault, dear," Morgan said softly. Then she looked intently into his amber eyes and kissed him gently on the mouth. As his eyes closed to hold back his tears, she kissed them each, and waited.

"But I didn't try to stop them!" he sobbed against her breast.

"You told me you were fourteen, and Aidan was only ten when it happened. There was nothing you could have done against an armed group of murderers except get yourself and your younger brother killed as well. You saved Aidan and yourself so that you could fight back another day. That was a very brave act. I am so proud of you, *mavorneen*."

"But they shot them point blank for no cause. We watched them!" Tears rolled down his face, and his whole body was shaking in their embrace.

For the moment, Morgan became the beloved Mother that Tadgh had so painfully lost and now needed. She let him cry it out, holding him and stroking the wavy locks from his forehead.

"Something must have triggered the outburst," Morgan thought.

"I saw them today, those bastards," Tadgh muttered through clenched teeth. "I'm going to kill them."

"Who? The ones who murdered your parents?" Morgan was astonished.

"The very same. The two Cork constables in Deidre's Pub this morning are the two ringleaders of the group that killed my Mam and Pa. I almost went after them today but realized the odds were against me. I didn't want to risk your life as well. But now I know their names and that they work out of Cork."

"Doesn't it strike you as strange that it's the same men that attacked both your parents and Aidan, only five years apart?"

"I see what you mean. It's almost as if they are targeting McCarthys, for some reason."

"Precisely," Morgan said.

"If that's true, then they may be a rogue group, not acting on Government orders, don't ya think."

"Possibly."

"One thing's for certain. They're never going to relent until we stop them, Morgan. And we will close down their operation, eventually, as only death can."

"At least we know where they work, and they don't know where we live," Morgan pointed out, letting Tadgh up from the bed.

"Let's keep it that way." Tadgh shook his fist in the air.

Tadgh returned to his love. They fell asleep in each other's arms, drained by the emotions of the last few minutes. For the first time in many years, Tadgh didn't have a tortured dream of failing to accomplish some ludicrous task. Instead he dreamed serenely and deeply of Morgan and children.

Saturday dawned rainy, consistent with Boyle's mood. Gordo was giving him a wide berth.

"Dammit, James, we lost him again. Did you track down Andy at the Temple Bar Hotel?"

"Yes, boss. He hasn't seen McCarthy since we chased him out of the hotel. I'm sure he's telling the truth."

The trail had gone cold. "Shite, Gordo. I want this guy. Did you see the DMP report that came in yesterday where Tadgh McCarthy assaulted one of them over by the City Hall?"

"So he's here as well. Fascinating."

"Let's check the birth records over at the Public Record Office in Four Courts and confirm that these two are related," Boyle commanded, pushing his underling through the doorway.

"I'm on it, boss."

Aidan woke up first on Saturday. His arm still hurt like hell, but at least the headache was gone. It seemed odd to him that his brother, who had always been a loner like himself, was sleeping soundly with Morgan by his side. He could plainly see that she was good for him, the lucky bastard. He liked her spirit, and she wasn't bad to look at either. He somehow felt better when she was around.

He stumbled about getting dressed and woke Morgan. Being

nude under the covers she was reluctant to get out of bed in his presence.

"Morning, Aidan," she said. "Would you bring me that robe over there, please?"

"Sure, don't have any clothes on, eh?"

"I guess you're feeling better then, are you Aidan?"

"Here's your robe," he said and he turned his back while she slipped out of bed and into it.

He had positioned himself so that he could see her in the wall mirror when she got out of bed, a family trait. Wow, she's a gorgeous creature, he thought.

This tactic had not gone unnoticed by Morgan, who was quick to cover herself up.

"We'll have none of that, now, my boy," she chided, to let him know that she knew what he was doing.

"Okay, Ma," he said, involuntarily, passing her boots over the bed.

Now there was a telling remark, she thought, but let it pass.

Morgan roused Tadgh from his deep slumber with a kiss on his cheek.

"Mmmm," he purred as he regained consciousness in the presence of his love in his dream. "I feel unbelievably great and liberated." He reached out to pull her down to him and suddenly stopped. "Morning, Aidan. How are you after feeling this morning?"

"Hungry, brother. How about you?"

"Feeling great. Never better."

"I can clearly see why, Tadgh," Aidan joked, as he winked at Morgan.

"All right, boys. Let's go down to breakfast. I'm famished," Morgan cajoled, throwing Tadgh his clothes. She was happy to see the repartee between the brothers.

After breakfast Tadgh announced that he needed to go and see Thomas. Aidan and Morgan went back to the room so that she could check his wound.

"Aidan, there is infection in your arm. I am going to get antiseptic ointment for it. You wait here," Morgan told him.

"Grand," he said.

She went out onto Frederick Street to find an apothecary. When she returned, Aidan was gone.

Morgan was frantic. Tadgh had left his brother in her care. She searched the hotel and the bars close by to the An Stad to no avail. How could he be so asinine? Where would she go if she was him, she wondered? Then she remembered. He had seen her naked.

It came to her. She made a telephone call to the Temple Bar Pub and Deidre picked up.

"Morgan, thank heaven you called. I didn't know where to find you. Aidan came here looking for Aileen and wouldn't tell me where you are. They're up in my apartment together. Like two peas in a pod, those two."

"My sentiments exactly, Deidre. Don't let him leave."

Tadgh was nowhere to be found, so Morgan hiked over to the Temple Bar Pub alone.

By the time she strode into the Pub, Aidan and Aileen had completed their *tête-à-tête*.

She found him nursing his second Beamish in the back. He looked very pleased with himself. Aileen fawned all over him. Deidre was back behind the bar.

"Deidre, can I use your apartment for a few minutes?" Morgan asked.

"Sure, Morgan."

"Hello, Morgan. What brings you here this time of day?" Aidan asked, oblivious to having broken his word.

"Come with me, you stupid boy!"

When he didn't move fast enough, she yanked him up by his

good arm.

"Whoa, lady, what's got into you?"

"Get up those stairs," she hissed at him.

When they were seated in Deidre's drawing room, Morgan let him have it, both barrels.

"Didn't you tell me that you would stay put?" she growled, pushing him down onto the plush settee. He had to be treated like a child. And, for some reason she knew how to deal with children.

"Ya, but . . ."

"But you were horny, right? Do you have any idea of the trouble you are causing? You are not only putting your life at risk, but your brother's and mine as well. Next time they won't just shoot you in the arm. They'll torture you and then kill you. Mark my words. If we hadn't been here yesterday, and if Deidre hadn't helped us, you would already be dead."

"What do I care?" He slouched down on the settee.

"Stop feeling sorry for yourself, young man. I'm truly sorry that your parents were murdered and that you had to witness it. But you aren't the only one who has suffered due to these bastards. There are thousands and maybe millions who have had to deal with such tragedies and who have come through them to be responsible and valuable people. Your Mam and Pa are gone. But you're still here and you can help to avenge their deaths."

"Not me," he protested, looking down to avoid her angry stare.

"We went looking for you at your flat in Cork, you know, after you ran off from Skibbereen. Tadgh was identified by the RIC, and we had to run for our lives. Your brother was almost killed. He got shot in the arm and had to kill two constables in self-defense. They know about me, and they think that we are constable killers."

"Jeez. But why do they want to kill *me?*"

"It's not all about you, Aidan," Morgan said, sternly, reaching down and pulling his head up by the chin until his eyes met hers. "Let me repeat this: Tadgh almost got killed trying to save you."

"Oh." He tried to look contrite.

"Furthermore," she continued. "You know where Tadgh lives and the true purpose of his home. If you don't immediately get control of yourself to their satisfaction, then the IRB will be forced to kill you to keep you from divulging his location under torture. Can you imagine what that would do to your brother?"

She stopped there to let her words sink in.

"Beyond that, we want to help you and wouldn't want to hear that you've been killed."

"But I can never measure up to Tadgh," he protested.

"Don't try to compare, Aidan. There will always be people more and less capable than yourself. Just try to be the man that you can be."

Aidan got up and paced the room, wringing his hands. "But I've got no skills."

"Whose fault is that, my boy?"

"I don't know where to start, and I've got no money."

"I've heard a lot of buts and cants from you. Where is the positive belief in yourself? You've got to change your way of thinking, starting right now, and I'm going to help you do it," she said, vehemently.

"We're going to show you how to learn to be a Republican and a gentleman in an environment that should keep you protected from the RIC. In this training program you will demonstrate that you can be a responsible and valued person to the IRB. If you don't agree to participate, or if you try to leave this program, then you will die very soon thereafter, I can assure you. But I believe that you can succeed."

Aidan was quiet for quite a long time as he paced. Morgan let him stew.

Finally he said, "Morgan, I respect you and know that you mean me well. You're the first person in a long time who has really cared about what happens to me. Thank you. But I don't know if I can have a belief in me."

"First of all, didn't you hear me? Your brother would give his life for you, you idiot. He almost did. Second . . ."

"But he's always criticizing me."

"Because of your actions, Aidan. He still loves you, don't you know?"

"But . . ."

"There you go with the negative buts again," Morgan chided, and she went over and laid a hand on his shoulder.

"It wasn't your fault, you know."

"But I just stood there and didn't do anything to save them," he groaned. He would have sagged to his knees if Morgan hadn't held him up.

"You were ten years old and they were very bad men with guns. Neither you nor Tadgh could do anything but save yourselves. And you did that, very bravely. That gives you a chance to make something of your life, and hopefully to bring your parents killers to justice, doesn't it?"

"But I didn't try."

"What if I told you that the men that tried to kill you yesterday are the same ones who killed your parents?"

"That can't be."

"Tadgh saw them yesterday morning when they came back here to the pub, but it was too dangerous for him to try to seek revenge."

"Damn. I could have helped."

"Except for that arm. Live to fight another day, lad."

Aidan looked down and rubbed his aching forearm. Then he nodded in the affirmative.

"So you see there's a trail to these men, and you can take the offensive. It's not hopeless. And your brother needs your help."

"I see your point, Morgan. I'll do whatever you suggest."

For the first time Morgan sensed sincerity in his voice and demeanor. "All right, then. Let's go do it."

She slapped him on the back and gave him another hug as they descended into the pub.

"Everything fine, then?" Deidre asked when they joined her. Morgan nodded.

Deidre pulled Morgan over to the bar and whispered, "There's an off-duty DMP constable over there in the far booth. I don't think that he has spotted you, but I would be careful that you aren't followed when you leave here."

"Thanks, Deidre. Thanks for everything," Morgan gave her a big hug. "We are two peas in a pod, don't you think?"

Deidre gave a wink and a wave as they headed off.

On the way back, Morgan gave Aidan the task of checking that they weren't being followed. For the first time, he seemed to take the assignment seriously.

When they arrived back at the *An Stad,* Tadgh was pacing their room.

"Well now. What happened to you two? I was worried."

"We were just out for some air. I thought it would be good for Aidan's condition. Sorry we were gone for so long."

"You could have been identified and apprehended."

"Well, we're here, safe and sound, as you can see."

Aidan was relieved and gave Morgan a silent thank you.

"Any luck with Thomas, Tadgh?"

"I found out that Thomas MacDonagh is the assistant headmaster at St. Edna's School here in Dublin. Aidan, I've got good news for you, brother. They are willing to admit you as a senior student. There you will learn our Gaelic ways and how to be a valued Republican. It includes clothes, room and board and you should be protected from the RIC there. What do you think?"

"I think that's a grand idea. When can I start?"

"Immediately. I'm glad you are in favor of this, lad."

Tadgh looked at Morgan inquisitively, so she said, "We talked about it while we were walking."

Morgan could see that Tadgh had some misgivings based on Aidan's recent disposition, but she could also see a slight lifting of his furrowed brows.

"I also got my nine-millimeter bullets from Thomas this morning."

"I'd like to re-dress Aidan's bullet wound with the ointment I purchased this morning, if that's agreeable to you both. It's the newest antiseptic that they're going to be using on the battlefield."

"How do you know that?"

"I don't know. It just came to me when I got to the chemist apothecary." Morgan was as puzzled as Tadgh.

"I'll go get us a table for lunch then."

"Your brother and I will be right down."

While the wound was being attended to, Aidan thanked Morgan for covering for him that morning.

"We did go for a walk, didn't we? I told you that I would help you."

"Well, thanks, Sis. Can I call you that?"

"Absolutely, Brother. I rather like that; especially since I don't know if I really have a brother."

Chapter Twenty-Seven
Riddle Revealed

Saturday, July 3, 1915

*W*hile the three were eating in the *An Stad's* Pub, Peader O'Donnell came rushing in.

"What's the matter, Peader?" Tadgh asked, seeing him in an agitated state.

"You'll remember our discussion yesterday about the riddle in your locket. Well, I think I know what it means!"

Tadgh and Morgan sat forward in their chairs.

"Remember that I said I was interested in tracing my lineage in the O'Donnell Clan?"

Tadgh stopped him there. "Would you like some lunch?"

"Never mind, I ate. Listen, this is important."

"I can see that, don't ya know. Can you give us a few minutes to finish and then we'll meet you in our room, lad."

Morgan handed him the key. "It's number 2B on the front."

Peader seemed impatient but took the key and departed.

Tadgh and Morgan raced to finish their food.

"What's the rush, Sis?"

"We've got business with that fellow, Aidan. Can you stay on the lookout for RIC here in the pub until we come back?" It was a test. "Come for us if they show up."

"Sure, I will. Tadgh, can I have a stout?"

"One, lad."

Peader was pacing around the room when they arrived. They hardly had time to sit him down before he began. "Well, I have been gathering historical and mythical information to help me in my quest. I don't know why I didn't think about this yesterday."

"About what?" Morgan urged him to continue.

"I need to give you some background history on The O'Donnell Clan, which grew from the great Irish King Niall of the Nine Hostages to rule the northwest of Ireland, around Donegal from 500 to 1600 AD—a mighty Clan indeed." He drew a long breath and continued, "One of my most famous ancestors was in direct line to be chieftain when in around 535 AD, he chose to give up all his worldly wealth to become our second greatest Saint of the Catholic Church, Colum Cille, or St. Columba, as he was called. His coming was foretold by our first Saint Patrick some 60 years earlier. It came to pass that St. Columba founded many monasteries in Ireland until, in 561, he copied a new Roman Vulgate Psalter on behalf of the people. When he refused to return the copy, a war ensued, with his forces winning. Under threat of excommunication by the Pope John III, he was forced to leave Ireland to minister to the Picts in the territory that would become Scotland." He continued, "Before he left he visited our Chieftain and gave him the Psalter, which he called *An Cathach* for safekeeping. He instructed the Chieftain to have a man with no sin encircle their army three times clockwise before battle carrying *An Cathach* to ensure victory. This was how battles up until 1602 were won."*

"But what has this story to do with the riddle in the McCarthy locket?" Morgan's hands clasped and unclasped.

"I am coming to that, Morgan. Be patient." He paused and then continued. "In 1084 this O'Donnell relic was enshrined in a *Cumdach* made for Cathbharr O Domhniall, the current O'Donnell king, by Domhniall Mag Robhartaigh, the Abbott of Kells. Do you know the meaning of the terms *An Cathach* and *Cumdach*?" He fixed his eyes on them.

"Out with it, man," Morgan urged him.

"The *Cumdach* is a very ornate and precious metal box made to hold and protect an historic relic. They was popular among the nobles in the Middle Ages, and their relics was typically from earlier ages. The unique *An Cathach*, means 'the battler'," Peader said.

"Seek ye the battler's box!" Morgan cried out, looking at Tadgh in disbelief.

"I didn't even think of it yesterday because we was focused on the McCarthy Clan, not the O'Donnells."

"Why would a riddle in a McCarthy heirloom, if it is that, be referring to a relic of the O'Donnell Clan, do ye think?" Tadgh opened his locket and looked intently at the inscription opposite his Mam's picture. "Surely this is just a coincidence."

"That's unlikely in my view. But there's only one way to find out, Tadgh."

"Does your family have the *Cumdach*?"

"No, lass. The hereditary protector/keepers of this relic were the MacRobhartaigh/McRoarty Septs of the O'Donnell Clan. By tradition, before a battle, it was customary that a religious man with no sin, usually McRoarty, would wear *An Cathach* in its *Cumdach* on a chain around his neck. He would walk three times clockwise around the O'Donnell army to ensure victory, as St. Columba had ordained. The box was turned over to the government in about 1840 after two centuries of traveling all over Europe. We have no idea where it went during those lost years. Lucky for us, it now resides in the National Museum of Ireland, just blocks from here."

"Well, now. We had better go examine it," Tadgh suggested excitedly.

"Easier said than done, my friend. The Museum is open until five today. We can probably go and view it from the outside through a glass case this afternoon, but access to examine it thoroughly will be problematic."

"What are we waiting for, then?"

"I know you are excited about this, Morgan, but I need you to stay here and make sure Aidan is safe until I get back. Peader and I will go inspect it."

Morgan looked disappointed, very disappointed. Her mouth turned down.

"You won't miss out, *aroon*, I promise." Teague winked.

They went down through the pub, where Aidan was still on guard nursing what looked like his first stout. Good news on that front, Tadgh concluded. *I wonder what Morgan said to him to change his attitude*, he thought. She was continuing to amaze him with her skills and understanding of human nature.

The archaeology section of the NMI was located on Kildare Street just opposite School House Lane East. They entered through the columned rotunda with its circular, zodiac inlaid marble flooring.

As pre-arranged, Peader asked to see the museum curator. They were told that he was not available, but that his assistant could meet with them.

"What can I do for you?" demanded the matronly woman looking up from her work, behind the desk.

"I am a descendant of the O'Donnell Clan, and I would like to examine the *Cumdach* that belonged to my family," Peader asked politely.

The term Clan appeared to set her off. "No one is permitted to examine our artifacts, young man, especially if you are one of those Republicans."

Tadgh tried to reason with her, to no avail. "The consummate bureaucrat," he muttered under his breath.

"Unfortunately, we need to go to find another way," he announced when they were alone again in the Rotunda.

It took a while to find the case containing the *Cumdach* located in the Treasuries section on the ground floor, to the right and behind the rotunda.

"This is a magnificent metal box," Tadgh marveled, taking close note of the details. "I'd guess that it's about nine inches square by two inches thick. Look at the silver, crystals, pearls and other precious stones adorning it. And notice the inlay Christ in Majesty flanked by the Crucifixion and a saint in gilt *repoussé*."

"Where did you learn those terms?"

"I've been studying up when looking into my ancestors. I wonder if that Saint might be St. Columba."

"Could be. *An Cathach* was his and this *Cumdach* was designed and made in Kells, one of the many Abbeys that St. Columba founded."

As they viewed the *Cumdach*, safely mounted inside its locked glass case, they realized that they still had no idea what the riddle was trying to tell them.

Tadgh had decided. "Well now. We've got to remove the *Cumdach* from this glass case right enough to examine it more closely. And then we need to put it back so no one knows we looked at it. "

"So, how do you propose to accomplish this, Mr. Houdini?" Peader challenged, sliding his hand along the edge of the locked glass door.

"I don't know yet. But we have all night to think about it, don't we now." Tadgh answered. "Tomorrow the funeral procession starts at noon and the oration at Glasnevin Cemetery will be about two p.m. The RIC and DMP should be out in force to control the crowds well into the evening after the service at the cemetery. That would be a grand time to access the *Cumdach*. It says here that the Museum is open from two to five on Sunday afternoons."

Tadgh spent a minute closely examining the glass case door and framework.

On the way out he noted the locked side door and the new-fangled door alarm pads. They walked around the building and Tadgh saw the external tradesman's entrance down into what must be a basement storage area.

When they returned to the *An Stad*, they found Morgan

anxiously waiting for them in the Pub with Aidan in tow.

"Your color looks better, brother. How are you feeling?"

"Much better, Tadgh, thanks to Miss Nightingale over here."

The nurse added, "The antiseptic ointment seems to be working. Mr. MacDonagh was here a while ago and said that Aidan can move into St. Edna's tomorrow afternoon after the funeral service at the cemetery."

"That's great, Aidan," Tadgh said. He left it at that since Morgan seemed to have succeeded where he had repeatedly failed.

"I'm actually looking forward to it, Tadgh. Morgan says it will bring out my good character."

"That it will, brother, for all that."

Despite Morgan's urgent desire to hear the results of Tadgh's afternoon investigation, he chose not to involve Aidan in the discovery. Peader agreed to stay over and got a room. After supper they left Aidan to rest and met in Peader's room. Morgan was fair bursting to hear any news.

At nine that evening, they started their planning meeting.

"That's quite a box," Morgan exclaimed after they had brought her up to speed. "Is it possible that the message is engraved on the outside in plain sight? That would certainly simplify the challenge of examining it."

"There may have been other McCarthys before me who figured out this riddle. This box has been in the museum since 1842, it says on the plaque. I would have thought that the outside had been carefully scrutinized before now."

"Maybe it took a chance meeting of the right O'Donnell and McCarthy descendants to put the two together."

"True, Peader, or maybe your meeting was destined and not just chance," Morgan mused waving her arms in the air as if some mystical force controlled their every thought.

Peader continued, "From the days of the Clan, between roughly 1100 until 1842 AD, when it was donated and placed in the

Museum, there was a belief that the powers of *An Cathach* would be lost if the *Cumdach* was opened. There must be a reason for that superstition, don't ye think? That would suggest that the message, if there is one, is inside the *Cumdach*."

"All right, then, it's settled now. We need to remove the *Cumdach* from its case," Tadgh stated bluntly. "I'm concerned about being able to silence the door and window alarms on the building on such short notice. So I think we need to enter and exit the museum during normal hours."

"But Tadgh, I noticed that there is a stationary guard in each display room of the Treasuries section. Not to mention the guards at the front door."

"That's why we have to enter tomorrow afternoon before they close and leave on Monday morning after they open. After all, we are not trying to steal the *Cumdach*. I noticed that they have a turn-stile to count how many visitors enter the museum, but there is no counting mechanism for those leaving."

"Clever, *Mavorneen*, but did you see a place where we can hide at closing time?

"There's the back tradesman's entrance to the basement. They probably have storage areas down there where we can hide. We'll have to play that by ear."

"They will, undoubtedly, have a roaming guard on rounds during the night. We'll have to watch the pattern for a few hours to see when we can access the relic. Hopefully there will be enough time."

"I'm thinking that if we can remove it without detection, then we can examine it in the basement and then return it without their knowing."

"That's a gutsy call, dear. How are we going to break into the case that holds the Cumdach?"

Tadgh really loved how Morgan thought so logically and clear-ly. "Great question, lass. The *Cumdach* is in a tall glass case about six feet high and three feet across. It has a metal frame with a full-height glass door on the front. This door's metal frame is piano-hinged on one side and there is a keyed lock on the other side at waist height. As part of my guerilla training, I learned to pick locks. I have the tools for this. What I am afeared of is the likelihood that the door is alarmed. When we open it, the alarm will go off."

"Not if the electrical contact across the door lock interface is never broken."

"How can we open the door without breaking the contact with the case frame, Peader?" Morgan was skeptical about this whole venture.

They thought about this problem for a few minutes without coming up with a satisfactory solution. Tadgh finally broke the reverie. "That's our homework assignment for this evening."

"What are we looking for, anyway?" Morgan asked. "Where could this mystery lead us? We don't even know when the locket was made."

Tadgh realized that it was his turn to inform. "As I have told you, I have been researching the history of my Clan in an attempt to prove what my father told me; that I am directly descended from the Clan Chieftain. Just like Peader, I have collected quite a few documents that give me some knowledge." He took a breath. "After Henry VIII founded the Anglican church to justify his adultery and murder of his wives, his daughter Elizabeth was plotting against and warring with Catholic Ireland in the last half of the 1500s. Spain threatened England and allied with the remaining Irish Clan Chieftains, mainly the O'Donnells, the O'Neils in the north and the MacCarthaighs in the southwest."

"So there was a connection between these two Clans, then?"

"Aye, lass. The Spanish did land an army in Kinsale in late 1601, and the O'Donnell and O'Neill armies marched south through the winter to join them. Unfortunately, my ancestor and the last true MacCarthaigh Clan leader, Florence, was incarcerated by

England in mid-1601. The English lured them away from guerilla tactics into a pitched battle in January 1602, and our once mighty Clans were routed. We've been terribly subjugated ever since." He returned her gaze fixed intently on him. The tale was ingrained in him and he knew it well. "The McCarthy Clans in the southwest that had settled in Cashel Ireland from Wales in the fifth century were some of the last to surrender after the Confederate Wars rebellion in 1642-52. My ancestors, the MacCarthaigh Reagh, lost their castle Kilbrittain in 1642, and the Muskerry Mor MacCarthy lost their stronghold Blarney Castle among others in 1646 when the hated Cromwell lay scourge to our lands and people." He stopped to take a breath, touched the handle of the glass of ale but didn't drink. "You want to hear more? The abuse continues." His eyes burned.

Morgan nodded, enthralled.

"The story goes that when Lord Broghill finally took Blarney there were only a few servants present. The others had fled with the McCarthy Gold Plate through the caves behind the castle. Many ruthless Englishmen have sought that prize over the centuries without success as far as I know." Tadgh pulled the locket out from under his shirt and examined it, turning it over and aright again. "Perhaps now, almost 300 years later, with this revelation from my locket, we will be more fortunate to reclaim what has been rightfully ours all this time and to establish my rightful leadership of our Clan. Then it can be used to help fund our glorious revolution.** And there you have it."

"Wow, what a story, Tadgh," was all Morgan could think to say. "This is all very exciting! It's as if the Clans will rise again."

"Precisely so, *aroon*. I think that's what my ancestors must have had in mind almost three hundred years ago when they hid the McCarthy treasure to protect it until the time was right."

"And maybe my ancestors also," Peader chimed in, "Although I don't have a locket."

"How so?"

"Because my ancestors' relic is showing up in your riddle."

They all went to bed that night with a myriad of unanswered questions yet with great hopes for the adventure that lay ahead.

The McCarthy/O'Donnell trio met for breakfast and sat in a remote corner of the pub. Aidan had already taken his breakfast earlier with Tadgh and was being introduced to some of Thomas's boys who had been allowed to come over for the funeral.

"Show Peader what you've come up with," Morgan suggested. "I think that it's quite brilliant."

"Well, I've scrounged some items this morning that should solve our little problem."

He produced from his pocket a package of the newly-marketed Wrigley's spearmint gum from America, a six-foot coil of thin bare copper wire, a broad yet pointed eating knife from the Pub kitchen, and a box of the recently-invented strike matches. He also announced that they would need to use his torch for the task ahead.

"Well, now. This is going to be tricky, and it will require all three of us to work in unison."

Tadgh explained in detail how they would do it with the tools that he assembled. "How does this sound to you two?"

"Complicated and risky, to be sure, Tadgh. And we'll be trapped in a locked building if the alarm goes off. But I can't think of a better method. Of course we could get lucky and there won't be a case alarm. They may think that the building alarm is enough."

"I'm in. We can do this." Morgan was remarkably enthusiastic.

"We won't be trapped, Peader. We will have already determined how to get out through the basement tradesman's door in a hurry if the alarm goes off. Unfortunately, if this happens, we will have to take the *Cumdach* with us and we'll all be fugitives with risk of

capture."

"Two of us are already fugitives. Hopefully, it won't come to that, Peader."

"Right, then. Let's rendezvous at 1:45 p.m. at the graveside at the southwest corner of the mourners area, away from where Padraig Pearse will give his eulogy. All eyes, including the RIC and DMP constables, should be on him and the casket as it arrives. Our black funeral attire should help us this evening in the Museum, I'm after thinking." His eyes met Tadgh. "I hope we've thought of everything."

On his way out of the pub, Tadgh grabbed one of the books in their small library.

Chapter Twenty-Eight
Burying a Hero

Sunday, August 1, 1915
The Castle, Dublin

"**The brothers are** the only direct offspring of Fergus," Gordo announced when they met at the Castle on Sunday morning. "And they've got a good-looking woman with them, according to the DMP constable they assaulted. Probably the same dame that we heard of in Cork." At least he had good news for his boss for once.

"That's what I thought," Boyle said. "If we find one brother, we'll find them both." All these years of searching; all those McCarthys interrogated and disposed of. He sensed he was getting close to the source and he could smell the money. *It's rightfully mine*, he gloated, *and I'm finally going to get it.*

For the first time in a long time, James saw him smile.

"So, Gordo, I'll bet that they're going to be at the cemetery this afternoon to hear the service. We'll be there to arrest them."

"Just arrest them, boss?"

"Well, you know what I mean."

Gordo knew the grisly details.

When they woke up they could hear the hubbub outside on Frederick Street.

"They're already lining up and it's only half-seven," Tadgh said, parting the curtains. "It's sunny. Even Mother Nature's co-operating for this glorious day for O'Donovan and our cause."

Tadgh, Morgan and Peader travelled together to the City Hall that fateful morning. It had been decided that Aidan should stay out of sight at *An Stad* in relative safety until the funeral procession passed by.

At precisely eleven a.m., Father Michael O'Flanaghan gave a moving oration to a packed audience in the Rotunda.

The funeral procession left the City Hall at noon. Morgan observed and later chronicled the pageantry of it all. The crowd of onlookers was so dense that it left barely enough room for the horse-drawn hearse to pass by. The four chestnut stallions were plumed and preened, a stunning site as they strutted east on Dame Street and then south on St. George's Street.

"This isn't the way to the cemetery. You said it's to the north."

Tadgh smiled. *Crafty.* "This is the IRB route to Glasnevin all right, *aroon*, See all these armed Volunteers marching along? This isn't only a grand funeral procession, but it's an armed show of force that I'll bet is going to pass by many of the British bastions of power here in Dublin. Marvelous!"

Sure enough, after passing by the Castle stronghold on the hill to their right, the black glass enclosed carriage hearse, with its liveried driver and six pallbearers riding regally high above it, turned east on York Street until it came to St. Stephen's Green.

"Here's an example, Morgan. This fenced park of the wealthy British was only recently made public after a lot of negotiating by Lord Ardebaum of Guinness Brewery fame."

"Look at the tall metal spikes, Tadgh. It goes all around the Park."

"Built to keep us vermin out, don't ya know."

As the cortege turned left when it reached the Park, Tadgh pointed. "See that statue just inside the Park? That's Lord Ardebaum. I'm not sure if he was loved more for his support to the common man or for the beer that is his lifeblood."

"It is a beautiful park," Morgan said, as they turned east around what Tadgh called the Fusiliers Arch at its northwest corner. Well-wishers were hanging off the Arch to get a better view above the throng. Perhaps because it was Sunday, yet more likely to pay respect to the unrepentant Fenian, the men, women and children were decked out in the finest clothing that they could afford. Tadgh looked right pleased.

"Where are the British authorities?"

"They're there in the background, lass, but they've obviously decided not to oppose us openly. Can you believe this turnout? It's a grand day, so it is."

The procession finally turned north on Grafton Street and ran into Trinity University, that bastion of British learning. Snaking around its western end, they then crossed the financial Fleet Street before arriving at The O'Connell Bridge over the Liffey River. There, on the other side of the bridge in the middle of north-running Sackville Street, or what was being petitioned to become O'Connell Street, was the larger than life statue of the man himself, ever looking southward, surveying the city he had helped build.

The jam-packed trams on Sackville were stopped while the swelling procession went by. People were hanging out of the commercial buildings along the route. They marched while Morgan observed the procession moving north at a stately pace past the General Post Office. A sense of foreboding struck her when they came even with that august edifice. Was it *déjà vu*, or a premonition of her future, she wondered? It sent chills down her spine. Come to think of it, she had felt the same sensation when they reached St. Stephen's Green. She hoped she wasn't coming down with the croup.

After they passed Parnell Square the *An Stad* finally came into view. Aidan slipped out and joined them for the final long march to Glasnevin Cemetery, as Tadgh, Morgan and Peader walked alongside the hearse and mingled with the solemn throng. They didn't mind the long walk, exemplifying the spirit of endurance and

411

perseverance through adversity of the man that they were honoring. Even Aidan kept up the pace. The Irish Volunteers, of which Tadgh was also a member, were marching in formation now ahead of the hearse in the cortege. Some of the rifles on their shoulders were the antiquated Prussian Maussers that had been acquired in the daring Howth gun-running episode. But many carried wooden mockup rifles for show. A drum band escorted the entourage. It was a splendid turnout. By the time that the procession passed the *An Stad,* the crowd had swelled to well over ten thousand and seemed to be growing.

"Well, don't ye think that this is a marvelous day for Ireland," Tadgh said. "Look at how much the Irish love O'Donovan Rossa, the people's champion. He may not have been the most gifted orator of his time, but he is the epitome of what we stand for with the common man, to be sure."

Peader produced a paper from his jacket. "Did you see this commemorative booklet by Terrence MacSwiney? It really helps the people to remember O'Donovan's lifelong leadership in the fight for our freedom here and abroad." They could see that many in the crowd had copies of the document.

"I'm astounded that so many people have come out to pay their respects. It seems that all of Dublin is here," Morgan marveled.

"And most of Ireland, *aroon.*"

By the time they reached the Irish Martyrs Cemetery, there was a huge crowd around the gravesite. Patriotic Irishmen were draped all over the Celtic crosses, trying to get a glimpse of the ceremony. The Irish Volunteers honor guard was ringing the enclosure. The hearse stopped, and the Irish tricolor flag-draped casket was slowly borne to the gravesite by the honored pallbearers. A hush fell over the crowd as it arrived at its final destination. Mary Jane and Margaret Rossa arrived, escorted by Thomas Clarke, the senior dignitary of the organizing committee. Finally, after some Catholic ceremonial graveside remarks by Father O'Flanaghan and others,

Padraig Pearse stepped forward to give the eulogy.

Tadgh was on edge. "This speech will be historic for our movement, so it will. For the first time in modern times he will publically enunciate what my play was trying to express, that is 'A Call to Arms.' "

At precisely one thirty, Padraig commenced, "It has seemed right, before we turn away from this place in which we have laid the mortal remains of O'Donovan Rossa, that one among us should, in the name of all, speak the praise of that valiant man, and endeavor to formulate the thought and the hope that are in us as we stand before his grave. The clear true eyes of this man almost alone in his day envisioned Ireland as we of today would surely have her—not free merely, but Gaelic as well—not Gaelic merely, but free as well."

Later, having praised O'Donovan's fortitude, along with others like him, while in prison, Padraig said, ". . . and speaking on their behalf, as well as our own, we pledge to Ireland our love, and we pledge to English rule in Ireland our hate."

And finally, referring to the oppressive English, he concluded with, "They think that they have pacified Ireland. They think that they have purchased half of us and intimidated the other half. They think that they have foreseen everything, think that they have provided against everything, but the fools, the fools, the fools! They have left us with our Fenian dead, and while Ireland holds these graves, Ireland unfree shall never be at peace."

There were tears in Tadgh and Peader's eyes when Padraig had finished, Morgan noticed. She, too, was moved.

As a fitting punctuation to the speech, and in honor of the great Fenian, the Irish Volunteers guard gave him a twenty-one-gun salute.

Finally, after composing himself, Tadgh said to his partners, "Wait here, will ye, while Aidan and I meet with Thomas MacDonagh."

Recognizing that this was the parting of the ways, at least

for the time being, Morgan gave her 'brother' a big hug and said, "Aidan. I know now that you can be a better man. I have confidence in you. Don't betray my trust, brother."

Aidan squeezed her back, looking her straight in the eyes. "Morgan, I won't let you down. Thank you, Sis."

"Goodbye for now. I'll write you. You do the same," she shot back. "Don't let yourself down, Aidan."

Tadgh returned, having turned Aidan over to MacDonagh and St. Edna's. His farewell had been less emotional, but just as encouraging.

"Let's get on our way, team. It's already two."

They hurried off through the crowd that was just starting to get vocal. Strains of "Tone's Grave" got louder as more and more citizens picked up the chant.

Boyle and James were observing the burial ceremony from the Finglas Street watchtower overlooking the southern entrance gates to the walled-in Glasnevin Cemetery. They had a birds-eye view at this choke point, from which they hoped to spot and apprehend the McCarthys. Their other two cohorts were roaming through the crowd below. The high walls surrounding this original portion of the cemetery had been built, along with the watchtowers, to combat the practice of grave-robbing prevalent during the 1800s.

From their elevated post, they could also see the burial site, which was directly east of O'Connell's Tower in what would become the revolutionary section of the cemetery.

As Tadgh moved through the crowd towards the exit just beyond O'Connell's Tower, he spotted Boyle high up on the watchtower. "Damn," he said softly to the others. "Stop and turn around. Now!"

"What's the matter, Tadgh?"

"That rotten RIC constable and his RIC lackey are up on that watchtower blocking the exit. He's probably looking for us. I don't think he saw us yet. Duck back behind O'Connell's Monument Tower while I think about what to do. If there weren't so many people here, and if we didn't have get someplace immediately, I would try to take them out. But not now. And I promised MacDonagh there'd be no gunplay at this event."

Tadgh had known that by entering this high walled cemetery, they were potentially walking into a trap. He had hoped that the crowd would hide them. Now he was counting on it. From behind the O'Connell monument, Tadgh could still see Boyle's head. But now he was pointing towards the O'Connell tower and energetically beckoning to someone below him. They'd been spotted. Boyle disappeared from view. Tadgh looked around frantically for a way out. Running for the north exit into the botanical gardens had been his first exit strategy, if they ran into trouble. With their pursuers so close at hand, that avenue was problematic.

Just then, as fate would have it, Tadgh heard the clop clop of the funeral hearse horses' hooves behind him. The hearse carriage driver had waited to hear Pearse's eulogy and was now guiding his charges slowly out through the crowd around the O'Connell tower on his way to the front entrance gates.

Tadgh grabbed Morgan's hand, whispering, "Quick now, *aroon.* Follow me and keep your head down." Peader needed no urging to follow suit. Tadgh timed it perfectly. While still hidden from the constables behind the monument, he intercepted the hearse just as it was rounding the tower. Waiting momentarily for it to pass, he flung open the rear door and pushed Morgan up into the carriage. He and Peader scrambled in behind her, and with one deft motion, Tadgh pulled the door closed.

"Lie flat," he ordered. "Cover yourselves up with some of those flower displays," he urged.

The carriage driver, from his forward looking post, did not see or hear their intrusion.

Boyle and James reached the bottom of the watchtower just as their cohorts got there. "Come on, you men. I saw the older McCarthy over by the O'Connell Tower. He and a woman ducked behind it. You two go around to the right, and Gordo and I will go left. They may make a run for it away from us heading due north towards the botanical gardens."

They were immediately lost in the crowd pushing against them to get to the exit gates.

As the hearse lumbered on towards the exit amidst this stream of humanity, Tadgh could see Boyle through the window come abreast of it and stop the carriage driver. Tadgh covered himself with a daisy garland. Then the murderer looked into the hearse through the window. Because of the afternoon sun glinting off the glass, he was squinting and hooding his eyes to see what was inside the vehicle.

From his position on the floor, looking up through the flower garland, Tadgh could examine Boyle's face in the glass side door. He could clearly make out the skull and crossbones tattoo on his left temple. The Constable put his right hand on the glass as if he was reaching to open the door; Tadgh could see that the man's little finger was missing.

Tadgh desperately wanted to shoot him, then and there, right through the glass. Instead, he held his breath and squeezed Morgan's hand. His other hand was holding his loaded and cocked Luger.

The sun-glint, a partial cover afforded by the open side curtains, and their black funeral clothes, saved them from detection, at least momentarily.

Gordo's face appeared alongside Boyle's at the window. Tadgh could plainly hear him saying, "Why are you stopping, boss? They'll get away if we don't hurry. The hearse looks empty to me."

Boyle hesitated and then his face disappeared. Tadgh heard

him tell the driver to move on.

A few minutes later they were out of the cemetery and clopping down Finglas Street towards Dublin Center.

"That was a close call," Morgan whispered.

"Don't you like the elegant carriage that I ordered to get us back to the City in time for our exciting museum adventure?"

"What do you call what we've just experienced?" Morgan quipped, her heart rate just starting to return to normal.

Chapter Twenty-Nine
Acquisition

Sunday, August 1, 1915

"**Why are they** after you, Tadgh?" Peader asked as they rolled south down what the Republicans already called O'Connell Street.

"That's a good question, comrade. They probably know that I killed two constables. My play can't be the only reason."

"They seem to be targeting you McCarthy boys for some reason, dear," Morgan added.

"I'm sure we will find out in due course, my love," he whispered. "We're coming to the river. There's the General Post Office to our right and then the monument of Daniel O'Connell on your left. Morgan, can ye see?" Tadgh pointed out as they passed the caped statue of the 'Catholic Liberator' standing high atop its granite base and friezed pillar for the second time in the day. "Those four winged victory statues below the circular frieze are quite beautiful."

"They stand for patriotism, courage, fidelity, and eloquence, as I understand it," said Tadgh. "All aspects of our hero's character, to be sure. Well now, it looks like the hearse is planning to turn west along the north side of the Liffey River. This is where we get off."

When the carriage slowed in the turn, Tadgh opened the river side door and they tumbled out onto Bachelor's Walk just west of O'Connell Bridge.

"Look out!" Morgan cried, and she yanked Tadgh sideways, off the road onto the river edge walkway just west of the bridge. They hit the side of the river railing with a thud and ended up behind the walkway barrier, sprawled on the ground. Tadgh heard a sickening crack that sounded like glass breaking. Peader was quick to follow their lead as he smashed down against them both. "I'm soaked," he announced, as they lay in a puddle.

"Shhhh," Morgan whispered, grabbing hold of Peader's arm to emphasize the order.

Lying there, holding his bruised ribs, Tadgh questioned, "What was that all about, Morgan?"

She put her finger to her lips and whispered, "Look up on the bridge."

He had been so intent on examining the O'Connell monument that he had failed to see the Dublin United Tramways Electric Tram that had been starting north across the bridge. The open upper deck of this tram was crammed with police officers.

"Jeez," Tadgh whispered back. "Good eyesight, *aroon.*"

They lay still while the tram passed close by, hoping that their exit from the carriage would not have been noticed. The tram lurched to a stop, just opposite where they lay in plain sight. Tadgh re-gripped the Luger. *This could get messy. Stay still, or run?* Seconds passed like hours, yet he held his team down and silent. A few people got off at the Bachelor Walk station, and then the tram started up O'Connell Street again. The DMP men were all still on board absorbed in animated discussion.

"So much for the observation powers of the DMP force," Peader said, once the tram was out of sight.

Tadgh checked his pocket. The torch that they absolutely needed that night had a cracked glass lens. He tried to turn it on with no success.

"We need to get going," he urged his companions. "It's after three already and we haven't gotten to the museum yet. We're running out of time."

Morgan checked the small satchel and was satisfied that the contents were still usable. On the lookout for more police, they darted south across the bridge and headed into the Trinity College campus. Fortunately, their short walk east on Nassau Street and

420

two blocks down Kildare Street was swift and uneventful.

"Here's the National Museum, Morgan. Impressive, isn't it."

"Like a fortress."

A guard paraded on the outside steps. Tadgh had tucked the kitchen knife down his boot and the book he carried in an inside coat pocket. "Well, now. Here we go then." Inside the rotunda they passed successfully through the turnstile at a quarter to four. The guard there did not appear to consider them suspicious and reminded them, "The Museum closes at five. You make sure you start for the exit at ten of."

As previously agreed, Tadgh was to go alone to Treasury Gallery One where the *Cumdach* was located to gain a better understanding of the locking mechanism and alarm system of its glass case. Peader had been assigned the task of determining the likely guard activity and office location. And Morgan was to wander to the basement area to assess the best location for them to hide just before closing time. It had been decided that she could act more naïvely than the others if caught prowling this area. They were to meet in the cafeteria at four-thirty to report.

Tadgh realized that his first critical task was to get the torch working. He stepped into a stall in the visitor's restroom and closed the door. The confounded contraption still wouldn't illuminate. He unscrewed the lamp front end and the two broken halves of the glass front fell out into his lap. They were soaking wet as was the battery chamber. Tadgh had hoped that the cell capacity would not have bled off in its partially shorted condition.

As if he were dismantling, cleaning and reassembling his Luger, a task he had learned to do in his sleep, Tadgh thoroughly cleaned and dried every piece of the torch. He noticed some corrosion on the end terminals of the two dry cell batteries, using the kitchen knife to scrape down to the bare metal. Then he reassembled the unit and, swearing at it through clenched teeth, he flipped the switch on the case. The bulb glowed dimly. He quickly switched it off.

They met in the cafeteria, as planned. It had been a light atten-dance day because of the Rossa funeral, giving them enough priva-cy for their discussion. Peader said, "I was right about the alarm for the glass door. The hinge is insulated and, with the viewing lights on, I think I can see the height of the alarm contacts, which are just below the lock. The guard in the room wasn't paying attention to me. He was flirting with a pretty colleen."

"The guard office is in the back of the building, opposite from the door marked 'Antiquities Storage'. They are buzzing around it like bees at their hive. We will have to wait until after closing to see the coverage pattern. I scouted out a place to stand where we can observe the office without being detected," Morgan announced. "The good news is that the storage entrance door is not locked. It doesn't even have a lock. I had a marvelous chat with a good-look-ing student custodian whom I ran into in the basement."

"What?" Tadgh sounded annoyed.

"It was no problem. I told him I was doing a story for the local paper on how they catalogue their pieces that aren't on display. I think he was more interested in my body than why I was down there with him. He even shared that he will be leaving at quarter to five this evening, because it is Sunday, and asked if I would like to go for a drink at the pub nearby. I told him, 'Sorry, I'm with friends. Maybe next time'."

"Won't be a next time," Tadgh growled and rose to give his girl a quick kiss on the cheek.

"There are several places down there where we can wait without detection, and a couple where we can turn on a light to examine the *Cumdach*, if we can get it out of its case, that is. How's the torch doing, Tadgh?"

"I got it working, but the light is very dim. It'll be decent if it doesn't deteriorate further. We just need to keep it off until abso-lutely necessary."

The other two, as if on cue, looked up to the ceiling and crossed themselves.

"Right. It's ten of five. Lead the way, Morgan." They were careful to avoid the guards as they made their way to the antiquities storage door. At one point, a guard saw them and suggested that they head for the exit then went back into his assigned display gallery to talk to other visitors who were getting ready to leave. He didn't follow up, and the team passed through the door undetected. The flirting student had left the basement storage areas unattended.

Tadgh did his own reconnoitering. The basement consisted of three cavernous storage rooms and one small but well-appointed office furthest from the stairs. In the second storage room there was a concrete ramp with a loading door. Tadgh examined the door. Locked and alarmed. Unless they could disarm the museum's alarm system centrally this would have to be an emergency exit only. He took out his pick and tried the lock. The tumbler clicked. Satisfied that he could open the door in a hurry if necessary, Tadgh returned to his team at the foot of the stairs.

At precisely five, a loud siren sounded announcing that the museum was now closed. They waited in the basement darkness. Tadgh spent the time making sure they knew their escape plan if they were detected by the guards. They also discussed the fact that they were in for the night since leaving the building would require disarming the central security system, an impossibility in Tadgh's opinion. So there was no reason to rush into action.

Half an hour later they heard the basement door open and footsteps on the stairs. They darted behind a pair of upright Egyptian mummy sarcophagi and waited. A guard flipped the light switch and the storage room they were in was flooded with light. He walked downstairs and along the main aisle among the antiques, peering from side to side. A mouse, startled by the light, scuttled across Morgan's foot. Involuntarily, she kicked it up and out into the aisle, and it squealed as it hit the floor. The guard wheeled around and headed in the direction of the sound. They circled the sarcophagi out of sight. Then, just as he was about to round their hiding screen and find them out, he saw the mouse scurry down the aisle. Laughing, he turned around and headed after it.

Close call, Tadgh thought. The whistling guard disappeared into other catacomb storage rooms only to reappear a few minutes later. Finally satisfied that all was in order, the sentry ascended the stairs and switched off the light.

Waiting until they could tell that the facility was completely shut down and under nighttime procedures, the three of them clustered in the dark. All was silent.

"Come on, Tadgh. Let's go and check out the security guard routine," Peader said.

"I'm happy to stay here until needed, *mavorneen.* The more of us that go up there, the more chance of detection, right."

It was night outside when they emerged from the basement. There were dim lights in the hallways, but the display rooms were cloaked in darkness, except for their baseboard night lights. The exit through the basement door had been the riskiest point since they couldn't tell if there was a guard passing by at that moment. Peader showed Tadgh the out of the way spot where they could watch the guard room. At 7:15, a guard left the office, torch in hand.

"Look, Tadgh," Peader whispered. "You can see through the open door that there are only two guards. One goes on rounds and the other monitors the status from the office. That's lucky for us, don't ya think?"

Tadgh nodded concurrence and noticed a second torch on the guard's desk.

At 7:45, the guard returned, entered the office and closed the door. At least he didn't bother to visit the basement storage area again.

The second guard appeared at 8:15 and headed down the hallway. He came back thirty minutes later. During this cycle Tadgh shadowed him. Given the timing of when he passed by the basement storage door and probed Gallery One with his light, Tadgh determined that they would have to strike sometime between a quarter to the hour, to a quarter after the hour.

Tadgh and Peader successfully re-entered their basement hideout. Morgan greeted them. "I'm really glad I didn't hear any alarms going off."

"Only in my head, lass."

Picking up her satchel, Morgan said, "While you were gone, I scouted around. I suggest that we retire to the well-appointed office down the hall to partake of our evening repast, such as it is." Tadgh agreed. "Can we do it in half an hour?" Morgan asked tentatively as she arranged cold sandwiches and fruit on the office desk.

"We have to," stated Tadgh, worrying about the torch and not being able to see a way to get one of the guard's. "We'd better watch for two more cycles to make sure before we act," he said, when they were done eating and cleaning up any evidence of their presence. He watched for two more cycles and found timing consistency of the rounds to within three minutes. Good enough, he thought. He came back down at 12:30. "Time to go in 15 minutes, you two."

At the appointed hour Morgan stopped him. "If we made it through the sinking, the B & C loading yard and the freighter at sea, then we can do this." She threw her arms around him and kissed him fiercely on the lips. "I believe in you."

"I believe in us," her *mavorneen* replied, hugging the breath out of her.

"We're eating into our half hour," Peader announced, peering closely at the second hand of his watch in the dim light of their sanctuary.

Tadgh led his team stealthily up into the hallway and down to Treasury Gallery One. He saw Morgan slip five sticks of Wrigley's gum into her mouth. There was enough light spilling into the chamber from the hallway to guide them to the glass case holding the *Cumdach*. It was in the center of the room. "See the display case over on the wall behind the *Cumdach*—the one with the Druid Ceremonial Robes?" Tadgh whispered to his team. "That's our backup hiding place if we see the guard approaching. The robes should give us some concealment. Remember, if any alarm goes off, we head immediately for the basement." The others nodded their agreement. Tadgh set to work on the lock while Peader stood guard by the entrance to the hallway. In the distance, music came from the guard's office. It was a constant reminder of the risks they were taking.

"I sure hope there is something of interest in or on this *Cumdach*," Morgan mumbled, waiting patiently by the case.

"Damn," Tadgh whispered. "This is a more sophisticated lock than I am used to. I need the torch on the keyhole for a second." Morgan switched it on. At first it flickered, then it glowed dimly.

"Good, now switch it off, lass." There was a faint clicking of the tumblers as he twisted his picks. Morgan announced softly, "It is now 12:58." Tadgh motioned to Peader who came over to the case. Pulling the kitchen knife out of his boot, he gave it to Peader, saying, "Well now. The door is unlocked. I am applying closing pressure. Easy does it. Make sure you can always feel the contacts, comrade."

Flicking on the torch and looking edgewise to the door at the height of the lock, Peader said he saw a metal strip in the contact between the door and the case. Then he said, "I see the interface slit of the alarm contacts. They are about one inch high. I'm sliding the knife blade in now." There was a scraping noise as the knife found the contacts and pried them apart. They knew that the only thing separating them from being discovered was the thickness of a knife blade. Peader was sweating profusely.

"Take it easy, Peader, "Morgan murmured. She mopped his brow with her handkerchief. "Give me the torch."

Cool under fire, Tadgh thought. *I hope she does regain her memory*

426

so I can find out why she is like this. No, wait a minute. I don't want that. Funny what strange thoughts come to you in dangerous situations.

"How far in did you push the knife, Peader?"

"About halfway to the hilt."

"Stop. I just realized that you won't be able to twist the knife and maintain contact if the pads are only one inch in height. You need to withdraw the knife so only the pointed tip is inserted. Then you can twist the knife to where the blade is horizontal while maintaining electrical contact. Then, if you push in the knife it will force the door open without breaking the electric circuit, understood?"

"Got it. Here goes." There was a quiet scraping. The torch flickered and threatened to go out.

"Damn," Tadgh muttered. "We'd best hurry."

"The more haste, the less speed," Morgan cautioned, rattling the light. "It's clicked back on."

Tadgh could see Morgan removing the wire from the pocket of her tunic and pushing a gob of chewing gum onto each end. She was holding the torch in her teeth. The dimming light shone steadily on the knife. Tadgh could feel the door starting to open against his closing pressure as Peader forced the knife in. When it was in to the hilt, Peader said, "Morgan, attach the wire."

She only had two inches of separation to work with. And she couldn't disturb the knife and its contacts.

Holding the knife steady with one hand, Peader took the torch from her mouth with his other. As he grabbed it from Morgan, it suddenly flickered again and went out. The case was left in darkness. "Don't move," he said. With his free hand he reached into his pocket and produced a packet of matches.

"Morgan, take the torch from Peader's hand and place it on the floor. Then take a match and light it. Give it carefully to Peader to hold near the knife." Morgan immediately did as she was told. "Do you have enough light now, lass?"

"It'll have to do."

Peader said, "You'll have to hurry, Morgan. My hand is starting to shake."

Morgan ducked under Peader's arm and squeezed one of the gum gobs, with its wire end against the contact on the door frame. "This is really sticky stuff."

"Make sure you push the wire hard up against the contact, *aroon*, We can't allow any gum to be between the two, don't ya know."

"Done," said Morgan. The match went out.

"Now, before you try to attach the other end of the wire, I want to pull very gently on the one you have attached to see if it pulls off. If it doesn't pull free, then push on the wire at the contact to see if it feels like it is still connected. Can you do this in the dark?"

"Yes!"

Thirty seconds later she announced that the wire did not pull free, but that she felt some movement when she tried to push the wire against the contact. Tadgh realized that they were inventing this procedure on the fly. One false or forgotten step and they would be discovered. Morgan lit another match.

"Attach the other end to the contact on the door, lass."

"Look out, Morgan. You are moving the knife," Peader cautioned.

"Thanks for letting me know. It's a cramped space even for my small hands. There, I think it is attached and touching."

The moment of truth had arrived. Morgan lit a third match and again put it into Peader's free hand. "Peader, hold your knife fast. Morgan, press the wire onto the contacts with both hands. I am going to open the door, but not enough to stress the wire contacts. If I get the door open three feet without an alarm, then I will grab the *Cumdach*. After that, as we discussed, I will mostly close the door. Morgan, gently tuck the wire inside the case as it closes. Everybody ready?" Tadgh mentally calculated that they probably only had 5 minutes. He slowly opened the door. The knife blade broke contact. The sound of silence was deafening. The plan was working.

When the door was open the prescribed amount, Tadgh let go of it. It was being held in place by the outstretched arms of Morgan. "Hurry, Tadgh," she muttered as the third match burned out. Peader tried to light a fourth match but it fizzled. Seconds passed as he groped in the box for another.

"There are only two left."

"Light one, for God's sake," Morgan implored. The fifth one lit and Peader held it near the open case for Tadgh to see. Then Tadgh pulled out the book he had brought. He had chosen it because it was about the same size and rough shape as the *Cumdach*. Peader was holding the match as close to the opening as he dared.

The box was standing in a picture frame tripod. Deftly, Tadgh inserted the book and removed the *Cumdach* in one swiping motion, trying to keep an even pressure on the frame throughout the maneuver. He took a breath expecting the worst, the noise of detection. But no alarm sounded.

His shoulder bumped the inside of the door, but Morgan had such a tight grip that no harm was done. The wire was still hanging slack from both contacts. Tadgh produced a hand towel from his jacket pocket and carefully wrapped the *Cumdach* in it.

The non-locking door closure was uneventful.

"The time is now 1:20, five minutes over our allotted time," Morgan whispered anxiously.

"The guard should have passed the basement door by now. He will be here in five minutes at the latest," Tadgh said, testing his mental acuity. "We can hide in Gallery Three until he passes this room. Then we will have five minutes to get through that basement door before he returns."

They had just taken up their positions in the darkness when they heard the guard's footsteps approaching. Then Peader remembered— "The torch," he whispered. It was still on the floor by the case—too late to retrieve it.

Tadgh could see the guard standing at the entrance to Gallery One shining his torch around to the various cases, and he could clearly see the slightly open door and the glint of light off the metal torch lying on the ground when the light panned by. The guard missed the incriminating lantern as he walked into the room.

Just as the light was about to pan back across the *Cumdach* case, the other guard passed by in the hallway. "Got to go to the loo," he yelled. Distracted, the guard moved on past the slightly opened case in the darkness and shone his light near the far end of the room.

Tadgh quickly gave Morgan the relic. Then he motioned his team to hurry to the basement door. But he bolted off into the darkness in a different direction.

"Where did he go?" Morgan asked once they were safely through the door and down the stairs.

A few minutes later the door opened and closed and Tadgh breathlessly descended, triumphantly holding two torches. "I realized that we had a unique opportunity to grab one of their lights from the office. Then I circled back and picked up our torch before anyone saw it. I hope they don't notice theirs missing." It was 1:45, and he had the *Cumdach* in hand.

"What was all that about with the book, Tadgh?" Peader asked.

"Well now. I was concerned that they might be using the newly-designed mechanical pressure switch on the stand to trip an alarm when the relic was removed. So I substituted the book.

"Well, we're halfway home, if the chewing gum holds. Let's see what secrets this *Cumdach* has to offer."

Chapter Thirty
Replacement

Monday, August 2, 1915

*W*hen they reached the underground office, Morgan carefully laid the cloth on the table and peeled back its folds. There, in all its medieval splendor, rested the O'Donnell *Cumdach*. She couldn't take her eyes off the lid of the beautiful box, shimmering in the desk gas light. "Is that gold sheeting and are those real jewels?"

"I think that the main sheeting is brass, but there looks to be silver inlay work around the precious stones," said Tadgh.

"Interesting crystal and moonstone jewels on the surface. What's the religious significance of those gem choices, I wonder?"

"I can help with that, Morgan," Peader chimed in. "Moonstone is as ancient as the moon itself. It holds the power of mystery. Its secrets are locked beneath a pearly veil, and with them, our own hidden truths."

"So, if I gaze into the big one in the top corner long enough, I may learn who I am?" Morgan took a corner of the cloth and polished the pearly surface.

"Perhaps. Where I come from the *Seanchai* used to say that moonstone is foremost a talisman of the inward journey that each of us makes to retrieve the parts of the soul left behind or forgotten."

Morgan looked quizzically at Peader.

Tadgh didn't like where this conversation was going. The craftsmen at Kells in 1078 AD couldn't possibly have envisioned a wayward lass in need of inner retrieval finding this relic, could they have? He could see Morgan pondering and knew why. She was getting that faraway look in those sultry green eyes of hers. *That's not good.* "Morgan, you can see Christ in Majesty in the middle, on the cross on the right and a saint who could very well be St. Columba on the left, all done in repoussé or relief."

"Yes, there's great detail in that gilt relief work isn't there. Amazing artistry for its time. What's that structure that Christ is sitting on in the middle? It's masked by the mounting of the missing rectangular gem."

"It looks to me to be the base of a peaked building. I've seen paintings that depicted Solomon's Temple in the Holy City before the fall to the Assyrians," Peader offered, looking closely at the figure. "There's a famous one like that as a wonderful illumination in the Book of Kells. I saw it on a field trip to Trinity College a year ago."

"That would make sense. Christ building on the ancient civilization of his people."

"Interesting. Didn't you say that this box was also crafted at Kells?" Morgan noted the potential connection.

"Yes, but the two were probably four hundred years apart."

"Yes, but Kells, right?"

"Well now, we've been talking about one figure on this ornate box. We have to broaden our investigation to figure out how all this is trying to tell us something important, don't ye know." Tadgh brought the conversation back to the purpose of this adventure.

"All right, if the message is not on the front of the lid then maybe it's on its sides." Peader suggested, tracing his right hand over the intricate patterns that he found there. "Look closely at all the animals and foliage on a crossed pattern on gold foil."

Tadgh squinted and bent his head closer. "There's an inscription, here: *A prayer for Cathbarr Ua-Domnaill, for whom this case was made; for Sitric, son of Mac-Aeda, who made it; for Domnall, son of Robartach; for the successor of Kells, for whom it was made,*" he translated.

Peader said, "I've researched Cathbarr. He was my ancestor in

432

1080, so he was."

"Surely the box itself is not all gold and silver," Morgan stated.

"I read up about it. It is probably a wooden box, completely covered with bronze for strength and then covered by foils of gold and silver respectively," Peader said.

"There could be any number of messages in all these exterior characters and figures," Morgan said. "Where do we start?"

"The outside of the main box is covered by silver foil with Celtic patterns," Tadgh observed. "More possible clues?"

It was perplexing, they all had to admit. "Let's open the box and see what's inside." Tadgh suggested.

"But what about the ancient superstition about not opening it?" Morgan queried.

"We've come this far. I think we need to open it," Tadgh said. With that, he undid the partially broken clasp and lifted the lid.

"It's empty, for all that," Peader exclaimed, removing the lid entirely and setting it aside on the cloth.

"Look. The bronze and silver leaf covers the entire surface of the inside as well as the outside. And the inside of the lid is similarly covered with folded sheets of the metal," Tadgh added.

"Why would the words engraved in a locket made at least five hundred years later direct us to this ancient relic?" Morgan questioned.

Peader expressed what the others were thinking. "Maybe we misinterpreted the riddle . . . a lot of work and risk for nothing."

Morgan stared at the box while Tadgh and Peader started discussing some of the possible clues that might be contained within the complex outer pictures and patterns. *We're missing something*, she decided. She thought about Peader's words: "Its secrets are locked beneath a pearly veil, and with them, our own hidden truths." That's when she noticed something that they had all missed. The folds of the metal surface on the inside of the lid were tucked neatly under each other. This was different from the way the metal was formed elsewhere on the box. "Tadgh, give me the knife please," she requested.

"Morgan, lass. Don't damage this relic. We are just examining it," he cautioned as he passed her his knife handle first.

Morgan flipped the lid vertical with the main fold tuck on the bottom. Carefully she inserted the knife edge up under the fold and partially separated the outer layer from the inner while gently shaking the lid.

While the others looked on in astonishment, gravity did the rest. Suddenly a corner of old paper popped out from between the folds.

"My God, Morgan, you've found something, lass!" Tadgh exclaimed, leaning close.

"It's right under the moonstone as Peader already said it might be," she said.

"I did?" Peader was taken aback.

While Morgan held the folds slightly apart with the knife, a yellowed document slid down from between the bronze layers of the lid. Tadgh cradled it softly as it appeared.

"This has got to be it, to be sure, to be sure!" Peader was ecstatic.

"This document is folded in four and is blank on both sides," Morgan stated. "It looks brittle to me. We might tear it, or worse if we try to unfold it here and now. It needs to be steamed first."

"I agree, but we can't do that here," Tadgh stated.

"We've got a dilemma," Morgan said. "This paper could just be padding with the real message on the outside of the box. What should we do? It's almost 3 o'clock." It had taken them a lot longer than they had expected to examine the *Cumdach*.

"I brought some paper and a pencil with me," Tadgh announced getting it out of his pocket. "I can take some brass rubbings of the outside surfaces in case the message is really imbedded there. That way we can hedge our bets. We will leave the document folded."

"There you go, now. I will go back upstairs and make sure the guards are still on their routine," Peader offered. "There are new guards now, but they are following the same schedule," he reported.

It took Tadgh the better part of an hour to carefully trace the characters and figures in repoussé on all sides plus the top of the *Cumdach*. He kept the folded document and gave Peader the tracings. "That way if one of us is apprehended . . ." He left the rest of the sentence unfinished.

"It is coming up on quarter to four," Morgan announced.

"We've got to replace the relic on this guard cycle before it starts to become light out," Tadgh said. "Everybody ready? Let's do it." He reluctantly put the ancient document down behind the sarcophagus. "It'll get damaged if we take it with us," he explained. The others looked worried.

"At least we have a torch that we know will work," Peader said, as they started up the stairs.

They timed their exit from the basement perfectly. Reversing their procedure, they set to work to return the *Cumdach* to its case. Peader held the guard's torch.

Tadgh reinserted his pick in the lock. But when Morgan slowly opened the door and tested the wire at one contact, she exclaimed, "Tadgh, we've got a problem. The gum has hardened in place."

"You need to scrape it off the contacts but not until the knife is in place. What can we use to do that, lass?"

Morgan fumbled in her pocket. "I have the door key to our room. It has a sharp metal edge."

"Good. Can you scrape the gum off without disturbing the knife, do ya think?"

"I think so. I stuck the gum just below where the knife was."

Tadgh successfully switched the *Cumdach* for the book and put the latter in his overcoat pocket. "Well then. So far so good."

Morgan checked her watch. "It's ten after four already," she announced.

"Peader, insert the knife blade on edge just above the gum," Tadgh said, as Morgan closed the door on it. Tadgh applied closing pressure on the door.

"Shut off the torch, Peader. Now!" he whispered. The area where they were standing was plunged into darkness.

Tadgh heard footsteps running down the hallway toward them. "Damn," Peader muttered under his breath. Holding the knife precisely on edge between the contacts was very difficult with the lights on, and almost impossible in the darkness.

The guard rushed past the entrance to their Gallery and kept running. Moments later they heard him slam a nearby door.

"Urgent bathroom break, I should think," Tadgh whispered. "Hold your position until he returns to the office."

Morgan could sense that this was not good news for Peader. "Tadgh, the wires are still attached," she whispered. "Let the door open somewhat and give Peader's arm a breather."

Peader was very thankful when the pressure on the door was eased. He withdrew and massaged his hand.

Three minutes later the guard returned down the hallway towards the entrance to their room, moving at a more leisurely pace, judging by the sound. Tadgh noticed that dawn was starting to shed a faint light through the high windows of the gallery. *If the guard looks our way when he passes by, then we're caught.* "Don't move a muscle," Tadgh whispered.

The guard came into view in the hallway opposite the entrance and stopped. His back was toward them. He hesitated there, and then turned and ran back down the hallway. Apparently, he still had urgent business to attend to.

Tadgh glanced at his watch—5:20. The other guard would now be passing the basement door and would be upon them in less than ten minutes. They couldn't wait. "We need to finish this now," Tadgh whispered and he started reclosing the door. "Turn on the torch."

Peader got the knife blade inserted just as the door closed on it.

"Morgan, scrape the contacts and pull out the wire now, lass."

It seemed forever before Morgan said, "The gum on one side is off. But there's still a bit of gum residue on the contact near the knife. I can't do any better."

"Leave it, Morgan," Tadgh whispered back. "We've run out of time, darlin'. Just get the other side free."

A minute later Morgan announced, "The other side is detached."

"Peader, withdraw the knife slowly," Tadgh murmured loud enough to hear. He had no idea whether the gum residue would insulate the contacts when the door closed. At the same moment that Peader was withdrawing the knife from the contact interface, Tadgh was pushing the door closed with significant force. There was a loud click as the door closed. Tadgh twisted the tumblers and the door locked. He breathed a sigh of relief. There was no alarm sounding.

Just then from nearby down the hall, they heard the guard-on-rounds yell out to his compatriot, "Henry, did you hear that noise in Gallery One?"

A few seconds later the guard burst around the corner and into the room, his torch scanning. He passed by the *Cumdach* case, fortunately looking down the Gallery.

The team behind the display of the Druid robes stood absolutely still. Although their heads and torsos were hidden, their legs and feet were exposed below the case. If the guard looked down, or came around that case, they were done. They held their breath.

As fate would have it, the second guard returning from the loo popped his head into the room at that moment and asked the guard why he had yelled. Although that might have made matters worse, it actually helped by diverting the guard, who went back to the entrance to explain that he had heard a clicking noise.

The one said, "That was just me trying to get the loo to flush. Dirk, you know how it sticks."

"Yah, Henry, I know. But I thought it came from in here."

They watched as Dirk, the guard, hesitated and started to turn back toward them. Then, to their relief, he looked at his watch and stopped. Spinning on his heel he announced, "I'm going to continue my rounds now." With that he moved down the room and proceeded into Gallery Two.

"That was close, to be sure," Peader gasped. Tadgh gave the guard two minutes to get back to the office. Then he ushered them all to and through the antiques storage door.

"I don't ever want to do that again!" Morgan announced breathlessly once they were back in the basement.

"We're okay for now you two. Relax," Tadgh suggested. "Good job, both of you. We just have to figure out how to mesh with today's visitors when they arrive without raising suspicion. "If we open the basement door in sight of a guard, we will be in trouble, to be sure."

He went over and held Morgan closely, kissing her sensuously on her mouth and then on both closed eyelids. "I can't imagine what I would do without you, my *aroon*."

Morgan could feel his body begin to relax against her as they clung to each other.

Tadgh retrieved the ancient document from its hiding place and carefully placed it inside the pages of the decoy book for safekeeping.

"You have a student identification card for St. Patrick's with you, don't you, Peader?"

"Yes I do. Why do you ask?"

"Because I have an idea. I think we should be students of Egyptology, and you are our leader, comrade," Tadgh announced. He was counting on some official coming to his basement office at the beginning of the work day. He explained his plan to the others.

"The museum opens to the public at ten in the morning," he said, having checked the sign on the way into the museum. "And now, I suggest we get some rest over there behind the sarcophagi. I will take the first watch."

Several hours of needed sleep later at 9:45, the basement door opened and the light came on. Peader, who was standing watch, jumped back behind their screen. With a finger to his lips, he silently woke the others. Peering cautiously around one sarcophagus, they watched as a bespectacled old man slowly, and unsteadily, navigated the stairs. They could easily hear his puffing and groaning in the otherwise silent subterranean world. At the bottom of the stairs, he paused to catch his breath, and to adjust his bottle-thick glasses. Then, without looking sidewise, he dragged his bent-over frame down the main corridor and into the next storage room. A few minutes later, they heard the storage office door close.

Now, with the light on, the folded document in the book in Tadgh's pocket became a magnet for their attention. They desperately wanted to open it.

"I know what you're both thinking, but we have to wait to look at it," Tadgh cautioned. We could destroy it and never see what's written on it if we try to open it now."

They all knew he was right, yet they continued to be intensely curious as to what they would find when they did. At 10:30, they straightened their attire as best they could after the strenuous events of the past day, and came out from their hiding place. As planned, Tadgh ascended the stairs and closed the door. The other two joined him, and then they started down the stairs together, laughing aloud.

When they reached the bottom, Morgan squealed, "Look, Frank, over there, near those sarcophagi. We've found the right place."

The old man heard the commotion and opened his office door, "You there, what do you think you are doing?"

They hurried through the storage rooms to him, and Peader shook the man's hand.

"Hello, sir," he said in an excited tone of voice. We're students at St. Patrick's, learning to be secondary school teachers. We are very interested in your Egyptology artifacts. They told us there were some more interesting pieces down here." He briefly showed the man his student pass for identification.

Morgan piped up. "We saw those magnificent sarcophagi over there. Can you tell us which period they came from?" She batted her eyelids at him as she spoke.

They struck a nerve. His eyes lit up behind his obtuse glasses.

"I'm Professor O'Toole, head curator at this museum. You're not supposed to be down here, you know."

"Well now," said Tadgh. "We were just curious."

They waited for his reaction. If he questioned their presence, they could be searched. And they couldn't allow that to happen.

Finally, after looking them up and down, the professor said, "Right then. Come with me. I'm very interested in Egyptology, as well. In fact, I am an expert in the field."

With that, he escorted them back to the sarcophagi and started to explain. "These are mummies from the Romano-Egyptian period during the second century AD. They're from the area of Hawara. Did you see our wonderful Egyptian exhibit upstairs?"

"Not yet, sir," said Tadgh. "Could we trouble you to show it to us, please?"

"Not at all, my boy," answered the Professor. "I'd love to. Student education is an important part of our program here at the National. Don't get many who are truly interested in the Egyptians, you know."

With that, he guided them up and out to the Egyptian, Roman

and Greek Exhibit Gallery. Along the way he informed them, "There are over three thousand artifacts alone in our Egyptian collection." They passed by the Treasury Gallery One. Tadgh smiled as he glanced in and saw visitors milling about the *Cumdach* case as if nothing had happened.

When they arrived at the Egyptian Gallery, the Professor exclaimed, "Over here is our most prized piece, the mummy and coffin of lady Tentdinebu of Thebes from the first millennium BC." He went on and on. And when he was finished, he insisted on escorting them to the front door of the Rotunda. The result was better than Tadgh had hoped.

The sun was shining as they exited the museum, sixteen hours after they had entered it. Exhausted, yet exhilarated, they headed for the *An Stad*.

"What an unbelievable adventure," Morgan exclaimed.

"Not bad for an evening's work, *aroon*," Tadgh agreed, as they jumped on the tram with no police in sight.

Chapter Thirty-One
Revelation

Monday, August 2, 1915

*B*oyle's **rage was** not subsiding. "How the hell did they get past us?" he raged. "They must have somehow escaped through the Botanical Gardens."

"Did you get a good look at the fellow who was with them?" Gordo asked his boss.

"Too far away. But it wasn't the brother Aidan. Different facial features."

"So we're back to square one, then, are we?"

"Not exactly. We've got the DMP checking the railway stations, the boat docks and the exit roads from the city. They've been at it since about an hour after the funeral. The McCarthys and that girl of theirs have got to head southwest sometime, and I think that there's a very good chance they haven't left yet."

"One more thing, Gordo. I have now come to the conclusion that they were still somewhere in that Temple Bar Pub when we went through it. Go back and watch to see if they show up there again. But don't rough up the bartender this time. It's not our juris-diction. Keep me informed."

It was mid-afternoon by the time that Tadgh and his team returned to *An Stad*, the folded document inside the book pressed close to his chest.

Thomas MacDonagh and Tom Clarke were conversing in the lobby. Morgan noticed that festivities were winding down.

"Hello, friends. Killed or maimed anyone since yesterday,

Tadgh?" MacDonagh kidded. It was his job as Chief Marshal to keep law and order, at least for the time being.

"Nah, just eluded the RIC and broke in and out of a National institution, don't ya know," Tadgh zinged back.

"Okay, joker. Just make sure you don't fire off any of those nine-millimeter shells in Dublin, my boy."

"Not unless I'm fired upon first," Tadgh answered.

"What's that book you have there, Tadgh?" Tom asked, stepping between Tadgh and Morgan. "Let me have a look."

He grabbed the book out of Tadgh's hand before he could react and turned its spine up to read the name. Morgan gasped as she saw the pages spread open and the parchment relic drop out and fall. Peader looked petrified. If the ancient folded page hit the stone floor from that height, it would potentially crumble to dust if someone tried to pick it up.

Tadgh's right arm swooped down and caught the parchment before it hit the floor. He cradled it so softly that you would have thought it was an eggshell. No harm was done.

Both Peader and Morgan let out audible sighs.

"What's that you're hiding, Tadgh?" MacDonagh asked, now getting curious.

Tadgh had to think fast. Just then he glimpsed the name of the book, *I'll Take the High Road*.

"It's just the folded map of country roads that goes with this book—nothing special," he lied, as he pointed out the title. Grabbing the book back from Tom, he delicately tucked the relic back between its pages.

Quick thinking, Morgan realized.

"Looks interesting," Tom commented.

"At least he didn't ask to see the map," Peader said, later, when they were on their way back to Tadgh's room.

Tadgh had been thinking about the method for softening the relic. "I think that we should make a small tent over the bathtub and then fill the tub with hot water. It won't produce steam but it will increase humidity while the water's flowing. The trick will be to remove the document before it gets too much moisture."

As the tub was filling with scalding hot water that the chambermaid brought in, they set up the tent using the blanket from the bed and the curtain rod from the armoire. Tadgh held the relic under the tent.

"I can feel the moisture starting to form on the bottom of my fingers," he announced after a couple of minutes. Soon, after gently separating the folds with a knife and pliable fingers, they managed to get it open to where there was just one stubborn fold left. Both sides were still blank.

"It's possible that the ink has dissipated over the ages," Tadgh suggested, laying the document on a clean towel on the side table.

"Now there's a cheery thought," Morgan said. "But I don't think so."

"Anyone want to guess how old this document is?" Peader was taking bets. "The paper looks really old. I think about 1700s."

"1800s," guessed Morgan, by the texture of the document.

"Well now, based on what we've discussed so far, I'm guessing early 1600s," Tadgh offered. "I suppose it's now or never."

"I suggest we close the draperies so that there is only subdued lighting. Who knows whether any text will already be too faded to read," Morgan said.

They worked together to open the final fold. As they inserted knives between the two folded sections of the document, they encountered strong resistance.

"Stop," Tadgh ordered them. "Withdraw your knives. It seems to me that the ink lettering or seals have somehow bonded together over the years. If we force the knives in, we may tear the document and obliterate the writing, or at least portions of it."

"So what do we do now?"

"It's risky, but I think we have to get the inside surfaces warmer and slightly moist to separate them," Tadgh advised him.

"Like heating the knives in a fire?" Peader asked.

"No, we don't want to scorch or burn the document," Morgan cautioned. "I recommend that we heat the knives in the scalding water and mostly dry them off. Then, immediately, we should push the knives in at the same time, slowly yet forcefully if need be. That might separate the sheets without damaging them too badly."

"Don't ye think that the moisture might smear the letters?" Peader wondered.

"I said there is risk. Any other ideas?" Morgan asked.

They couldn't come up with any. They moved the table over beside the claw foot bathtub and poured new hot water into it. After immersing the knives for a minute to get them hot, they simultaneously dabbed them with a towel and began the insertion process.

Suddenly, the fold popped open. If there had been any seals, they were cut. The relic opened fully and revealed its secret.

"This is unbelievable, to be sure," Tadgh exclaimed, as he pored over the parchment.

Morgan, who couldn't read Gaelic, could only marvel at the precision of the manuscript scroll with its colorful illuminations and the flourish of the original sealed signatures. "Well? Well? What does it say, for Heaven's sake?"

Peader was trying his best to interpret the ancient Gaelic, but Tadgh read it with ease.

Tadgh's throat had gone dry from the shock of what he had just read, and he had trouble mouthing the words. Finally, somewhat composed, he announced, "Before I read it verbatim—translated for you, Morgan—I must first say that I now know why an O'Donnell relic is called out in my McCarthy locket." He stopped to let that statement whet their appetites.

Finally he started, "This is what it says." Before he could begin, there was a pounding on the door.

"Tadgh. Open up. There is urgent news," MacDonagh announced through the door.

"You two wait here," he said quietly to his friends. "Guard that document. I'll be right back." With that he opened the door only far enough so that he could squeeze through without letting MacDonagh see into the room.

Closing the door behind him, he said, "What's so important, Thomas?"

"Pearse has just announced that he has won over the Gaelic League to our side at the Ard Fheis annual meeting. Eion MacNeill is now the President and Douglas Hyde is out. He called for you to help him prepare a speech for the League's assembly outside their offices at Nine Lower O'Connell Street this evening."

"What? Now?" Tadgh queried.

"Yes, now. Come along then."

"Let me tell my friends where I'm going, first," Tadgh requested.

"No time for that, my boy," MacDonagh stated. "They'll catch up with you later."

Morgan and Peader waited for Tadgh to return. After several minutes Morgan checked the hallway outside their room and it was empty.

"That's strange," she said, "It must be really urgent and private IRB business. Can you translate the document, Peader?"

"Despite coming from a galltacht area of Dungloe, I'm still learning, and this is old Irish script," he said. "We'll have to wait for Tadgh for the main text, I'm afraid. But we can see who signed the document." Peader lowered his head close to the page. "Tadgh guessed right," he added. "I'm astonished. It is dated on the 8th day of October, 1600 at Donegal Castle, and signed and sealed by none other than the two Clan Chieftains, Florence MacCarthaigh Reagh, King of Desmond, Tadgh's ancestor and Red Hugh O'Donnell, King of Tir Conell, my ancestor." His face shone as he looked at Morgan. "I'll be," he whispered.

Tadgh met with Padraig Pearse at Liberty Hall, the headquarters for the Irish Volunteers. Most of the senior members of the secret IRB were also staunch members of the growing Volunteers brigades. He noticed that Padraig was smartly dressed in the same Volunteers officer's uniform that he had worn at Rossa's funeral.

"Thanks for coming on such short notice, Tadgh," he said. "I value your counsel. I couldn't convince Douglas to transition the League from a solely cultural to a political force, so he resigned and the assembly voted Eion MacNeill President. I want to strike while the iron is hot and make a statement to all the Volunteers while the funeral of our forefather is still fresh in their minds. I'd like to take a slightly different slant to the message from what I spoke at the eulogy. I want to appeal to the cultural side of our movement to show them that we aren't just a militant group hell-bent on martyrdom." They sat and talked through a draft of the speech.

"I think that you should acknowledge the cultural contributions of the Gaelic Athletic Association and those of the members of the Irish National Theatre Society and their Abbey Theatre," Tadgh suggested, even though he knew that one of Society's founders, W. B. Yeats, was dead set against military action.

When they had completed their discussion, Padraig thanked Tadgh and said, "I would like you and your friends to be present for this brief speech this evening at eight o'clock."

Tadgh agreed to be there, but added, "Then after that, Morgan and I have to get back to Skibbereen, sir."

Just before they parted, Padraig commented, "I'm glad you found Aidan; it was a brilliant idea to get him to come to St. Edna's. I spoke with him earlier today, and he seems motivated and stable. I don't know what you said to him to turn him around, but it seems to be working. Leave him in our hands. We'll take very good care of him."

Tadgh thanked his boss, thinking to himself once more of the treasure he had already found in Morgan. He hurried back to the *An Stad* and up to his room to share the news. But his compatriots were gone. *Bloody buggering bollocks!* He stormed around the room looking for the document to no avail. *Did Boyle somehow get to them?* Then he stormed downstairs to the pub. There they were, gobbling down some Irish stew and drinking Beamish. He approached them with, "Why the hell didn't you leave me a note?"

"Sorry. We weren't sure when you would be back and we were famished," Peader admitted, looking chagrined.

Tadgh realized his stomach was growling. It was supper time and, with all the excitement about the relic, he hadn't eaten since their meager supper in the basement office a day ago. "You had me worried. Where did you …?"

"Between the mattresses," Morgan answered the unfinished question. "We thought it would be safe there and it would help to press it, too. What happened to you, anyway?"

"I'm sorry for leaving you in the lurch, but Padraig needed me to help him prepare a brief speech for tonight at eight o'clock. We're asked to attend," Tadgh said.

"We're having a wee celebration here, although we don't exactly know what we're celebrating about," Morgan giggled, downing the last of her second Beamish. "We're dying to know what it says, you know."

"And I'm dying to tell you both . . . but not here in public. Presumably you saw the date and signatures, I'm sure."

"Yes, unbelievable," Peader chimed in. "But I couldn't understand the main text."

Despite the subject on all their minds, they forced themselves to enjoy their well-earned meal. Before long, Jeffrey Wiggins strode into the Pub. He spied them sitting there and sat down in a booth not too far away, by himself.

"Hello," Morgan started to greet him, but Tadgh put a hand on her arm and a finger to his lips.

"When are we going home?" Morgan asked Tadgh.

"First thing tomorrow, *aroon*," he answered. "I needed a way to get us out of Dublin without being apprehended. I know those blaggards will be looking for us with a vengeance. I got a message to Jeffrey and he has been kind enough to bring our Ablingdon on his truck as part of his Beamish delivery."

Peader said, "I'm already late and will need to return to class at St. Patrick's tomorrow morning. But not before we learn what is written and what we are going to do about it."

"After supper in our room and before the speech," Tadgh suggested. "And, by the way, this should be a major celebration, so it should," he stated, as he ordered his first, and as it turned out, only Beamish of the evening.

After supper, Tadgh stopped by Wiggins' booth. Morgan could see them talking quietly. Then she saw him pat his Beamish boy on the back and shake his hand.

On the way back to the room he told Morgan, "Wiggins left the locked bike behind the building by the tradesman's entrance. I've got the key."

"Finally, I can tell you what this Clans Pact says," Tadgh said after they returned to their room and had taken out the document. It was starting to look like a flat piece of parchment.

"Did you say Clans Pact?" Peader asked expectantly.

"Yes that's right, comrade. Exciting isn't it? Here it is verbatim:

'I, Red Hugh O'Donnell, King of Tir Connell, and I, Florence MacCarthaigh Reagh, King of Desmond, do hereby form a solemn Pact between our two remaining Clans, North and South. Now, as a result of our lamentable loss to the English swine in the Desmond Rebellion, we recognize the possibility of overthrow of our beloved Clan system

and Kingdoms. Therefore, united, we shall employ a strategy of active aggression and then, if necessary, passive defiance against the English invader.

Further, we have constructed a plan to hide the treasures of our estates from the English overlords, if and when that becomes necessary, each in a place of historical religious significance. Each firstborn male heir, alone, shall inherit the knowledge until the time of concealment, if needed, and shall swear secrecy at risk of eternal damnation for betraying Ireland. We do this to protect the monetary strength of our heritage so it may be used by our worthy descendants after they uncover it, when the time is right, to lead the march for independence for all Irishmen, and to restore the glory of our Gaelic way of life.

The markers of the path shall hereby be passed to the rightful firstborn son heirs of the Great O'Donnell and MacCarthy Clans through interlinked talismans and other family relics.

The Cumdach containing our sacred An Cathach Psalter given to us by our blessed and beloved ancestor, Colum Cille, has protected the O'Donnell Clan for centuries in battle and in peace. It also forms a bridge to our ancient past, which is linked to religious resurrection. It is, therefore, fitting that these sacred O'Donnell relics shall form a part of this path to freedom.

Blessed be the Alpha and the Omega and the Balance of Justice.

Witnessed, signed and sealed by us alone, Florence MacCarthaigh Reagh, King of Desmond and Red Hugh O'Donnell, King of Tir Connell this the 8th day of October, 1600 at Donegal Castle.

When Tadgh had finished there was a prolonged silence, the three taking in the tremendous significance of the document.

Peader was first to speak. "My God, Tadgh. Do you realize what this means?"

"Well now, it means that we three are joined on a journey of discovery on behalf of our forefathers and our Gaelic Nation. Since our countrymen are on the verge of a great revolution to regain our freedom, perhaps our generation has been chosen to finally unearth the family treasures to support our cause."

Being somewhat perplexed, Peader asked, "Chosen by whom?"

Morgan grasped it immediately, "By Divine intervention, Peader. By Divine intervention."

Looking around the room, Morgan whispered, "So then that is why it was acceptable to open the *Cumdach* and discover it, without concern for bad luck. Here now must be what they meant by 'when the time is right'. I can feel their presence."

"Whose presence?" Tadgh reached for his Luger and scanned the room.

"It's as if the spirits of Red Hugh, Florence and Colum Cille are here with us."

Peader chimed in. "I see what you mean. None of this could have happened if our paths had not crossed serendipitously, and if I hadn't asked about your locket. It took the two of us, the two Clans, to work together."

"Precisely," agreed Tadgh, holstering his side-arm. "It fulfills the prophecy and intent of the Pact. And we are now sworn to secrecy."

"So you two are joined in our crusade to find your families' treasures on behalf of freedom for Ireland, just like Mr. Pearse and Mr. Connolly, joining forces despite having different ideologies," Morgan observed, quite proud of herself.

"That's very astute of you, *aroon*."

"It means something else important, my love."

"What's that, lass?"

"If that locket was handed down through the ages to the first-born as you said it was, and since your Pa is dead, then this document proves that you are the rightful head of the McCarthy Reagh Clan."

The reality of this statement took a moment to sink in.

"That's right, Tadgh," Peader agreed. "But if there was an

O'Donnell locket, it was either lost in antiquity, or I'm not the first-born heir of the O'Donnell Clan."

"But are you an only child, Peader?"

"One of nine, but I am the oldest boy, and my Pa is dead."

"Lost in antiquity, then."

"That's fine with me. I'm just interested in knowing my lineage. I'm more motivated to help to restore the Gaelic way of life for our women and men. I think that the rights of women continue to be neglected in our society, by the way."

"Thanks for that," Morgan exclaimed, clapping her new friend on the shoulder.

"They might not have used a locket as a talisman for the O'Donnell path," Tadgh offered.

"That brings us to the question of where we go from here," Peader commented.

"Well now. We've used the clue in my locket, so we have. What other family talismans or relics do we have to work with?" Tadgh asked.

"On my side, the only one I can think of is *An Cathach* itself," Peader replied.

"Does your family have it?"

"No, I think that it is a national treasure, housed in the Royal Irish Academy here in Dublin."

"Not another break-in, I hope," Morgan stated, looking alarmingly at Tadgh.

"It's too risky for us to stay in Dublin now. We'll have to find another way," Tadgh concluded. "I've got an old family bible with a partial, handwritten family tree that may provide a clue. I'll have to look into that, to be sure."

"Wouldn't it be likely that both Clans would have had a copy of the Pact someplace?"

"You would think so, my love. What really happened in the aftermath of the defeat at Kinsale that set our two Clan leaders plans into action, do ye think?"

"And how did the Pact get into the *Cumdach*, which was never to be opened?" Peader wondered. "Especially if this was a closely guarded secret and the box was being protected by the McGroarty sept of our Clan during the battle."

"And when would they have found it necessary to hide the treasures, and who did so, if they did?" Tadgh added.

"And, most importantly, where?" Morgan emphasized.

"It is time to go to the speech, so we need to terminate this conversation for now," Tadgh concluded. "This Pact raises a lot of questions that we cannot answer today. These mysteries are all very intriguing, aren't they? We will need a plan of action."

With that said, Tadgh placed the Pact in a large picture book he had borrowed from the pub, and he bound the book in both directions with twine.

"I'm not letting this out of my sight," he vowed. With this package under his arm, they headed for the Gaelic League Headquarters.

True to form, the Irish Volunteers had brought out a crowd. Lower O'Connell Street, as the Republicans were wont to call it, was packed, Tadgh observed as they pushed their way to the steps of the Gaelic League Headquarters building just opposite the O'Connell Monument.

"It looks as if it was excellent timing to win over the League on the heels of this historic funeral for Mr. Rossa. This is a rollover crowd," Tadgh exclaimed to his compatriots.

Peader summarized the thought, "Great to build momentum, isn't it."

Padraig Pearse stood to address the crowd in his crisp Volunteer uniform, and started his speech. "My fellow Irishmen and women. I have good news."

Tadgh, who had been watching the throng for their reaction, saw that both the DMP and the RIC were present to witness the speech and suppress any untoward enthusiasm by the participants.

"Duck into the crowd," Tadgh suddenly commanded Morgan and Peader. "I saw Boyle on the southern fringe of this gathering. I don't think he saw us yet, but we should make ourselves scarce. Peader, we'll be in touch. I suggest you get back to St. Patrick's this evening. Morgan and I will make our way home to Skibbereen."

They snaked northward through the maze and heard Padraig continuing, "Tonight I'm here to announce the alignment of the Gaelic League with the goals and objectives of our Irish Volunteers."

Morgan noticed that Peader had disappeared.

Tadgh grabbed Morgan's hand and whispered, "We've got to hurry. There is someone waiting for us."

Boyle had seen them and was frantically trying to push through the crowd. He signaled to a DMP officer near him to follow him. *Damn. Why did I assign Gordo to stakeout the pub? I need him now.*

Tadgh had seen Boyle bolt towards them. He and Morgan broke free of the crowd and sprinted north.

"It's about half a mile north to *An Stad,* Morgan," Tadgh yelled. "We can outrun Boyle if he doesn't get help."

"What do you think I am, a gazelle?" Morgan gasped.

As luck would have it, something Padraig said incited the crowd to rally at that moment, and most of the DMP officers present needed to do their duty. Boyle could only commandeer two of them. He always relied on Gordo to do the heavy work.

By the time the Head Constable's squad got free of the agitated crowd, Tadgh and his girl had already reached Cathel Brugha Street.

"Damn," Tadgh muttered when, glancing back, he saw the three pursuers gaining on them. A minute later, when they crossed Parnell Street, Tadgh knew that there would be no way for Boyle to commandeer a private vehicle since their route, northern Parnell Square East, was one way southbound for traffic. He took the time to look over his shoulder again and saw that his pursuer was about a hundred and fifty yards behind.

"How are you doing, Morgan?" he called out. He saw that she was lagging behind and he dropped back to pace her.

"I'm getting really tired, Tadgh," she panted.

"We're halfway there. You can do it. Let's go, lass," he urged.

By the time Boyle reached Parnell Street, the two were one hundred yards ahead of their pursuers, continuing northbound on Frederick Street North. Looking back once more Tadgh could see that Boyle's squad was making up ground and that he was not that winded at the loping stride he had settled into. He saw him draw his Webley.

"We're almost there, Morgan," Tadgh urged. "Turn left down Frederick Lane North just ahead to get to the back of the *An Stad*." He had the Ablingdon key in one hand and the package in the other.

Boyle saw the couple veer left off of Frederick. He was swearing when a DMP police car approached him southbound.

"Need some help, Head Constable?" The officer asked, "I see that you are in pursuit."

"Thanks, yes," Darcy said as he jumped in the passenger seat leaving the other officers in his wake. "They went down that alley to the left."

Just as they reached the alley, the policemen saw the Ablingdon motorcycle with the Watsonian wickerwork sidecar flash out from behind the buildings turning west down the alley away from them.

"They're the ones. After them."

Tadgh looked behind and saw that they had problems. Their pursuer was now mobile.

"Hold on, Morgan. Boyle's in a police car. This is going to get dangerous, to be sure."

Tadgh knew that the car was faster than his motorcycle, but his bike was narrower than the police vehicle. His only hope was his cunning and agility. "By God, we're not going to get caught now, especially with the Pact in our possession," he yelled over to Morgan.

She hunched over in the sidecar in exhaustion, the package tucked safely between her feet. The lane turned north and headed to Dorset Street Upper. At the intersection, Tadgh craftily wheeled left. The bank was so tight that the sidecar left the ground and crashed back down a moment later.

"I see that you're awake now, *aroon*," Tadgh yelled, above the shrieking motor.

"Why are we on the bike if they're going to have all the roads blocked?" she yelled back.

"You'll see, my love," he shot over to her.

"I knew it," Boyle swaggered. "They're headed southwest. We're gaining on them. Step on it."

The police car accelerated, and the gap between the pursued and the pursuers closed to two hundred feet.

"We've got 'em now," Darcy cried with glee. "Finally."

Tadgh could see the Granby Row intersection coming up. There was a lot of cross traffic ahead, especially for nine in the evening. Good, he thought. He was supposed to stop before proceeding.

"Brace yourself and hold tight to the package," he shouted.

Gauging the distance between two converging hansom cabs on the cross-street ahead, he ignored the stop sign and accelerated into the intersection. Timing it just right, he dodged right then left and narrowly squeaked between the hansoms just before they reached each other.

The police car was only five seconds behind them. It hit the nearest cab just behind the passenger door, knocking the driver off his perch. Spinning around, the back of the cab hit the cab going the other way. They all ended up in the middle of the intersection with the two horses rearing up and fighting to get free.

"You blithering idiot," Boyle screamed. "I can't see past this mess. Back up and go around."

"But there are people injured," the officer cried.

"I don't care about them. Do as I say!" Boyle was livid.

Tadgh heard the crash over the din of the motor and turned briefly to survey the scene. He had seen his opportunity and had taken it. "Hold on, Morgan, we're turning right," he yelled as he spun the bike right and up onto the Tarmac of the Number 2 Fire Station. He shot past the far side of the building and skidded right to a stop behind the building.

The police car engine sounded ragged but it functioned as the officer backed up and spun forward around the carnage. Angry passengers and Hanson drivers were yelling and shaking their fists at the car. Boyle ignored it, wiping the blood from a cut around his chin.

Once they had cleared the intersection, he could not see the motorcycle.

"Keep going. They must have gotten ahead of us. I'm sure they're heading southwest. We need to get a message to reinforce the barriers on all south and west exits from the city."

"Whatever you say, Head Constable," the officer complied.

Tadgh waited several minutes to ensure they were out of sight. Then he pulled back out onto Dorset Street and turned east, tooling within the legal speed limit.

"Where are we going?" Morgan queried. "Seems like the wrong direction to me."

"Be patient, *aroon*. All things will come clear in the fullness of time."

They had a leisurely ride and eventually wound their way onto the Clontarf Road, and east along the north shore of Dublin Bay past North Bull Island.

"It won't be long now," Tadgh said, as looked over at his love's beautiful, yet perplexed face.

Fifteen minutes later they passed through the Sutton crossroads onto the Howth peninsula and soon they arrived at a secluded dock just west of Howth Harbor.

"Here we are," Tadgh announced as they drove onto the dock, up a ramp and gingerly down onto the deck of *The Republican.*

"Ahoy there, Martin," Tadgh called out, and a salty old mariner in a stained yellow Macintosh poked his head around the yard arm.

As they dismounted the bike, Martin pulled an old tarpaulin up and over, covering the 'Kerry' Ablingdon and its sidecar completely. Then they tied it down.

"Thanks for picking us up, old man," Tadgh offered in salutation. "Jeffrey said that you would be here. Have any trouble with the old girl?"

"None, young lad. She's a corker."

"Let me introduce my partner. Morgan, this is Martin Murphy, Mr. Wiggins' ship's captain. He takes those lovely kegs of Beamish to all points of the compass, don't you Martin."

"Aye, son. We best be shoving off, don't ye think." Tadgh noted that he was clearly nervous about this assignment that his boss had given him.

"Off we go, then," Tadgh agreed, throwing off the stern mooring rope. "They won't be looking for us at sea now." He could smell the fish and knew that Martin had done his job well.

"Even in August there was a chill in the night air." Murphy noticed Morgan was shivering.

"Here's some blankets and coffee ta warm ya," Martin offered.

Morgan was still speechless as they pulled out into the Irish Sea under the moonlight. She watched the shore for any sign of the police, but only the wharf lights winked back.

Chapter Thirty-Two
The Sighting

Tuesday, August 3, 1915

*B*y mid-afternoon *The Republican* was abreast of the Roche's Point, Cork Harbor Galley Lighthouse on a path into Queenstown harbor.

"Ye can drop me off on the dock near my home, lad," Murphy announced, pointing northward. "It's that colorful yellow row house in that group way over yonder on the south shore of Great Island in the harbor, don't ye see."

Tadgh's attention was diverted elsewhere. "Do you see that police launch coming in from the Celtic Sea?" he asked, pointing south.

Is that a problem, dear?"

"Don't be alarmed," the captain replied. "These patrols do be commonplace nowadays in the coastal waterways during this confounded war, especially here in the supply corridor so close to England. They be after U-Boats that are sighted almost daily hereabouts."

"Hold on, now. It's turning to starboard and heading right for us, Capt'n. Morgan, I need you to duck under the tarpaulin, now," Tadgh commanded.

Morgan did as she was asked but wondered, "What business could they possibly have with us?"

"Don't underestimate the RIC, *aroon*. Martin, let's spread that fish catch out in those buckets around the edges of the tarpaulin with some on top, if ya please."

"Aye, laddie. At least we're tired and scruffy enough to look like we're coming back from the fishing grounds, don't ya think?"

Tadgh imagined that he looked ready for the grave.

461

It was hot under that tarpaulin, especially with the cockpit decking underfoot. The air was foul and the green cover cast a sickly color over Morgan's close surroundings. She was nauseous from the rocking of the boat and sweating profusely. That's when the anxiety hit. Claustrophobic? Maybe. No, déjà vu again. Impending doom. *Lusitania? Damn, the memory won't come to me.*

Five minutes later the launch pulled alongside.

"Ahoy, *The Republican*," an officer on the launch cried out when they had closed to five feet. "Checking your haul, here. Routine. What's under your tarpaulin?"

"An unusually good catch of cod and ling sir, so it is," Tadgh yelled back. "Got it on ice."

"Where from?"

"Well, now. Nymphe Bank, of course. Ten leagues south of Dungarvan."

The officer on deck bellowed. "We need to confirm this by looking under your tarpaulin. Prepare to be boarded." One officer jumped across and approached to inspect.

Martin joined the fray. "'Paddy, is it yourself in the wheelhouse, you old salt?"

"Murphy, you fouling barnacle! What are you after doin' fishin' off a hooker?" the police captain boomed. "I thought you was allus runnin' Beamish up the coast."

"Not today, cap'n. I'm helpin' me son here with his catch, don't ya know."

The officer started to pick up a corner of the tarpaulin. At that moment, Tadgh could clearly see the bright spokes of the front wheel glinting in late afternoon sun and illuminating Morgan's anxious face.

"Right, men. Leave these fine gentlemen be," the captain instructed his crew.

The officer turned and dropped the tarp back in place without peering under it. Then he hopped back onto the launch as it revved up to pull away.

"Have a nice day, me boyo, "Martin yelled to his maritime buddy, as the launch nosed away.

When the vessel was a speck on the horizon, Morgan poked her head out from under the tarpaulin. "The fish under here really stink," she joked. "Mixed in with smell of motor oil and wet wicker. Do you think that Boyle alerted them to look out for the motorcycle?"

"I wouldn't put it past him, lass," Tadgh replied. "It's unlikely they'd be lookin' at sea. On the other hand, if they had found the Kerry, they would have suspected something and brought us in for questioning."

"We are *wikkit* glad that you were here," Morgan said to Martin. "You saved the day."

"Where did *wikkit* come from, *aroon*?

"I don't know actually. It just came out. Maybe from my past. Could that be a clue as to where I'm from?"

"Possibly. I've not heard that said around these parts before," said Tadgh.

"Glad to be of assistance ma'am," Martin replied as they pulled in to the fishing docks east of the Liner Terminals.

"Well then. Give our best to Jeffrey, and thank you for all your assistance, Martin," Tadgh said, as the elder mariner jumped nimbly onto the dock.

"Sinn Fein, me boyo," was the response, which seemed to echo off all the fishing boats in the harbor.

Before heading back out to sea, Tadgh took *The Republican* west along the south shore of Queenstown to show Morgan what it looked like from the water.

"Tadgh, I love the quaint village atmosphere of these colorful stepped homes, nestled on the hillside. I could be so happy here with you for the rest of my life."

Tadgh let that remark pass. Now was not the time nor the place.

They passed the liner terminal docks near Scott Square before heading out of the harbor.

"Is this where we came to the Cunard offices to try and find out my identity?"

Tadgh realized that he had made a mistake.

"Could we stop and ask if they have any news?"

"We're a bit vulnerable on *The Republican,* don't ya know. And that patrol boat is still protectin' the harbor entrance."

"But there's still a chance, right?"

"Aye, though slim to none, I would think, at this point."

"But they don't know how to contact us, do they?"

"I gave them Wiggins' contact information if they found out anything," Tadgh lied. God he felt awful about it. She had a right. But Jordan could easily have been wrong.

"I see. We need to talk to him again then. It's still important to me, you know."

"I know, *aroon.*"

Throwing her arms around Tadgh as he guided the tiller, she added, "Don't feel bad for me. I have a new life now with you, *mavorneen.*"

"Even after I have dragged you through all these harrowing dangers?"

"Especially because you let me be your partner in all these exciting adventures, sweetheart!"

Jack was in a funk. The physical therapy was going slower than he had hoped. Oh, he was building up his arm muscles with all the exercises that they had given him, but he had only managed to stand on his own a few times while holding on to his wheelchair. His legs still wouldn't work properly. And his inquiries into who might own that singular-looking motorcycle that he thought Claire was riding in had come up empty so far. She had become his second fantasy, the first being the act of walking.

As the sun was beginning to set that evening, he had wheeled himself out to the end of the empty Cunard Pier and was gazing out to where the harbor emptied into the sea. How much his life had changed in 18 short minutes because of one German torpedo. But at least he was alive. That was more than you could say for 1,198 lost souls.

Oh, how he wished he could go to sea again, like the couple on that Galway hooker he saw glide by.

His pulse quickened as his focus centered on the figures in the cockpit. "My God," he shouted. "There she is."

"Claire, Claire," he shouted waving his arms frantically.

The figures swiveled to look his way, but they obviously couldn't hear him, since they were turning out to sea into the onshore breeze.

He looked around for someone to help, but he was alone.

"Tadgh, look at that man in the wheelchair at the end of the Cunard pier back there," Morgan pointed as they turned south towards the harbor exit. He's waving at us and shouting something. I can't make it out."

Alarm bells went off in his head when he saw the man. *My God. Jack Jordan.*

"Tadgh. Let's go back and talk with him, Maybe he knows me."

"He's probably one of the lucky ones off the *Lusitania* still trying to recover, just like you, my love." That much was true. "He probably never met you."

"It looked to me that he had a uniform on. Maybe a Cunard official."

"I'm thinkin' it unlikely if he's in a wheelchair."

Tadgh had tacked to port with the land on his stern as he lined up to exit the harbor.

"I can hardly see his features, but he's still waving his arms."

"He's probably wishing he was able to sail off into the sunset, like we can," Tadgh answered. "Which is what we are doing. It'll be dark soon and we've miles to go before we're home safe and sound." His focus returned to trimming the main sail in preparation for the tricky tack through the narrow harbor opening to the sea.

Morgan turned away and clasped her arms around her man from behind, feeling his rippling muscles as he worked the mainsheet. He pulled away, growling. "Not now." Then he saw her consternation, hugged her briefly, and said, "Back to work, lass."

Tadgh and Morgan were exhausted when they finally guided *The Republican* home to her berth inside the Skibbereen boathouse at 10 o'clock.

"The Pact is still intact," Tadgh announced triumphantly, holding the bound book high in the air to signify a small victory for his team.

"Poetic, even for a playwright," Morgan kidded, as they trudged up the boathouse stairs towards their warm bed.

At that same moment, Darcy Boyle was being disciplined in Sir Neville Chamberlain's office, all the while trying to make light of his demolition of two Hanson cabs and the attendant injuries to both drivers and three passengers.

"What were you thinking?" the Inspector General was lecturing. "Running a police car into a busy intersection without stopping? Officer Gregory said that you ordered him to do it, and then left the scene without tending to the injured including one horse that had to be destroyed."

"We were in pursuit of dangerous criminals, likely German spies," Boyle stated, holding his ground. There was no apology in his voice.

"Did you catch them, Head Constable?" Chamberlain asked sarcastically, knowing full well that he had not.

"Not so far. It's only a matter of time. Can I go now, so that I can continue my pursuit?"

"There is no question that I want you out of my office," the superior snarled. "You could be held on charges, Boyle. Against my better judgment, you are free to go, but get out of Dublin and don't come back unless I authorize it. You will be notified of your financial accountability in this matter. Now, get out of my sight and out of my city!" the Inspector General ordered.

"I'll do as I please, you bastard," Boyle muttered to himself as he noisily closed Chamberlain's door behind him.

"That bastard Chamberlain. Who does he think he is?" Boyle ranted at Gordo on the way back to Cork, letting off steam. "The McCarthys could still be in Dublin for all we know."

"They're located somewhere around Cork, boss. We know that much," Gordo said to appease the monster. "And you said you can identify the motorcycle they were using. So we're a step ahead, right?"

"Yah. I found out that it's an Ablingdon with a Watsonian wicker side car," the Head Constable answered. "There are only six licensed in Ireland and only three in Cork/Kerry. But, I didn't see a plate. It might not be registered at all, damn it."

As they rolled into the RIC headquarters at the Constabulary Barracks on Union Quay, District Inspector Maloney was waiting for them.

"Boyle, I want to see you in my office, now."

"Fine," Boyle replied, nonchalantly.

"What's this I hear from Neville?" the Inspector asked.

Boyle decided to take a conciliatory approach. "No harm done sir. We're one step closer to finding a German spy."

"A German spy, you say," Maloney said.

Boyle marveled at how easily Maloney could be diverted from his line of questioning. All he had to hear was an opportunity to add a feather to his cap.

"Yes, sir. I chased him. He was riding an Ablingdon motorcycle with a wicker sidecar."

The Inspector thought for a moment. "That's strange," he mused. "I saw a missing persons bulletin about one of those machines somewhere around here the other day."

Well, keep up the good work, Head Constable," he added. "Keep me informed."

With that said, the Inspector dismissed his Head Constable, forgetting completely that he was going to reprimand him for his recent behavior in Dublin.

"What an idiot," Darcy commented to Gordo as they headed for their offices.

It took three minutes for Gordo to find the bulletin. "Looks like the Cunard manager in Queenstown thought he saw one of the *Lusitania* victims riding away from the *Lusitania* recovery site in Scott Square on the twenty-second, Darcy. She was a passenger in a motorcycle with a wicker sidecar."

"Does it say who was driving the motorcycle?"

"All it says is 'an Irishman', boss."

"Does it give a name?"

"They figured it out from the manifest. Claire. It's Claire O'Donnell, from America." Gordo answered, expecting his boss to explode.

"Coincidence?" Boyle wondered but left it at that for the moment.

"Organize for us to meet the Cunard manager tomorrow, Gordo."

When the police car rolled out onto the Cunard wharf early the next morning it was foggy; so much so that the headlights only penetrated a few feet. Boyle sent Gordo ahead to find Jordan's office. No point getting wetter than he had to. James returned a few minutes later and led his boss to the office. Boyle took one look at the pitiful cripple in the wheelchair and muttered, "This one looks like a total waste of time."

"Mr. Jordan. I am Head Constable Boyle from the RIC. How can I help you?"

Jack explained his experience the day of the sinking and that he was pretty sure that the woman he saw in the motorcycle sidecar was the one on the deck that day.

"How do you know that woman's name was O'Donnell?"

"She said her name was Claire and that she was travelling with someone named Byron," Jack explained. "From the manifest we put two and two together." Then he added, "And, by coincidence, I think that I saw her again yesterday."

"Really? Do you know how unlikely a coincidence that is?"

"Very, I'm sure," answered Jack. "But I know what I saw. Her mane of black hair is distinctive. She was with a man on a Galway hooker out there in Cork Harbor."

"Same man that you saw on the motorcycle?"

"I don't know. I only got a glimpse of the back of his head in both cases. All I can really say is that he was probably dressed in an Irishman's clothes."

"Did you catch the name of the ship?" Gordo asked.

"No, but she had a dark gray main sail. Most hookers have all dirt-red sails."

"Where was she headed, sir?" the Head Constable asked.

"Out to sea through the Harbor entrance."

"Did you see if she went east or west?" Boyle persisted.

"West, I think. Hard to tell, really, from this distance."

Telling the Cunard manager that they would look into the

matter, Boyle and Gordo headed back to the city.

"So what do you think now?" Boyle asked his deputy.

"I think that Jordan saw a motorcycle that fits the description of the one we're looking for. It's possible, therefore, that the rider was McCarthy. If that's the case then the girl is also likely the one we're after. But I also think that Jordan could easily be imagining that the girl was the one on the *Lusitania*. He's obviously been traumatized. As for the ship in the harbor, I think it is unlikely that it was the same couple. Wishful thinking, I would venture."

Boyle was less analytical than his underling. He grunted, "Probably right. But let's check it out anyway." *Could they have escaped from Dublin by boat?"* he wondered. The motorcycle was too much of a coincidence.

Jack was encouraged that the police had come to see him. Maybe now I'll get some support. He was also encouraged to find a relative in Canada who was searching for his lost sister. He decided that he would contact the brother directly the first chance he got. An ally in the search wouldn't hurt even if he was four thousand miles away.

Chapter Thirty-Three
Home Again

Wednesday, August 4, 1915
Creagh, Ireland

*M*organ awoke. Her first sensation relief—how good it felt to be home in her own bed. Technically, it wasn't her bed at all. But she'd spent so much time in it during the last three months, that she had decided she had squatter's rights. The next sensation was one of sexual awakening. Tadgh's hand was cupping her right breast causing it to tingle and swell. He was sound asleep, with his nude body snuggled deliciously up to and over the top of hers. She thought how tender he could be in dreamland compared to the well-oiled fighting machine he was when provoked by the English. She loved both sides of him and wondered what other characteristics he might display for her in the future. He was as charming as he was alarming.

This brief respite from their hectic activities gave Morgan time to reflect. She knew that her age was probably twenty-something, but she could only remember the last 40 days or so. Oh, she'd had a couple of times when the veil had momentarily parted. Like yesterday under the tarpaulin. In these few instances under duress, she wasn't granted knowledge of her past, only a deep sense of foreboding. Her history must have been filled with danger and pain, she decided. Maybe it was best to let it die, like she had been told that she had almost done. Maybe the truth would be unbearable.

What utterly amazed her was that she had fallen in love with this crusader for freedom in such a short time. And it was uncanny that she instinctively knew how to nurse the injured, when she couldn't remember any of the training or experience for this profession. These were such positives.

She had no idea if her life before had been easy or hard, exciting or boring, but she did know that it was becoming anything but dull since she was reborn. Reborn, she thought. That's a great way to look at it. And she was thrilled with the life that Tadgh had decided to share with her.

But a voice inside kept saying, *You did not die. Don't you have an obligation to find out if there are relatives pining and hoping for your return?* It was as if someone was calling to her from behind the veil.

Morgan studied the man by her side. Muscular and hairy. And very sexy. She wondered if he was the first lover that she had been with. It had seemed that way. Then she decided that it didn't matter. He was the only one she ever wanted to be with from now on.

As her libido started to take over, she instinctively began to gently stroke Tadgh's body, feeling the warmth and strength of it through her fingertips. And still he slept.

This led her to his manhood, which lay sleeping along with its master. Initially, she felt its softness and marveled that it could rise to fill her up so perfectly. As if her thoughts were being telegraphed, it began to swell. It grew and grew, until it had inflated and arched to its fullest extension. And it pulsed as if it had a life of its own. There it stood, like its master, seemingly struggling for freedom itself. And still he slept.

She couldn't resist stroking it to let it know she cared. When she did, its master started to groan and slowly thrust the air. And still he slept.

She opened her legs and pulled the throbbing fellow and its master into her. What a magnificent feeling. Moments later, she and it both climaxed simultaneously, sending shivers down her back.

Startled into consciousness, Tadgh gasped as he tried to understand the situation. He had been having the most erotic dream, where Morgan had been leading him into delirium. And now, here she was, voluptuous, in the flesh. They were both panting and quivering together.

The power of the moment seized him, and he clung on to savor it. It was unbelievable how this woman had worked her magic on him in such a short time. Before she had appeared, he had no interest in women. Now, he couldn't imagine life without her. It was as if he had been reborn, he thought, as they both collapsed into each other, spent for the moment.

Tadgh awoke again later to the smell of bacon cooking. He was alone.

"Get up, you sleepyhead," he faintly heard from the floor below.

When he came down for breakfast, Morgan was standing at the stove, spatula in hand. He noticed that the apron she wore did little to cover up her otherwise nude body.

"Did you have a nice sleep, dear?" Morgan laughed, pirouetting for his benefit.

"Yes, *aroon*, until I was so rudely awakened."

"Rudely, indeed. I had a marvelous time."

"So did I when I was asleep," he joked, as he pinched her cheek.

After breakfast Morgan asked, "So where do we go from here?"

Tadgh had been giving that a lot of thought on the long boat ride home. "Well now. Let me show you something," he offered, as he led her back upstairs.

"You showed me plenty earlier this morning. I meant, about the Clan Pact."

"Me, too. Have you ever wondered about anything up here?"

"I've wondered why I was so lucky to have you show up in my life, and save me."

"I mean, does anything seem out of place, lass?" he clarified, as they stood in the bedroom.

She thought for a moment and said, "It does seem as though this room is shorter than the outside house dimension."

473

"Thatta girl. That far wall, the one without windows, is a false wall." He went over and pushed on the standing wardrobe, which pressed against that wall.

Morgan could see a waist-high door that had been covered up by the furniture.

"This house is full of surprises, isn't it?" she marveled, her smoky eyes now flaming in wonder.

"It is, indeed. I added the basement operations center, but this hidden room was part of the original house construction. I only found it when I restored that wooden oak wall. It was covered over with chipped plaster when I first moved in."

"I'd love to know the history of what went on in this old house," Morgan mused, feeling the rough texture of the old oak. "I can almost feel it. There are secrets here. Old secrets."

"Really? That's the second time you've said something like that after feeling the building."

"I don't know why I sense it. But I do. I wonder if that's a result of almost dying in the sea."

"I have no idea. Quite out of my military world. If I can't see something, it doesn't exist, right enough."

"Oh, but there is so much more, Tadgh. If only we knew the story of this strange house."

"It is strange. That's part of the reason why I chose this place, for all that. The mystery and the history."

"As I've said before, you're a mystery yourself, Tadgh McCarthy."

"Step into my parlor, said the spider to the fly," Tadgh quoted as he unlocked and opened the small door, and led her inside. Turning on an overhead light, he explained, "This is my secret office where I study the history of my family. It's where I store my keepsakes."

Morgan looked around at the long, skinny chamber. It was about four feet deep and the full twenty-foot length of the bedroom. The outside wall consisted of rough stonework. At the far end, she noticed a ladder mounted to it with a trap door above it in the old beamed ceiling.

"This room looks positively ancient," she said. "How quaint."

"When I found it, it contained this built in roll-top desk that spans the full width of the room at this end. You'll notice that it's carved up with initials, sort of like the banister of the circular staircase."

"F . . . J . . . v . . . S is an odd set of initials, isn't it," Morgan noted. "Do you have any idea who may have lived here?"

"None, at this point," Tadgh admitted. "Maybe it was a left-over Barbary Pirate's ghost," he joked, and let out a mournful wail for effect.

"That's not funny," Morgan gasped. "I get claustrophobic in small spaces like this." She had a vision of people crushing her in a staircase and then the veil dropped. "My God, the *Lusitania.*" She covered her eyes with her outstretched hands.

"What is it, lass?" Tadgh was immediately at her side.

"I . . . I . . . saw it for a second."

"What did you see?"

"The terror on the ship, I mean *in* the ship."

"Can you see it now?"

"No, it's gone, thank God. Oh Tadgh, I think that my brain has blotted out a very evil and dangerous past so I won't go crazy."

"There, there, *aroon*. It's just the uncertainty. But maybe it would be better not knowing, do ya think?"

"I don't know anymore. Of course I don't know anymore. I have amnesia."

"Bits are maybe coming back, lass."

"Not the important bits, like whether I have family."

"Why don't we focus on our future together then, *aroon*? Don't trouble yourself with your past. If you are meant to remember, you will."

Tadgh gave her a big hug and kissed her forehead. "I was just kidding you, my dear, about the ghosts."

Mostly to gain control over her odd emotions, Morgan asked, "So, what are all these papers tacked to the inside wall here?"

"Those are my notes tracing my ancestors . . . trying to document each person in the Bible family tree. As you can see there are many missing links, to be sure."

"What are your sources?" Morgan asked.

"There are some Parish records, which I have cross-checked with cemetery tombstones," he showed her. "And then there are records and book copies that I obtained from the Old Cork Library." He pointed to the small bookshelves attached to the stone wall. "But the largest gaps occur in the 1700s and early 1800s when my ancestors were out of the country. That's one reason that I was coming back from Wales when I found you in the Celtic Sea. I was after doing some research the day before."

"So I can thank your Welsh ancestors for my rescue, can I?"

"Partly, yes," Tadgh admitted. "And for your name, don't forget."

"I haven't remembered anything before I saw your face from the bed over there, but I have remembered every detail since then, my love," Morgan murmured, snuggling into the crook of his right arm.

"Me, too."

"I'm impressed at all the work you've done here, dear. But I think that your locket and the Clan Pact bypass all this detail," Morgan wisely observed. "What are those drawings on the wall?"

"That one is a cross-sectional drawing of Kilbrittain Castle, my ancestral home I believe, as I mentioned earlier," Tadgh instructed. "It was the principal castle of the MacCarthaigh Reagh Clan. Florence, who signed the Clan Pact, was the last real Clan Chieftain before the English overran Munster Province in the south of Ireland back at the beginning of the 1600s." He went on, "And this one over here is Blarney Castle. You can see the old castle tower and keep. The castle dates from before 1200 when a wooden structure was purported to have been built on the site. Around 1210 this was replaced by a stone fortification. That was destroyed in 1446, but subsequently rebuilt by Cormac Laidir MacCarthy, Dermot McCarthy Mor, Lord of Muscry."

"You told me about what happened to the Blarney Castle, but what happened to your Clans' Estates?" Morgan probed.

"Well now, it's quite the history, so it is, if you've a mind to hear it."

"Yes of course. Shoot away. Will there be a test when you're done?"

"A test of your patience, perhaps, lass."

"In that case, Tadgh, let me summarize what I thought I heard from you in Dublin." She was quite anxious to get out of this cramped space as soon as possible.

"Fine."

"The various McCarthy Clans ruled southwest Ireland for centuries until the British invaded and took away your lands, your culture, your religion, in fact your civilization."

"Dead right, girl."

"Let's see. After the British won a decisive battle around 1600, the Clans were essentially defeated. All wars after that have been rebellions."

"You were listening then, weren't you."

"At least I can remember this, even though my own history is totally unknown."

"What did I say about the Confederate War, smarty pants?"

"Just that it started in 1641 and involved both your clan, the McCarthy Reaghs who owned Killbrittain castle near Kinsale, and the McCarthy Mors who owned Blarney among other castles, the latter being besieged by Cromwell's evil forces in about 1647."

"And the McCarthy gold?"

"Went missing and has never been found after the taking of Blarney Castle."

"And what of your ancestral home, Kilbrittain Castle?" Morgan continued. "I don't know about that part of your history."

"Most of the planted English families that had taken over the lands of the Fitzgerald Clan after the Desmond Rebellion in 1598 fought on the side of the English Protestants. One example is Sir Richard Boyle, who was the first Earl of Cork at that time. He purchased Sir Walter Raleigh's Irish estates from him in 1603 while Walter was imprisoned in the Tower of London, including Lismore Castle east of Cork City," Tadgh explained.

"In 1642, one of Boyle's nephews named Lord Kinalmeaky led the English assault on Clan Chief Cormac MacCarthy Reagh at Kilbrittain Castle as I mentioned before. My Clan's lands fell to the English that day. The center of MacCarthy power then rested with Lord Muscry at Blarney. In 1643, Lord Muscry led a retaliatory attack on Boyle at Lismore, but he did not succeed in capturing the castle. It was, in fact, Richard Boyle's son Roger, Lord Broghill, a member of ruthless Oliver Cromwell's forces, who led the siege and capture of Blarney Castle in 1646."***

"So the Boyles and the McCarthys didn't get along, I take it." Morgan sat down against the wall, cross-legged, her back up against the stone.

"Mortal enemies."

"Tadgh, now it makes sense." She looked up at him.

"What? The losses in the Confederate War?"

"No, silly. What is the name of the RIC bastard that has been hunting down Aidan and yourself? What did you say his name was?"

"Boyle! Dammit that's right. Morgan, you're a genius."

"So they never give up trying to kill you McCarthys, do they?"

"If you're so smart, then why would they be doing this 270-odd years after the defeat of the McCarthys?"

"The McCarthy gold, maybe? That's got to be it."

"The swine. They killed my grandfather and my parents looking for it, then. They've got to be killed."

"Remember Mr. Pearse's warning to you to stand down and not jeopardize the cause until he calls on you again."

"Family honor, Morgan."

"Does it come before the Revolution, Tadgh?"

"Well no, but I will kill them before they kill us, lass."

Morgan dragged the conversation back to her original question. "What happened to the MacCarthaigh Reagh wealth?"

"Knowing what we now know from the Clan Pact letter, I think that there must have been a well-thought-out plan, created by Florence MacCarthaigh Reagh and Red Hugh O'Donnell back in 1600," Tadgh suggested.

"And Cormac then maybe moved his treasures over to Blarney when he was being attacked?" Morgan asked.

"Cormac would likely have done so if he had time to react before being overrun," Tadgh responded. "As you can see from these drawings on the wall, Blarney was considerably better fortified."

Morgan arose to take a closer look at the drawings. "But, certainly they must have implemented the plan for safeguarding at least the Muscry McCarthy fortune during the Broghill siege, right?" she asked

"I would think so," Tadgh agreed. "Can you see the caves below the battlements at Blarney on my map?" Tadgh said. He pointed to them.

"Yes, I see them. Badgers Caves?" Morgan examined the Blarney drawing more closely.

"And you said that it was never found, right?"

"Right."

"So, after all that, now it's our job to find that treasure," Morgan concluded.

"I love how you cut to the chase, my dear," Tadgh laughed, and gave her a hug for luck.

"That's enough of a history lesson for now, Tadgh," Morgan interjected. "I'm amazed I can remember all of it. Your history goes back for centuries and centuries. As far as I know, mine goes back a mere six weeks."

"Ah, but what a wonderful six weeks, *aroon*," Tadgh offered.

"To use your vernacular, to be sure," Morgan replied giving Tadgh a peck on his stubbly cheek. "Although I could have done without the near sinking of *The Republican, mavorneen*," she whispered, nibbling on his earlobe.

" 'Tis true and you were a brave lass out there when I needed you to be," Tadgh stated, grasping her by the shoulders and pinning her back against the brick wall. He could feel her starting to melt into him as he kissed her hard on the mouth.

"Whoa there, Casanova," Morgan exclaimed coming up for air. "Not in this closet space."

"Later then," Tadgh sighed and let her slip out from under him.

"Back to my original question. Where do we go from here?" Morgan asked, straightening her blouse and re-centering the conversation.

"On our side we only have my family bible," Tadgh answered. "On Peader's side, we only have *An Cathach*, as far as we know today."

"Where's your family bible? Let's have a look at it," Morgan asked.

Tadgh turned to his old roll top desk and extracted an ancient tome from its locked drawer.

Morgan noticed that it was a huge, dog-eared volume, leather bound and well used. The leather was badly in need of some oiling, she thought.

"Be careful with it," Tadgh cautioned. "It's pretty worn."

"I'll be careful, dear," Morgan said as she opened the front cover. "I see here where the faded lettering states it is a Douay-Rheims version, 1610."

"It's a collector's item, that one, to be sure," Tadgh agreed.

They spent an hour poring over the bible, looking at the family tree and the various scribbled marginal notes written against presumably profound passages that Tadgh's ancestors found either perplexing or inspirational, or both.

"I don't see anything in here that points us in the right direction," Morgan finally announced.

"That's what I had already concluded," Tadgh responded glumly.

"So that leaves us with *An Cathach,* which is safely stored, where, again?" Morgan asked.

"In the Royal Irish Academy on Dawson Street in Dublin. It's only a couple of blocks from the National Museum."

"Tell me that you're still thinking of a way to prevent us from breaking into another museum," Morgan exclaimed with mounting anxiety in her voice.

"I don't know yet. Hopefully we can find another way," Tadgh offered. "We need to avoid going back to Dublin for the time being. It's too risky."

"Surely there would have been two lockets, don't you think?" Morgan asked.

"You'd think so, Morgan, but maybe there was just one to lead us to the Clans Pact."

"That doesn't feel right for some reason, Tadgh. If there was another one it could easily be lost in antiquity."

"If that's true, then we're lost. It would have contained another essential cross-Clan clue. We'll have to wait until we can get with Peader again. Maybe he'll have some other O'Donnell information."

"That's not going to be until next year when he says he will finish school and head home to Donegal."

"That's all right, lass. I have a lot of work to do here at Creagh in preparation for our military offensive."

"Speaking of which," Morgan chimed in. "I've been thinking about that. Is there no other way to gain your freedom? Peader and Mr. Casey favor a legislative process with trade unions. Something inside of me tells me that we should be saving lives and not taking them no matter how evil our opponents. And besides, your leaders don't seem to be very military. How can you stand up to the well-equipped British army?"

"How can you still think that after what we've discussed about those bastards?" Tadgh exclaimed. With that he withdrew to the bedroom and opened the nightstand drawer. When he rejoined Morgan he was brandishing his Luger.

"*Si vis pacem, para bellum*—If you desire peace, prepare for war," he repeated over and over.

"Then prepare, if you must," Morgan said. "And I'll follow you into hell itself, if necessary. But don't you dare go getting yourself killed, Tadgh McCarthy," she implored him. "I want you around for the rest of my life, don't you know."

"It'll be a life that's free of the damned British," Tadgh assured her.

In his anger, Tadgh failed to notice the tear in Morgan's eye as she clung to his arm trying to get him to lower his gun.

Chapter Thirty-Four
Remembrance

Friday, August 6, 1915

*I*t had taken a month and a half to arrange for Governor Lippitt to come to Toronto. Kathy wanted to make sure that he was present for Claire's remembrance service at St. Aidan's Church. She had taken the lead in making calls to invite the guests. About forty people had agreed to attend. Sam coordinated with Canon Dixon and made the funeral arrangements while Liz started baking for the Wake. Collin's only task, and it was a painful one, was to choose the casket. He chose Sessile Oak, which is sturdy and native to Ireland.

Kathy had wired the School of Nursing, whose director had sent Claire's acceptance letter and a nurse's uniform. Governor Lippitt had collected signatures on a letter of thanks from many of the orphanage children, which he would bring to the Service. Collin had used the facilities at the Paper to have two enlarged photographs made from the small photo he had of Claire at age eleven. Just two days before the event, Collin and Kathy met at the Finlays' home to co-ordinate final arrangements. The dust had settled, and the plan went from chaos to order.

"I would like to put all these positive remembrances of Claire in the casket," Collin said. "Sam, one of these photographs of Claire should be put on one of your painting easels by the casket."

"That's a terrific idea." Sam and Kathy agreed whole-heartedly. It was good to see Collin engaging in the process.

Sunday afternoon, August 8th, was sunny and warm. That helped. At the appointed hour of two in the afternoon, the church filled with well-wishers. It was heartening to see the sun streaming through the first of Sam's west-facing stain glass windows, casting a rainbow of sparkling colors into the center aisle of the church. Collin thought *There's Claire now, right on time.* He went and stood where the colors were converging and felt warm and strangely at peace, for once.

"Kathy walked down the aisle and joined him, marveling at his composure.

"She's here with us. Right here where I'm standing. Can't you feel her?"

Kathy threw her arms around her man and whispered in his ear, "You have a heavenly glow around you, my love. Yes, I can feel her." Kathy looked around at the myriad of well-dressed attendees. "Where did all these people come from, dear? I've counted seventy or so."

"Many hail from the *Telegram*. Many more than I thought would come."

"The flower arrangements surrounding the casket, including a special draped Lily of the Valley bouquet, are beautiful aren't they?"

"I remembered that they were Claire's favorite back in Ireland— back when life was happy and grand. I hope that she can smell them."

"Are you going to be all right?" Collin asked, looking at Kathy anxiously. "You looked quite ill at the luncheon."

"Yes, dear, of course. It's just stomach indigestion. Maybe a few butterflies until this service is over."

An eleven-year-old Claire smiled down from her photograph.

Sam played the church organ, starting with "Amazing Grace."

After Canon Dixon gave a standard religious introduction, he asked for speakers from the congregation. There was a surprise orator. Governor Lippitt had brought Lucy to speak on behalf of the orphans. Kathy was delighted.

Lucy began, "I am here today, me, to represent the thirty prisoners from our orphanage. Claire was one of us, and she was our best friend. She nursed us when we were sick or injured, even if she was sick herself. She was our 'Florence Nightingale,' and we loved her. She gave us hope that someday we would be free, always she did. We are so sad to hear that she has died, but we know she was free, and doing what she wanted to do; the selfless vocation of nursing others." Then she went on, "And we would all like to thank Collin and Kathy for getting to Governor Lippitt so that he could set us free. We love you all and are forever in your debt. In a sense, Claire did help us escape. It is because her brother and his wife came looking for her, that most of us are back with our families today. What a legacy she has left us, and what an example for us to follow."

She doesn't know that we're not married, Collin thought. He could see the smile spread all across Kathy's face when Lucy said that, right there in the sanctity of the church. *I need to make Kathy truly happy.*

Then the Governor got up and spoke. "I didn't know Claire, although she worked in my woolen mill. She rose up above the oppression at the orphanage to be a leader of these children. And she is the only one who escaped the orphanage with a goal of trying to stop the tyranny. How many of us could say that we could have done what she did?" He went on, "Claire, her brother Collin, and now his partner Kathy, have opened my eyes wider to the presence of an evil in our society—that of misusing our youth in our new industrialized world. Because of Claire I am making changes in our company's business practices to reduce the workload and to increase the educational opportunities for our young workers. Thank you, Claire. And thank you, Kathy and Collin."

Finally, with tears in his eyes, Collin got up to speak. It was just one week after, and a world away from, Padraig Pearse's eulogy for O'Donovan Rossa. Collin first spent a moment kneeling at the casket and then he kissed his sister's photograph. His remarks were choked and brief. "I want to thank you all for coming to honor a person whom most of you have never met. It means a lot to my sister, myself, my Ma and to my betrothed. We were a close family until Claire was taken from us nine years ago. We had survived tough times in Ireland and in America. Claire was a wonderful and strong girl who knew her own mind. I am very proud of her. And now I can see that God chose her for this ordeal because he knew she would prevail to bring this wicked process of child slavery to an end at that orphanage. So, Claire, I can sense your presence here today. I love you and I will always love you."

Collin sat down and grasped his lover's hand while she gazed lovingly into his glistening eyes.

Kathy could see that all present were emotionally affected by the story of tragedy and triumph of that brave young woman.

Did he intend to use the term betrothed? She could feel her heart beating uncontrollably and her face was as hot as the dickens.

Kathy thought that Sam's choice of closing music was very appropriate, "Clair de Lune." She was a beacon of light in an otherwise dark world, mirroring the title.

The Governor, despite his age, insisted on being one of the pall bearers. Collin, Sam and three of the rowing buddies completed the honor guard. Collin was at Charles' shoulder to help minimize the load on his back.

The graveside service was solemn, and when the casket was being lowered, Collin made sure that the bouquet of Lily of the Valley was squarely resting on it. His final words were, "Rest in peace, my love."

As they walked back from the gravesite, Collin said to Kathy, "She is really here, eh."

"Yes, my dear, she is for sure," Kathy answered and smiled.

Along with all four Finlays, Collin and Kathy were the first to arrive back at the family abode. The girls had been seated on their laps, entertaining them and keeping them from talking to each other.

Liz and Kathy jumped out of the Lizzie to attend to the food for the wake. Before they could get to the kitchen, Collin grabbed his true love's hand and led her back into the living room. He dropped down on one knee and said, "Dearest Kathleen, you are the love of my life. You have shown me such love and support throughout my ordeal with my sister. I know now that we are meant to be together forever. Will you marry me, darlin?"

Kathy was flabbergasted. She had not expected this so soon, but she was ready with an all important question of her own. "Do you believe in yourself enough to be my soul-mate without reservation?"

"I finally see that we have done all that can be done to lay my past to rest, darlin. So yes."

"Then—yes, yes, I will marry you, my love," Kathy gushed, throwing her whole body behind the hug for her man, knocking him over on the carpet.

Their laughing and hugging brought in the two girls who thought this great fun. They jumped on top.

"Now there's a marvelous turn of events," Sam exclaimed, peering back from the kitchen.

"It's just as it should be," a smiling Liz replied.

The first guests were astonished to find the four of them laughing and rough-housing on the floor when they arrived.

"I would like you all to know how much I appreciate your support," Collin announced when all the guests had arrived and assembled. "And I want to especially thank Sam and Liz for being such good friends and mentors. And mostly, I want to thank the love of my life, Kathleen O'Sullivan, for her unwavering affection and support. It seems fitting that today, when one dear woman in my life has been laid to rest, that there should also be a beginning for me with the other most important woman in my life. A few minutes ago, I asked Kathy to be my wife and she has accepted. We are to be married."

Sam was the first to step forward and congratulate the two. "That's terrific, my boy," he exclaimed, grabbing Collin playfully in a headlock and ruffling his hair with his knuckles.

"I am so happy for you," Liz whispered in Kathy's ear during their embrace.

"Please be my Matron of Honor," Kathy whispered back.

"Of course," Liz replied. "Do you know when?"

"Not, yet, but soon," Kathy exclaimed, beaming with joy as she grabbed her fiancé's arm and held tight.

An Irish wake is something to behold. And Claire's was no exception. How Ten Balsam was able to accommodate that many people, no one knows. But it did. There was great *craic*, and someone insisted on playing the infernal Irish bagpipes most of the evening. Dot sang along to the beat of her own drummer while Norah headed for higher ground. Despite all the baking, Liz and Kathy had to scramble to ensure that all were fed. And Sam needed that proverbial pot at the end of the rainbow to pay the bill for all the liquor and beer that was consumed. But that didn't matter. Claire had a marvelous sendoff, and Collin was proud.

Doctor Gordon Stewart, the young community counselor and GP, and good friend of the Finlays, was Scottish but he loved a good wake as much as the next man. And he was here on a mission, a happy one, he hoped.

"Kathy, can I talk to you a minute?" he interjected, when there was a lull in the conversation.

"Does it need to be in private, Doc?"

"Yes, that would be best."

They retired to the front lawn outside among the roses.

"I am sorry to take you away from this auspicious event but I have some additional important news for you. You know the annual exam that I just gave you last week," the doctor started.

"Yes?" Kathy replied cautiously.

"Well, I'm happy to inform you that you are soon to be a mother."

"What? That's impossible." Kathy cried. *Wait. The marriage night. Father. Mother for that matter.* Her mind went into fear. *What will they think?*

"Well now, young lady. The test was conclusive."

"But I'm not even married yet! What am I going to do?" she moaned.

"It's not the end of the world, lass," Doctor Stewart replied calmly. "It's the beginning of the world for a new life, your child's life. It should be cause for celebration."

"You don't know my father, do you? Trust me. It's the end of my world. Oh, Doc, what am I going to do?"

"When the time comes, I can help you. There are places to go."

Just then a Western Union courier came riding down Balsam Avenue. He dropped his bike at their feet and strode up to the front door. Sam answered his knock, expecting the police to be complaining about disturbance of the peace. But he came back to the party with a small piece of paper in his hand.

"Collin, there's a telegram here for you," he said.

Above the din, Collin asked, "What does the *Toronto Evening Telegram* want of me tonight, of all nights, boss?"

"No, no," Sam corrected. "Not the Paper. It's a real telegram for you, marked Urgent."

Collin took the paper and he and a dazed Kathy, who had followed the courier in, went off into a corner to read it in private.

Suddenly, everyone from the party hushed up and looked at the couple. Collin was openly crying and Kathy, with tears in her eyes was in a state of shock It took a minute for both of them to collect themselves before addressing the group. Finally, through his tears, Collin announced, "This is an urgent telegram from the Cunard Steamship Company in New York. I'll read it to you.

Claire O'Donnell may have been spotted by Queenstown Manager Jack Jordan departing Cunard Recovery Center by motorcycle on July 23 - stop. Contact us immediately -stop. Anthony Fry, Operations Manager, Cunard Steamship Company, NYC, NY."

You could hear a pin drop. Everyone waited for Collin to speak. With his typical "glass-half-empty" mentality, he said, "This unlikely turn of events would be wonderful news if it were true. I'm gonna telephone Mr. Fry. Sam, can I use your telephone?"

"What? At this time of night, on a Sunday?" Kathy asked. This was all too much for her to bear.

"He said he was still working around the clock on the *Lusitania* affairs. I've got to try." Sam agreed and showed him into his art studio, where he had just installed a telephone. It took half an hour for the Bell operator to make the connection. There was an officer in charge at the Steamship office, who gave the operator Mr. Fry's home telephone number.

Finally, on a line full of static, Collin was put through to the Operations Manager.

"Oh, Mr. O'Donnell. Thank you for calling. I thought it best to contact you as soon as I was informed."

"Please tell me what you know, Mr. Fry."

"Let me start from the beginning. Mr. Jack Jordan was the third mate on the *Lusitania* when she was sunk. On the boat deck, he was in charge of trying to save as many passengers as possible during those terrifying and tragic 18 minutes. It was bedlam, and not many boats could be launched successfully. Jack saw a young woman on the port deck, all alone, and holding a basket with a baby in it. She was attempting triage to a passenger who had been crushed by a falling lifeboat. He thought her quite brave.

When he approached her and tried to direct her to the starboard side where the last of the boats were trying to be launched, she, at first insisted on continuing her work. She said her name was Claire and that she was waiting for someone named Byron. She was positive that he would save them both. Jack convinced her that the people on the port side could not be saved and got her to come to the starboard side by saying that he thought he had heard Byron calling for her there. Of course, he had not, but it was a good motivator.

Jack was amazed that someone would be that selfless in that horrible circumstance. He desperately wanted to make sure she and her baby were saved. He managed to get her baby into the last boat to be lowered, and she was in the process of getting in, when the bow rope broke and the lifeboat was sent hurtling vertically into the sea. Jack said that he could see her, holding on to the back transom, still on the outside when it struck another boat already in the water. After that, there was nothing more Jack could do for the passengers and crew, so he jumped overboard, just before the *Lusitania* went under.

One of the few lifeboats to survive the launching found Jack clinging to a piece of decking. His back was broken and he was almost frozen, but they managed to save him. Afterwards, the hospital in Queenstown brought him back, although, so far, he is paralyzed from the waist down. But Jack is a leader and a fighter, so we recently made him the Manager of the Recovery Center in Queenstown. It helps him cope with the tragedy.

A few days ago a woman came to the Recovery Center, accompanied by an unknown Irishman. She said that the Irishman with her had found her drifting on a piece of wreckage far out to sea. She had amnesia from a bump on the head. The officer said that when she arrived at the Recovery Center, she didn't look very well. She was seeking to find out her identity. Our officer on duty took her picture and said he would attempt to find out. But the photograph was spoiled. Then, as this young woman was leaving the Center on a motorcycle driven by the Irishman, Jack came out of his office and caught a glimpse of the two. He thought he recognized her as being the woman on the port deck, but he's not completely sure. It was just a fleeting image. He wasn't able to communicate with her and has no way to reach her since she didn't leave her contact information with our officer."

"But how do you know that this Claire would be my sister?"

"We put two and two together from the manifest. Although there were several Claires who were lost at sea, this young woman was the only one who said she was connected to a Byron."

"So, I don't want you to get your hopes up too high, but I thought you should know what we found out. We will continue to search the surrounding area for her, and we will keep you informed."

Collin thanked the man and urged him to keep looking. Then he returned to the party and told the group what he had found out. He presented it as a possibility, and Kathy chose to agree with him. The consensus of the inebriated crowd was that it sounded more like a probability, and the party immediately switched purpose from wake to a celebration. And, unbeknownst to all but Kathy and the doctor, there was another new life to celebrate.

The party got even rowdier. Collin got drunk, and Kathy fell asleep on the chesterfield.

Chapter Thirty-Five
Conundrum

Wednesday, August 11, 1915

After the revelations at the remembrance service, Collin and Kathy had a lot to discuss. The biggest albatross around Kathy's neck, and in her womb, she couldn't talk about, at least not with Collin.

"I want to go to Ireland immediately. I could go as a war correspondent," Collin pressed.

"They need war correspondents in France, not Ireland, dear."

Collin thought a minute and then said, "No matter, then, I'll go to Queenstown and conduct my own search."

"In Brooklyn you had a starting point. Here you have a fleeting potential sighting in a place you've never been. You could search for years and not find her. Better to let the authorities try with their resources."

"I'm going to contact this Jack Jordan myself."

"Just remember what you promised me at the party."

"That was before we knew that Claire is alive."

"May *possibly* be alive, you mean." Kathy had a bad feeling, and it wasn't just the butterflies in her stomach. How strange that Collin had gone from a glass-half-empty person to this glass-overflowing insanity. *I can't bear all this right now.*

After a day of anxious stewing, Kathy called her best friend on Friday afternoon when school got out. "Liz, I need to talk to you as soon as possible."

"About the wedding, I gather. How about having lunch at the *Georgian Room* at Eatons tomorrow? I can pick you up in the Lizzie. Since it's Saturday, the department store will be open until 5. Then we can look for a wedding dress."

Kathy felt a little bit better sitting in the grand and sumptuous Eaton's restaurant downtown. In the midst of the diners, embraced by the building's vaulted ceilings and ornate lighting, she felt like a lady, albeit a pregnant one with no engagement ring. No ring of any kind, actually.

"So let's talk about the wedding," Liz started, clasping her hands in delight, and then stopped herself, noticing that Kathy looked like Norah after she'd just stolen a cookie from the cookie jar. "What's wrong, honey?"

"Everything's wrong."

"How so? You've just accepted a proposal of marriage from the man you love. Now you can start that family you are always talking about with your very own schoolhouse of little O'Donnells."

"That just it," Kathy blurted out. "I've already started."

"Started what?"

"That little schoolhouse." She looked down at her abdomen, started crying, and Liz suddenly understood.

"Oh, dear. Did it happen on the trip?"

"I guess so. It was just once. I didn't think it *could* happen."

"It just takes once, dear. Does Collin know?"

"Heavens, no. And I'm not going to tell him, either."

"Why not? He's the father. Doesn't he deserve to know?"

"You're right."

"Did he take advantage of you, dear?"

"No, it was the other way around. Because of the trauma that we had been through together, you know. I remember thinking that we'd better live for the moment since we don't know if we'll be dead tomorrow."

"But what about your father and his beliefs?"

"I said to hell with him and what he stood for. Life's too short."

"So. Are you going to tell him—your father?"

"Definitely not."

"But you need to face him, dear. He has been so mean to you. We've talked about this before."

"He'll kill me."

"He would do nothing of the kind. You've got to face him for the sake of your future happiness with Collin and with your child."

"I won't contact, him and that's final," Kathy exclaimed, burying her head in her hands.

"Well, then. How about your mother?"

"She's got her hands full with father, and the shame of it could well exacerbate the situation. I'm lost," she wailed not looking up.

Liz decided to leave that subject for the time being. "Have you thought about the wedding timing, then?"

"There won't be any wedding," Kathy sobbed, pulling a hanky to daub her streaming eyes.

Liz put the her glass down. "But why?"

"I got pregnant. That's what's happened. Collin will find out and then he will blame himself, like always. He already wants to run away to Ireland to find Claire now that there's a chance that she is alive. That's already affecting his ego again. He'll probably think that I seduced him to trap him into marriage. I didn't. I didn't—" her words trailed off.

"Just remember. He asked you to marry him without knowing about the baby."

"But that was when he believed that Claire had died."

"I don't think that you are giving him enough credit, Kathleen. Hear me out, now. He has come a long way, mainly due to your love and support. And he knows that. He's the father of your child, and he'll do the right thing out of love, not just obligation. Mark my words."

"I know he loves me, but guilt is so strong within him. I am not sure anymore."

"Well, there's only one way to find out. It's better that you tell him now before he finds out on his own. Come on now. It's not the end of the world."

"That's what Doc Stewart said. He said he could help when the time comes."

"There, you see. Gordon is always right," Liz concluded offering Kathy her handkerchief. "Let's have lunch."

Liz thought that the chicken pot pie, a favorite at the *Georgian,* was having a positive effect."Have you thought about the timing, dear?"

"The timing to tell him?"

"No, the wedding, silly."

"I haven't been thinking about a wedding at all after all this mess."

"Well, as your reliable Matron of Honor, I think that we had better get down to brass tacks and set a date."

"You and Collin have a lot to be thankful for together. I was thinking about a Thanksgiving wedding. Let's see. It's August 14th and Thanksgiving Sunday is October 10th this year. That gives us almost two months. That should be enough time. And we can have your wedding shower on Labor Day weekend three weeks from now."

"How appropriate," Kathy moaned.

"What do you think about that schedule?"

"I don't know what to think right now."

"That's all right, dear. That's why I'm here. I'll help get the process started. You talk to Collin tonight, to be sure."

"We'll see."

"Maybe we should look for a dress another time," Liz suggested, patting Kathy's hand.

Kathy shot her friend a feeble smile.

Kathy had planned for a quiet supper at Collin's place on Lee Avenue adjacent to Kew Beach Park Saturday night. All the way back to the Beaches in the Lizzie, she agonized. Liz let her stew in silence.

When Liz dropped her off at Collin's apartment Kathy said to her, "I want to thank you for listening to me today. I love you dearly. I have decided to speak to Collin this weekend. If everyone could be as non-judgmental as you, I could face this. But they're not."

Leaning out the window, Liz replied, "Just try him, dear. I believe that you will be pleasantly surprised."

Collin met her at the door. "Did you have a good time downtown with Liz?"

"It was just grand," Kathy replied absentmindedly. "Girl talk, you know."

During supper of Collin's favorite Irish stew that she had prepared herself, Kathy asked, "How would you like to spend the afternoon with me at the Scarboro Beach Amusement Park tomorrow?"

"I thought that we were going to go to Sam's for lunch after church?"

"I'd like to be alone with you. Liz said that it would be fine."

"Can we go on the *Shoot the Chutes* ride?" Collin asked.

Liz thought about the queasiness she had been feeling—mostly in the morning.

"I guess that would be swell if we can go through the Tunnel of Love."

"I love that Tunnel of Love, all that closeness and darkness," Collin replied, admiring her sensuous figure.

Kathy was taken aback until she remembered that night in New York. "That's a switch then."

Throughout the Sunday service at St. Aidan's, Kathy prayed for deliverance. Two hours later, after two turns on the roller coaster, she was feeling sick. This was going to be another turning point in her life. Right here, today.

"You've been very quiet today, darlin'," Collin commented. "I appreciate your tolerance for my love of thrill rides, but you look a little green at the gills. So why don't we try that Tunnel of Love now?"

Unlike their earlier journey through the tunnel, it was now Kathy's turn to be reluctant and Collin's to be enthusiastic.

When they were inside in the dark Collin went for a kiss. Kathy recoiled at the touch. "Are you all right? You seem real jumpy and distant today."

It was now or never, she thought. "Collin, you know that I love you and would never do anything to hurt you, right?"

"Of course, darlin.' You don't have to ask that."

"I'm pregnant," she blurted out.

The kicking horse flashed out toward the boat. Kathy flinched backward and almost fell overboard. The red light illuminating the scene caught Collin's face in its glow. Kathy could see that he had a look of utter amazement. Or was it anger? Then they were back in the dark again.

"You're what?" he sputtered.

"I know that I told you it would be all right in New York. But I miscalculated. It was our real wedding night, wasn't it?" Her face fell. She put her face in her hands and sobbed.

"Are you sure? When did you find out?" Collin was numb.

"Very sure. I've known it, but I've been afraid to tell you," she cried. "During the wake last Sunday, after you proposed and before you got the telegram. Doc Stewart had examined me the week before. Look, Collin. I never intended for this to happen. I am as shocked as you are. Talk to me." She held her breath. Her future was on the line. The red devil leaped out of the darkness at them, cackling and fuming. She almost threw up, but held it down.

"Why don't we get married now?" he asked.

She said, "We can't get married yet—there's the banns to post, and meeting the pastor, and then there are my parents!" her eyes widened, as she broke down in tears again. Collin took her in his arms and caressed her back to reassure her. "No, no, darlin, we can do this."

"Just think, by this time next year we may have two Claires in our lives," he grinned.

Kathy marveled. In the midst of this dire situation, Collin was finally looking at the glass half full.

"Oh, darlin'. I think it's wonderful," Collin said, as he pulled her closer to him. "I love you so!"

Kathy melted into his arms sobbing for joy just as they emerged into the sunlight. Onlookers must have thought that there was something special happening down near that tunnel as Collin, oblivious to the world around him, showered his fiancée with kisses. "My God, I'm going to be a father!" his eyes shone brightly in the dappled light.

By the beginning of the last week of August, with no news from Ireland, Collin was melancholy.

"Why hasn't Mr. Fry gotten back to me with how to contact Jack Jordan?"

Kathy was saturated with the start of the fall semester, and the bridal shower was only a week away. Her mind was in a whirl. Without Liz she would be utterly lost. She needed Collin to focus on her now instead of fixating on his desire to leave for Ireland.

"Dear, you're swamped at the Paper. They're doing everything they can to find Claire.

If she survived, then we know she has at least one friend who is helping her. We have no idea where she might have gone. She could be in Toronto for all we know. And if she regains her memory, then she will likely contact Cunard and they know where to find us. If she didn't survive, then we have held a wonderful memorial service for her. I need your help, and we need to get on with our lives now."

Kathy grasped his hands and held them, like caging restless birds.

"Yes, right enough," Collin replied, but his tone was less than enthusiastic.

On Thursday, with the Sunday Labor Day shower just around the corner, Collin finally heard from Jack. He abandoned the Paper and rushed over to the Kingston Road School, pulling Kathy out of class mid-day to tell her on her lunch break.

"What's the matter dear? Why aren't you at work?"

"Claire's a fugitive. This telegram I got today from Mr. Fry says so." He brandished the piece of paper over his head and bunched his other fist into a ball.

"What does it say?" Kathy tried to be calm, but her insides were churning again.

Collin read it aloud, word for word. "*Note from Jack, Stop. Saw Claire again on a boat in the Bay. Stop. Called the Cork Police Head Constable Boyle. Stop. He said the woman on the motorcycle is a fugitive from justice. Stop. Her friend is a police murderer and a suspected German spy and terrorist. Stop. I don't believe it. Stop. I am still looking. Stop. Jack Jordan. Stop.*"

"I've got to save her—from herself," he cried. "Now."

"But what about our wedding?"

"We will have to postpone it unless I can find her first."

"No, I'm tired of playing second fiddle." Kathy exclaimed, grabbing her betrothed's collar in both hands and shaking him. "I am barely holding my life together as it is. A delay would be disastrous. There's no way that you alone can find her where the authorities have failed, even if it is her at all."

"I have to try," Collin insisted, breaking free of her grasp. "If you loved me, you'd realize that." His face looked pained.

"You're not being fair to me, *to us*. I will start to show, and if we don't get married by Thanksgiving, everyone will know. It will be disastrous."

Kathy's students could see through the window in the school-house door that she was getting upset. Three of the older boys decided she needed their support. Michael, the eldest, opened the door and asked, "Are you all right, Miss O'Sullivan?"

"Yes, boys. Go back to your seats. I will be there in a minute." She turned back to Collin, glaring, as the boys quietly closed the door. He was already in motion.

"I'm going to send Mr. Jordan a telegram to get passage on the next troop transport," Collin yelled over his shoulder as he started back down to the streetcar stop. "I'll call on you later."

Kathy barely made it through the shortened school day. *He is setting the wrong priority* kept cycling through her thoughts. The schoolchildren must have thought she had gone daft. When school let out, she rushed over to Ten Balsam in the hope that Liz would be there.

Liz met her at the door. "Here to talk about final preparations for the shower? Oh dear. That's not it, is it?"

Kathy broke down crying at the salutation from her best friend.

"Just a minute," Liz said, scooping up the girls and installing them in the double pram. "Let's take a stroll on the Boardwalk. It will help clear our minds."

As they walked past the Scarboro Beach Park, the leaves on the oak and maple trees were uncharacteristically starting to have a tinge of gold and crimson in the radiant afternoon sunshine of the mid-summer day.

"It's more nippy than usual for Labor Day, don't you think?"

"He's postponing the wedding," Kathy sobbed.

"What? Why?"

"He got a telegram today that says Claire has been seen again and that the police say she is a fugitive associating with a police murderer who is also a German spy. He's intent on going to Ireland right away on some troop ship. He won't take no for an answer."

"I see," Liz said, trying to absorb the situation.

"He's never going to be truly content until she's found safe and sound or dead, is he, Liz?"

"I'm just worried about what will happen if no one finds her, or if it turns out that it isn't her," Kathy lamented. "They've got his hopes up so high. And I can't wait for the fall."

"Most certainly not. I always say don't worry about a thing until you know there's something you can do about it."

"I feel so alone," Kathy moaned.

Dot started to cry.

"Sam and I are here for you, dear. Don't worry. It will be all right. Sam will help you come up with a solution. He always does."

"All this is piling up on me. I just got up the courage to tell my father. Collin came with me and tried to ask for my hand in marriage."

"That was brave. How did it go?'

"He's disowned me and threw both of us out of his house."

"Surely not."

"Oh yes. I am the disgrace of the O'Sullivan Clan."

"What a callous, pompous ass," Liz hissed. "Let me talk sense into him, the idiot."

"It won't do any good."

"So he won't be walking you down the aisle, I take it?" Liz asked to steer the conversation away from Collin for the moment. "Not unless hell freezes over."

Liz could see that Kathy was crestfallen, tears flowing down her cheeks. "How about your mother, then?"

"Mom and I don't see eye to eye, either, since she won't stand up to him. I told her that just before Father had his blow up. He's ruined her life as well as mine."

"But you haven't *let* him ruin your life, have you, dear?"

"Well, no. Collin has seen to that."

"Correction. You took care of it that day when we met you at Scarboro Park."

"I guess so. . ."

"Would your mother come to the wedding?"

"He won't let her come, I'm sure."

"To see her only daughter wed? That's terrible."

"For her and me both."

"Sam told me that if your father was going to be obstinate, then it would be a great honor if you would ask Sam to walk you down the aisle and give you away."

"Would he, really?" Kathy exclaimed, her tears abating. "I would love that. I'll ask him tomorrow." Liz thought she saw a slight smile curl up at the corner of her friend's mouth.

Changing the subject for a second time, Liz said, "It's going to be a boy for me, this time. I know it." She patted her abdomen.

"Both of us in the family way? Doesn't that man of yours ever leave you alone? You're a veritable baby-making machine."

Liz smiled and said, "If it is a boy, we're going to name him Ernest." With that, Dot, as bubbly as ever, voiced her opinion from the pram, squealing. The women took it as an affirmative. "Listen, Kathy, Sam and I have discussed it and we want to have your wedding reception at our house," Liz offered, taking a positive attitude. "And we won't take no for an answer."

"Well, since you put it that way, we accept. Correction—I accept, for both of us, Kathy responded. "Or, at least I accept if there is still anything to accept for." She threw her arms around her best friend and started to cry again.

"It's going to be a joyous and glorious event," Liz assured her. "And you have that radiant glow, if you know what I mean. Two blessed events in your life. Are you having any morning sickness these days?"

"Feeling somewhat queasy, but saltine crackers do the trick."

"Are you hoping for a boy or a girl?"

"Oh, a girl, a girl," Kathy cried, picking up Dot and dancing her around the pram. "And she's going to be called Claire,'" she added. Norah reached up to join the party and Kathy pulled her up into her arms as well.

Liz saw what a rejuvenating force her daughters could be. Having turned the conversation to a more positive note, Liz ventured, "As matron of honor, I think it is high time you chose the final design of your bridal gown. What are your thoughts?"

Before she could respond, Dot piped up with her suggestions.

"I'm not sure that 'grbl okin' is such a good color for Kathy's dress, dear," her mother laughed as she looked down into the pram. It was a good thing that she did, for at that moment Norah was hanging way out over the side trying to touch the spokes of the wheel as they spun by.

"Norah, sit down!" Liz exclaimed in a chastising voice, and Norah reluctantly flopped back down into the carriage with a scowl.

"Gracious, girl, you could lose a hand doing that, or fall out on your head, don't ya know." But then she leaned down and gave her daughter a hug and kiss.

"Mommy loves you and doesn't want to see you get hurt, Norah," she cooed. Norah's smile returned. "What color do you think Aunt Kathy's wedding dress should be, Norah?" Liz asked to bring her daughter into the conversation.

"Pink, Mommy," she immediately answered.

Both women laughed. "Ladies always wear white dresses when they get married, dear," Liz instructed.

"But pink is my favorite color."

Kathy jumped in. "I want you to be my flower girl, Norah. How about if you get to wear a pink dress and we'll have all the bridesmaids' dresses in pink like yours?"

"Can I, Mommy, please?" Norah's eyes were wide with wonder and glee.

"Yes, of course, dear," her mom agreed. "Do you know what a flower girl does in the wedding?"

"No. What?"

"She gets to carry a basketful of pink rose petals and throws them down on the floor as she walks down the aisle of the church before the bride comes down," Kathy explained. "It's a very important job. Do you think you can do it for me and Uncle Collin?"

"Yes, yes please, I want to do that!" came the immediate response.

Liz turned to Kathy and gave her a big smile, thinking to herself, she's not only a good teacher, but she is going to make a great mother.

They walked and talked of dresses and flowers and cakes and receptions and music and all the things wonderful about the final wedding planning. And their mood shifted to match the splendor of the summer day. But when Liz dropped Kathy off at her walk-up flat on Leuty Avenue just up from the lake, her friend's face had clouded over.

She reiterated, "Don't worry, dear. Sam will help you find a solution for Collin." But she knew from her best friend's saddened demeanor that she would be agonizing until Collin switched his priorities, if indeed he would.

"What's all this?" Kathy exclaimed when she opened the front door and tripped on several boxes blocking her way.

Liz, who was just starting to push the pram back south towards the boardwalk, yelled after her, "Are you all right?"

Kathy reappeared at the doorway. "Someone's been here and left a lot of boxes."

At that moment Liz could see an older woman appearing behind Kathy. They were the spitting image of each other save for the 20 years between them.

Liz twirled her finger in the air and Kathy turned around.

"Mother! What are you doing here? Are these your boxes?"

"You were right from the first, Kathleen. Your father is selfish and egotistical. I've left the old buzzard. Can you put me up for the time being?"

"Oh, Mother," Kathy sobbed, pulling her mother to her in an embrace. It was all just too much. Fiona's tears mixed with her daughter's.

"Your Collin seems like a fine young man and your father had no right to talk to him that way. I can't live with him anymore."

"Of course you can stay here, Mother, for as long as you like. I have a spare bedroom."

"Thank you, Kat. I won't be a bother, not for long at least."

Kathy hadn't been called that since she was ten.

"Let him stew in that big old mausoleum of his. See how he likes it. Speaking of stew, he doesn't even know how to boil water," Fiona grinned. "Let's see how he fares without me."

"Does he know you're here?"

"No. I just walked out after telling him off."

Kathy's eyes were glistening with pride. She never thought her mother had the nerve to stand up to him.

Liz left the pram briefly at the bottom of the steps and ascended to the women.

"Mother, this is Liz, my best friend and matron of honor."

Liz embraced the woman warmly. "Fiona is it? Could you help me plan your daughter's wedding? I need your help. And the shower's this weekend."

Kathy knew that she really needed no help. What a thoughtful gesture to engage Mother and make her feel welcome and needed. Liz acknowledged Kathy's radiant smile.

Fiona seemed overwhelmed with it all, but she nodded her assent. Liz thought she saw a momentary flash of excitement behind those otherwise sad brown eyes.

"I'll make tea," Kathy offered. "That'll perk us up."

"I've my kids to tend to," Liz said, disengaging and starting down the stairs. "I'll talk to you both tomorrow and we'll get organized."

Mother and daughter went in and closed the door. They had a

lot to talk about.

Just after Liz arrived home with the girls, the storm hit. One of those doozies sweeping east out of the blue off Georgian Bay. By six that evening, the rain was torrential and lightning crackled all around. "Who'd have thought this would happen?" Liz said as she comforted her daughters who had started crying out of fear of the noisy thunder hammering overhead. "It was so nice an hour ago." Thinking of Kathy's predicament, she hoped that this wasn't Mother Nature's harbinger of what was to come.

Chapter Thirty-Six
O'Donnell Wedding

Thursday, September 2, 1915
10 Balsam Avenue, Beaches, Toronto

*S*am loved his new teaching job, but the three-mile trip to and from Riverdale High was wearing him down. He had taken the Lizzie to work that glorious morning, but he had left the car at the school in the storm. It had a tendency to short out when wet. So the streetcar was his only mode of transportation. The Toronto Railway Company operated the Kingston Road Line, which got him to and from the school, but he had to walk about a half mile at each end from the stations. And since the Beaches district was still considered a cottage community, electrified streetcar service could break down during severe weather events. Collin had it a little easier, since the relatively new main Queen Street line passed very close to his house in the Beaches and took him right downtown to where the *Toronto Evening Telegram* building was located.

Sam arrived home exhausted by dark, having trudged the last half mile in the downpour.

"Hello, my darlings," he announced, trying to be as exuberant as ever. "What's for dinner?"

"*Coq au vin*, dearest," Liz yelled from the kitchen. "Did you hear the news?"

Sam thought that his wife's tone sounded alarming.

"What news is that?"

"The wedding's only five weeks away and Collin's just now postponed it," she exclaimed as she popped her head into the living room, spatula in hand. "What are we going to do?"

Sam didn't have the emotional energy to deal with that

509

dilemma before dinner.

"Do we know why?" he asked as he slumped down into his easy chair by the door to take off soaked oxfords. He could see the concern in her face.

"Are you heeding Doctor Stewart's advice to take it easy in bad weather, dear?"

"My heart is in my work come rain or come shine," Sam replied. "Unless the good doctor can invent some new mode of door-to-door transportation in a monsoon, you and the girls will have to rejuvenate my ticker with your love on flood days."

"Don't ya know that this is not a laughing matter, Samuel."

Quickly changing the subject he reiterated, "Do we know why?"

"Why what?" Liz asked, still preoccupied with his physical condition

"Why Collin postponed the wedding."

"Kathy said that he got another telegram from Jack, the Cunard Manager, yesterday. Our dear boy got excited and said that he has to go to Ireland immediately. The wedding would have to wait."

"What did the telegram say?"

"I don't know. But with the wedding all planned, Kathy put her foot down and said no. It's all off. She told me that they had a big blowup and Collin stormed out."

"That sounds serious, all right. "Let's eat, and then I'll try to talk to him."

The house was decorated for the Bridal Shower already. Liz, with some help from Norah, and encouragement from Dot, had created a very festive ambiance. There were colored balloons everywhere, and flickering lights from the candles on the fireplace mantel danced on the handmade banner draped there. The girls had helped their Mommy with the words *Congratulations Collie and Caffie*, although Dot's contribution was an outside-the-lines scribble in bright orange. The dining room table was festooned with paper Valentine lanterns, red with white hearts.

"Did you help Mommy with all these wonderful decorations today?" Sam asked the girls at dinner.

Norah proudly produced a paper heart which she had cut out by herself and gushed, "Yes, Daddy. Look what I made for you."

Always the artist, Sam looked at the lopsided humps and said, "This is lovely, Norah. See how these wings look like they are flapping?"

Liz noticed her husband's loving and encouraging remarks, and how Norah responded so delightfully by throwing her arms around her Daddy.

Not to be left out, Dot hurled a pearl onion off her spoon in the general direction of her Dad. He caught it mid-flight and popped it into his mouth, saying, "Great throw, Dot." Dot started giggling and wouldn't stop until Liz admonished her for playing with her food and Sam for encouraging her.

"Really, you two. Food's for eating, you know. We're not playing baseball."

"You're a marvelous cook, my dear," Sam offered. "Thank you for a scrumptious dinner."

After dinner was over, Sam felt better. Spending some time with his three girls was indeed his elixir of health.

Collin went underground and even Sam had trouble reaching him that evening. Finally, on Saturday morning he surfaced.

"What's going on, Collin, my boy?" Sam asked nonchalantly. He listened while Collin told him the story that he had already heard from Liz. They matched except that Collin had now established a direct telegraph contact with the Cunard manager in Ireland. He was working on trying to get Collin on their troop transport ship, the *HMS Olympic*, which they called *Old Reliable* because it had run the gauntlet successfully so many times. It was clear that Collin had no intention of honoring the wedding date he and Kathy had planned for. This was indeed a serious setback.

"How about going fishing tomorrow while the girls have their bridal shower?" Sam suggested. "We can talk then." He needed the night to formulate his strategy.

"Are you sure they are still having it? I thought Kathy would call it all off."

"Yes, of course it's still on, my boy. Be at the boathouse at ten. I'll meet you there."

"Are there any fish left in this lake?" Collin asked, as he rowed Sam's dingy, trolling under the Scarborough Bluffs near the mouth of Highland Creek the following morning.

"You know that this is my favorite fishing spot," Sam whispered. "It is a little late in the season, I'll grant you. The water's getting colder and the steelhead trout are heading deeper. But the Chinook salmon are still running to spawn in the creek."

Sam was using a northern king spoon with a downrigger, Collin noticed.

"How's work going at the Paper?" Sam asked.

"Hectic. There's new technology that we're tryin' out to get higher speed images. The fixing process isn't workin' just yet," Collin started to explain. He knew that Sam would be keen to hear about all the new techniques for improving art, whether paint, sculpture or photography.

Sam waited for his protégé to broach the main subject. He didn't. After a few minutes discussing the new Kodak processes, he steered to a different topic. At this point he was rowing and Collin was trolling.

"How's all your family plans affecting Kathy's parents, my boy? If you don't mind my asking."

"Her Pa's a devil. He's disowned her and won't be coming to the wedding."

"I thought as much. Do you think that there can ever be a

reconciliation between them?"

"I don't think so," Collin sighed, head down. "And it's all my fault, you know."

"Nonsense, my boy. It takes two to tango, as they say."

"Yes, but I'm supposed to be the responsible one. I've gone and made a mess of things."

"You told me that you asked her and you were told it was a safe time of the month."

"It was still my responsibility."

"Don't try to load this onto your other misguided burden, Collin. Speaking of which, I know that you need to find Claire if she is really still alive. But you're going to lose the love of your life if you continue to obsess and put Claire ahead of Kathy. Is that what you want?"

"I've got to get over there. I'm trying to get on the next troop transport ship. It leaves Montreal next Friday."

"Hold your horses. Let's review what we know. What are the facts?"

"Claire's a fugitive."

"Not as I understand it," Sam corrected, forcing Collin to look at him. "Here's what I have heard. First, Claire was on the *Lusitania*. Second, Jack Jordan was the bosun, third mate responsible for getting the lifeboats launched. Third, he helped Claire whose boat came apart when it hit another boat already in the water. Fourth, Jack survived but is paralyzed, and he is the Manager of the Cunard Office in Queenstown. Fifth, the police were notified to look for Claire. Those are the only facts we know."

"But what about Jack seeing Claire on the motorcycle?"

"Speculation, not fact, my boy. Jack thinks he saw her but he only really saw a girl's hair from the back, at a distance. And the police may be after the girl on the motorcycle, but it is not confirmed that this was Claire. Furthermore, the 'Florence Nightingale' who was described by that delightful Lucy from the orphanage doesn't sound to me to be someone who would be running around with a German spy and terrorist, does she?"

"I see your point. But what if it is Claire, eh?"

"What if it isn't?" Sam countered. "Are you willing to risk losing your true love, your baby, and your good job here, on the chance that an employee from the *Lusitania* who was severely traumatized may have seen her or someone else, at a distance?"

"But what if it is her?"

"Do you love Kathy?" Sam changed his approach.

"Yes, of course I do."

"How would you feel if she told you, for some reason, that she wanted to postpone, and maybe cancel your wedding?"

"I guess I'd be right fuming."

"Do you want to marry her?"

"Yes, yes I do."

"I rest my case," Sam concluded, resting on his oars.

"But . . ."

"But nothing, my boy. If it were me, I'd marry her *tout de suite* and wait for more information from Ireland before traipsing off in search of a shadow."

"But I've got to find her."

"You're not listening to me. This situation with Kathy is serious, lad."

After a prolonged silence, Sam stated, "I agree with Kathy, Collin. You've got responsibilities and a new family life starting next month here. You've got to put them first in my opinion, don't ya know, or you're going to lose them and leave Kathy in an awful predicament."

"I know you're right, but I can't let go of my responsibilities to my birth family, either."

"Give it some more time, my boy. Then if she is not found, maybe you and Kathy can take a trip to Ireland during summer break next year."

"The trail will have gone cold by then," Collin argued.

"But you found the trail in New York after nine years. Postpone your trip, my boy."

"If I had only gone to New York just a few months earlier. . ."

Before he could finish his sentence, there was a tug on the line and the rod in his hands almost sailed overboard.

"Yeow," Collin yelped as the spinning out line burnt a groove into his finger.

"Lock the reel, boy," Sam yelled as he stopped rowing and picked up the net.

Collin jammed the reel lock and held on.

"Look at that rod bend!" Sam cried as the fish tried to dive under the boat.

"It must be a big one!" Collin grunted as he struggled for his balance against the gunnels. "How many pound test is this line?"

"Fifty, I think, but it's old. Not sure what it will hold."

"Get that net ready then," Collin shouted, as he struggled with the rod.

The boat started to spin around as the fish tried to use to boat keel to break the line. Collin deftly jumped to the other side of the dingy while swishing the tip of the rod around the bow.

"Give him some slack and then jerk him back."

Collin flicked off the reel lock and the line spun out once more.

"Now," Sam yelled and Collin locked the reel and jerked back as hard as he could.

They watched as the line went slack, springing the rod straight.

"I think I lost him," Collin moaned.

"Just wait and hold on," Sam coached him.

Then they saw the wily fish heading back towards the boat and picking up speed. Suddenly the line went taut and almost pulled Collin overboard.

"He's on the other side of the boat again," Collin yelled as he tried to bring the rod back around the bow. "He's a monster!"

515

"Now it's time to start reeling him in, me boyo."

Slowly and painfully Collin ratcheted in the line. The boat was being dragged slowly in the direction of the fish.

"I think he's tiring, eh." Collin finally exclaimed. "I know I am."

After thirty minutes of reeling in the line, the monster was brought along side of the boat. They both seemed spent.

"Look. He's blue-green and purple on his back and looks silvery on his sides," Collin noted. "Is he a salmon?"

"That's a very big Chinook, my boy," Sam shouted gleefully. "We'd better not lose him after all this work."

"Is that net big enough to hold him?" Collin asked, straining on the line.

"I don't think so," Sam guessed. "He's got to be at least thirty inches and forty pounds."

"I suggest we beach him, eh."

Sam dropped the net into the boat and started rowing for shore. He guessed that they were a hundred yards away.

As soon as he started to row to shore, the Chinook tried to hightail it back out into the lake. "Clearly he was only playing possum while he gathered his second wind."

"Row faster," Collin yelled as he tried to hold the rod from going overboard, his arms and back aching from the fight. This was the last ditch effort by the salmon, he suspected. Collin held the reel locked, but then he noticed the line starting to fray at the rod's outboard eyelet.

As soon as the bow touched the shore, Collin leaped out onto the beach and simultaneously yanked the rod and fish shoreward. The line snapped with a great twang which caught him across the side of his face. But the fish was airborne and landed with a thump on the beach about a foot from the water.

Collin was momentarily dazed, but Sam sprang into action. The fish was slithering and its head was now entering the water.

Whap! Sam's oar caught it squarely on the head and the battle was over.

"What a team effort," Sam shouted with glee as he held the monster from floating away.

Collin was sporting a red bloodline from his jaw to his cheekbone. "Did we do it, eh?" he asked tentatively.

"Great job, my boy. We'll have a fish feast for Labor Day dinner tomorrow."

Suddenly, Sam clutched his chest and plopped down on the shore next to the fish with a pained look on his face.

"You all right, boss?" Collin sounded anxious.

"Just a stitch in my chest. Had it before." Sam's words came in halted gulps as he tried to ride out the pain.

A minute later "There. See? It's gone now. Just something I ate."

"That didn't look like just something you ate. Didn't the doctors tell you . . . ?"

"Some doctors are quacks you know. It's the food, I tell you."

"Now who isn't facing reality? I'm going to mention this to Liz."

"Don't you dare, my boy. Don't you dare."

"Promise me then that you will talk to Doc Stewart about what just happened."

"Fine. I promise."

Collin insisted on rowing all the way back.

"I'm not sure that I will be coming tomorrow," he said as they approached the boathouse.

"Nonsense, my boy. You are the hero of this fish story."

They rowed up on to the concrete ramp of the Balmy Beach Canoe Club chests out, victoriously displaying their forty-five pound trophy. It turned out to be the second biggest salmon ever caught by members of the Club.

Collin and Kathy both showed up separately, the latter with her mother, Fiona, for the salmon dinner the next day. There was a chill in the air. Collin was shocked to see Kathy's Ma. It put him off-guard. Sam took an immediate liking to the lady and went out of his way to make her comfortable in his favorite seat in the parlor.

The talk at dinner was superficial, skirting the issue.

"All right, Liz. That's enough talk about the glorious shower," Sam requested after he had heard the story four times. Kathy looked less than pleased despite the success of the day before.

Even the salmon story seemed to fall on deaf ears. Some of the balloons were still hanging around in a semi-deflated state. This was not going well, Sam concluded. Clearly Collin had not yet taken his advice and there had been no reconciliation. Even Dot picked up on the frigid atmosphere, motor-boating "brrr" with her lips while applesauce dribbled down her chin. No, this was not going well at all.

It was now September 6th with the wedding planned to be less than five weeks away. If it was still on, that is. Sam could see that Kathy was waiting for him to come up with a win-win suggestion. All the girls seemed to be ganging up on him in their anticipation of him saving the day. But he was, uncharacteristically, coming up empty. Collin looked like he was about to get up and leave.

Sam could see that he was not getting through to the lad. He hated to have to use his trump card.

"You know, in many ways you are just like my younger brother Liam," Sam stated.

"Younger brother, boss?" Collin asked. "I've never heard you talk of him before. Is he still in Ireland?"

"In a matter of speaking, yes."

"Maybe I can look him up when I get there."

"I don't think so, my boy, unless you throw your life away completely like he did."

"What do you mean?"

"He's dead, Collin. He had everything to live for and he threw it all away."

"I'm sorry for all that. How did it happen?"

"Street brawl, the hothead. Knife to the heart. He mistakenly thought he was defending our family's honor."

"Shite. A terrible way to go. I saw some things in Brooklyn . . ."

"I should have been there," Sam agonized, turning it all over in his mind and heart once more.

"What? You too?"

"Yes. I was selfishly away at school. And afterwards I thought that I could make amends by staying with my Ma. But I couldn't. She died of a broken heart. I thought that all of it was my fault."

"I can relate to that."

"That's why I'm telling you this."

"What do you mean?"

"If Liz hadn't convinced me to come to Canada, I'd still be in Lisburn pining away, wasting my life over something I couldn't change in a million years. It took the love of a good woman . . ." Sam grinned, glancing at his wife.

"Liz, is a good woman. And Norah and Dot are priceless," Collin added, reaching over and enfolding the two daughters in a big bear hug. You are a lucky man, boss."

"Precisely my point, brother."

Suddenly Collin realized why Sam was calling him brother. "God, Sam, we're two peas . . . ."

". . . in a pod," Sam finished the sentence. "I think that you have as much chance of finding Claire by going to Ireland now as I did of trying to keep my mother alive."

"But there must be something I can do."

Kathy and Liz looked helplessly at Sam who was uncharacteristically at a loss for words.

"Here you go, Daddy." Norah broke the prolonged and

pregnant pause in the conversation, breaking free of Collin's grasp and handing her Daddy the Sunday funnies section of the *Telegram*. "You didn't read us the funnies yet."

Sam reflected on how astute his three-year-old daughter was about people's moods. Amazing. She was just trying to break the ice in the living room. Then Sam smiled. He picked her up and gave her a big kiss on the top of her head, exclaiming, "Out of the mouths of babes."

Not to be outdone, Dot ran to her daddy to get a similar osculation.

"What is?" Kathy asked, grasping at straws.

"I should have thought of this sooner. It took Norah to show us the way, bless her heart."

Norah looked pleased as punch, but no one had an idea what Sam was thinking.

"Look," he started. "At the risk of restating the obvious, you two lovebirds are lovesick. Collin, you love Kathy but you also love Claire and you are torn between the two. Kathy, you love Collin but you also love your unborn child and you want to get married quickly. It seems to me that you both have the wonderful opportunity to start your life together here in Toronto with your wedding on Thanksgiving. But it is understandable that Collin would be compelled to help find Claire if at all possible. We don't really know if she is really alive in Ireland. The Cunard officer may certainly be mistaken as to the identity of the woman that he saw from a distance. We hope not. Going to Ireland in the middle of the War to help in the search would completely disrupt your plans for your life together here and would, in my opinion, have very little chance for success. So, what could you do from here to help without destroying your life's priority at home?"

"What?" Collin asked, starting to take an interest.

"How about putting a missing persons notice in the local Cork/Queenstown newspapers saying that we know who the young woman is who went to the Cunard office and giving your contact information," he offered.

"That sounds like a fine idea," Liz exclaimed. "If she sees that, she will likely get in touch, I would think."

"Wouldn't Mr. Jordan have already thought of that?" Kathy questioned.

"I don't think so," Collin replied. "He has been relying on the police and their missing persons search. Jack said she has amnesia."

"Put that in the notice. There can't be two of them from the *Lusitania* running around over there."

"You know, Sam, that might just work. It's worth a try."

Sam was pleased. This gave Collin a positive initiative to personally try to find his sister while still fulfilling his timely commitments to his future wife and unborn child. Kathy was starting to smile for the first time in days.

"Collin, that could be your labor of love for Claire," Sam concluded. "And after your child is born, and if Claire has not been found, you both could go to Ireland together during the summer break to try to find her. Liz and I would be happy to care for your child, wouldn't we, my dear?"

"Absolutely, my love," Liz exclaimed. "The more the merrier."

"Liz, you or my mother are the only people I could entrust my new child with and you may be nursing again by then, anyway."

"I know dear, don't worry."

"What do you think, Collin?" Kathy asked. Her future depended on his answer.

"I think that this is a grand idea. I will contact Cunard and ask them to do this immediately."

"What about the transport ship?" Kathy asked, anxiously.

"I'll tell them that I am postponing my trip until we see what happens with this," Collin agreed.

Kathy looked at Sam to say thank you with her eyes and the girls pushed the funny papers in front of their Daddy. Then Kathy went over and sat beside Collin on the chesterfield.

"So I take it that the wedding is back on for Thanksgiving?" Liz stated, giving her man a big smooch on the cheek.

"Yes," the two lovebirds replied in unison.

"No longer lovesick, then?"

"Nope," they both confirmed.

"Daddy, Daddy. Teddy Tail please." Norah pleaded.

They all listened, spellbound, as Sam narrated. "The cartoon mouse chased the cat up a tree."

With the help of Mr. Jordan, Collin placed an advertisement in the Cork *Southern Star* newspaper the next day. He was enthused with the idea.

The next five weeks sped by, a whirlwind of wedding planning and preparations. Even Fiona got into the spirit, insisting on taking care of the flowers for the church. Kathy was concerned for her mother's health. There was no reconciliation with her father, and as far as Kathy knew no communication whatsoever with him. Her mother seemed so lost. Certainly not a confidant for her only daughter, as Kathy explained to Liz on more than one occasion.

The fact that there was no positive word from Ireland escaped the attention of all concerned except Collin. And he was up to his neck in alligators at the Paper.

Then, on Thanksgiving Sunday the big day arrived. The sunshine lit up the multi-hued leaves of the fall foliage, making Sam wish he could be out in the crisp autumn air painting glorious landscapes.

On the center aisle at the back of St. Aidan's Church, Norah was scared. Of course, she loved her pink dress. The ruffles on her neck and wrists were pretty, but they itched. And the pink ribbons in her hair matched the belt and sash around her waist. She also saw that the color of the rose petals in her basket and the flowers on the ends of the church benches were the same as her outfit. It was all made to match *her.*

She had been quite fidgety while her Mom curled her hair in ringlets that morning, but that was nothing compared to the butterflies that were now fluttering around in her tummy.

The church was full of dressed-up people she didn't know. Norah could see them all looking at her as she waited until she was told to walk. She glanced around and saw the three bridesmaids lined up behind her, waiting for her to do her job. All of a sudden doing this thing seemed to be a huge mistake.

Norah looked frantically behind her for her Mommy, but then she remembered that she was around the corner making sure that Auntie Caffie's hat was on straight. The music started to play and she knew it was time for her to start walking slowly down the aisle between all the staring people. *I want to run away*, she thought. She couldn't make her legs move.

The first song was ending and still she was stuck to her spot. Finally she spied Unca Collie up at the front of church with some other men. They were all dressed like the penguins she had seen in her animal book. He was waving at her and motioning her to come down and join him. She loved his smile, that smile that he had when he saw her after they came back from their long trip. She wanted to be beside him. She focused on his smile and pretty soon she forgot all the people and just started walking towards him.

She wanted to run, but somehow she forced herself to walk slowly, just like they had practiced. At first she forgot to throw the petals down in front of her, until one of the guests on the aisle reminded her to do so. After that she just put one foot forward after the other until she was hugging her Unca at the front of the church.

She turned to see the bridesmaids and then her Mommy walk down the aisle until they were standing in a row on the side away from the men. She thought that Unca Collie looked like a handsome prince in his dark gray suit. A prince of penguins that is.

Then she saw Auntie Caffie appear at the back entrance. She was really, really beautiful, Norah thought, all dressed in white, with ruffles and a sash just like her pink ones. They were all dressed to match her. How wonderful. And how wonderful that her job was over and all the guests were now focused on her auntie and not her any more. Norah thought how Auntie Caffie must be scared, too, in front of all those people looking at her.

But there was Daddy holding her arm. He would make it all right. She wished that her Daddy had been there to hold her hand and walk her down the aisle.

At that very instant Kathy was petrified. Everyone was looking back at her. *They can see the swelling beneath my dress.* She realized that emotion had overtaken logic. There were so many folds of material that the congregation wouldn't have known the truth. That thought made her smile.

"Are you ready, my dear?" Sam asked quietly, patting the back of the hand he was holding. "You look amazing, you know, lass."

"My veil seems crooked."

"Nonsense, it's just at a jaunty angle, well within proper decorum,I can assure you. Ready now?"

"Mmmmm."

Sam nodded to the organist who started playing the wedding march.

Before they could take a step, the rear door of the church flew open and a very distinguished man in appropriate formal attire entered and stepped forward. The music stopped and Kathy turned, annoyed that someone had come in late. Then she saw who it was.

"Father! What are you doing here?"

"To ask forgiveness of his only beautiful daughter."

"Really? What's the catch?" *Why do I have to bear this cross on my wedding day?"*

Sam put up his hand and the organist switched to a standard religious hymn.

Then he took a step back around the corner pulling Kathy with him. She wasn't expecting it and almost tripped over her train. Then Sam motioned for Mr. O'Sullivan to follow suit. Now they were outside visual sight and muted from the attendees.

"You and your Mother have made me see . . ."

"That you need women slaves to do your bidding?"

Collin saw what had transpired at the back of the church and realized it was a big problem. After a private word with Reverend Dixon, the groom turned to face the congregation.

"Ladies and Gentlemen, we are so happy that you have come to share our wedding with us. And this is the appointed hour. But we have a small technical delay, so if you will bear with us for a few minutes we will get this wedding underway."

By this time the Reverend had left through the door leading to his office. Without waiting for any response from the friends present, Collin stepped down and took Fiona O'Sullivan's hand.

"Could you come with me, please?"

She had not seen the brief altercation that had occurred at the back of the church. But she did not resist when Collin raised her up out of her front row seat and escorted her up the aisle and out the back of the church. Collin noted that Liz had stepped across the dias and taken confused Norah's hand.

As the church organ played *Nearer my God to Thee*, Collin led Fiona to the Reverend's study where they found Kathy and her father in animated conversation, with Sam trying to mediate.

"What's the meaning of this, Ryan," Fiona cried. "Can't you just leave us alone today of all days? Haven't you done enough damage for one lifetime?"

"That's why I am here, albeit late. I have been so selfish and stuck in the old ways of trying to protect my family, that I have lost you altogether. I have only come to realize it after you had the courage to leave me, Fiona. I know I don't deserve you both, but I have to try and make amends before it's too late. And the thought of not walking my only child down the aisle on her wedding day propelled me to confess my sins to you today, and ask for your forgiveness."

"He just needs slaves to take care of him," Kathy screamed. "He doesn't mean it."

Collin felt sympathy for the man. True, he had been a stern master with Kathy and her mother, but there was some parallel to his own situation, having certain beliefs of behavior that got in the way of truly loving and protecting his family. And wasn't Collin doing the same thing with Kathy and their unborn baby because of his need to find his sister? Different circumstances but the same misguided good intentions. How is it that Kathy's father's situation clarified his own dilemma better than all the helpful counsel from Sam and others?

Ryan was on his knees now, crying.

Collin grabbed his hand, lifting him up and supporting him with an arm around his waist. Ryan was beside himself with grief.

"I think that we should all take a deep breath," Collin said. "Come over here to me, Kathy."

Collin could see Sam smiling.

Fiona sat down in the Reverend's chair while he consulted the Good Book for an appropriate passage.

"I have had an epiphany thanks to Ryan here. Yes, that's right my love, an epiphany, and I do know what that word means."

All but Sam looked confused. By the look in Kathy's eyes, she felt betrayed by her fiancé.

"I think that Ryan here, Da, if you will permit me, is genuinely seeking forgiveness and inclusion." Mr. O'Sullivan nodded with his head lowered.

"I am not condoning his past behavior, it was beastly. Stop me if I'm wrong, Reverend, but the Lord's Prayer says, *forgive me my trespasses as I forgive those who trespass against me.*"

"Yes, my son, it does indeed." He put down his Bible.

"I think that Da, here in his own twisted way, was trying to protect his family as only he knew how, with tough love. I would guess that his father ruled his household with an iron fist, am I right, sir?"

Again a nod from the intruder.

"I have been obsessed with finding my sister, a noble cause, like Ryan's. But I have been endangering my family in that pursuit, just like Ryan. So on his behalf and my own I would like to seek your forgiveness, Kathy and Fiona, in accordance with God's word."

Sam was fairly beaming and the Reverend was crossing himself. "Well, Kathy, what do you say? At least for today and hopefully forever, we can let bygones be bygones and bring our whole family together to share in our wedding. This is your father and fathers walk their daughters down the aisle."

Fiona stood up and came over to Collin with tears in her eyes. "Thank you, son," she said, as she took over the burden of supporting her husband.

Kathy looked pleadingly into Collins' eyes for a minute. He thought she found solace there. They all waited for her response.

Finally she said, "I thought that the groom wasn't supposed to see the bride before the wedding. Isn't that true, Dad?"

At this, Ryan lifted his head. Fiona let loose her grip, and father and daughter embraced as they had never done before.

"But what about . . . ?" she moaned.

"How wonderful," he replied, stroking her cheek. "A grandchild."

"But I did see you at the wedding already, my love."

"What?"

"At the back of the church. A vision of loveliness to be sure."

Sam stepped in. "Places everyone. We have a wedding to

perform."

Five minutes later, Collin and Reverend Dixon reappeared through the side door into the church and took their positions in front of the altar. The Reverend shook Collin's hand warmly.

Then Sam and Fiona, arm in arm, came down the aisle. There was a spring in her step. After seating her back in the first pew, Sam went and stood beside Collin.

"Fine piece of work, lad," he said quietly.

Sam signaled, and the organist started playing the wedding march.

The bride appeared at the back of the church once more, this time on the arm of her beaming father. As she floated down the aisle, her smile got bigger and bigger.

Norah could see Kathy smiling through her veil. And Norah noticed that Unca Collie seemed amazed by her beauty. It all seemed like the pictures in the storybook that her Mommy read to her and Dot some evenings before bed. She wondered if Auntie Caffie was wearing glass slippers under that flowing bridal gown.

Then Norah noticed the big picture of Unca Collie's sister standing up at the end of the line of bridesmaids. She remembered that picture in this church a few months ago when they carried a big box out of the church, and she wondered why it was there.

When Auntie Caffie got to the front of the church, the man with her lifted her hat veil. Then he gave her a big kiss and went to sit with the woman Daddy had just brought down the aisle. He was crying a little. Why would he cry at a time like this? Norah wondered.

Then this man all dressed in a bathrobe of white and gold lifted up his arms and started singing funny. Everybody in the church sat down and started to pray. Norah was looking at a girl in the third row who was about her own age. She wondered who she was, and the girl noticed her too. She was focused on this when her Daddy asked her to give Unca Collie two gold rings that he handed her.

As she went to do that, one of them slipped out of her tiny hand and rolled down the three steps and under the feet of an old man. Oh no. Now everyone was looking at her again. She started to go and get the ring but her Daddy held her tight. She watched as the old man bent down and picked up the ring. Smiling, he brought it back to her. Everyone was smiling.

"Here you go, Unca Collie," Norah exclaimed in her loudest voice, as she handed him the rings. *Why was everyone laughing? Did she do something wrong?* Her Daddy bent down and gave her a kiss on her cheek, which made her feel much better. And her Mommy was smiling at both of them.

After Unca Collie and Auntie Caffie put the rings on each other's fingers, they both said, 'I do'. Do what? Norah wondered. She waited for them to do something.

Pretty soon afterwards the man in the bathrobe said, "I now pronounce you husband and wife. You may kiss the bride." Norah's eyes opened wide when Unca Collie grabbed Auntie Caffie around the waist and bent her backwards with a really long kiss on the mouth.

"That's just a taste of what's in store for us later, my love," Collin whispered.

"You mean for us three," she whispered back."

Everyone clapped and Daddy gave a loud whistle.

Norah decided that this is what they said they were going to do. After that, everything happened at once. Norah waited while Auntie Caffie and Unca Collie marched, arm in arm, to the back of the church. Unca Collie looked back at the picture of his sister as they walked and he blew it a kiss.

Then her Daddy and Mommy with her in between, marched right after them. Norah was happy to be with them on the way through all the people. She saw the guests waving and cheering.

Then they were all out on the steps of the church and people were throwing rice at them, handfuls of it.

"Why are they being so mean, Daddy?" Norah asked

"It's for good luck, sweetie," Sam answered. "It's a good thing."

The bride and groom came over and Unca Collie picked Norah up.

"You were the best flower girl ever," he said and he and Auntie Caffie both gave her a big kiss on each cheek.

Norah felt really good.

And with that, the wedding was over.

Chapter Thirty-Seven
Crossroads

Tuesday, October 19, 1915
Creagh, Ireland

*I*t had been more than two rainy months since Tadgh and Morgan had arrived home from Dublin, and there had been no word from the IRB leaders. Tadgh paced the kitchen while Morgan made breakfast. Finally she had to speak.

"You're going to wear a hole in the oak floor if you don't stop circling this table. You're making me dizzy."

"Why the hell haven't we heard anything from Padraig?"

"Because they told us to lie low and because they know you're apt to use that Luger you keep cleaning over and over. They don't want notoriety. Of course it might just be that they are concentrating on training Aidan and that's taking up all their intellectual time.

"But I want to be rid of Boyle and his lieutenant. We know where he works."

"I know you do, but you can't right now. Can you imagine the repercussions if they hunted us down for killing a Head Constable and his assistant? No, Tadgh. You've got to be satisfied with preparing the safe house."

"But it would be so easy . . . I'd just slip in and out of RIC headquarters."

"You'll do nothing of the kind, so get that nonsense out of your head." She plopped a ham-and-eggs plate down on the table which scattered the utensils. "Breakfast now. You'll feel better."

Tadgh wolfed down his meal in silence.

"How about doing something for me for a change?" Morgan asked, buttering her toast.

"Meaning?"

"It's been almost three months since you inquired for me at the Cunard office. Surely they'll know something by now."

"Morgan, you keep asking me." He believed with all his heart that her *not* finding out was the best thing for his sweetheart. *Or is it only best for me? Same thing, right?* "I have contacted that man Jordan twice since we've been home when I've been into Cork to inquire about the revolution from Tomas. You may have to face the fact that there are no surviving relatives." He regretted saying it the moment it came out of his mouth. *Surviving?* And he lied about contacting Jack Jordan.

"Do you think my whole family was lost at sea?" Morgan started tearing up once again at the thought.

"There, there, *aroon*, there's no point speculating now, is there, lass. If they existed it wouldn't do you or them any good worrying now, would it. And if you were a lone young woman, you're not alone anymore."

Morgan finished her breakfast and started clearing up the dishes. "I can't leave it like this, Tadgh. I won't. I'm going to go and find out for myself."

"So you don't trust me then, is that it?"

"I just need to know what they found out, if anything."

"It's a waste of time and an unacceptable risk, don't ya know." Tadgh realized that this circular discussion, as usual, was only serving to heighten the tension between them.

They were fugitives, holed up and going stir crazy.

Tadgh opened his kitchen door and scouted out his rain-soaked property. For what seemed like the first time since they got home, the sun was shining. True enough, it was cool, what with the freshening breeze out of the east, but it was perfect sailing weather.

Stepping back into the kitchen, he was met with, "Why don't we get out of here and go sailing?"

It was still uncanny to him how Morgan could simultaneously enunciate his own thoughts before he could speak them. Definitely a strange yet alluring woman. If only she would give up her improbable search for her past and focus on their future together.

"I was thinking the same thing now the sun is shining, *aroon*. We could take a sail down to Baltimore for lunch and then see if we want to venture out further."

"That's a grand idea. I'll just get dressed."

Tadgh spent the next hour checking out and outfitting *The Republican*. It was to be the first use of his prize possession in over two months, the longest time away from the sea that he could remember. No wonder he was so aggravated. The main sheet looked a little frayed, so he replaced it. While he worked he stewed. He had crossed the line months ago and he knew it. It probably didn't matter anyway in terms of her personal history knowledge, but he had lied to her, for the good of both of them. Or was it just his selfishness, his possessiveness. And she wasn't going to let it lie. Why should she? He wouldn't if it was him.

Tadgh decided that he had jeopardized his goal of being with her for life. She would insist on talking to Jordan somehow, and he would be exposed. *Eejit!* Better to have told her the photograph was ruined. Too late now.

"You ready?" he heard as Morgan came clopping down the stairs, heavy sweaters over her shoulder. "I thought you might need this." She tossed him his favorite one.

"Thanks. I will if we go out to sea." Tadgh pulled open the monstrous 10- by 25-foot high back doors that swung from the centerline of the boathouse and was reminded that he needed to oil the hinges sometime soon. Then together, with ropes, they walked the hooker that was so unwieldy in the confines of his boathouse back and out into the river. Tadgh jumped on board and paddled *The Republican* around until it was moored at the dock. Grabbing Morgan's hand and then encircling her waist, he lifted her up off the dock and set her down light as a feather in the cockpit.

"I'm truly sorry," he mumbled.

"It's all right. We've both been frustrated and housebound. Let's just make a fun day of it."

Morgan now knew how to help with setting the sails and within half an hour they were on their way southwest on the Ilen River. There were places where this river narrowed, and sand bars had to be avoided, but Tadgh knew every protuberance, every twist and turn by heart. And it helped that the wind was favorable. They exited the Ilen estuary into Baltimore Bay just past noon.

"I'm going to moor in the harbor. Then it's a short walk back up the coastline to my favorite pub hotel here. It's called the Algiers Inn. I think you'll love it."

"That's an odd name for an Irish establishment, isn't it?"

"Not if you remember the history."

"Right. The Barbary Pirates attack in 1631."

"Thatta girl. After they carried away 109 slaves, the town was devastated. Most of the remaining residents vacated the town and moved inland for protection, past where we live to Skibbereen and beyond. Baltimore never really came back as a port town until the 1800s."

"It looks thriving enough now, doesn't it?" Morgan said as Tadgh neatly maneuvered the hooker up to the dock. Hopping out herself with the bow-line, she clove-hitched it to the dock cleat like a veteran sailor looking to Tadgh for praise.

He had landed on the dock and snugged the stern-line down. "There. That's got it." Fifteen minutes later, after the sails were furled, they headed out into Baltimore.

When they arrived at the Inn, Morgan noticed the pub shingle, showing a turbaned, pipe-smoking renegade with a giant scar across his face. "Not a very friendly looking sort, that pirate from Old Algiers, is he?"

"No, I suppose they were fierce marauders, them Barbary corsairs."

"I wouldn't want to wake up in my bed at night with five of

those devils staring at me."

"They wouldn't have just been staring, *aroon*."

Morgan shuddered as they passed under the shingle and into the warm, cozy pub. There was a fiddler practicing in the back corner near the open fireplace.

Tadgh decided that this was just what they needed.

When they were seated, Morgan said, "I see they've got the 1631 raid described on the wall over there. They can't be that concerned about the event."

"Maybe not now that it's a tourist magnet. At least it was before the war. But when it happened . . ."

"It's true that we tend to remember the good things and the buried bad things we lock or explain away."

There it is again. The elephant in the room, Tadgh thought.

The subject was averted while they munched on their delicious, yet standard-fare Irish stew and ale. They talked of Tadgh's love for the ocean and some of his sea-faring adventures. It seemed like all was right with the world.

"Fancy a turn on the open ocean, *mavorneen*?" Morgan asked as she was just sopping up the final juices with freshly-made soda bread with raisins.

"My thought precisely, *aroon*. The afternoon looks bright, the sea relatively calm and the wind has now switched out of the west."

"Give me a minute to freshen up," Morgan said as she rose.

"I'll meet you out front." Tadgh paid the bill.

There was a comfy chair and table at the entrance with newspapers spread out for the clientele.

I wonder what the locals read down here? That's when he spied an outdated copy of the Cork *Southern Star*, a regional newspaper that he never read. It was certainly not Republican. September 7th. More than a month old. *They're somewhat out of touch here.*

Tadgh was just throwing it back down face first when a small article in the personal section on the back page caught his eye.

HELP ME FIND MY LOVING CLAIRE!!!! Lost on the Lusitania 5-7-1915. Had amnesia. 21 years old, black hair, green eyes. Seen near Cork by Mr. Jack Jordan, Cunard Steamship Lines, Queenstown. Reward! Contact Mr. Jordan at . . .

Tadgh's gut tightened in a knot. He couldn't breathe. *Sweet Brigid!* He saw Morgan advancing to him through the pub. He quickly ripped half the back page off and shoved it into his pocket just before she reached him. *Damn, why'd we have to come to this pub today?*

"Ready to go? Wait. You don't look well," she said as she stepped forward and felt his forehead. "Hmm, no fever."

"I'll be all right. Right as rain. Let's get out into that sunshine." Air was finally filling his lungs. "C'mon." He wanted to put as much distance between them and this pirate pub as quickly as possible.

By the time they had taken ten steps from the pub, color was starting to return to Tadgh's face, although behind that beard it would be hard to tell. "Better now?" Morgan asked as they stepped along together.

"I'm fine, really." *Another lie.* He carried the devastating proof in his own pocket. Exactly what Morgan, er Claire needed. It wasn't just a chance sighting from afar that probably was just the wishful thinking of a debilitated Cunard employee any more. Now it was a woman with amnesia, fitting Morgan's characteristics who has a man who loves her and who is desperately, by his words in the article, looking for her. And she for him, unknowingly.

"A penny for your thoughts," Morgan said.

Just then they reached the dock. "What? What did you say? Can you help me with the sails?"

"I just asked what you were thinking about, that's all."

"Nothing really." *Just my life going forward,* he agonized as he unfurled the main lug sail.

Ten minutes later they were knifing out of the harbor south towards the Celtic Sea. For the time being Tadgh could let his cares go and enjoy being in his element. There were enough tasks to keep them both busy until they passed beyond Cape Clear Island. Seemingly they were alone on the sea which was a good thing. Morgan came back into the cockpit and sat beside her man.

"In which direction should we seek our fortune as pirates on the bounding main?" Tadgh asked, waving his arms first west and then east.

"Definitely east, Capt'n."

"Why east, *aroon*? You've never been west with me."

Morgan wetted her finger and held it in the air, "Because, uh, because the wind is favorable."

Well, that was a logical answer. The wind had shifted westerly while they were eating. But it would be harder tacking back if the wind didn't shift again.

For two and a half hours they both drank it in, the wind, the waves, the sunshine and the billowing sails as they scampered along with the coast well inside the horizon. It was marvelous, just what they needed. There was no need to talk, just sit arm in arm. Every once in a while, Morgan would go and trim a sail at her captain's command, and once, Tadgh had left her in charge while he scrounged for the two bottles of stout that he had provisioned on-board.

Finally, when they were opposite Courtmacsherry, Tadgh stood up and stretched. "It's time to turn about, lass, and head home if we want to be in our berth before sunset. Prepare to come about."

Morgan kissed her beau on his cheek and asked, "Why don't we just go on to Queenstown and talk to Mr. Jordan? We're more than halfway there, aren't we? Wouldn't that be safer than going on the roads past Cork City?"

Tadgh, who was always the decisive one, was tongue-tied. The paper in his pocket was crying out to him. He could say no, keep quiet and no one would be the wiser. Except of course himself, the deceitful one. He could show her the notice in the paper himself.

But why didn't he say something three hours ago? Or he could go to Queenstown and let Jordan tell her about the notice in the *Southern Star*. And as far as Jordan knew, he was talking to Sir Neville Chamberlain.

"Well, what do you think about my suggestion, Tadgh? I really want to know."

She was tugging on his arm. Her smoky green eyes were pleading, as close to begging as her constitution would allow. At that vulnerable moment he realized the depth of love he had for her, beyond himself. He couldn't ignore her needs any more. If he just told her about the newspaper notice, they could avoid the risk of going to Cunard. But he didn't want to demonstrate that he had withheld that from her. He would have to let Morgan make her own choice.

"All right, we can go on to Queenstown, but we have to very careful. Hopefully, Mr. Jordan will be sympathetic and not call the police."

"Thank you, *mavorneen*." Morgan pulled him down into his seat at the tiller in the cockpit and held him tight. "We'll be safe. You'll see."

Having made that decision he felt better, much better.

Tadgh figured it was going to be another hour and a half until they were berthed in Queenstown. He had decided to come ashore where they had dropped Martin off and then walk to the Cunard office. That way their boat might not be compromised.

Half an hour later, the sea height started to swell, maybe six feet, he thought. No need for alarm. The wind had freshened and they were now moving along at quite a clip. He estimated almost 15 knots. He was thinking that, depending on the outcome of their meeting with Jordan, if he was even at his office, and the weather, he might have to contact Martin to see if they could stay with him overnight. That's when Tadgh saw it coming over the horizon from the east. Twin stacks headed their way, plying the commerce route from Europe to America. Running the gauntlet if it was British or French.

"Trim the forward jib, Morgan." He wanted to optimize the wind.

"Aye, Capt'n." She seemed in good spirits now. He had no idea what she would be like two hours from now, when she learned that her lover was alive and looking for her.

"You see that freighter heading our way?" Tadgh asked. "We need to get closer to shore to give her a wide berth. With these six-foot swells, I don't want to get swamped by her wash."

"Aye, Capt'n."

When they were about five minutes from passing, by Tadgh's reckoning, he steered a few degrees to port to avoid an intercept. Morgan trimmed the sails tighter. The freighter just kept plowing along, obviously expecting the hooker to get out of her way.

"She's smaller than the *Talmooth,* isn't she, Tadgh."

"Probably, but it was too dark remember. Things look bigger in the dark."

Suddenly there was a flash of light as the port side of the approaching freighter burst into flames, aft of the cargo holds.

"Torpedo," Tadgh yelled. "That ship's been torpedoed." He could see that it had lost forward thrust and was starting to wallow in the sea.

"Look!" Morgan cried as the main aft deck and bridge burst into flames.

Tadgh had already taken action, altering course on a bee-line for the stricken ship.

"I don't see any sign of life," Morgan called out from the bow. "Wait. There." A figure appeared from the wheelhouse, staggering, fully engulfed in flames.

"My God. Burning Man." They watched and the figure gyrated to the rail and plunged himself overboard to his certain death.

Now *The Republican* had come alongside the dying freighter. It was, indeed, smaller than the *Talmooth*. But it was also inaccessible given the wave heights and lack of support on the vessel. Now the aft of the freighter was fully engulfed. It was sinking by the stern. They could feel the heat as they passed.

"We've got to see if anyone is alive on board," Tadgh yelled forward.

"I can see some men clustering near the bow. Up there," Morgan pointed above and in front of the hooker.

"I'm going to tie up at the bow and attempt to board her. We should have a good half hour before she sinks," Tadgh yelled back.

Morgan acknowledged what he said with a wave, but she was obsessed with what was going on the ship. This is what it must have been like on the *Lusitania*. *Why can't I remember?*

"Do you see what I'm seeing, *mein Kapitan*," the second in command of U-19 asked, glued to the periscope.

"Let me look Fritz," Kapitanleutnant Raimund Weisbach said, pushing his second in command aside and hunkering down over his primitive periscope.

"Mein Gott im Himmel!" That munitions ship is not launching any boats. And what's that alongside?"

"It looks like that Galway hooker we saw after we sank the *Lusitania,* sir. You know, that unique gray lug sail," Fritz, his second in command replied.

"They're trying to save the crew. Up 15 degree bubble. Surface, surface," Weisbach yelled over the IMC.

Morgan saw it first as they approached the bow. The black nose shooting up out of the water 100 yards off to their starboard.

"Tadgh, help."

Tadgh diverted his attention to help Morgan and saw the familiar shape of a U-boat. "Them's the lads what torpedoed the freighter. Believe it or not they are on our side."

"Are you crazy? They just destroyed this freighter and most if not all of its crew."

"Believe me, you can trust them." He could see running figures on the outer deck of the sub. It looked like they were trying to launch a raft. He returned his focus to the intercept with the freighter's bow.

"This is absolutely insane," Morgan cried. "How are you going to get up there in the first place? Let them jump first."

"The jump would likely kill them. We've got to go get them."

Tadgh had brought a coiled rope with a grappling hook on the end. He was looking up. Deck level loomed high above them. It wasn't clear he could throw it that high.

A moment later the main storage hold of the freighter caught fire and erupted, sending plumes of smoke a hundred feet in the air. Seconds later the freighter split amidships, the aft end almost submerged in less than a minute.

Tadgh realized that it was too late to save any men on the freighter. "Coming about," he yelled to Morgan who seemed transfixed. "C'mon, c'mon," he cried in frustration as it took time for the sails to refill.

Seconds later he had *The Republican* turned perpendicular to the freighter and moving away, but slowly in the direction of the U-boat.

That's when the magazines in the hold exploded sending shrapnel and fiery debris hundreds of feet in all directions. The blast knocked Tadgh and Morgan down onto the deck. The freighter sank fifteen seconds later and their own boat didn't fare well, either. *The Republican* was foundering. Its sails were shredded and on fire. The main mast was broken off five feet above the deck, the transom and tiller were gone, and the decks were awash with flaming debris. Water was filling the space below the deck and it was keeling hard to port. To make matters worse, the sea around them was covered with burning wreckage.

"Abandon ship, Morgan," Tadgh cried, trying to get past the burning sails and decking to get to her. She just stood there mesmerized, dazed, as if she didn't even know he was there. She was looking shoreward, her hands outstretched. Eight miles away, the lighthouse on Old Kinsale Head threw out its beam. By the time he reached her, she was crying. "Where is my love?" she was sobbing.

"I'm right here. Morgan, you've got to go now, *aroon*," Tadgh said, grabbing her around her waist.

She turned and stared at him with vacant sea green eyes. "Have you seen my love? He'll be here shortly. He's bringing the babies."

She wasn't making any sense. The German captain in the rubber dingy, now only 50 feet to the starboard of his once beautiful hooker, was familiar to him. Why was he out there in the raft personally? He was urging his men onward in German through the six-foot swells.

They were standing together on what was left of the forward deck, splintered and smoldering. The water under the decking reached a critical point, and the boat started to roll violently to port-away from the Germans. Tadgh went to steady himself and his left foot broke through the damaged decking and lodged in the ragged opening with a large splinter piercing his calf muscle below deck. He was stuck.

There was no time left. "Give this to Aidan," he yelled, ripping his locket from around his neck and shoving it down her bodice right to her waistband. *That should secure it.* It wasn't clear that she understood.

He kissed her hard on the mouth and then, in one fluid motion against the sea's fury, he heaved her, the love of his life, up and over the starboard gunnels, toward the raft, into the maelstrom.

As the broken hooker rolled precariously to port, he clawed at the deck opening to free himself, fingers bleeding.

Weisbach dove over the side of the dingy when he saw that the girl, now 20 feet away, was going under. He caught her tunic when she was already sinking below the surface. It was just a lucky grab. Seconds later he had pulled her up to the dingy that was now only 15 feet from the hooker. His men were paddling with all their strength. The girl was sputtering. One second the young Irishman was bending down and frantically working to free himself from the debris. The next, what was left of his boat flipped over to port. He was pulled into the wreck like a rag doll and disappeared from sight underwater.

Weisbach pushed Morgan up and over the gunnels of the dingy, then turned toward the overturned broken hull of *The Republican* and started swimming with all his might. What was this crazy war proving anyway? That munitions czars can make a fortune over the killing of millions of able-bodied men in the name of Nationalism? The fact that he was the one who had pushed the torpedo launch button that sent the *Lusitania* and almost 1,200 innocent souls to the bottom of the Celtic Sea had been eating away at his soul. Now to give him some peace, he would save this Good Samaritan Irishman trapped beneath his sinking boat, or he would die trying.

Cast of Characters

North America – Historical

John Devoy	Leader of Clan na Gael in America
Reverend Dixon	Minister, St. Aidans Church, Toronto
Samuel Stevenson Finlay	Artist & Director of Art at Riverdale High School, Toronto
Elizabeth Finlay (Liz)	Sam's Wife
Norah Finlay	Sam's Eldest Daughter
Dorothy Finlay	Sam's Youngest Daughter
Mr. Charles Warren Lippitt	Former Governor of Rhode Island and Mill Owner
Joseph McGarrity	Leader of Clan na Gael in America
Dr. Gordon Stewart	General Practicioner, Beaches, Toronto, Canada

North America – Fictional

Lucy Daggett	Inmate of the Providence Orphanage and Claire's Friend
George Fredricson	Captain of the Providence Rhode Island Police Force
Anthony Fry	Cunard Operations Manager, NYC
Rudy Gann	Head of Longshoremen, Toronto Harbor
Monsieur Gauthier	Operations Manager at the Lippitt Textile Mill
Hank Handelman	Barkeep at Benny's in Brooklyn
Byron Harrison	Orderly and Savior of Claire
Officer Mulrooney	Toronto Metropolitan Police Force
Collin O'Donnell	Young Irishman in Toronto
Claire (Morgan) O'Donnell	Collin's Younger Sister
Shaina O'Donnell	Collin's Ma
Kathleen O'Sullivan	Young Irish Woman in Toronto

Cast of Characters

Ryan O'Sullivan	Kathleen's Father
Fiona O'Sullivan	Kathleen's Mother
Enrico Salazar	Shaina's Pimp in Brooklyn
Detective Williams	Second in Command to Captain Fredricson

Europe – Historical

Thomas Clarke	Lead Member of Irish Republican Brotherhood (IRB)
Michael Collins	Member of Irish Volunteers
Florence MacCarthaigh	Last Independent Chieftain, MacCarthaigh Reagh Clan
Thomas MacDonagh	Member IRB and Chief Marshall for Rossa Funeral
Sean O'Casey	Irish Playwright
Peader O'Donnell	College Student, Later to be a Revolutionary Leader
Red Hugh O'Donnell	Last Independent Chieftain, O'Donnell Clan
Niall O'Donnell	Red Hugh's Cousin
Padraig Pearse	Lead Member of the IRB and School Master
O'Donovan Rossa	Irish Fenian Leader and Patriot Exiled to America
Mary Jane Rossa	O'Donovan's Wife
Walther Schwieger	Kapitanleutnant of U-20 that Sank the *Lusitania*
Will Turner	Captain of HMS *Lusitania*
Herr Voegele	Quartermaster on U-20
Raimund Weisbach	Watch Officer on U-20

Europe – Fictional

Tom Clancy	Owner of Clancy's Bar, Cork Ireland
Deidre	Owner and Barkeeper of Temple Bar Pub, Dublin, Ireland
Alex Henderson	General Manager, Beamish & Crawford Brewery, Cork City, Ireland
Gordon (Gordo) James	Sergeant RIC Cork, and Taggert's Henchman
Jack Jordan	Third Bosun's Mate, HMS *Lusitania*
Aileen Mahoney	Aidan McCarthy's Girlfriend, Waitress at Temple Bar Pub
Tadgh McCarthy	Young Irish Revolutionary. Member of IRB
Aidan McCarthy	Tadgh's Younger Brother
Martin Murphy	Captain of Supply Ships for Beamish and Crawfords
Morgan O'Donnell	Young Irish Woman Rescued by Tadgh McCarthy
Professor O'Toole	Head Curator, National Museum of Ireland, Dublin
Derek Slocum	Deidre's Cook and Bodyguard
Darcy Boyle	Head Sergeant Royal Irish Constabulatory (RIC)
Jeffrey Wiggins	Transportatio Leader, Beamish and Crawfords Brewery, Cork City, Ireland Tadgh's Collegue

Background History

The Tir Conaill/Domhnaill/O'Donnell Clan
*Reference 1, Chapter 27, Page 397

In ancient days the Tir Chonaill Clan ruled the northwest of Ireland. We are talking now about the time between 500 and 1600 AD. These were Peader's ancestors, who evolved as the O'Donnell Clan, centered in what is now Donegal. In 521 AD a son was born there who was the great, great, great grandson of Niall of the Nine Hostages, an Irish High King. They named him Colum Cille, meaning "dove of the church."

St. Patrick, founder of the Roman Catholic Church in Ireland, had predicted 60 years earlier that this lad would be a great leader of the Christian faith in Ireland. St. Columba, as he became known, discarded all of the materialistic riches due him as an inherited King at a very early age. He gave his life to the monastic order, creating many monasteries in Ireland among the Celtic Christians.

I could go on and on about St. Columba's self-sacrifice, his church leadership, and so on. But to make it brief, in about 561 AD, long after studying at the famous Clonard Abbey, he decided to make and keep a copy of a unique Roman vulgate manuscript of the Psalms owned by St. Finnian while he was at Movilla Abbey. St. Finnian found out about it and demanded that the copy be turned over to him. St. Columba refused, claiming that the words of the Bible are open for all people. A battle ensued over the ownership of this Psalter, as it was called, and 3,000 men died. St. Columba was victorious and retained the document. This is the first known battle over copyright infringement. St. Columba was almost excommunicated by Pope John III over this issue.

St. Columba self-exiled himself from Ireland to live and work miracles among the Picts for the rest of his life based at a monastery he built with his disciples on the island of Hy, which would later be called Iona, in the Inner Hebrides of what would be called Scotland. Before he left his beloved Ireland, he met with his relative and King of Tir Conaill and gave him the Psalter calling it *An Cathach*. He claimed that if the Clan leader would carry this Psalter into battle, with a soldier without sin encircling his army three times in advance with it, that the Tir Conaill Clan would always be victorious. They followed his direction and, until 1602, they always came out the victors. Near the end of the eleventh century, an ornate, jeweled box to house *An Cathach* was created at the Kells Monastery and called a *cumdach*. It had a chain to go around the neck of the soldier without sin, usually from the McGroarty Clan. The O'Donnell Clan continued to

547

prevail as the ruler in Northwest Ireland for eleven hundred years.

Red Hugh O'Donnell was born to be Clan Chieftain of northwestern Ireland. In 1587, at the age of fifteen, he was abducted by the English and imprisoned in Dublin Castle. He and his comrade Hugh O'Neill, prince of northeastern Ireland, escaped in 1592. Only three prisoners have ever successfully done that. Red Hugh became Lord of Tir Conaill. He was deeply religious and just, to both his army and to his enemies. Accompanied by his brother Rory, and his ally Hugh O'Neill, Red won several battles against the English using guerilla warfare in what was named the Nine Years War in the 1590s. This included the Battle of Curlew Pass in 1599 where he soundly defeated the Earl of Essex, Robert Devereux's forces, sending the Lord Lieutenant back to England.

Unfortunately, Red Hugh's cousin Niall Garve O'Donnell defected to the English in the hope of being made O'Donnell Chieftain after an English victory. Niall, with many followers, enabled the English to take the city of Derry and thus establish a northwestern stronghold from which they could attack Red Hugh and Hugh O'Neill.

In early 1601 during the siege of Donegal, Red Hugh was forced to burn his own castle stronghold in Donegal Town to avoid its capture by Niall and the English. He headed south to Ballymote Castle in Sligo, which he had acquired earlier. His forces amassed there in the fall of 1601 in order to march south to meet with the Spanish at Kinsale. The march was an amazing achievement through the early winter, covering forty miles a day. He met up with O'Neill's forces and the Spanish under Juan del Aguila on the south coast, west of Kinsale. The Spanish had chosen Kinsale because it had a fortified harbor, and it was a provisioner town for ships headed for the New World.

Red Hugh stopped en route at the Holy Cross Abbey in Thurles to visit the relic of the True Cross on the Feast of St. Andrew, November 30th. From there he sent an expedition to Ardfert to recover territory of his ally, Fitzmaurice, Lord of Kerry that had been lost during the earlier Desmond Rebellion.

Tragically, this combined Irish-Spanish force was soundly defeated by the superior strength of the English army under Lord Mountjoy, Charles Blount, in an open field battle at Kinsale on January 2, 1602. It was not at all the guerilla warfare that the Clansmen were good at. The northern clans scattered homeward with the English at their heels. The invading force turned northward.

Clan Chieftain Red Hugh O'Donnell went directly to Spain from Munster to try to get more support from the Spanish King, now King Phillip III, while his brother Rory led his O'Donnell kinsmen back to Donegal. One of the English generals and President of Munster in the south, Sir George Carew, sent James Blake, a spy, after Red Hugh to poison him. Within the year the Clan Chieftain was dead in Spain and there was no more assistance forthcoming from that country.

Within five years, the Clan leaders in the north were forced to flee Ireland or be captured and executed. Rory O'Donnell and his family were a main part of the flight of the Earls to the European continent in 1607. Rory went to Rome and met with the Pope. Then he died mysteriously in the Roman port of Ostia.

Niall was eventually incarcerated after an abortive uprising in Derry (now Londonderry) was quelled by the English in 1608, and he and his son died in prison.

With that, the English had taken over Ireland from the native Irish, and they planted their own nobility into the castles and lands of the Northern Clans.

The Eoghanachta/Mac Carthaigh/MacCarthy Mor/McCarthy Clans
**Reference 2, Chapter 27, Page 405

There is much I could tell you about the history of the MacCarthy Clan, from its beginnings as the previously Welsh Eoghanachta dynasty who migrated to Cashel, Ireland, in the fourth century AD to today. I will leave out the detailed story of King Brian Boru who united Ireland in about 1,000 AD and drove our Clan south from Cashel. Suffice it to say that by the 1500s, the MacCarthy Clans ruled the southwest portion of Ireland, from Kerry to Cork and from Tipperary to the sea. There were four main branches of the Clan, with respective Kings. The Mac Carthaigh Reagh Clan, from whom Tadgh McCarthy is descended, settled in Carbery, the southern most region, west of Cork. They fought alongside the O'Donnells and O'Neills at nearby Kinsale, which was close by in 1602. Their Chieftain Florence MacCarthaigh Reagh was incarcerated by the English in mid-1601 prior to the battle, and remained in gaol, in the Tower of London, until 1626. He stayed in London until his death in 1640. After Kinsale, all the wars for Irish independence became uprisings against the English overlords. Florence's main castle home, Kilbrittain, was finally overtaken by the English in 1642 during the startup of what was called the Confederate Wars. Lewis Lord Kinalmeaky, nephew of Richard Boyle, 1st Earl of Cork, managed to take Killbrittain Castle in that year, defeating Cormac MacCarthy Reagh.

Another branch, the Muskerry MacCarthys, who ruled north of Carbery, had several castles. Their primary residence was Blarney Castle just northwest of Cork. At the time of the Battle of Kinsale, which was in their backyard, Cormac Teige MacCarthy Mor, Lord of Muscry had already been severely pressured to give up his throne and lands to the English Queen Bess, as she was called. In 1602 he avoided this defeat by parlaying with the Queen's emissary, Sir George Carew. This prompted the English Queen to say of him, "This is all Blarney. He never says what he means." So, around the time of the Battle of Kinsale, the MacCarthy Mor Chieftain had learned the art of passive defiance, believing that military battle was a losing proposition.

This tactic worked throughout most of the first half of the 1600s, principally when King Charles I ruled England, since he was Roman Catholic. But in the 1640s, Charles I was overthrown and eventually executed in 1649 by a junta led by the brutal Parliamentarian Oliver Cromwell. By 1642 the civil war in England was drawing military forces away from Ireland. As a result, the Confederates were successful in consolidating control over much of the country except Dublin, Cork itself, and much of the Protestant northeast. They tried to negotiate with King Charles I, but he was too busy fighting for his Kingdom, and as it turns out, his life. During the next three years there were many skirmishes, and much of the country was devastated by the burning of crops and killing of livestock and civilians. It was a terrible time. By then, what was called the Long Parliament in England, was gaining control over the King. It was a brief anarchist period when there was no monarchy in England. Cromwell was a ruthless tyrant. He and his murdering Roundhead troops decimated the Irish and particularly the Roman Catholic Irish in the latter part of the 1640s

In 1646, one of Cromwell's generals, Lord Broghill, lay siege to Blarney Castle. Lord Broghill was Robert Boyle and the son of Richard Boyle, 1st Earl of Cork, who had been instrumental in the British victory over the FitzGerald Clan during the 1590s Desmond Rebellion. Boyle lorded over the lands around Lismore castle, east of Cork City. Donough MacCarthy, 2nd Viscount Muskerry, attacked Lismore castle in 1643 in retribution for the loss of Kilbrittain Castle the year before, but he was not successful in taking the castle for the rebels.

Lord Broghill wanted Blarney Castle and all the treasures that the Muskerry MacCarthys had accumulated, and he wanted to annihilate the power base of the Clan by killing off its leadership. Cromwell was doing this all over Ireland. It was the beginning of the reign of terror where the English started the belief that the Irish were vermin to be exterminated. They called their murderous tactics "slash and burn."

The inhabitants of Blarney castle were well prepared for this assault. Their leader, Donough, was off leading the fight against the English. They had a plan. After a siege, when the Cromwellian forces finally took the castle by force from a gun emplacement to the south on Card Hill, they found that the occupants had fled through escape tunnels, along with the McCarthy "gold plate." This was an abbreviation for the accumulated wealth of at least the Muskerry MacCarthys. So they temporarily acquired the severely damaged castle and its lands, but they didn't get the leaders and the riches. The story is told that there were three tunnels in Badger's Caves under the castle—one that led west to Kerry, one that led southeast to Cork, and one that led south to the lake. It was speculated that the "gold plate" was hidden in the lake by the retreating MacCarthys. Passive defiance.

Years later, a man named Jeffereys bought Blarney Castle, then a shell, and its surrounding land. He spent a fortune searching for the MacCarthy "gold plate" in the lake. But it was never found, and its whereabouts remains hidden today . . . or does it?

England Invasion Overview
***Reference 3, Chapter 33, Page 478

The English had been ruthlessly subjugating the Irish, and particularly the Roman Catholic Irish, for centuries. The attacks escalated in the 1500s when the King of England, Henry VIII, couldn't produce a male heir for his kingdom. He created a new religion based on the Protestant faith and called it the Church of England to avoid the eternal damnation of the excommunication invoked against him by the Roman Catholic Pope Paul III. This enabled him to justify to himself, and to his subjects, that he could divorce and execute his various wives in his futile attempts to gain that male heir. Since Ireland remained true to the Roman Catholic faith, this set up a bitter religious rift between the two countries. And, of course, England was in the business of acquiring territory all over the world starting at that time. Ireland, so close to home, was a major prize to be won. As long as the Irish Clans were strong, they could protect Ireland from English occupation.

Back in the time of Henry's daughter, Queen Elizabeth, who ruled the English Empire in the last half of the 1500s, this terrible domination started to take hold. We know that during the late 1500s, Queen Elizabeth started to take away the property of the Southern Clan chieftains by force to give it to English and Scottish noblemen, in many cases the soldiers in her army. This implantation was resisted by all the Clans. That included both native Gaelic, for example the McCarthys, and landed "Old English" Normans who had become quite Gaelic themselves. The British started closest to their strong base in Dublin, called the Pale, and moved to the southeast first. There were two periods of war in the south called the Desmond Rebellions in the 1570s and 1580s. The main attack was on one of these Norman families, the Fitzgeralds of Desmond. They ruled the southeast of Ireland and often fought for territory with the McCarthys in the southwest. Who wouldn't fight for their own land and territory? That, and family and honor were the essence of life then, as they are now. The second rebellion ended in 1583 after the massacre by the English at Smerwick on the Dingle Peninsula. The Pope's forces that had been sent to help the Fitzgeralds and their allies the FitzMaurices, as well as many Irish men, women and children, were all beheaded and thrown into the sea.

There was a famous adventurer who had the Queen's favor. His name was Sir Walter Raleigh. He was a member of the English forces during that massacre. As a result of his valor in the minds of the English, he was granted some forty thousand acres of Fitzgerald land in the southeast after the war. This included Lismore castle and areas around Youghal east of Cork.

The English carried out a slash and burn policy during that period, which killed off one third of the Irish population in the south of Ireland, thirty thousand in all, either by murder or resultant famine and disease. Bubonic plague ran rampant as a result, and the Desmond dynasty was over.

Richard Boyl, later to become the 1st Earl of Cork, acquired the sizeable estate granted to Sir Walter Raleigh when he was incarcerated by the Queen for marrying one of her ladies-in-waiting without her permission in 1591. In other parts of the country, the English were able to "plant" Englishmen with families into the fractured fabric that was the

Irish Clans society.

The McCarthys still had their lands at this point, but the end was in sight.

Thereafter, in the 1590s, the two major Clans in the north, the O'Donnells in the west, and the O'Neills in the east, were waging war with the advancing English. They had some successful battles in the rugged countryside using guerrilla tactics, and they drove the English leader Robert Devereux out of the country in 1599. But then the English brought in reinforcements under the command of Lord Mountjoy. That's when the Northern Clans decided that they needed help. Clan Chieftain Florence MacCarthaigh Reagh in the south was in contact with King Phillip II of Spain. Florence convinced him to support the Irish as a means to get back at England. The English got word of Florence's involvement, and he was arrested and taken to the Tower of London prison in the middle of 1601.

In October of that year, the Spanish fleet landed in Kinsale, near Kilbrittain Castle, prepared to fight the English. Red Hugh O'Donnell and Hugh O'Neill and their armies marched down from the north through the gathering winter, which was an amazing feat by itself. They all fought, including the remaining MacCarthaigh Reagh clansmen, against Lord Mountjoy's forces there outside Kinsale on January 2, 1602, and an all-out battle ensued. It was live or die for the Clan system of Ireland.

The English won the open field battle of Kinsale. To the victor go the spoils.

That was not the end of the wars, but from then on, Irish wars would be uprisings against the English-occupied conqueror. And the conqueror was ruthless.

The English imposed what were called the Penal Laws to prevent the Catholic Irish from becoming strong again to try to force them to convert to the English protestant religion. As examples, Catholics were not allowed to hold public office or be in the army. They couldn't bear arms and the Catholic religion could not be practiced. Eventually they were not allowed to own land or horses. They were relegated to being tenants on the land that they once owned. The intent was to break their will as well as their bodies. It was inhumane.

So the Catholics in Ireland rebelled with a major uprising starting in 1641 against the ruling Protestants in the northeast and Dublin. It started up north in Ulster. Thousands were brutally killed on both sides. By early 1642 most of the country was involved, including in Munster. The leader of what were now called the rebels there was Donagh MacCarthy, Viscount Muskerry, headquartered at Blarney Castle as discussed above. So far, he had managed to keep his castles and lands, as had Tadgh's ancestors, the Mac Carthaigh Reaghs headquartered at Kilbrittain Castle. They were two of the last holdouts.

The English brought in reinforcements and the Irish Catholics banded together to form the Catholic Confederation headquartered at Kilkenny in the southeast. They controlled the southeast ports of Wexford and Waterford so that they could get help from Catholic Europe. This period was called the Confederate War of Ireland, and it lasted until 1652 when Lord Muskerry finally surrendered at the last MacCarthy stronghold of Ross Castle, west of there, under duress from Oliver Cromwell's forces.

Most of the planted English families that had taken over the lands of the Fitzgerald Clan fought on the side of the English Protestants. One example is Sir Richard Boyle, who at this time was the first Earl of Cork after the Battle of Kinsale. At the insistence of George Carew he had purchased Sir Walter Raleigh's Irish estates from him in 1603 while Walter was imprisoned in the Tower of London. He became 1st Earl of Cork, operating from Lismore Castle. He and his relatives became a major force in the final overthrow of the MacCarthy Clans during the Confederate Wars as discussed above.

There is much more to discuss regarding Anglo-Irish history, which will be addressed in Books Two through Four of the continuing saga, **The Irish Clans.**